LET THE OLD DREAMS DIE
AND OTHER STORIES

Also by
John Ajvide Lindqvist

Let the Right One In
Handling the Undead
Harbour
Little Star

LET THE OLD DREAMS DIE

AND OTHER STORIES

John Ajvide

LINDQVIST

**Translated from the Swedish
by Marlaine Delargy**

Quercus

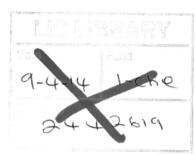

First published in English in 2012 by The Text Publishing Company, Australia
First published in Great Britain in 2012 by

Quercus
55 Baker Street
7th Floor, South Block
London
W1U 8EW

First published in Swedish as *Pappersväggar* by
Ordfront Stockholm, 2006
'Let the old dreams die' first published in
Låt de gamla drömmarna dö by Ordfront, 2011

Published by arrangement with Ordfronts Föelag, Stockholm
and Leonhardt & Høier aps, Copenhagen
First published in English by The Text Publishing Company, Australia, 2012

A CIP catalogue record for this book is available
from the British Library

ISBN 978 0 85738 549 9 (HB)
ISBN 978 0 85738 550 5 (TPB)
ISBN 978 1 78087 387 9 (EBOOK)

10 9 8 7 6 5 4 3 2 1

Printed and bound in Great Britain by Clays Ltd, St Ives plc

To my mother, Anne-Marie Lindqvist.
To the memory of my grandmother, Maj Walhqvist.
Love and strength.

CONTENTS

Border

As soon as the man appeared, Tina knew he had something to hide. With every step he took towards the customs post, she grew more certain. When he chose the green channel, Nothing to declare, and walked right past her, she said, 'Excuse me, could I ask you to stop for a moment?' Glancing over at Robert to make sure he was on board. Robert gave a brief nod. People who were about to be caught could resort to desperate measures, particularly if they were smuggling something that would attract a prison sentence. Like this man. Tina was sure of it.

'Could you put your suitcase here, please?'

The man heaved a small case up onto the counter, unlocked it and opened the lid. He was used to this. Not surprisingly, given his appearance: angular face, low forehead. Small, deep-set eyes beneath bushy eyebrows. A beard and medium-length hair. He could have played a Russian hit man in an action movie.

Tina pressed the hidden alarm button as she leaned across the counter. Her instincts told her with absolute certainty that this man was carrying something illegal. He might be armed. From the corner of her eye she saw Leif and Andreas position themselves in the doorway leading to the inner room, watching and waiting.

The case contained very little. A few clothes. A road map and a couple of Henning Mankell crime novels, a pair of binoculars and a magnifying glass. There was also a digital camera; Tina picked it up to examine it more closely, but her gut feeling was that the camera wasn't the issue.

Right at the bottom of the suitcase lay a large metal box with a lid. In the middle of the lid there was a round meter with a needle. A cable ran from the side of the box.

'What's this?' she asked.

'Guess,' the man replied, raising his eyebrows as if he found the situation enormously amusing. Tina met his gaze. She saw a kind of exalted calm in his eyes, and that could be down to one of two things. Either he was crazy or he was certain she wouldn't find whatever he was hiding.

She didn't even need to consider a third option—the idea that he *didn't* have anything to hide. She knew.

The only reason she was working in Kapellskär was that it was so close to home. She could have worked anywhere. Customs posts all over the country sought her help when they knew that a large shipment of illegal drugs was on the way. Sometimes she would go, staying in Malmö or Helsingborg for a couple of days until she spotted the courier and taking the opportunity while she was there to point out a few miscreants smuggling cigarettes or people. She was almost never wrong. The only thing that could mislead her was if a person was carrying something that wasn't illegal, but that they wanted to hide anyway.

Usually that meant sex toys of various kinds. Dolls, vibrators, films. In Gothenburg she had stopped a man coming off the ferry from England whose suitcase had turned out to contain a huge amount of newly bought science fiction: Asimov, Bradbury, Clarke. The man had stood there looking around nervously with the suitcase wide open on the counter, and when she caught sight of his clerical collar she closed the case and wished him a nice day.

Three years ago she had been in the United States, monitoring the border crossing in Tijuana. She had pointed out five people carrying heroin—two in their stomachs, inside condoms—before the delivery they were waiting for actually arrived.

Three trucks with hollow wheel drums. Twelve hundred kilos. The biggest haul in ten years. She had been rewarded with a consultation fee of ten thousand dollars; they had also offered her a post with five times the salary of her job in Sweden, but she had turned it down.

Before she left she suggested to the head of the operation that he might like to investigate two members of his team. She was virtually certain they were being paid to facilitate the transportation of heroin. It turned out that she was absolutely right.

She could have become a multimillionaire by travelling around the world carrying out temporary assignments, but after her trip to the US she had turned down every offer. The two team members she had unmasked had secreted not only a high level of anxiety, but also *threat*. For safety's sake she had stayed with the chief customs officer and travelled to work with him. Knowing too much is dangerous, particularly when big money is involved.

And so she had settled in Kapellskär, ten minutes from her house in Gillberga on the island of Rådmansö. The number of seizures had increased dramatically when she first took up her post, and had subsequently fallen and continued to fall. The smugglers knew that she was working here and Kapellskär was now regarded as a locked-down port. Over the past few years she had dealt mainly with spirits and the odd disorganised chancer with steroids stuffed in the lining of his suitcase.

Her shift patterns changed from week to week so that the smugglers wouldn't know which times to avoid and which times they could exploit.

Without touching the box, she pointed at it and said, 'This is not a game. What is that?'

'It's for hatching out larvae.'

'I'm sorry?'

The man was smiling almost imperceptibly beneath his beard as he picked up the box. She could now see that the cable ended in an ordinary plug. He opened the lid. The interior was divided into four compartments, separated by thin walls.

'For breeding insects,' he said, holding up the lid and pointing at the meter. 'Thermostat. Electricity. Heat. Hey presto! Insects.'

Tina nodded. 'And why do you have such a thing?'

The man put the box back in his case and shrugged. 'Is it illegal?'

'No. I'm just curious.'

The man leaned across the counter and asked her in a low voice, 'Do you like insects?'

Something very unusual happened. A cold shiver ran down Tina's spine and presumably she began to secrete the same anxiety she was so good at detecting in others. Fortunately there was no one here who was capable of sensing it.

She shook her head and said, 'I'd like you to step in here for a moment.' She gestured towards the inner room. 'You can leave the case here for the time being.'

They examined his clothes, they examined his shoes. They went through every single thing he had in his case, and the case itself. They found nothing. They were only permitted to carry out a body search if there were reasonable grounds for suspicion.

Tina asked the others to leave the room. When they were alone, she said, 'I know you're hiding something. What is it?'

'How can you be so sure?'

After everything he had been subjected to, Tina thought he deserved an honest answer. 'I can smell it.'

The man laughed out loud. 'Of course.'

'You might think it's ridiculous,' said Tina. 'But—'

The man interrupted her. 'Not at all. It sounds eminently reasonable.'

'And?'

He spread his hands wide and gestured towards his body.

'You've examined me as thoroughly as possible. You're not allowed to go any further. Am I right?'

'Yes.'

'There you go. In that case I'd like your permission to leave.'

If it had been up to Tina she would have liked to take him into custody, keep him under observation. But she had no legal grounds for doing so. And besides…There was after all one option left. The unlikely third option. The possibility that she was wrong.

She accompanied him to the door and said what she had to say: 'My apologies for the inconvenience.'

The man stopped and turned to face her.

'Perhaps we'll meet again,' he said, then did something so unexpected that she didn't have time to react. He leaned forward and kissed her lightly on the cheek. His beard was rough, the hairs pricking her skin like soft needles just before his lips touched her.

She gave a start and pushed him away. 'What the hell do you think you're doing!'

The man raised his hands defensively as if to show that he wasn't going to do anything else, said, '*Entschuldigung*. Goodbye for now,' and left the room. He picked up his suitcase and made his way out of the entrance hall.

Tina stayed where she was, gazing after him.

She finished early that day and went home.

The dogs welcomed her with their usual angry barking. She yelled at them as they stood there behind the fence, their hackles raised and their teeth bared. She loathed them. She had always hated dogs, and of course the only man who had ever shown any interest in her just had to be a dog breeder.

When she first met Roland, his dog ownership had been restricted to a single breeding male—a pit bull by the name of Diablo that had won a number of illegal fights. Roland allowed him to mate with promising pure-bred bitches for five thousand kronor.

With the help of Tina's smallholding and her financial support, he had been able to increase his stock to two breeding males, four bitches and five young dogs that were next in line to be sold. One of the bitches was a real champion, and Roland often took her to shows and competitions where he made new business contacts and screwed around.

It happened as a matter of course, it had become part of their everyday life. Tina no longer asked him about it. She could smell when he had been with another woman, and never reproached him. He was company, and she had no right to hope for anything more.

If life is a prison, then there is a moment in a person's life when she realises exactly where her walls are located, where the boundaries to her freedom lie. Whether there are walls, or possible escape routes. The end of year party when she left school had been one of those moments for Tina.

After everyone in the class had got fairly drunk in the hired venue, they drove down to the park in Norrtälje to sit on the grass and finish off the last of the wine.

Tina had always felt uncomfortable at parties because they

usually ended up with people pairing off. But not tonight. On this occasion it was the *class* that counted, this was their last evening together, and she was part of the group.

When the wine had been drunk and the in-jokes had been trotted out for the very last time, they lay sprawled on the grass, not wanting to go home, not wanting to say goodbye. Tina was so drunk that what she thought of in those days as her sixth sense was no longer working. She was just one of the group, lying there and refusing to grow up.

It was very pleasant, and it frightened her. The fact that alcohol was a kind of solution. If she just drank enough, she lost the thing that made her different from everyone else. Perhaps there was some sort of medication that could block it out, stop her from knowing things she didn't want to know.

She was lying there thinking along these lines when Jerry shuffled over to her. Earlier in the evening he had written in her hat: 'I'll never forget you. Love Jerry.'

They had worked together on the school newspaper, written several things that had circulated all around the school, been quoted by their fellow students. They had the same dark sense of humour, took the same pleasure in writing poisonous articles about the teachers who deserved it.

'Hi.' He lay down next to her, resting his head on his hand.

'Hi yourself.' She was almost seeing double. The pimples on Jerry's face faded away, became blurred, and he looked almost attractive in the semi-darkness.

'Bloody hell,' he said. 'We've had so much fun.'

'Mmm.'

Jerry nodded slowly for a long time. His eyes were shiny, unfocused behind his glasses. He sighed and adjusted his position so that he was sitting cross-legged.

'There's something…something I've been wanting to say to you.'

Tina rested her hands on her stomach and gazed up at the stars, piercing the foliage with their needles of light.

'Oh?'

'It's…well…' Jerry ran a hand over his face and tried to stop slurring. 'The thing is, I like you. I mean, you know that.'

Tina waited. She had thought she needed a pee, but now she realised it was a kind of tingling feeling. A warm nerve trembling in a previously unexpected place.

Jerry shook his head. 'I don't know how to…Right. I'm just going to say it, because I want you know how I feel, now we…now we might not see each other again.'

'Yes.'

'Well, it's like this. I think you're a bloody fantastic girl. And I wish…this is what I wanted to say…I wish I could meet someone who's exactly like you, but who doesn't look like you.'

The nerve stopped trembling. Grew, went cold. She didn't want to hear the answer, but she asked the question anyway:

'What do you mean?'

'Well…' Jerry banged his hand down on the grass. 'For fuck's sake, you know what I mean. You're…you're such a bloody fantastic girl and you're great to be with. I…oh, what the hell: I love you. I do. There. I've said it. But it's just…' He banged his hand on the grass again, more helplessly this time.

Tina finished the sentence for him. 'But it's just that I'm too ugly to go out with.'

He reached for her hand. 'Tina. You mustn't…'

She got up. Her legs were steadier than she'd expected. She looked down at Jerry, still sitting on the grass holding his hand out to her, and said, 'I don't. Why don't you take a look at yourself in the fucking mirror.'

She strode away. Only when she was sure she was out of sight and Jerry wasn't following her did she allow herself to collapse into a bush. The branches scratched her face, her bare arms, finally embraced her. She drew her body in on itself, pressed her hands to her face.

What hurt most was the fact that he had been trying to be kind. That he had said the nicest thing he could say about her.

She lay there in her prickly cocoon and wept until she had no tears left. No doors. No way out. Her body wasn't even a prison, more like a cage inside which it was impossible to sit, stand or lie down.

The passing years hadn't improved matters. She had learned to tolerate life inside the cage, to accept her limitations. But she refused to look in the mirror. The revulsion she saw in the eyes of other people when she met them for the first time was mirror enough.

When all hope was lost for the people she caught smuggling, they sometimes started screaming at her. Screaming about the way she looked. Something about Mongols, about the fact that she ought to be put out of her misery. She never got used to it. That was why she let others do the tough stuff once she had pointed out a miscreant. To avoid the horror when the acting stopped and the mask slipped.

An elderly woman was sitting on the steps of the little cottage, reading a book. A bike was propped up against the fence. The woman lowered the book as Tina went by and carried on staring for just a little too long after they had nodded to one another.

The summer had begun. The woman's eyes burned into her back as she walked into the house and found Roland sitting at the kitchen table with his laptop. He looked up when she came in. 'Hi. The first guest has arrived.'

'Yes. I saw her.'

He turned his attention back to the computer. Tina looked at the guest book that lay open on the table and discovered that the woman's name was Lillemor, and her home address was in Stockholm. The majority of their guests came from Stockholm or Helsinki. Plus the odd German en route to Finland.

Renting out the cottage for the summer had been Roland's idea, after he heard how well things were going for the hostel a couple of kilometres down the road. That had been early on in their relationship, and Tina had gone along with it because she wanted him to feel he had a role in deciding how the place was run. The kennels came six months later.

'Listen, I think I'll probably go down to Skövde this weekend,' said Roland. 'I think we might just do it this time.'

Tina nodded. Tara, the pit bull bitch, had been named Best in Class twice, but still hadn't won Best in Show, which would really put Roland's kennels on the map. It was like an obsession. And a good excuse for going away, of course. Having a bit of fun.

Even if Roland had been in the mood for talking, she wouldn't have been able to tell him what had happened at work. Instead she went out into the forest, to her tree.

Summer comes late to Roslagen. Even though it was the beginning of June, only the birch trees were in full leaf; the aspens and alders were a pale green shimmer amid the eternal dark green of the conifers.

She went along the little track leading to the flat rocks. In the forest she was safe, she could think without worrying about pointing fingers or drawn-out looks. Even as a little girl she had been happiest in the forest where no one could see her. After the accident it had been several months before she was brave enough to go out again, but when she did go out, the pull was so much stronger as a result. And she went straight to the scene of the accident, then as now.

She called it the Dance Floor, because it was the kind of place where you could imagine the elves dancing on summer evenings. You went up a slight incline, then the forest opened out into a plateau, a series of flat rocks with a single tall pine tree growing out of a deep crevice. When she was little she had thought of the pine as the central point of the earth, the axis around which everything spun like a merry-go-round.

Nowadays the pine was no more than the ghost of a tree: a split trunk with a few bare branches sticking out from the sides. Once upon a time the rocks had been covered with fallen needles. Now there were no needles left to fall, and the wind had blown away the old ones.

She sat down next to the tree, rested her shoulder on the trunk and patted it. 'Hello, old friend. How are you?'

She had had countless conversations with the tree. When she finally got home from Norrtälje that night after the end of term party, she went straight to the pine tree and told him everything, weeping against the bark. He was the only one who understood, because they shared the same fate.

She was ten years old. The last week of the summer holiday. Since she didn't really like playing with other children, she had spent the summer helping her father work on the cottage, and walking and reading in the forest, of course.

On that particular day she had taken one of the Famous Five books with her. It might have been *Five Go to Billycock Hill*. She couldn't remember, and the book had been ruined.

She had been sitting under the pine tree reading when the rain caught her unawares. In just a few seconds it went from drizzle to a downpour. After a couple of minutes the rocks were a delta of gushing rivers. Tina stayed where she was, the dense crown of the pine tree forming such an effective umbrella that she was able to carry on reading, with only the odd drop of rain landing on her book.

The thunderstorm moved across the forest, drawing closer.

Eventually there was a crash so loud that she could feel the vibration in the stones beneath her, and she got scared and closed her book, thinking it might be best to try to get home in spite of the weather.

Then there was nothing but a bright white light.

Her father found her an hour later. If he hadn't known that she often went to the tree, it could have been days, even weeks.

She was lying underneath the crown of the tree. The lightning had snapped off the top of the tree, raced down the trunk and continued on its way into the girl down at the bottom, at which point the crown had fallen and landed on top of the child. Her father said his heart stopped when he reached the plateau and saw the shattered tree. Exactly what he feared most had happened.

He pushed his way in among the branches and caught a glimpse of her lying there. With a strength he didn't know he possessed he managed to overturn the crown and get her out. Much later he said that what had really stuck in his memory was the *smell*.

'It smelled like...like when you're trying to start the car with jump leads and you accidentally short-circuit the whole thing. You get sparks and...that exact same smell.'

Her nose, ears, fingers and toes had been black. Her hair had been a single clump stuck to her head, and the Famous Five book in her hand was almost burnt to a crisp.

At first he had thought she was dead, but when he put his ear to her chest he had heard her heart beating, a faint ticking. He had run through the forest with her in his arms, driven as fast as he could to the hospital in Norrtälje, and her life had been saved.

Her face, which had been less than attractive before the accident, was now actually ugly. The cheek that had been turned towards the trunk was so badly burned that the skin never healed properly, but remained permanently dark red. Incredibly, her eye had survived, but her eyelid was stuck in a half-closed position that made her look constantly suspicious.

When she started to earn decent money she looked into the possibility of plastic surgery. Yes, skin could certainly be grafted, but since the nerve damage was so deep it was unlikely the new skin would take. They wouldn't even consider touching the eyelid because an operation could damage the tear duct.

She gave it a go. Paid to let them scrape skin from her back and graft it onto her face. The result was as expected. After a week the skin was no longer getting any oxygen, and it shrivelled and died.

Plastic surgery had made great strides in the intervening years, but she had accepted her fate and had no intention of trying again. The tree hadn't got better, so why should she?

'I don't understand it,' she said to the tree. 'There have been times I've had my doubts, when I thought someone might just be carrying an extra bottle or two, and I've let it go. But this man, he...'

She leaned her healthy cheek—the one that had today received its first spontaneous kiss since she was a child—against the trunk and rubbed it up and down on the rough bark.

'I was absolutely certain. That was why I thought it was a bomb, that metal box. Something major. And after all, they do say there's a risk that the ferries will be the next terrorist target. But why should anyone coming *off* the ferry smuggle a bomb, now there's a question...'

She kept on talking. The tree listened. Eventually she got around to the other issue.

'...and I don't understand that either. It must have been a way of showing that he had the upper hand. A kiss on the cheek, there there, you have no idea what's going on. Like some kind of revenge. What do you think? And it's hardly surprising after what he'd been subjected to, but it's a funny way of doing it...'

Dusk had started to fall by the time she finished. Before she got up she patted the tree and asked, 'And what about you? How are you getting on? Aches and pains all the time. Life's hell. I know. OK. I know. Take care of yourself. Bye bye.'

When she got home, Lillemor was sitting on the porch with a paraffin lamp glowing. They waved to one another. She would have a word with Roland. No more after this summer.

That evening she wrote in her diary: *I hope he comes back. Next time I'll have him.*

————·————

For the same reason that her shifts varied from week to week, her holidays were spread throughout the summer. A week here, a week there. If she had asked for a continuous break they would have agreed because they valued her, but she didn't feel the need for it. After all, work was the place where she felt most at ease.

She took her first week so that she could go down and help out at the customs post in Malmö. An unusually sophisticated press for printing euro notes had been discovered in Hamburg, and they knew that hundreds of millions had already been printed, ready to be spread right across Europe.

On her third day the couriers arrived in a campervan. A man and a woman. They even had a child with them. The situation became clear to Tina only when she realised she was picking up signals from the man, not the other two. The woman and child knew nothing about the false floor and the ten million in hundred-euro notes hidden underneath it. She explained this to the police, and they said the information had been noted.

However, she also made contact with the public prosecutor in Malmö, whom she knew from a previous case, and repeated that the woman was innocent (the child was eight years old and subject only to the worst punishment of all: being taken away from his parents). The prosecutor promised to do what he could.

When she got back to Kapellskär at the beginning of July, she let a few days pass before she asked.

She and Robert were taking a coffee break in the cafeteria in the entrance hall. The next ferry wasn't due for an hour, and when they had finished their coffee she leaned back in her chair and asked, quite casually, 'That guy with the insects. Has he been back?'

'What guy?'

'You remember—I thought he was carrying something, but he wasn't.'

'Are you still thinking about him?'

Tina shrugged. 'No, I just wondered.'

Robert folded his hands over his stomach and looked at her. She glanced over at the pinball machines, and at first she thought she had turned her head so that the sun was catching it, because her healthy cheek suddenly felt hot.

'No,' said Robert. 'Not as far as I know, anyway.'

'OK.'

They went back to work.

During her second holiday week at the end of July she went to a dog show in Umeå with Roland. He took the car and she took the train because she didn't want to travel in the car with the dogs, and the dogs didn't want to travel in the car with her.

She didn't actually go to the dog show either, but she and Roland had two free days together. They spent the first wandering around Umeå, and on the second day they went for a long walk in the surrounding area. Occasionally he stroked her arm or took her hand when there was nobody else in sight.

She couldn't work out exactly what it was that made them a couple. They were much too different to be friends, and the only time they had tried to have sex it had been so agonisingly painful that she had been forced to beg him to stop. It was probably a relief for him.

He slept with other women, and she didn't blame him for that. He had been kind enough to try with her, and she had told him to stop. The morning after their failed attempt, she remembered saying, 'I don't think I'll ever be able to have sex with you. So if you...if you want to do it with someone else then...then that's OK.'

She had said it out of despair, and had hoped that he would say— well, whatever. She had said it. And he had taken her at her word.

During the rest of her week off she went to see her father a couple of times. Took him out in his wheelchair so that he could escape from the residential home in Norrtälje for a little while; he had gone there after the death of his wife.

After the death of my mother, Tina forced herself to think. They had never been close. Unlike Tina and her father.

They sat down by the harbour eating ice cream. Tina had to feed her father from a carton. His mind was completely clear, his body almost completely paralysed. When they had finished their ice creams and watched the boats for a while, he asked, 'How are things with Roland these days?'

'Fine. He had high hopes in Umeå, but they ended up with Best in Class as usual. People don't like fighting dogs.'

'No. Perhaps things will improve if they stop attacking children. But I really meant how are things between you and Roland.'

Tina's father and Roland had met once, when her father called in to say hello, and it had been a case of mutual dislike at first sight. Her father had questioned the wisdom of both the kennels and renting out the cottage, wondered if Roland was intending to go the whole hog and turn his family home into some kind of theme park, with carousels and goodness knows what.

Fortunately Roland had been diplomatic, but when her father left—after coffee drunk in an uncomfortable, brooding silence—he had launched into a tirade about old farts who couldn't accept change and senile fools who wanted to block any kind of progress; he had stopped only when Tina reminded him that was her father he was talking about.

Her father normally referred to Roland as the Small Businessman; it was rare for him to use his name.

Tina didn't want to talk about it. She went off and threw their serviettes and empty cartons in the bin without answering him, and hoped he would drop the subject.

No chance. When she came back, ready to take him to the residential home, he said, 'Stop right there. I asked you a question. Am I so old that I no longer deserve an answer?'

Tina sighed and sat down on the plastic chair beside him.

'Dad. I know how you feel about Roland...'

'Yes, you do. But I have no idea how *you* feel.'

Tina looked out across the harbour. The Vaxholm ferry, which had been converted into a restaurant, scraped gently against the quayside. When she was little there had been a plane on the other side of the channel. The counter had been inside the fuselage, you could sit at a table out on the wing, drinking your coffee. Or juice. She had been sad when it was taken away.

'The thing is...' she said. 'It's a bit difficult to explain.'

'Try.'

'It's nothing like...what about you and Mum, anyway? Why did you stay together? You had next to nothing in common.'

'We had you. And to tell the truth, things weren't too bad in bed either. When we got around to it. But what about you two? What have you got?'

The sun struck Tina's cheek again.

'I really don't want to discuss this with you, Dad.'

'I see. And who are you going to discuss it with, exactly? The tree?' He turned his head towards her just a fraction, which was all he could manage. 'Do you still go there?'

'Yes.'

'I see. Good.' He blew air out through his nose, sat quietly for a few seconds, then said, 'Listen, sweetheart. I just don't want you to be exploited.'

Tina studied her feet through the straps of her sandals. Her toes were bent; even her feet were ugly.

'I'm not being exploited. I want someone to be with and…it can't be helped.'

'Darling girl. You deserve better.'

'Yes. But it's not going to happen.'

They made their way back through the town in silence. Her father's parting words were: 'Say hello to the Small Businessman from me.' She said she would, but she didn't.

She was back at work on Monday. The first thing Robert said after they had exchanged the usual pleasantries was: '…and no, he hasn't been here.'

She knew what he meant, but asked anyway: 'Who?'

Robert smiled. 'The Shah of Iran, of course, who do you think?'

'Oh, you mean…Right. I see.'

'I checked with the others too. In case he came through when I wasn't on duty.'

'It's not that important.'

'No, of course not,' said Robert. 'I've asked them to let me know if he comes through, but you're not interested then?'

Tina got annoyed.

'I got it wrong once,' she said, holding up a rigid index finger in front of Robert's face. 'Just once. And I don't think I did get it wrong. That's why I'm wondering what he does. Is that so strange?'

Robert held up his hands and took a step backwards.

'OK, OK. I thought we'd agreed it was something to do with that—what was it called—insect hatching box.'

Tina shook her head. 'It wasn't that.'

'So what was it, then?'

'I don't know,' she said. 'I don't know.'

The summer rolled back its warmth and the holidays came to an end. The ferries began to run less frequently, and the little cottage was empty, thank goodness. When Tina brought up the idea of not renting it out in the future, Roland got annoyed. She let it be.

During the summer the house next door had been sold to a middle-aged couple with two children from Stockholm. The woman, who was pregnant with what she referred to as Tail-end Charlie, was always popping round. No doubt she thought that's what people did in the country.

Tina liked the woman, whose name was Elisabeth, but she kept on and on about the fact that she was pregnant. She was forty-two years old, and slightly obsessed with the fact that she was going to be a mother again, and Tina sometimes found it painful to listen to her.

She would have liked to be able to have children herself, but as she was incapable of doing what was necessary in order to create a child, it was never going to happen.

She envied Elisabeth, but she liked the particular aroma surrounding the pregnant woman. A secret aroma, filled with expectation.

Tina was also forty-two, and from a purely theoretical point of view she could have talked to Roland about IVF, but that wasn't the way things were between them. Not at all.

So she sat and breathed in Elisabeth's aroma and longed for something that could never be.

The weather had been unusually warm during the summer, and the autumn was taking its time to arrive.

In the middle of September he turned up again.

The feeling was just as powerful as it had been on the previous occasion. So powerful that there was an aura around him, a flashing neon sign with the words HIDING SOMETHING.

She didn't even need to say anything. He walked straight to the counter and heaved up his suitcase, then linked his hands behind his back.

'Hello again,' he said.

Tina made an effort to sound normal: 'I'm sorry? Do we know each other?'

'No,' said the man. 'But we have met.'

He waved one arm towards the suitcase in an inviting gesture. Tina couldn't help smiling. She waved her arm in turn, indicating that he should open the case.

He's treating the whole thing like a game, she thought. *But this time I'm going to win.*

'How was your summer?' he asked as she went through the case. She shook her head. He might be treating this like a game, and she might have thought about him now and again, but when it came down to it they were on opposite sides of the counter. He was trying to bring in something illicit, and she forced herself to think *Drugs... drugs that will be sold to thirteen-year-old kids.* The man in front of her was one of the bad guys, and she was going to break him.

The contents of the case were largely the same as before, except that the Mankell novels had been replaced by Åke Edwardson. She picked up the insect hatching box and looked inside. Empty. She tapped on the base to check that there was no hidden space. The man followed her movements with amused interest.

'Right,' she said when she had established that the case contained nothing more than the eye could see. 'I am convinced that you are hiding something, and this time I intend to have a more thorough search carried out. Could you come this way, please.'

The man didn't move. 'So you do remember,' he said.

'I have a vague recollection, yes.'

He held out his hand and said, 'Vore.'

'I'm sorry?'

'Vore. That's my name. What's yours?'

Tina met his gaze. His eyes were so deep set that hardly any light from the fluorescent tube on the ceiling reached them, and they looked like faintly reflective black mountain pools. Most people would probably be frightened by such a gaze. Not Tina.

'Tina,' she said dryly. 'This way, please.'

Since the search was of an intimate nature, Tina did not participate. No ferries were due for some time, and while Robert carried out the external physical check she wandered around the entrance hall making bets with herself, fixing the odds on what might be found.

Drugs of some kind: two to one. Heroin: four to one. Amphetamines: eight to one. Something to do with spying: ten to one.

But the more she thought about it, the more the odds on spying shortened. He wasn't the type to smuggle drugs.

Vore's suitcase was still lying on the counter. She took out the two detective novels and flicked through them. No words were highlighted or underlined. She held the pages up to the light. Then she looked around and took out a lighter. Ran the small flame to and fro underneath a page to see if any invisible writing might appear. She

21

singed the edge of the paper, but no writing emerged. She quickly put the book back in the case, its blackened edge glistening.

This is ridiculous. Kalle Blomqvist.

But what *was* it, then?

She walked between the pinball machines and the panorama windows and back again. Her job, her ability was something she simply took for granted. This was something completely new. The man spoke with no accent whatsoever. But *Vore*? What kind of a name was that? She supposed it must be Russian, Slavonic.

At any rate, if the external physical examination didn't produce any results, she would apply for a warrant allowing a doctor to carry out a proper search. Check every orifice.

Robert came out, made a comment to the occupant of the room, and closed the door behind him. Tina hurried over. Her heart sank when she was only halfway across the hall; Robert was shaking his head.

'Nothing?' she asked.

'No,' said Robert. 'Well, nothing that concerns us, anyway.'

'What do you mean?'

Robert drew her a little distance away from the door.

'Let me put it this way: you can rest easy. He did have something to hide, but nothing punishable by law. The problem is that we've now stopped him twice without...'

'Yes, yes. Do you think I don't know that? So what is it, then?'

The thought had struck her, but she hadn't seriously considered what Robert was suggesting: the fact that they might have been guilty of professional misconduct. Subjecting Vore to an examination on two separate occasions without any solid evidence for doing so. If Vore made a complaint, they would probably be reprimanded.

'The thing is,' said Robert, 'he's...he's a woman.'

'Come on, stop winding me up.'

Robert folded his arms and looked uncomfortable. With

exaggerated clarity he said, 'He...or rather she, does not have a penis but a vagina, to use the technical term. *You* should have carried out that search, not me.'

Tina stared at him open-mouthed for a few seconds. 'You're not joking?'

'No. And it was rather...embarrassing.' Robert looked so miserable that Tina burst out laughing. He looked at her, his expression furious.

'Sorry. Has he got...breasts as well?'

'No. He must have had an operation or something. I didn't actually ask. He's got like a big scar just above his bum, by his tailbone. Whatever that might be. Now it's *your* turn to talk to him and try to explain that—'

'What did you say? A scar?'

'Yes. A scar. Here.' Robert pointed to the bottom of his back. 'If you want to take this any further, you can do it yourself.' He shook his head and headed off towards the cafeteria. Tina stayed where she was, looking at the closed door. When she had thought things through she opened it and went in.

Vore was standing by the window looking out. When she came in, he turned to face her. It was impossible to think of him as 'her'. If you wanted to define the repellent aspect of his appearance in a few words you could perhaps say: exaggerated masculinity. He looked *too much* like a man. The coarse, broad face. The squat, muscular body. The beard and the powerful eyebrows.

'So,' he said, and now she noticed how unusually deep his voice was. Up to now she had taken it as a natural complement to his body. 'Are we done here?'

'Yes,' said Tina, sitting down at the desk. 'Could you spare a few moments?'

'Of course.'

He showed not the slight sign of being angry or offended on this occasion either. He sat down opposite her.

'First of all,' said Tina, 'I would like to offer my sincere apologies. Again. I must also inform you that you have every right to make a complaint against us. You can—'

'Why would I do that?'

'Because of the way we've treated you.'

'We can forget about that. What else did you want to say?'

'Well...' Tina's fingers began to twist themselves around each other under the desk, where he couldn't see them. '...I was just wondering. Who you are. This is purely...private.'

The man looked at her for such a long time that she had to lower her gaze. She shouldn't be doing this. To begin with, she was completely on the back foot after what had happened. A position she hated. In addition, it was against regulations to have any personal contact with those she was supposed to be investigating. She shook her head.

'Forgive me. You're free to go. We're done.'

'I'm in no hurry,' said Vore. 'Who am I? That's something I'm not too sure about, like most people I suppose. I travel. I stay somewhere for a while. Then I continue my journey.'

'And you study insects?'

'Among other things, yes. Although perhaps your question is mostly concerned with my...physical attributes?'

Tina shook her head. 'No. Not at all.'

'And what about you? Do you live locally?'

'Yes. In Gillberga.'

'I don't know it, unfortunately. But perhaps you know the ramblers' hostel here in...Riddersholm, I think it's called. Would you recommend it?'

'Absolutely. It's good. Beautiful surroundings. Are you thinking of staying there?'

24

'Yes. For a while, anyway. So we might see one another.' He stood up and held out his hand. 'Goodbye for now.'

She took his hand. His fingers were thick, strong. But so were hers. A strange excitement was growing in her stomach. She led the way to the door. As she stood there resting her fingers on the handle, she said, 'Otherwise I have a cottage that I rent out.'

'In...Gillberga?'

'Yes. There's a sign by the side of the road.'

Vore nodded. 'In that case I'll call round one day and...have a look. That would be nice.'

She stayed where she was, looking at him. The moment was exactly the same as last time. Perhaps it was a desire to pre-empt him, to regain control. Perhaps it was something else altogether. It was impossible to say, it was beyond everything she was capable of knowing or determining. She quickly leaned forward and kissed him on the cheek.

This time it was her lips that were pricked by his sharp beard, and the moment they touched his skin a hammer of regret struck her on the forehead, making her jerk backwards.

She quickly opened the door, refusing to look him in the eye. He went out, picked up his suitcase and disappeared.

As soon as she was sure he had gone, she scurried off to the toilets, locked herself in a cubicle, sat down and hid her face in her hands.

Why did I do that how could I do that what's the matter with me?

Something had fallen apart inside her head. The mistake had made her confused. The ground had been snatched away from beneath her feet, and she wasn't responsible for her actions.

What's the matter with me?

She rocked back and forth, whimpering to herself. What would he think of her? She! What would *she* think of her?

Why...why?

But somewhere she knew the answer. When she had calmed down and managed to stop her hands shaking, she got up and pulled down her trousers and her panties.

It was difficult to turn her head so far, it was just on the edge of her field of vision, but it was still clearly visible. It was years since she had last looked at it in a mirror: the big red scar just above her tailbone.

She rinsed her face and dried it with a paper towel.

There was a better reason why she had invited Vore to her home.

Robert could think what he liked, and the information about Vore's body was certainly a surprise, but she was still sure that wasn't *it*. She couldn't put her finger on how she knew, but she definitely knew.

Whatever he was hiding, it wasn't his own body. It was something else, and she *had* to find out what it was. Which meant that having him close by was the most sensible thing to do.

Wasn't it?

As Tina drove home from the harbour the sky was a dark grey lid covering the world, and the treetops swayed alongside the motorway. It didn't take an expert to realise that an autumn storm was on the way.

The first drops fell as she turned into the drive. During the short time it took her to walk up to the house they began to fall more heavily, and with a sudden squall the downpour was upon her. She ran the last few steps and pulled the door open.

The dog came racing towards her across the hall. She probably wouldn't have had time to react if she hadn't heard the patter of claws before she realised that the black mass of muscle was a dog.

Just as Roland yelled 'Tara!' from the kitchen she slammed the outside door and heard the dog crash into it with a thud that made the handle vibrate. The dog barked and scrabbled at the door, eager to get at her.

Use the handle, you stupid bitch.

She backed away from the door and ended up beyond the plastic roof covering the porch. The rain ran down the back of her neck. The door opened a fraction. Inside stood Roland, hanging on to the furious, barking dog with some difficulty while at the same time trying to plaster on a conciliatory smile. Above the noise of the dog he yelled, 'Sorry. Had to put some ointment on her, she's got an attack of mange on her—'

Tina stepped forward and slammed the door shut. She didn't need to know where the dog had mange. Through the door she could hear Tara being dragged across the floor, still barking.

The landscape beyond the porch was beginning to disappear. A grey veil covered everything and the noise of the rain was like a TV channel with nothing on it. White noise. The water splashed over the guttering, made a fan shape in the water butt.

Between the dog and the rain she had a strip about two metres wide in which she could move, and she was sharing the space with a box of old newspapers and a broken bilge pump. She picked up a copy of *Dagens Nyheter*, held it over her head and ran the hundred metres across to the cottage.

A thermostat ensured that the temperature in the cottage never dropped below twelve degrees. If a guest arrived it took no time at all to get the house pleasantly warm. As soon as she got inside she turned the radiator full on, took a towel out of the cupboard, dried her hair and sat down at the desk just in time to witness a scene she found remarkably upsetting.

The neighbours' sheets were pegged out on the line. They were flapping wildly in the growing storm, tugging at their moorings like fettered ghosts. Just as Tina sat down, Elisabet and Göran came out of the house. Elisabet's belly was so big by now that her body was an appendage to it rather than vice versa.

They ran across the garden in the pouring rain. If you could call what Elisabet was doing running. It was more of a fast waddle. For some reason they were in a really good mood, laughing as they tried to grab hold of the flailing sheets. Elisabet was slow and only managed to take down two, while Göran seized the other four and rolled them up into a big ball, which he stuffed under his jumper. It was impossible to say whether this was a practical measure to protect the sheets or a joke right from the start, but as he waddled off with his false belly, Elisabet laughed so much that Tina could hear her inside the cottage.

She spun her chair around so that she was facing into the room. *How silly can some people be?*

They were like something out of Astrid Lindgren's *Life on Seacrow Island*, one of the scenes that was cut because even the director thought it was too nauseating.

Although this was real, of course. People can be this happy.

Tina made a conscious effort not to hate her neighbours because they were happy. For a moment she sat there at the desk staring out of the window and wishing that Elisabet's child would be stillborn, just so that she could have a taste of the other things life serves up.

Then Tina excised the thought because she wasn't that kind of person.

But Tina is exactly that kind of person.

No I'm not. Haven't I promised to drive them to the hospital when the time comes, if I'm home?

You're hoping you won't be home. You don't want to do it.

Because I don't like hospitals, that's all.

You saw it so clearly: Elisabet bent double by the washing line, clutching her belly. The sheet torn free, entangled in her flailing arms. Her screams, her—

Stop it, stop it, stop it!

28

Tina got up and pressed her hands to her temples. The wind, gaining strength, tore a flurry of leaves from the trees, set them whirling in the air outside the window. The small television aerial on the roof shook and swung like a tuning fork, sending a single long, mournful note through the house as if it were a sound box.

With her hands still pressed to her temples Tina fell to her knees and sank down until her forehead was resting on the floor.

Help me, God. I'm so unhappy.

No reply. Prayer requires humility, self abasement. That was what her mother had told her in front of a picture in the church.

The picture showed Jesus and three fishermen. They were out at sea in a small boat. There was a storm. The three fishermen, portrayed in the time-honoured way, with seamen's caps and beards, had fallen to their knees in the boat and were gazing at the bright figure in the stern.

Her mother explained what the picture meant: the fishermen had placed their fate in the hands of the Lord. They had let go the oars and the rudder, abandoned all attempts to save themselves from mortal danger. Now only Jesus could save them. And that is exactly what man must do if his prayers are to have any power: let go of everything, hand it over to the Lord.

Tina had disliked the idea even at that early age, and as an adult she had decided that holding onto the rudder and the oars was her preferred option, not falling to her knees.

But help me anyway.

It took another ten minutes before there was a knock at the door. Roland was standing outside with an umbrella.

'Are you there?' he asked.

'Yes,' Tina replied. 'Where else would I be?'

Roland had no answer to that. He held out the umbrella towards her, exposing himself to the rain.

'Come on,' he said. 'I've locked her in my bedroom.'

'You take the umbrella,' said Tina, holding up the towel she had used to dry her hair. 'I've got this.'

'Don't be silly. Here.' He shook the umbrella, wanting her to take it. The rain had already soaked his hair, plastering it to his scalp.

'Roland, you're getting wet. Take the umbrella and get inside.'

'I'm already wet. Here.'

'I've got the towel.'

Roland stared at her for a few seconds. Then he closed the umbrella, placed it at her feet and walked back to the house. Tina waited thirty seconds then followed him, using the towel to protect her. When she was a few metres away from the cottage, she stopped.

Silly. Now who's being silly?

But she still didn't take the umbrella. The rain was so heavy that it had soaked through the towel before she got back inside the house. Roland was standing in the hallway pulling off his wet clothes so that he could drape them over the stove. He pulled a face when he saw her arrive without the umbrella, but said nothing.

She put her blouse on a hanger in the bathroom and thought it was going to be one of those evenings. Just as they hadn't huddled together to share the umbrella, so they had no way of dealing with conflict.

They didn't *want* to solve their problems, so disagreements always ended up in a mutual silence that went on until it ebbed away. On the rare occasions when they really did quarrel, there was a huge store of assorted unresolved issues to be tipped out and hurled at one another.

Tara was whining in Roland's room, and Tina had just started wondering how she was going to get through the evening when the problem solved itself: Göran rang to say the baby had started. Did she have time to drive them to the hospital?

She certainly did.

Elisabet and Göran sat in the back of the car, their arms wrapped around each other. Their older children were fifteen and twelve, and were fine on their own. Göran explained that they had had the foresight to buy a new video game a month ago, ready to hand over when the time came.

Tina murmured something appropriate and concentrated on her driving. The windscreen wipers were working at full speed, swishing spasmodically back and forth without managing to clear the water completely. Her tyres were worn down to the point of illegality, and she didn't dare go over fifty in case of aquaplaning. There might have been an evil Tina inside her wishing miscarriage and misery on her passengers, but the Tina behind the wheel had no intention of crashing the car with a pregnant woman in the back seat.

Just as long as we don't have a thunderstorm.

Thunder and lightning could still knock her completely off course. Admittedly the car, with its rubber insulation on the ground, was the place she preferred to be during a thunderstorm, but not while she was *driving*.

As they passed Spillersboda the rain eased off and visibility improved. She glanced at the back seat. Elisabet was bent over, her face contorted with pain as she leaned against her husband.

'How's it going?' asked Tina.

'Fine,' Göran replied. 'But I think the contractions are quite close now.'

Tina increased her speed to seventy. She was revolted by the thought that the child might be born in her car. The smell emanating from Elisabet was anything but pleasant. It would cling to the upholstery for months.

They arrived at the hospital and Göran half led, half carried Elisabet to the maternity unit. Tina stood by the car for a moment, unsure what to do, then she followed them. It had more or less stopped raining; there was just a film of drizzle hanging in the air.

As they walked into the hospital a couple of nurses immediately came over to Elisabet, and the little group set off with Göran two paces behind. He didn't even glance in Tina's direction. Her job was done, and she no longer had anything to do with the proceedings. She stood in the corridor and watched them disappear round a corner.

How were they intending to get home?

Did they expect her to sit here and wait?

If so, they were going to be disappointed. Tina opened and closed her hands, gazing at the spot where they had vanished.

A nurse came over and asked, 'Has someone been to help you?'

'No,' replied Tina. 'But I don't need any help, thank you.'

The nurse smelled more strongly of hospital than the building itself, and Tina quickly made for the exit. Only when she was outside in the carpark did she dare to breathe again. That smell of disinfected clothes and antiseptic soap almost brought on a panic attack. It went back a long way. She remembered being terrified all the time when she had been in hospital after being struck by lightning. Just wanting to go home.

It was quarter to seven, and the storm had blown over as quickly as it had come. There wasn't a cloud in the deep blue evening sky, and the half-moon was as sharp as a blade. She pushed her hands deep in her pockets and strolled over towards the residential home for the elderly.

Her father was watching *Jeopardy*. 'Viktor Sjöström, you idiot!' he muttered at a contestant who thought *The Phantom Carriage* had been directed by Ingmar Bergman. The next question was about the director of *Sir Arne's Treasure*, and when the same contestant went for Bergman again, her father said, 'Turn it off, for God's sake. It's driving me mad.'

Tina leaned forward and switched the television off.

'A trained gibbon could do better,' her father said. 'I don't know why I watch it, I always end up getting really annoyed. Could you be an angel and give me some of that orange drink?'

Tina held the plastic cup with the straw up to his mouth, and her father drank for a while as he gazed into her eyes. When she took the straw away, he asked, 'How are you? Is something wrong?'

'No, why?'

'You just look as if there might be. Is it the Small Businessman?'

'No,' said Tina. 'It's just that…I was at the hospital. I gave my neighbours a lift—she was having a baby. I don't know why, but being in a hospital always shakes me up.'

'I see. Right. But otherwise everything's OK?'

Tina looked around the room. It was sparsely furnished so that it would be easier to clean. No rugs on the lino. Only a couple of pictures from home and a few framed photographs above the bed indicated that the occupant was someone who had lived a life of their own.

One of the photographs was of Tina herself, aged perhaps seven. She was sitting in a garden chair gazing into the camera with a serious expression, her small, deep-set eyes buried in her skull. She was wearing a floral-patterned dress that looked all wrong on her angular body. As if someone had put trousers on a pig to make it look presentable.

Ugly little bugger.

'Dad? I was wondering about something.'

'What's that?'

'I've got a scar here.' She pointed. 'When did I get that?'

There was a brief silence. Then her father answered, 'But I've already told you. You fell on a rock when you were little.'

'How little?'

'I don't know…four, maybe? A sharp rock. Can you give me another drink? The stuff they give you in here is horrible. Could you bring me some proper juice next time you come? Without all these preservatives?'

'Of course.' She held up the beaker again, and her father drank without looking her in the eye. 'But I was wondering...was I in hospital then? I think I ought to remember it, because...'

Her father spat out the straw. 'You were four years old, maybe even three. How would you remember that?'

'Did I need stitches?'

'Yes, you needed stitches. Why are you thinking about this now?'

'I was just wondering, that's all.'

'Well, that's what happened. That's probably why you're frightened of hospitals, for all I know. Have you got anyone staying in the cottage at the moment?'

'No, not just now.'

They carried on talking about summer visitors, tourism in general and the cheap vodka from Russia that was flooding in across borders where Tina wasn't around to stop it. At half past seven she got up to leave. As she stood in the doorway, she said, 'It was Mauritz Stiller, wasn't it?'

Her father, who seemed lost in thought, said, 'What was?'

'*Sir Arne's Treasure.* Mauritz Stiller.'

'Yes. Yes, of course. Take care of yourself, sweetheart.' He looked at her and added, 'And don't spend too much time thinking about... what's in the past.'

She said she wouldn't.

When she got home she stood outside for a long time checking things out before she went in. Even if there hadn't been a real storm, the wind was still quite strong and she could see the silhouettes of the pine trees swaying against the night sky. The air was chilly and she breathed in deeply through her nose, picking out rotting apples, damp earth, rosehips and a host of other smells she couldn't place or identify. There was an animal close by, probably a badger. The smell of its wet fur was coming from the forest behind the house.

A blue glow flickered in one of the windows at the neighbours' house. The children were busy with their video game. There was a blue glow from their own living-room window. Roland was watching some sports program.

As so many times before when she stopped and thought about it—rather than automatically getting out of the car and going inside—she had no desire to walk into her own house. Into any house. She just wanted to keep on walking past the lights and the warmth, out into the forest. To push her way through its dark wall and allow herself to be surrounded by the smell of badger, pine needles, moss. Allow the trees to protect her.

She looked over at the house next door. Should she knock on the door, check that the kids were OK? Nobody had mentioned it, and she didn't like the idea. The children shunned her because of the way she looked. As if they thought she might do them some harm. No, she would leave it. If they wanted anything they could come to her.

Roland was indeed watching sport. Ice hockey, even though it was only September. There were no seasons these days. A chemical smell hovered in the air, presumably the ointment Roland had used on the dog. She could also smell the dog from behind the closed door of Roland's bedroom.

As she walked through the living room, Roland said, 'Oh, by the way—someone called round.'

She stopped. 'Oh yes?'

Without taking his eyes off the screen, he went on, 'Some guy wanting to rent the cottage. Shady-looking character. Said he'd spoken to you.'

'Yes.' Tina clasped her hands together, tightly. 'What did you say to him?'

'I told him straight. That we don't usually rent the cottage out in the autumn. But it was mainly because…' He glanced up at her. 'Well, he didn't exactly look…nice. And you said you didn't want to carry on renting the cottage out anyway, so…' Roland shrugged his shoulders, looking pleased with himself. 'He looked like some kind of arsonist or something.'

Tina stood there for a while just looking at him. The glow of the television gave his skin a greyish tone, bringing the incipient rolls of fat around his neck into sharp relief and flickering in his eyes, making him look like a monster.

She shut herself in her room, read *The Old Man and the Sea* and got through the hours until it was time to sleep.

She started work at ten o'clock the following day, but left home at quarter past nine and drove to the ramblers' hostel. There was only one car in the carpark: a small white Renault which proudly proclaimed in blue letters that it had been hired from OKQS at a cost of only 199 kronor per day.

She knocked on the main door of the hostel.

When nothing happened she opened it and stepped into a small hallway. There was a stand displaying tourist leaflets, and a sign on the reception desk explained that the hostel was open only on request. The building exuded desolation and soap.

She foolishly pinged the bell on the desk, as if it might magically produce someone who could help her; perhaps the autumn staff, a little old man who slept in a cupboard and woke up only when guests arrived.

When the bell had no effect, she shouted, 'Hello? Is anyone there?'

She knew his name, of course, but she had no intention of shouting it out. The situation was already sufficiently absurd. A police officer shouting for a thief so that she could ask if he'd like to come and live with her.

She had just thought *Right, I'm going*, when a door opened along the corridor in front of her.

Vore emerged from the room and she gasped.

In the spacious expanse of the ferry terminal he had looked big, but here between the narrow walls of the hostel he was enormous. In spite of the fact that he was wearing only a singlet and pants, he seemed to fill the entire corridor. Tina could understand why Roland had felt a little nervous. Vore looked as if he could crush Roland between his thumb and forefinger.

When he spotted Tina his beard shot up on both sides of his face in a great big smile. He covered the corridor in a few thundering steps and extended a hairy arm.

'Good morning,' he said. 'I do apologise. I was fast asleep.'

She shook his hand. 'No, I apologise. I didn't mean to wake you.'

'No problem. It's time I got up anyway.'

Tina nodded and looked around. 'I've never actually been here before.'

'But you still recommended it?'

'Well, it was actually the surroundings I recommended, if I remember rightly.'

'I've no complaints on that score. I went for a long walk yesterday afternoon. I love forests like these, where man hasn't had the chance to destroy everything.'

'Yes. It's a nature reserve.'

'Let's hope it stays that way.'

Tina herself was very fond of the forests around Riddersholm. Since the area was protected, no one was even allowed to chop up a fallen tree unless it was lying right across the track, and in that case permission was needed.

Just for something to say, she came out with, 'It's just a pity they hunt elks.'

Vore frowned. 'Yes, it's a terrible thing. You don't go in for hunting with dogs around here, I hope?'

'Not as far as I know. Why?'

'Because you end up with dogs running around all over the place with that kind of hunting.' He looked at her. 'But you have dogs, I noticed.'

'They're Roland's. He's my...' She waved her hand vaguely. 'He lives there too.' She took a deep breath. 'Which actually brings me to my reason for coming here. If you're interested in renting the cottage, then of course you're welcome to do so.'

'He...That's not what Roland said.'

'No. But it's not his decision. It belongs to me.'

'I see.'

'So...if you're interested, just turn up.'

'I'll give it some thought. How are you?'

'Fine. Why do you ask?'

'He said you were at the hospital.'

Tina laughed with relief. 'Oh, I see. I'd just given my neighbours a lift—they were having a baby.'

Now he's going to ask if I have children, she thought, and decided to bring the conversation to an end. Admittedly Vore was a woman, and it shouldn't be difficult to discuss this kind of thing with a woman. But as he stood there in front of her...she would have had to pinch her arm until it was black and blue to remind herself of that fact.

'Did it all go well?' he asked.

'I don't know.' She looked at her watch. 'I have to go to work.'

'In that case I'll see you this afternoon. What time do you finish?'

'Five.'

'Good. Then I'll call round in the early evening.'

They said goodbye, and Tina walked back to her car. As she drove out of the carpark she glanced in the mirror to see if he was waving to her. He wasn't. She shook her head.

How did we get to be so familiar with one another?

It was impossible to say. If she was threatened with torture, she might perhaps admit that she had felt some kind of…affinity. Once the torture was well under way, she would add that the feeling had been there the very first time she saw him.

But red-hot pincers wouldn't get any more than that out of her. Because there wasn't any more. But there was an affinity. Just as difficult to grasp as a perch with your bare hands, but it was there nonetheless. Beneath the jetty on a sunny day. The warmth of the planks against her stomach, the sun glittering on the water. A shimmering movement.

Work was dull, to put it mildly.

A lorry driver she had been on nodding terms with for years had suddenly decided to bring in ten cases of cheap Russian vodka. He was furious with her when she explained that she had to report the matter and confiscate the liquor, as if she had broken some kind of trust.

A hundred bottles, what would he make on those? Five or six thousand, max. His son needed a new violin if he was going to be able to continue playing—did she have any idea what a violin cost? And now he would be facing fines and all hell would break loose. He would probably lose his job, and how would they manage to pay the mortgage then? Couldn't she just let it go, just this once, for fuck's sake, Tina. Won't happen again, promise.

No, she couldn't let it go. Dearly bought experience had taught her that the situation became impossible in the long run if she started ignoring this kind of thing. Secret smiles, unspoken complicity. When he had been going on for a while, still talking about the violin and the fact that she had no heart, she suddenly snapped.

'Heikko, for fuck's sake! Give it a rest! How many times have you brought in more than you should?'

He said it was the first time. She shook her head.

'I'd say it was eight or ten times. Smaller amounts, admittedly. Perhaps a case or two above the limit. And I've let it go every single time, without saying a word. Thought it was for personal use, as they say, but now you've gone too far, you understand?'

The rough lorry driver shrank before her; he looked terrified. She waved in the direction of the lorry, which was parked down below the window.

'If you bring in one extra bottle, or two or three, I can't be bothered doing anything about it, but this can't happen again, is that clear?'

Heikko nodded. Tina took out her notebook.

'Right. This is what I'm going to do. I'm going to report you as a private individual. You'll be fined and all hell will break loose as you so rightly pointed out, but you can keep the firm out of it. Next time you won't be so lucky, OK?'

'Yes. Thank you.'

She pointed to her chest. 'And I do have a heart. It's here, in exactly the same place as yours.'

'Yes, yes. Thank you.'

'And if you say thank you one more time I'll change my mind. There might have been amphetamines hidden in those cases, now I come to think of it.'

Heikko grinned, held up his hands in defence. 'You know I never—'

'Yes, I know. Now get out of here.'

When Heikko had gone and Tina had watched him climb into the cab of his lorry and drive away, she was seized by a sudden melancholy.

The tough approach was necessary and it was like a second skin as far as she was concerned, but it wasn't really her, just an essential façade that enabled her to do a job she was increasingly beginning to feel was pointless. What did she care about those cases of vodka? Who would suffer, apart from the state-owned liquor monopoly?

Heikko would have sold a couple of bottles to one neighbour, three to another. Everyone would have been happy, the boy would have got his new violin. Sweetness and light all around, if it hadn't been for that witch on customs. Perhaps she should pack it in, just do consultancy work. Drugs were another matter. She had no pangs of conscience there.

She could see Heikko in her mind's eye, arriving home. His wife. His son going sadly to his room, closing the door. Continuing to practise on his old violin, far too small for his big fingers.

Damn it, she thought. *He was probably lying.*

But he hadn't been lying, and she knew it. That was why she had let him off lightly. The customs witch.

SEPTEMBER 18

Vore came last night. I knew it was him when the dogs started barking. He's rented the cottage for a week, to begin with.

Roland wasn't happy. Said it was down to me if there were any problems. He sounds like the Muddler from the Moomintroll stories. The only thing missing is the button collection.

The neighbours came home with a baby girl. Haven't been to see her yet, but I suppose I'll have to.

I'm not happy with my life. Bloody Heikko, he showed me that. I don't like catching people out. Maybe there are those who do. The other people at work don't seem to have a problem. Perhaps because it's still a challenge for them.

41

Roland sulked all evening. The strangest thing about him is that he's not an alcoholic. It would suit him very well. But then again, he has the TV. I asked Vore if he'd like me to put the small TV in the cottage. He said televisions gave him a headache. Yet another thing we have in common. We talked for a while about herbal remedies.

I'm not allergic to electricity, I don't want to be allergic to electricity.

But if I had the choice, I wouldn't want to be indoors at all during the warmer months. It makes my skin itch. Is being allergic to electricity actually an illness? Everybody who has it seems to be loopy.

Went for a walk this evening. Everybody says there are no mushrooms at all this year, but as usual I still keep finding them. They're few and far between, though.

SEPTEMBER 21

Very windy, the TV aerial is making a noise. Roland has sold two of the puppies and is thinking of getting a satellite dish. Good. That will keep him occupied, and I won't have to listen to the sound of the aerial.

Pulled up a bodybuilder with eight hundred cartons of M. He got aggressive, smashed the table in the little room. Had to lock him in until the police arrived. He broke the window overlooking the carpark. Didn't try to jump, fortunately.

The autumn changes the forest. The conifers regain the upper hand. That's it. That's exactly how it is. In the summer the forest is a fairground. Bright, laughing colours. All welcome. It's still like that, with more colours than ever. But everything is moving towards the colours of the conifers. In a couple of months they will be in charge, because they will be the only ones still breathing.

Went to see the addition to the family next door. The other children were playing video games. Looked at the little person all wrapped up in her blanket, and wondered how long it would be before she too was sitting in front of the television. The neighbours were tired but happy. The whole house smells of breast milk and static electricity. I can't cope with it.

Something has just struck me: perhaps Vore took/takes hormones? How could he be the way he is otherwise? Perhaps that was what I sensed. After all, I have no problem knowing when someone is under the influence of drugs.

He's hardly ever home. Either he's off out in the car, or out walking. What does he actually do? I've never had a proper conversation with him.

The storm is picking up. The noise from the aerial is terrible. It sounds as if the entire house is moaning.

SEPTEMBER 22

Checked the cottage this afternoon.

Yes, there was a reason. This morning when I was on the way to work I thought I heard a child crying in there. Well, not exactly crying, it was more of a whimper. Of course it could have been something else (I think it was something else, or perhaps it was coming from the house next door), but...

When I got home his car wasn't there. So I did it.

There was no child, of course. Everything was neat and tidy. The bed was made, everything in its place. Piles of paperback crime novels and *The Brothers Karamazov*, also in paperback. On the desk lay his binoculars, his camera and a notebook.

Yes. I did read it. And I was none the wiser.

(Did I think there might be something about me? Yes, I did. I admit it.)

But it wasn't a diary. Just numbers and abbreviations. Terrible handwriting. The numbers might have been times. The abbreviations could have been anything. Insects, maybe. The times when he saw them. Do people do that kind of thing?

The metal box was plugged in. I listened, heard a humming noise from inside. Didn't dare open the lid. Thought a load of insects might come swarming out.

Now I'm going to say what I think: my life lacks excitement. I make things up. I pick on just about anybody and try to use whatever clues there are to piece together that person's life. It automatically turns into a mystery. Why did he go there? Why did he do that? What did he mean by that?

It's only in old-fashioned detective stories that everyone is gathered in the library for the final explanation. In real life there is no explanation. And if there is an explanation, it's unbelievably banal.

After I'd finished poking about I stayed in the cottage for a long time. Why? Because it smelled so good in there. If anyone ever reads this diary I will immediately commit seppuku. I slipped into the bed. Terrified the whole time, listening for the sound of his car, for the front door of my house. The sheets smelled...I don't know. But I wanted to stay there. Lie in that smell.

I lay there for just a few minutes, then made the bed exactly the way it had been.

In the afternoon Roland put up the satellite dish. He spent the evening trying to get a picture, but no luck. We played Scrabble. I won.

SEPTEMBER 24

I hate my job, and I hate myself.

I don't know what got into me today. Out of sheer bloody-mindedness I stopped every single person who was carrying anything. One extra bottle of whisky, a few boxes of Marlboro.

44

Suppressed rage, vicious words directed at me all day. A little old lady weeping, her suitcase full of brandy.

Went into the forest for a few hours when I got home. Grey skies, cold. Went out in a T-shirt but didn't manage to get really cold. Met an elk. One of the placid ones. He stood there and let me pat him. I wept, pressed my face against his coat. Tried to explain that it was the hunting season, that he should keep away from cleared areas. I don't think he understood.

Autumn depression, it's called. As if it were natural to think that life is shit. I don't want to be here, I don't want to do what I do.

Elisabet called round this evening with the baby. Burbled on. I got even more depressed, but tried not to show it. 'Melancholy', that's what it always says in the Moomintroll books. Never depressed. If only I could be melancholy instead. Have a sorrow that is somehow enjoyable.

I hated Elisabet too. The baby's sleeping really well at night. Only wakes up twice for a feed, blah blah. Her cheeks are glowing, her eyes shining. One bullet in the middle of her forehead. I'm a bad person.

Vore came to tell me that he's staying for another week. That's good. He asked if he could take a photograph of the baby, and Elisabet said yes. She kind of stiffened up. What is it with people?

Roland has managed to sort out the dish, he was gawping at some film. I chatted for a while with Vore after Elisabet had gone. Didn't get very far. But I don't hate him. No. Now I come to think of it. I can actually cope with him. I'm thinking about him now. I feel happier. There you go.

He's travelled all over Sweden, lived in lots of different places for short periods. Travels to Russia sometimes. On business. But he spends most of his time out walking. Collecting insects and looking around. That's good. That's what I'd like to do. No more poking about, no more talking, just…looking around. Like Snufkin.

Now I'm going to bed. Perhaps I'll feel better tomorrow.

SEPTEMBER 25

Saturday. My day off.

I'm as good as certain. He's got a child in there. Or some kind of animal that sounds like a child.

When he'd left I risked checking the cottage again, even though the car was still there. Like me, he goes for long walks.

Nothing.

But this time I did it. I opened the lid of that metal box. I don't know what I expected to find, but there were definitely insects inside. Or they might all have been flies, I don't know. Masses of larvae, hundreds, maybe thousands. And a few little ones that had already hatched, crawling around on top of the piles of white larvae. Perhaps I should have found them disgusting, but I didn't. I thought they were beautiful, somehow.

Felt excited when I left the cottage. I don't understand myself.

SEPTEMBER 27

Met Vore in the forest yesterday. I think he knows I've been in the cottage. He's started locking the door. (As if I didn't have a key, ha ha.) But I suppose he's making a point. It frightened the life out of me when I saw him locking the door as he left. Then I followed him.

Something strange is going on in my head. I hardly pay any attention to what Roland says anymore. Not that he ever says anything important, but we do live together after all. I think he's going to some show or other this weekend, I don't know.

I'm going to try writing it down: I've fallen in love with Vore. I'm in love with Vore. (I said it out loud as well, but quietly.) No.

It isn't true. I can tell when I write it down, when I say it. That's not the way it is. It's something different. Something...better?

I don't understand it. It's making me feel slightly unwell.

We bumped into one another down by the rocks I call the Dance Floor. Sort of. I mean, I'd followed him, and he was standing there...waiting?

We talked about the forest. How the autumn changes things. He said he never really felt comfortable indoors (!!!).

I told him I felt the same. And then...I showed him the Dance Floor. He said such a strange thing. When I told him I called this place the Dance Floor because you could imagine the elves dancing there, he said, 'They used to. Once upon a time.'

And he said it perfectly seriously, without the slightest hint of a joke. (And I believe it's true, actually. How can I think that? Elves?)

I told him about the tree, the lightning.

And I laughed, I just couldn't help it, because it's so ridiculous how everything...I laughed when he told me *he'd* been struck by lightning too! His beard hides the scars. He let me feel. The skin was knobbly underneath his beard on one side.

We stood there looking at one another, until I started laughing again. What else could I do? How many people have been struck by lightning? One in ten thousand? If that. There was nothing more to say, somehow.

It goes against the grain to write this, it's not my style (I'm a rational person, I wear a uniform at work), but is there actually such a thing as twin souls? If such a thing really does exist, it would explain a great deal.

Of course that leads to a question. Does he feel the same way? I think he does. To use a childish phrase: he started it. When he kissed me on the cheek last summer. He knew back then.

Or did he?

Yes, I know. All I have to do is ask, right? Of course. Just ask him. I'd rather die. No, I wouldn't. But it's difficult. If he says...I don't know. If he gives the wrong answer. Something will break inside me.

I didn't pull up a single person at work today. Robert stopped one just out of routine. Five bottles of Kosken over the limit. As I knew perfectly well. Robert gave me a funny look.

I don't want to do it anymore. I've had enough. I just want... what do I want?

SEPTEMBER 29

He's leaving the day after tomorrow.

We met in the forest yesterday, picked lots of mushrooms. He has the same radar as me when it comes to finding mushrooms (of course). I asked about his childhood. He said he was adopted. I could tell he didn't want to talk about it, so I dropped the subject.

I spent all evening blanching mushrooms. Roland's suspicious. So what. Tomorrow he's going to Gothenburg for a dog show that lasts all weekend, doing his own thing. Getting laid.

Vore is going away. I'll never see him again.

So my behaviour can be excused.

When I got home today, his car wasn't there. I fetched the key and went into the cottage. I felt like a thief. I lay in his sheets for a long time, feeling pleasure and fear at the same time. Panic. Even now while I'm writing this I feel as if I want to die.

I'm not going to kill myself, of course I'm not. But I want to die. That's the way it is. As I lay there in his bed, I knew it was the last time. (Yes, I've done it several times.)

I just want to be erased, to disappear.

But I expect it will pass. (It will never pass.)

Help me! What am I going to do?

As I was about to leave, I saw something strange. There was a plate and a bowl on the draining board. Very strange, don't you think? Well no, but it was what was on the plate. At first I thought it was some kind of pudding. When I took a closer look I could see that it was larvae. Mashed up larvae.

Yes, I did have a taste. It was pretty good. A bit like snails, but a bit more grainy.

Sometimes it feels as if I'm living outside my body. My body does things, and I stand next to it thinking, 'What are you doing? You're getting in the bed, you're eating larvae, what are you doing?'

What am I doing? What am I going to do?

I think I'm coming down with something. He's going away. I'm not in love, but I...I have to be near him. Perhaps I do love him. Her. Maybe that's what it is.

Love.

Yes.

I'm falling apart.

———·———

On Thursday afternoon Roland packed a suitcase and put it in the car along with Tara and some dog food. The attack of mange had turned out to be a mild one, and he decided to risk going to the show even though he shouldn't have done. There was virtually a price on the head of anyone who brought mange into kennels.

Tina stood at the bedroom window and watched him go. She had taken the day off work because she wasn't feeling well. Something to do with her stomach, her chest, her heart. It was the first time in her entire working life that she had been off sick. When she rang work to say she wouldn't be coming in, they asked if she'd called the local health insurance office. She didn't know what to do, so she didn't bother.

When the Volvo had disappeared down the drive she went and sat on the patio for a while and read *Comet in Moominland*. It was an unusually warm autumn day, and there was the same feeling in the air as there was in the book: a damp, highly charged warmth as if everything was holding its breath, waiting for a change.

The air pressure made her head ache, and she found it difficult to concentrate. She went inside and stood by the kitchen window for a while, looking down towards the cottage.

What's he doing in there?

As usual when Roland went away she had been shopping for a private party. The snails were on ice in the fridge. This time she had bought extra, but hadn't yet dared ask the question. She was afraid. Everything had conspired to create a situation where this evening could be crucial. Roland was away, Vore was leaving the next day.

And what is it that's going to be resolved tonight?

If she had been in her right mind she wouldn't have been standing here dithering about, putting off asking Vore if he'd like to come over for dinner. She would have called the police. Because she was convinced he had a child in there. Her hearing was better than most people's, and she'd heard it.

She ought to ring Ragnar at the police station in Norrtälje and explain the situation. They'd come straight away. They knew her.

Nobody knows me.

A long time ago she had read an article about how people choose their partner by smell. At least women did, she thought. Five women had been allowed to smell five T-shirts that had been worn by five different men. Or it might have been more women. The whole thing had seemed slightly shady and perverted—the combination of a laboratory environment and sweaty clothes.

She had felt some sympathy with the result, and snorted at it. As if you could choose.

She had chosen Roland *in spite of* his smell. Not that he smelled unpleasant, exactly. But he smelled wrong. Wrong for her. He wasn't the only one who had answered her ad, but he was the only one who had shown any interest after the first meeting. There's your freedom of choice.

But Vore. The smell of him, the aroma of him was like coming home. It couldn't be described in any other way. Lying in his sheets was like crawling into Mummy and Daddy's bed. Tina's parents had slept in separate beds, and it wasn't that smell she was thinking of, but something different, something safe and associated with home rather than anything based on a real memory.

So she didn't call the police.

Night fell quickly, helped along by black clouds rolling in from the east. The air was heavy, pressing down on her head. Odd raindrops trickled down the kitchen window, and the light went on in the cottage. Anxiety was a trembling sparkler inside her body.

There's going to be a thunderstorm.

She went around the house pulling out every single plug and electrical connection, the television, the phone. Switched off the power. She couldn't bring herself to ask him, didn't dare invite him over. Didn't know where it might lead. But she wished he would come, come of his own accord.

She drank a glass of white wine, then another. The anxiety pulled and tore at her. She would have liked to go out into the forest, but didn't dare. The storm would start at any moment. She could feel it, and it was like being trapped inside a castle, waiting for an unconquerable army to arrive. If you fled you would be killed, if you stayed where you were you would be killed.

She sat down on the kitchen floor and pressed her forehead

against her knees. Got up quickly, poured herself another glass of wine and sat down again. Her hand shook as she brought the glass to her mouth and knocked the wine straight back. After a few minutes she felt slightly better.

Then the storm arrived. It started close by; she only had time to count one thousand and one, one thousand and two, one thousand and thr— between the lightning and the crash of the thunder. The rain started pouring over the gutters, hammering on the window ledges. She clenched her teeth, folded her arms over her head and stared at the floor so she would be able to see the flash of the lightning.

The next one was closer. She only got as far as one thousand and two. As soon as she stopped clamping her jaws together, her teeth started chattering. The storm came rumbling in from the sea, an enraged, gigantic ghost getting closer and closer, wanting to crush her, to sweep her away in its white light.

When the next crash came she didn't know if it was the floor or her own body shaking. It was close now. Soon it would be on top of her.

She leapt to her feet. Without bothering with a coat or shoes she ran outside. The rain plastered her blouse to her back, splashing up around her bare feet as she sprinted across the grass to the drive.

Vore's car was a blurred, white shape behind the veils of rain, and she ran towards it as if the ground were electrified, which was exactly what she was afraid of all the time.

She opened the passenger door, threw herself inside and slammed the door shut. The rain pelted against the metal, the landscape burned in the phosphorescent flash and the trees were riveted to the sky. The crash came only a second later; two coffee cups in the space below the glove compartment clinked against one another.

Beneath the hire car aroma of upholstery cleaner she could pick up his smell. Her heart slowed down slightly, the worst of the shaking abated. It was an unexpected relief. She had been looking for the insulation of the rubber tyres against the ground, but his smell was here and it calmed her more than technical considerations. She took a deep breath, then gave a start as the driver's door opened and Vore folded himself into the car.

His eyes were wide open. He was just as scared as her. With some difficulty he got into the driving seat and slammed the door shut. The car was like a suit four sizes too small for him. Even though the seat was pushed back as far as it would go, his knees were rubbing against the steering wheel. She realised what he must look like when he was driving, and laughed out loud.

He turned to face her with a wan smile. 'A thunderstorm,' he said. 'Most amusing.'

'No, I just…' She pointed to his head, which was almost touching the roof. 'Wouldn't you be better with a bigger car?'

He said something in reply, but she couldn't hear him. A deafening clap of thunder drowned out everything else. She clenched her fists, felt the tears welling up. Vore grabbed hold of the wheel and stared fixedly out through the windscreen.

She did it without thinking. She shuffled closer to him. The handbrake dug into her hip as she leaned her head against his chest and inhaled the smell of his shirt. He placed one hand on her cheek, her ear. She closed her eyes.

The storm continued to rage around them, but after a while she could hear his heart slowing down too. The solace was mutual, and the thought calmed her even more. Which made him feel calmer. By the time the storm started to move away, they were almost not afraid anymore.

They were sitting in their seats like normal people. Didn't know where to start. The storm was far away now, a mumbling reminder of what they had gone through. Eventually Vore said, 'Roland.'

Tina pulled a face. 'What about him?'

'He's unfaithful to you.'

'Yes,' said Tina. 'How do you know?'

'The smell.'

Of course. Why had she asked? She nodded and looked out through the windscreen. Now the lightning had stopped it was almost pitch-black outside. The light inside the car picked out the odd dancing raindrop on the bonnet, nothing more. Vore opened his door.

'Come on,' he said.

She took his hand and they walked to the cottage. When they got inside, they both sat down on the bed. They didn't switch on any lights, and there was nothing but sounds, smells. Tina had a lump in her throat. She fumbled in the darkness and found his cheek, stroked his rough beard.

'Vore,' she said. 'I want to. But I can't.'

'Yes, you can.'

His answer was so definite that it should have been enough to convince a stone. But still she shook her head. 'No. It hurts too much. I can't.'

'You've never done it.'

'Yes I have.'

He took her face between his hands. 'No,' he said. 'Not your way.'

'What do you mean?'

He ran his hand over one breast and a swarm of ants ran through her body, gathered in her diaphragm, grew.

'Trust me,' he said.

He undressed her. The feeling in her diaphragm was something she had never experienced before, as if a previously unused part of her body had suddenly blossomed. When he took off his shirt and vest and she pressed her face to his bare chest, she felt a throbbing, pulsating sensation down there.

Her eyes were wide open in the darkness. It was as if something was being turned inside out, unfolding in her belly. When he pulled away from her for a moment to take off his trousers, she ran her hands over her sex. She gasped out loud.

A stiff erection was pointing upwards from what she had thought was her vagina. She groped along its root and found no opening. The sensation had been exactly right: she had been turned inside out.

Vore's hand touched her. 'Now do you understand?'

She shook her head. The bed creaked as Vore lay down. 'Come here,' he said.

She lay down on top of him. He gently guided her, and she pushed into him. The bed made a terrible noise as she pulled back, pushed in again. She ran her hands over his chest. The pleasure she was getting from this new part of her body was terrifying. Like phantom pains, but in reverse. She was experiencing pleasure in a place that didn't exist.

How...how?

After a while she stopped worrying. Stopped thinking. She fell on him and thrust into his wet, soft darkness. Vore groaned, grabbed her bottom and caressed the scar, the dead skin. They were no longer man or woman, just two bodies finding one another in the darkness. Moving apart, reuniting, rolling on each other's waves until the white light poured through her body, her belly cramping and contracting; she screamed as the burning ants were hurled out of her and into him.

He lit candles. Tina lay on the bed feeling her sex as it softened, withdrew inside her. When Vore stroked her breasts it hesitated for a moment, then disappeared into her.

She looked at his back. The big, curved scar at the bottom of his back was dark red in the candlelight. She touched it with her middle finger.

'I didn't know,' she said.

'No,' he said. 'That was very clear.'

'Why didn't you say anything?'

'Because…' His hand moved slowly over her body. '…because I didn't know if you wanted to know. I mean, you've made a life for yourself. Adapted to the world of human beings. There's a great deal you don't know. A great deal you might not want to know. If you're going to carry on living as you have done up to now.'

'I don't want to carry on living the same way.'

'No.'

She thought he was going to continue. Tell her something. Instead he sighed deeply and folded his body into an uncomfortable position so that he could rest his head on her stomach. After a while he started shaking, and she thought he was cold. She leaned forward to pull the covers over him, then realised he was crying. She stroked his hair. 'What's wrong?'

'Tina.' It was the first time he had used her name. 'There aren't many of us left. It's better for you if you…forget about this. Don't let it influence your actions from now on.'

She carried on stroking his hair as she gazed at the ceiling. The cottage wasn't well insulated; the candles flickered and flared in the draught, making the shadows move across the ceiling. Life everywhere.

'You've had a child in here.' His body stiffened on top of hers. 'Haven't you?'

'Yes.'

'Who was it? Where is it now?'

He raised his head and slid down onto the floor by the bed; he knelt there gazing searchingly into her eyes.

She could just get up and leave right now. Go back into the

house, have a hot shower and drink several glasses of wine until she fell asleep. Tomorrow he would go away. Roland would come back. On Monday she would go to work. She could carry on living within this—

lie

—security that had been her life up to now.

Vore got to his feet and opened the wardrobe. Moved the pile of hand towels on the top shelf. Reached in and pulled out a cardboard box, about the size of two shoe boxes. Tina pulled the covers over her. Vore's head almost reached the ceiling, he towered over her holding out the box. She closed her eyes.

'Is it…dead?' she asked.

'No. And it's not a child.'

She felt the bed dip under his weight as he sat down. She heard the lid being lifted off. A faint whimper. She opened her eyes.

Inside the box on a bed of towels lay a tiny baby, only a couple of weeks old. The thin chest was moving up and down, and Vore caressed the child's head with his forefinger. Tina leaned forward.

'It is a child,' she said. It was a girl. Her eyes were closed, her fingers moving slowly as if she were dreaming. There was a little blob of dried milk at the corner of her mouth.

'No,' he said. 'It's a *hiisit*. It hasn't been fertilised.'

'But it is a child. I can see it's a child.'

'I was the one who gave birth to it,' said Vore. 'So I ought to know, don't you think? It's a *hiisit*. It has no…soul. No thoughts. It's like an egg. An unfertilised egg. But it can be shaped into anything at all. Look…'

He prodded one eyelid and the eyes opened. Tina gasped out loud. The eyes were completely white.

'It's blind,' said Vore. 'Deaf. Incapable of learning anything. It can only breathe, cry, eat.' He picked off the white blob at the corner of the child's mouth. As if to reinforce what he had just said, he added, 'A *hiisit*. That's what they're called.'

'Is that what the…larvae are for? Food?'

'Yes.' He was rubbing the white stuff between his fingers. 'I thought you'd seen it. When you came in here.'

Tina shook her head. A slight feeling of nausea was growing in her stomach, crawling up into her throat. She tore her gaze away from the child's milky white eyes and asked, 'What do you mean… shaped?'

Vore pushed his finger hard against the spot where the child's right collarbone should have been, but the finger simply sank right in, leaving a dent behind. The child did not react. 'It's like clay.'

Tina stared at the hollow, which showed no sign of springing back, the shadowy dent in the child's chest, and she had had enough. She crawled out of bed, leaving Vore sitting there with the box on his knee. He made no move to stop her. She gathered up her clothes, which were strewn across the floor, and bundled them up in her arms.

'What…why have you got it?'

Vore looked at her. Where she had seen warmth and love just minutes before there was now only the loneliness of a tarn in the depths of the forest where no one ever goes. In a thin voice he said, 'Don't you know?'

She shook her head and took a single step to the door, opened it. Vore was still sitting on the bed. She walked out onto the porch and the wind showered her naked body with light rain. The candle flames flickered wildly inside the cottage, cascading patterns over the big man on the bed with the little box on his knee.

I was the one who gave birth to it…

The white eyes opening, the finger pushed into the chest.

She slammed the door and ran over to the house. When she got inside she locked the front door. She dropped her clothes on the hall floor and went straight into the kitchen where she knocked back the last of the wine straight out of the bottle. Then she opened another and went into the bedroom, put on a CD of Chopin's piano sonatas, turned the volume up high and crawled into bed.

She didn't want to know. She didn't want to know anything. When she had drunk half the bottle she ran her fingers over her sex. She could feel a sticky wetness, and brought her fingers up to her nose. They smelled of germinating sprouts and salt water. She caressed herself. Nothing happened. She had another drink.

When the bottle was empty and the pattern on the curtains was beginning to move, wriggling around before her eyes, there was a knock on the door.

'Go away,' she whispered. 'Go away.'

She staggered over to the stereo and turned up the volume until the piano was reverberating off the walls. There might have been another knock at the door, there might not. She crawled back into bed and pulled the covers over her head.

I don't want to. Don't want to don't want to…

The pictures in her head became confused. Big hands grabbing at her. A forest of enormous tree trunks that disappeared into shadow, then everything was white, white. White hands, white clothes, white walls. Hands that seized her, lifted her. She travelled along a sloping chute down into the darkness, and fell asleep.

She opened her eyes and knew nothing. Grey light was pouring into the room, and her mouth was stuck together. She had a splitting headache, and her belly was hurting because she was desperate for a pee. She managed to get out of bed and into the bathroom.

When she was sitting on the toilet letting it all go, she remembered. She looked down to where the urine was pouring out of her in a jagged stream, tried to imagine what things looked like inside her. It was impossible. An illustration from her school biology lessons flashed through her mind.

It's not true. I'm a freak.

She leaned against the washbasin, turned on the tap, half pulled herself up and drank. The sharpness of the water was real. She clung onto it and drank until her stomach was cold. When she straightened up and walked into the kitchen, the water began to reach the same temperature as the rest of her body. The contours blurred once more. She sat down on a chair, thought: *there's the coffee machine, there's the magazine rack, there's the clock. It's a quarter past eleven. There's a box of matches. All of these things exist. I exist too.*

She took two painkillers out of the medicine drawer, swallowed them with another swig of cold water from a glass that was hard and round in her hand.

Quarter past eleven!

For a moment she panicked, thinking she was late for work. Then she remembered she was off sick. She went back to the bedroom, looked out of the window. The white car had gone. She lay down on the bed, gazed up at the ceiling for an hour.

She thought she understood everything. But she had to know.

At a quarter past one she was standing at the stop waiting for the bus to Norrtälje.

Her father wasn't in his room. She asked one of the care assistants, and was told he was in the dayroom. The carer's eyes flicked down to her feet as if to check that she hadn't brought any dirt in with her. No doubt she looked like shit.

He was alone in the room, sitting in his wheelchair facing the window. At first she thought he was asleep, but when she walked around him she saw that his eyes were open, looking out towards the sparse pine trees outside the window. He quickly rearranged his features into a smile.

'Hello, love. Another surprise visit!'

'Hi, Dad.'

She pulled over a chair and sat down.

'How are things?' he asked.

'Not so good.'

'No. I can see that.'

They sat in silence for a while, looking into one another. Her father's eyes had acquired the transparency of old age. The clarity, the wisdom were still there, but somehow diluted, like blue water colour. Tina's mother had had brown eyes, so she had never thought about it. But she was thinking about it now.

'Dad,' she said. 'Where did I come from?'

Her father's gaze sought out the pine trees. After a while he said, without looking at her, 'I presume there's no point in...' He frowned. 'How did you find out?'

'Does it matter?'

Back to the pine trees. In spite of the fact that he lived in a nursing home, in spite of the fact that he was confined to a wheelchair and that his hands, once so capable, could no longer even wave away a fly, Tina had managed to disregard his age. Now she was aware of it. Or perhaps it was just that old age had taken hold at this particular moment.

'I've always loved you,' he said. 'As if you were my own daughter. You *are* my daughter. I hope you realise that.'

The lump in her stomach was growing. It was the same feeling as when Vore held out the box. The moment before the lid is opened. When you can still run away, close your eyes, pretend there's nothing to see. She had thought she would have to coax her father, hadn't been prepared for the fact that they would reach this point so quickly. But perhaps he had been ready since the day she asked about the scar. Perhaps he had been ready for many years. Ever since he...took her in.

He said, 'I see you didn't bring any juice.'

'No, I forgot.'

'You will still come and see me, won't you…in the future?'

She placed a hand on his arm, then on his cheek, and held it there for a few seconds. 'Dad. *I'm* the one who should be afraid. Now tell me.'

He leaned his cheek almost imperceptibly against her hand. Then he straightened up and said, 'Your mother and I couldn't have children. We tried for many years, but it never happened. I don't know whether you ever thought about the fact that…well, we were ten or fifteen years older than your friends' parents. We'd started the process of applying to adopt a child three years before…before they found you.'

'What do you mean, found?'

'You were…two years old at the time. When they found this couple deep in the forest. Only five kilometres into the forest from where we lived. Where you live now.

'I think people knew they were there, but it was only when it turned out they had a child that…steps were taken.'

He closed his mouth, opened it again with a sticky sound. 'Could you get me some water, please?'

Tina got up, went over to the tap, filled a feeding cup with water—

deep in the forest

—went back and gave it to her father. She watched him as he drank, the wrinkled neck moving as he swallowed tiny, tiny amounts. He was thin now, but he had been fine-limbed even in his heyday, just like her mother. She had seen photographs of her grandparents on both sides—

She gave a start. A little water spilled onto her father's chin, dripping down onto his chest.

Everything is disappearing, she thought. Her maternal grandparents, her paternal grandparents. The family home. The album of black and white photographs, the house built by her

62

great-grandfather, the whole line stretching back through time was erased. It didn't belong to her. Tall, sinewy people in fields, standing next to houses, swimming. An unusual farming family. To which she did not belong, of course.

'Steps…' she heard herself say.

'Yes,' said her father. 'I don't know how much of this you want to hear, but it was a serious case of…neglect, if I can put it that way. You were crawling around without a stitch on even though it was October, and they didn't really have any food. No electricity, no water, and you couldn't talk. Nothing. They weren't even living in a house, it was more a kind of shelter. Just walls. They built a fire on the ground. So you were…taken into care. And eventually you came to us.'

Tears welled up in her eyes. She dashed them away, covered her mouth with her hand and stared out of the window.

'Darling girl,' said her father, his voice expressionless. 'I can't reach out and touch you. As I should do right now.'

Tina didn't move.

'And my parents? What happened to them?'

'I don't know.'

She caught his eye. Refused to look away. Her father sighed deeply. 'They ended up in a mental institution. Died. Both of them. Quite soon.'

'They were killed.'

Her father flinched at the harshness in her voice. His face aged a few more years. 'Yes,' he said. 'I suppose you could look at it that way. That's what I think, looking back.' His eyes sought hers, pleading. 'We did what we thought was best. It wasn't us who decided you should be taken into care. We just welcomed you…as our child. When it had already happened.'

Tina nodded and stood up. 'I understand,' she said.

'Do you?'

'No. But perhaps I will.' She looked down at him, sitting there in his wheelchair. 'What was my name?' she asked. 'Had they given me a name?'

Her father's voice was so weak she thought he said 'Eva'. She leaned closer to his mouth. 'What did you say?'

'Reva. They said Reva. I don't know if it was a name or just… just something they said.'

'Reva.'

'Yes.'

Reva. Vore.

On the bus home from Norrtälje she peered out of the windows as they drove along. Beyond the fences, into the forest. The significance of the nondescript mass of fir trees had deepened. She had always felt that she belonged to the forest. Now she knew it was true.

Reva.

Had they called out her name, locked inside white rooms?

She imagined padded cells, heavy iron doors with peep holes. Saw her mother and father hurling themselves at the walls, screaming to be let out, to be released back into the forest, to be given back their child. But there were only rigid, closed institutionalised faces around them. Not a trace of green, of greenery.

Not a stitch on even though it was October. Didn't really have any food.

She had never really needed a great deal of food, and she didn't like the food that was served in cafés, in the cafeteria at work. She liked snails, sushi. Raw fish. She was almost never cold, however low the temperature fell.

They had doubtless known how to look after their own child. But the early sixties, the art of social engineering—smiling mothers in floral aprons, record years, the building project known as the Million Program. Lighting a fire on the ground and no food in the larder, if they even had a larder. Such things couldn't be permitted.

Tina had heard that people were sterilised well into the 1970s. Was that what happened to her parents?

A mental institution.

She couldn't get away from the image of those white cubes, her mother and father each locked in their own space, screaming themselves hoarse until they died of grief. She tried to think that perhaps it was for the best. That otherwise they would have neglected her until she died. But she had survived at least one winter, hadn't she? The most difficult winter, a baby's first winter. They had brought her through that.

Tears blurred the view as she looked over towards the fir trees along the side of the road, enclosed by fences, wire fences keeping the wildlife away.

Keep the forest away from us. Tame it. Enclose it.

Vore. How much did he know about all this? Had he always known what he was, or had he also had a moment like this when everything came crashing down on him and he was forced to reinterpret his entire life?

She rubbed the tears from her eyes with her fists and rested her forehead on the window, following the forest with her gaze.

The cottage was empty. The furniture was still there, of course, but his suitcase, the hatching box, his camera, his binoculars and his books were gone. She lifted up the towels on the top shelf in the wardrobe. The cardboard box had gone too.

He had left her without a word of farewell.

No. His notebook was still lying on the desk. She picked it up to see if there might be a note underneath. When she didn't find anything, she flicked through it. It fell open in the middle, revealing a small pile of photographs. She looked at the top one. It was a picture of his…*hiisit.*

She went through the book page by page to see if he had written her a message. Nothing. Only the lists of times, the illegible notes. She sat down at the desk and tried to decipher them. They were worse than a doctor's prescriptions; they looked like something written by someone pretending he could write.

After a while she managed to identify a number of consonants, and with their help she was able to guess at others. It took almost two hours before she had a comparatively legible alphabet, and was able to put the letters together to work out longer words:

0730 man leaves

0812 window open

0922 post

1003 dishes. asleep?

1028 outside. raking leaves.

1107 wakes up?

She turned to other days, saw the same schedule repeated. She closed the notebook, rubbed her eyes and looked out of the window. What she saw made her heart flutter.

No...

She picked up the photographs, looked at them one by one. At first she was convinced they were pictures of his *hiisit*, but in the later photographs she could see a woman's hands holding it. And in the last picture, the woman was there.

Elisabet.

She was standing in Tina's kitchen holding her child, a beaming, slightly strained smile on her face. The child was identical to the child that had lain on a bed of towels in a cardboard box. The child that was not a child. The child that was a *hiisit*, that could be—

shaped

—that could be made into an image of anything whatsoever. As long as you had something to go on, a model. Like photographs.

Tina looked out of the window again. Saw the neighbours' house.

The cottage was the perfect spot if you wanted to spy on them. If you had a pair of binoculars, made notes on their movements…

Why have you got it?

Don't you know?

She knew now.

Suddenly she threw back her head and laughed. A coarse, terrible laugh that sprang from the same original source as rage, as tears. She laughed, she screamed. It was all so obvious, so simple. The only thing that had stopped her from seeing it was that it had been right in front of her nose.

She slapped her head with the palms of her hands.

'Idiot!' she yelled. 'Idiot! Every single person knows what we do, after all!' She laughed again, panting. 'We swap children! We steal their children and leave our own in their place!'

She didn't want to do it, but she had to.

There was a strange car parked outside the neighbours' house. A dark blue Volvo 740 with the same ominous authority as a police car, an undertaker's car.

She knocked on the front door. When no one came she pushed it open slightly and called out 'Hello?' Elisabet appeared in the living-room doorway. She looked like a *hiisit* herself: her face was grey and empty, her body somehow soulless, heavy.

'What's happened?' asked Tina.

Elisabet made a vague movement with her head in the direction of the room, and moved back inside. Tina walked in, took off her shoes. She walked across the rag rug on sensitive feet. She was a living lie, she was a remnant of a tribe, a traitor. She had become all of these things in just a few hours.

Göran was sitting on the sofa, talking quietly to a man who was presumably a doctor. Elisabet sat down on an armchair and gazed vacantly into space. The cot was standing next to her. She was holding on to one of the bars. Tina walked over to her.

The child was lying there naked, with no nappy or blanket. Presumably the doctor had just examined it. As it lay there now in a child's natural environment, Tina could see how...unalive it was. The *hiisit*. Its skin was waxy, it looked neither soft nor warm, and lacked the flowing blood of a child. The face was immobile, closed, with only the lips moving a fraction. The eyes were closed, fortunately. She wondered if Elisabet had seen the white eyes. She probably had.

'I...' Elisabet said in a dead voice. 'I just went up to the mailboxes to fetch the post. When I got back...'

She made a feeble gesture towards the child. Tina walked around to the other side of the cot and crouched down. The child was lying on its side. Even though the light in the room was subdued, as if they were keeping vigil with a corpse, she could clearly see the small appendage beginning to grow at the bottom of the back. The tail.

Vore hadn't mentioned it, but Tina had a feeling that was confirmed by the resolutely neutral expression on the doctor's face: a *hiisit* didn't live for very long. Not long enough to have to grow up in the world of human beings.

Human beings who didn't believe in trolls. And if they found any, they locked them up in mental institutions, operated to remove their tails, sterilised them and forced them to learn the language of human beings. Tried to forget that such a thing even existed.

Until we come and take your children.

She murmured a few words of sympathy that grated in her mouth like rusty metal, and left the house. Left something else behind her at the same time. She went over to the cottage, crawled into bed and let the hours pass. She could lie there as long as she wanted. Nobody was going to come. Ever again.

When Roland got home on Sunday evening, she told him she'd had enough. He could find somewhere else to open his kennels. She locked herself in her room and communicated via a series of terse messages through the door. It took a few days before he realised she was serious. And a few more days before he gathered up his possessions, along with some of hers.

When she checked the house after his departure, she also went through her jewellery box, not really thinking he would stoop so low. She was wrong. A couple of diamond rings and a heavy gold chain were missing. He probably thought she wouldn't bother to contact the police, and he was right. She didn't care.

That's one thing the fairy stories have got wrong, she thought. He could have taken the whole box as far as she was concerned. This particular troll didn't collect treasures.

She spent November searching the forest. She had signed herself off sick for the foreseeable future, and as she wasn't claiming any benefits she didn't need a doctor's note.

No more doctors, no more hospitals.

It was hardly surprising that she had been afraid, even panic-stricken. They had snatched her out of the environment in which she had grown up, the entire world of smells and light that her two-year-old brain recognised. They had shoved her in a hospital, operated on her, spoken to her in a language she didn't understand and tried to press her into their mould, reshape her into one of them.

They make us into their image. We make ourselves into their image.

A few days before the first snow fell, she found what she was looking for.

She was a long way from home, and if she had a been a human being she would probably have thought she was lost. She had been walking at random for hours without bothering about landmarks; she simply relied on her own internal compass.

There was nothing to see at first. A dense, nondescript part of the forest with moss-covered rocks and tall, straight fir trees with needles only at the very top. Hardly any undergrowth, because the light didn't reach the ground. Odd trees that had fallen down because of age rather than the wind, and had been caught by their peers to rot away in their embrace. The ground covered in an undisturbed layer of pale brown needles. No one had walked here for a long time.

It wasn't something she saw, it was something she felt.

In a small glade she was suddenly aware of the trees soaring up into the sky, of everything growing *bigger* around her, then shrinking and growing smaller, all at the same time. She spun around. Once. Twice. The tree trunks appeared to flicker. She closed her eyes.

There, she thought, extending her arm and pointing. *There's an anthill right there.*

She opened her eyes and walked in the direction her arm was pointing. Thirty metres away there was indeed an anthill so immense that from a distance she had assumed it was a hillock. She laughed out loud.

It was the biggest anthill she had ever seen. It reached the top of her head. As it should. She was seized by something similar to dizziness, and leaned against a tree. Everything around her was exactly the same, but smaller than she remembered. Only the anthill had kept up with her, distorting all sense of perspective.

This is where I crawled to, she thought. She smacked her lips, recalling the bitter sting of the ants' jaws against her tongue before they were crushed by her teeth, filling her mouth with an acidic taste. The house was no more than a square of logs overgrown with moss. When she dug in the needles around it she found a few rough, half-rotten planks. She went and stood in the middle of the square. Knelt down. Lay down on her stomach.

The shifting light among the trees. The number of trunks and the way they stood. She hid the view to the sides by cupping her hands. Yes. She was looking out through the door.

'Reva!'

The voice filled her world, the voice was arms embracing, fingers smelling of earth and moss. The voice was come to me, softness in her mouth, warm milk.

She was breastfeeding me. She was still breastfeeding me.

What had they given her instead, in hospital? What had they done to force their food into her mouth?

Reva, Reva, sisimi...

She lowered her head to the needles, pressed her forehead against the ground, rubbing it back and forth until it hurt.

'Mommi...Mommi...'

For several days she went to the glade that had been her home. One day she took a sleeping bag with her, but realised she didn't need it. When she woke up in the morning with her head resting on a clump of moss, she was covered in a thin layer of snow.

She started doing some research. It took three weeks of telephone calls and papers being sent here and there before she managed to find out where her parents were buried.

The graves in the churchyard in Norrtälje were like no others. It was the first time she had seen a grave without a name. Just two wooden crosses and the words Rest in Peace. Like a memorial marking an unidentifiable mass grave, or an ancient monument.

She emptied two plastic bags full of earth from their home onto the graves, placed a branch of fir on each.

How *should* they have been buried? She didn't know. She knew nothing about her own race. If she were to believe the fairy stories and her own feelings, the crosses were wrong. But that was all she knew. There was nothing she could do.

From the churchyard she went to the supermarket and bought

a bottle of organic strawberry juice. Then she went to the nursing home. She and her father drank almost the entire bottle as they sat talking for hours. She promised to bring another bottle next time she came. Soon.

January came and went with plenty of snow and water that shone like oil and never froze. She walked in the forest, tracking animals and trudging through the snow to her tree. She sat there trying to understand what she should do. The tears froze on her cheeks. She was the spoils of war in her own country, an unpleasant reminder.

In the middle of February the letter arrived. It was postmarked St Petersburg, and the handwriting on the envelope looked like a child's. Big, sprawling letters, laboriously printed to make them legible.

The beginning of the letter was written in the same painstaking style, but after just a few lines the hand holding the pen began to slip into its natural routine, and by the end it was just about illegible for anyone who was unfamiliar with it.

Tina

I knocked on the door. You didn't answer. Do you still feel the same?

My job was selling children. If I had been a human being, I would have been evil. I don't know how you judge. But the law would put me in prison for life. I've stopped now.

I am carrying our child. A *hiisit* is an unfertilised egg. A child is a fertilised egg. It will grow up to become a creature like you and me, if all goes well. I am intending to give birth to it and let it grow up as it should. Perhaps in the northern forests. I want you to be with me.

I will come to Kapellskär on February 20.

Vore

———·———

She went back to work on February 16, and was welcomed with a cake, which she took home and left in the fridge until it went off. Too much cream. Her colleagues had never been nicer to her, and she had never felt more alienated from them. Her instincts were on full alert, and every false note grated on her ears.

On February 20 she pulled in every minor smuggler who came in on the morning ferry, and was rewarded with a plethora of dirty looks and muttered imprecations. There was a kind of pleasure in it.

I do not belong here.

He arrived on the afternoon ferry.

As soon as he appeared she knew he had something to hide, and this time she knew what it was.

A child. Their child.

She lifted the desk flap and went to meet him.

Village on the hill

'So you're walking along between the buildings, and you just feel that...no. No, no, no. You shouldn't *be* here. It's *wrong* here, you see?'

Let the Right One In

The first time Joel Andersson became aware of the problem, he felt nothing more than a vague unease he couldn't quite put his finger on. He was standing with his hands in his trouser pockets looking up at the building that had been his home for twenty-three years and four months.

It was a quarter past six, and the sun was so low that the entire block, except for the apartments on the top floor, lay in shadow. As he watched the shadow moved further up, nudging at his kitchen windowsill.

Seized by a sudden desire to see the sun before it disappeared, Joel dashed inside and found the lift waiting on the ground floor. As he pressed the button for the eighth floor he realised he was stiff after gazing upwards for such a long time. He rubbed the back of his neck and the ligaments crunched beneath his fingertips as the ageing lift moved upwards.

He didn't know what it was. He'd stood outside for a long time looking at the sturdy rectangle of the apartment block, dotted with windowpanes, experiencing something like seasickness: a sinking feeling in his stomach as if he were about to lose his balance.

'Midlife crisis,' he muttered to himself as he unlocked his door—one of four on the top floor. He ignored the post and junk mail and went straight over to the kitchen window, where he was rewarded with the sight of a bright red sun waving goodbye to Sweden before continuing its world tour across the Atlantic, via Hässelby.

The sun went down, its rim notched by pine trees, and the feeling of nausea returned. A subway train the size of a toy train slid into Blackeberg station and Joel tried to focus on it, to visualise the straight, familiar tracks, the timetable that was being followed, everything in its place, but the feeling of unease grew so strong that he had to move away from the window and sit down.

What's going on? What's wrong?

He didn't suffer from vertigo, of course not, otherwise he wouldn't have been able to live here. He'd had the odd moment of dizziness when he moved in twenty-three years ago, but there had been other reasons for that: Lisbeth had decided she wanted a divorce after two years of marriage, she and the twins had stayed on in the apartment in Vällingby and Joel had taken the first decent place he could find nearby. Which turned out to be in Blackeberg.

In those days when he stood by the kitchen window feeling dizzy, it was mainly due to the immediate possibility of suicide. Just open the window and jump. Like sleeping with a razor blade under the pillow, but even more straightforward.

As time went by he got used to his role as a weekend dad, but swore solemnly that he would never be tied down again—a promise he had had no difficulty in keeping, since he had never fallen in love again.

Anita?

Well, yes. That was something else. *They were seeing one another.*

His stomach was churning. He tried to suppress the feeling by going into the living room to look at the ship.

The model of a three-masted schooner took up approximately a quarter of the floor surface, but appeared to take up even more space because it had been placed right in the middle of the room, and wherever you wanted to go in the apartment, you had to walk around it.

Joel caressed the miraculously smooth surfaces and felt the usual reverence for that life, that era. His stomach settled and he was able to breathe deeply and with a sense of relief. It had taken him a few years to realise it was probably this reverence that had made him start building the ship. He never felt sorrow. Others who had seen his model did. First of all amazement, reverence. And then sorrow. Or perhaps it was envy, who can say?

He knew the exact number of matchsticks. Eighty-seven thousand eight hundred and sixty-three. He calculated that it would take approximately another twenty-three thousand to finish it. In the beginning he had been able to place fifty matches in one session. These days he worked more slowly, less frequently. He was afraid of finishing it, because what would he do then? Put it in the water?

The idea was as ridiculous as it was obvious. The ribs and planks were made with microscopic precision. It wasn't a question of just snapping the heads off the matches and gluing them in place. No, every match was carefully cut to the perfect shape with a miniature electric band saw, then fixed in place with waterproof epoxy resin. The hull was completely watertight and would be able to float.

The first obstacle when it came to launching the ship was that it was far too wide to fit through the door of the apartment. This was a conscious decision; he had chosen this scale to eliminate any impression that the ship could have been *brought* into the apartment. He wanted people to see and appreciate that it was built here.

However, the balcony window was an option.

Yes. He would have to send for a crane when the time came. Or the fire brigade, perhaps. 'Hello, I have a ship that needs to go in the water right away! Come quickly!'

So no launch, then.

The other obstacle was that he didn't know a thing about ships. If he put the schooner in the water he wouldn't have a clue how to set the sails to stop it heading off towards the end of the world. He had immersed himself in the details of constructing this particular model, certainly, but he knew nothing about sailing.

What really impressed new visitors—the woman who came to read the electricity meter, the man who fitted new kitchen cupboards—when they had got over their initial amazement at the size of the model, was the *precision*. There wasn't one incorrect angle, not one discordant relationship between two details. This was partly thanks to those who had built the original ship, bringing together the practical and the beautiful, but visitors saw only Joel's work.

It might have been his imagination, but he thought the woman who came to read the meter might have been interested in him. Not *that* kind of interest, necessarily, but the fact that he had built the ship gave Joel an air of dignity, sincerity and...yes, reliability. He had done something with his time. He had assembled his hours, his years into a creation that was something more than himself, something greater.

When he walked out onto the balcony, the feeling in his stomach returned. He tried to dismiss it as hunger, and succeeded so well that he actually did feel hungry. He couldn't be bothered cooking anything, so he pulled on his jacket and got in the lift, intending to go down to the square for a pizza. He stopped on the ground floor and rang Anita's doorbell to see if she wanted to go with him.

The nameplate on the door said 'Andersson'. No one answered. They had joked about the fact that they wouldn't need new nameplates if they got married. They lived just about as far from one another as possible within the same building. Anita was on the ground floor, right-hand side, Joel on the top floor, left-hand side; joking apart, they were quite happy with the situation.

Joel went out, passing the swimming pool where the windows were still boarded up with black planks of wood after the terrible events twenty years earlier. Two children had been killed and one had been kidnapped by some lunatic who thought he was a vampire. Neither the perpetrator nor the kidnapped child had ever been found.

As he walked beneath an oak tree that formed a gateway leading to the carpark, something hit his head and he looked up. A couple of giggling children were perched among its branches. He recognised their faces; they lived in his block.

'Sorry, granddad. It was an accident.'

Joel considered scooping up a handful of acorns and throwing them back, for fun. Couldn't be bothered. Instead he said, 'I don't think it was an accident, but I forgive you anyway.'

The joke, if it was a joke, went over the children's heads. They looked at one another and giggled again, more because he'd said something weird than because it was funny.

He carried on. Another acorn came whizzing down, but missed his head and bounced away in front of him. A thought along the lines of *Young people today. No respect* began to take shape, and he cut it off before it managed to develop into a rant. That's the way miserable old farts think. He didn't want to be a miserable old fart. His bitterness towards life had bloomed in all its black glory when he was between twenty-eight and thirty-two, approximately. Since then the flowers of bitterness had withered. He was neither happy nor sad, neither disappointed nor contented. He stuck one match to another and went on living.

At the pizzeria he had a marinara and a beer. The feeling of unease had left him as soon as he walked out of the apartment block, and had been replaced by his current sense of stillness. A few regulars were sitting at a table filling in their coupons for the harness races. He knew their names, they knew his. Nothing more.

It was just after seven. He thought about ringing Lasse to ask if he fancied going to the movies, but when he checked the ads in a paper someone had left behind, there was nothing he wanted to see that he hadn't already seen. Besides, Lasse had said he was working overtime almost every evening at the moment. Some building project in Hammarbyhamnen that was running behind.

Not much on TV either. Perhaps he would go to the movies on his own. No. He knocked back the last of the beer and belched quietly. He hadn't really wanted to go to the cinema when he locked up the ironmonger's, it was just that now he didn't want to go back to the apartment. To the problem. He closed his eyes and tried to see. Couldn't catch it.

'Joel!'

He opened his eyes. Berra, one of the regulars, had turned around on his chair and was looking at him.

'Are you sitting there dreaming?'

'No, I just…' Joel spread his hands in a gesture that might mean anything.

'Give me a number.'

'Err…twenty-seven.'

Berra shook his head. 'They're not running that many horses yet. We can't agree here, so you have to decide.'

'What are the alternatives.'

'Doesn't matter. Just give me a number.'

'Five, then.'

Berra looked down at the papers in his hand and raised his eyebrows.

'*Five?*'

'Yes?'

The others at the table were guffawing. Berra scratched his head, looking as if someone had just come up with incontrovertible proof that two and two made five. He looked sceptically at Joel.

'But that's Black Riddle. Definitely...long odds, if I can put it that way.' Berra pursed his lips, made his decision and turned back to the others. 'OK, let's fill it in.'

The others protested, but Berra stuck to his guns, and since they couldn't agree anyway, Black Riddle it was. Joel heard something about 'Three hundred kronor straight down the toilet' and 'Better hedge our bets'. He placed his knife and fork neatly on the plate, stood up and held out a hundred-kronor note to Berra.

'Can I join in?'

Berra looked at the note, at Joel, at the others. Joel folded the note between his fingers so that it wouldn't look threatening. 'If I'm sabotaging the system, I can at least make a contribution.'

'No,' said Berra, and the others shook their heads in agreement. 'We were only joking. If you want to join in that's fine, but you don't have to feel...'

Joel moved the note closer, and Berra took it. 'But in that case we'll hedge our bets on a couple more, because Black Riddle...well, you know.'

'No,' said Joel. 'I'm in if you *don't* hedge your bets.'

Berra looked at the others, who shrugged. It didn't make any difference, after all; they wouldn't have been able to hedge their bets anyway without Joel's fresh capital. Berra waved the hundred-kronor note at the coupon. 'So what shall we put it on, then?'

'You know better than me.'

Berra nodded and a new discussion began. When Joel had pulled on his jacket, Berra pointed at the lines and said, 'Don't you want a copy?'

'No. Let me know if I win anything.'

'There's not much chance of that with Black Riddle, but...sure.'

Joel set off home. As soon as he started down the hill from the square, the feeling came creeping up on him again. He placed his hand over his heart. Wasn't it beating faster than usual?

Fear.

It was a form of fear. He hadn't felt like this for a long time. He had read a series of articles in *Dagens Nyheter* last summer about panic attacks. They were most common among young people, but could affect a person at any age. The fear itself wasn't dangerous, but the premonition led to panic, which led to...

A rose is a rose is a rose...

The tower blocks stood out like darker silhouettes against the grey sky. From where Joel was standing, the buildings were almost exactly in a line. He stopped, looked. Tilted his head to one side, squinted.

What the hell...

The sides of the buildings stood next to one another, two lines running from the ground to the sky. Joel blinked hard and looked again. No. He wasn't seeing things: the lines were not parallel. They weren't parallel because the closest block, his block...was at an angle. Only a degree or two, but enough to make the two sides next to one another form a very long, upside-down V instead of two Is.

He took a few steps back, a few steps forward, to the side, but however he looked, the phenomenon remained. The building was listing towards the east. When he stood at his kitchen window watching the sunset he had been standing on a sloping surface, about to fall over backwards.

People on their way home from the subway looked at him as he stood there motionless, staring up at the building. They looked in the same direction to see if they could spot what he was gazing at, but didn't seem to notice anything odd. Nothing was *moving*, thank God. The block wasn't about to collapse. In the end he couldn't help himself; he stopped a young man.

'Excuse me?'

The man took off his earphones.

'What?'

'Sorry, but...would you mind looking at those apartment blocks and telling me if you can see anything strange?'

The man immediately did as Joel had asked. He stared for a few seconds, then shook his head. 'No. Like what?'

'It's listing. The building nearest to us is listing.'

The man looked again. For a little while longer this time. Music was whispering from the earphones round his neck.

'Yes,' he said eventually. 'Yes, it is. A little bit.' Joel looked at him encouragingly and the man pushed his lips forward, repeated, 'Yes, it is.' He was about to put the earphones back on, but stopped and said, 'Maybe that's normal?' He replaced the earphones and went on his way.

Joel stayed where he was. Did tower blocks list slightly? He couldn't remember ever reading about any such building falling over all by itself. Not in Sweden, anyway. But the bad feeling had only come today. It must have happened overnight, during the storm.

He'd called Anita around ten, because he couldn't stand the way the building *swayed* when the wind was strong enough. Couldn't sleep. So he had called Anita, and as soon as he said who it was, she asked, 'Is it the wind?'

'Yes. Can I come down?'

He could. He had spent the rest of the night in her apartment. Been beaten at Scrabble then made love routinely, without passion or any sense that something was missing. It was fine just the way it was. Neither of them wanted more, neither of them wanted to stop. They didn't want to merge their lives. If differences of opinion arose, they simply stayed away from one another for a few days and let things settle down. Then they got together again.

They had parted in the morning with a dry kiss, a caress on the cheek, and Joel had gone off to the ironmonger's feeling relatively happy. That was the state he was aiming for: relatively happy. Happiness could easily tip over into its opposite, and depression was hard to break. You could be relatively happy all the time, if you took it easy.

At the bottom of the stairs Joel stopped and looked at the list of names. Column after column of names he couldn't put a face to. Right at the top of the left hand column: Andersson. Down at the bottom of the right hand column: Andersson. Between these known poles an undivided village on a hill. Plastic letters that could be swapped around all too easily, rearranged into new names without faces.

He didn't bother ringing Anita's doorbell because there were no lights on in her apartment; instead he went straight up in the lift. Now that he had something concrete to which he could attribute the bad feeling, it was no longer so strong. His building was falling down, that was all. Probably quite normal.

But he couldn't shake off the thought. As soon as he got inside he took the spirit level out of the bottom drawer in the kitchen and placed it on the floor. He lay down on his stomach next to it so that he could see properly and studied the little air bubble. It was possibly a fraction of a millimetre closer to the window. He changed position and lay alongside the spirit level with his feet pointing towards the kitchen window.

Yes. He could feel it. He might possibly have been a little oversensitive, but his head was definitely lower than his feet. He took a pair of pliers, broke open a bearing that was lying among all the rubbish in the drawer and tipped the balls on the floor. They didn't roll away.

Hard to stop once you've started. He thought for a while, then remembered what to do. He took out a reel of thick string and tied a heavy nut on the end, opened the kitchen window and lowered the nut until it reached the ground, tied the end of the string to the broom handle, fixed it in place with a stool and measured so that it was protruding exactly thirty centimetres through the window. Then he wound the string around the handle several times so that it was hanging free above the ground. A plumb line.

With the ruler in his hand he went back down in the lift. Outside he met the kids who had been sitting in the oak tree earlier on. They were looking up at his kitchen window. They were both wearing identical black jackets, and were presumably brothers. The older one pointed up at the window and asked, 'What are you doing?'

'Measuring,' said Joel, unfolding the ruler.

'Can we help?'

'Come on then.'

The younger one held out his hand for the ruler. 'Can I measure?'

'No,' said Joel, walking over to the weight that was slowly swinging to and fro among the bare rose bushes. He had had bad experiences with children and folding rulers. Five seconds and they were busted. The rulers.

He could have managed without the ruler. As soon as he stopped the weight from moving, he could see with the naked eye that it was less than ten centimetres from the wall. He measured anyway. Eight centimetres. A difference of twenty-two centimetres, therefore, between the ground and his apartment.

How tall is the building? Thirty metres? Twenty-two divided by three thousand makes...

No. What were you supposed to do? Joel turned to the older boy. He was about eleven or twelve years old, and looked clever.

'How do you calculate degrees?' he asked.

The boy shrugged his shoulders. 'With a thermometer, I suppose.'

'Not that kind of degree.'

'What kind, then?'

The younger boy, who might have been about nine, pointed to the nut. 'Can I have that?'

Joel tried to undo the knot. When he couldn't do it he used his door key to break the string and gave the nut to the boy. 'Just don't drop it on anybody's head.'

Together they stood looking up at the building. Joel wanted to tell the boys it was listing, but didn't want to frighten them. The younger boy pointed halfway up, a few windows below Joel's.

'That's where we live,' he said. 'There's a mouse in our kitchen.'

'There is not,' said the older boy.

'There is too! Daddy showed me the mousetrap so I wouldn't hurt myself on it.' The boy measured something in the region of twenty centimetres between his hands. 'It's this big.'

'The trap,' said Joel.

'Yes,' said the little boy and his older brother laughed out loud. The younger one realised some joke had been made at his expense, and looked crossly from Joel to his brother and back again.

'Daddy said it had taken things from the bathroom, so there!'

'In that case,' said his brother, 'why didn't he put the trap in there?'

'So we wouldn't *stand* on it, of course!'

As if to emphasise the danger posed by the mousetrap, he stamped on the ground and marched off towards the sandpits. The older one looked at Joel and raised his eyebrows: *Kid brothers, what can you do,* and followed him.

Joel went back inside and rang Anita's doorbell. When no one answered, he took the lift up to his apartment. As soon as he walked in he could feel the tilt.

Hasn't anyone else noticed anything?

He considered going over to see Lundberg on the other

side—they were on nodding terms—but didn't know how to explain the situation. Lundberg would probably react in the same way as the man with the earphones: 'Yeah? And?'

He sat down and took out his modelling tools. Instead of gluing the matchsticks in place one at a time, he worked in the same way as a real shipbuilder: first of all he made a plank out of three hundred and twenty matchsticks, then hammered the plank in place with rivets and strengthened it with glue. He had half-finished one of the final planks for the deck. Since he didn't have the heart to completely cover the construction of the hull on which he had spent so much time and effort, he was planning to leave part of the deck unfinished so that it would be possible to admire the intricate skeleton of the framework through the gap. He might even put a small lamp inside.

He had been working for perhaps half an hour and had put eight matchsticks in place when he looked up at the ship and the feeling of seasickness came over him again. The ship was listing to one side.

It's my imagination. I'm listing as well, in that case. I can't see it.

However, the unpleasant feeling was still enough to break his concentration. He took a turn around the ship; it was as if he was walking on a swaying deck, and he had to sit down. He picked up the phone and called Lasse, who answered on the fifth ring.

'Yes?' He sounded annoyed.

'Hi, it's Joel.'

'Hi. Listen, I'm in the bath. I just got home. They're absolute slave-drivers down there, you know. Was it anything in particular?'

'No, I was just wondering how to calculate degrees.'

'Degrees?'

'Yes, the angle if a building is listing one way, that kind of thing.'

'Were you away when we did that in school?'

'I was probably standing in the corner.'

Lasse laughed. 'I'll ring you back in quarter of an hour, OK? Are you going to build something, or is it for your ship?'

'No, it's…I'll speak to you later.'

Joel hung up and sat on the sofa for a while, rocking back and forth to relieve the churning in his stomach. Then he went into the kitchen and looked at the spirit level, which was still on the floor. He lay down on his stomach, put his ear to the floor and looked at the bubble. Had it moved a fraction? He would make a mark and check it again the following day.

He was about to get up and fetch a pen when he heard something. From downstairs. In order to hear better, he stuck his index finger in the ear that wasn't next to the floor and closed his eyes.

It could of course be his neighbour downstairs doing something or other, but the boy's talk of mouse traps immediately evoked the image of a mouse moving around under the floor. A slow, sinuous movement. Joel sat up and stared at the linoleum. He wasn't scared of mice, but he couldn't work out how they could possibly have got into an apartment block, all the way up to the top storey.

He knocked on the floor. The response was a dull, solid sound against his knuckles. Concrete. Mice were supposed to live in wooden buildings, in the spaces between the walls where they could build nests and do whatever it is mice do when they're not shitting and eating and shitting. It was unthinkable that a mouse could have eaten its way through the concrete. It must be making its way through drainpipes, ventilation shafts.

Joel looked around the kitchen. It was easy to summarise the phenomena he had observed during the course of the evening:

This building is going to hell.

In his mind's eye he could see an army of mice gnawing through the concrete, perforating the block like a roll of toilet paper, making it soften, tilt. Al-Qaeda mice, working with a long-term objective. He snorted at the image of bearded mice in turbans infiltrating the swanky buildings of the western world.

The telephone rang. Lasse was out of the bath.

'So,' he said. 'What was it you wanted? Something about angles, you said.'

Joel told him about the unpleasant feeling he'd had that morning, how he could see the building listing to one side with the naked eye, the measurements he had taken. Lasse wrote down the numbers, and Joel could hear a faint tapping sound of fingers on a calculator.

'OK,' said Lasse. 'If what you say is accurate, then you have a divergence of approximately one degree.'

'Which means?'

'You know that already. The building is listing about twenty centimetres.'

'So how bad is it?'

'Well, you say bad…It's not *good*, definitely not, but I mean it's not going to fall down tonight, if I can put it like that. It was built in the sixties, wasn't it? Part of the Million Program, all that stuff?'

'I think so.'

'Mm. We've had a certain amount of trouble with those buildings. The strange thing in your case is that you say it kind of happened overnight. Are you sure about that?'

'Quite sure.'

'There ought to be cracks in the façade, down at the bottom. Concrete doesn't like to bend, as you know. When there are problems it's usually the main load-bearing girders. But the concrete cracks. Listen, I'll come over and have a look tomorrow evening, I'll bring a few bits and pieces with me. Maybe we could rent a film or something. Have you seen the new Coen brothers film, whatever it's called?'

'No. Sounds like a plan.'

'OK. I'll be there around seven, God and the boss willing.'

They said goodbye and hung up. Joel remembered the mice, picked up the phone again and started to key in Lasse's number, but stopped. They could discuss it the next day. They were best friends, admittedly, but Joel didn't want to sound like some hysterical lunatic: 'Lasse, the building's listing! Lasse, there's a mouse in the kitchen! Lasse, help!' Clearly there was no immediate danger.

He got up and took a walk around the ship.

No immediate danger.

But he wasn't convinced. At least the boat had stopped listing, and Lasse's comments had made Joel feel calmer. He would have a couple of glasses of wine, watch TV for a while, then go to bed. He went into the bathroom and scooped some wine into a jug from the big plastic container. Sometimes he took the trouble to decant the wine into bottles, but he had noticed that it matured almost as well in the container, and he didn't have to bother fiddling about with a load of empty bottles.

The container was half full. When it was empty he would start a fresh batch, drinking wine from boxes in the meantime. He didn't have room for two containers side by side in the bathroom. Perhaps he was a bit of an alcoholic; he drank three glasses of wine each evening, but seldom more. Alkie lite.

A person has to have something.

When he lifted the toilet lid to pee, he noticed that the water level in the bowl was low, much lower than usual. He wouldn't have paid much attention if it hadn't been for the fact that it was all part of the same problem. There was something wrong with the building. He had a pee anyway, and the flush worked normally. He'd give the company that owned the building a call if it got any worse.

The evening passed in the usual way. He watched a debate about Economic and Monetary Union in the EU, with both sides predicting a disaster if they didn't get their way. At a quarter to ten he rang Anita, but there was no reply. Perhaps she'd gone away on a course or something. He thought about using his key and going downstairs to sleep in her apartment, but decided against it. It wasn't a lasting solution.

When he did get to bed, he lay tossing and turning for a long time. Thought he could hear mice scrabbling and scuttling through the pipes. Or maybe it was the building creaking as it bent down further towards the ground.

The first thing he did when he woke up in the morning was to go into the kitchen and check the spirit level. Unfortunately he had forgotten to make a mark, but still, he was more or less certain that the bubble had moved towards the window. The feeling in his stomach told him the same thing: the tilt had got worse. He couldn't manage any breakfast before he went to work.

When he reached the spot where he had spoken to the man with the earphones, he turned around and studied the building. At first he thought nothing had changed: the top intersected with the building next door in the same place. Or did it?

Hang on a minute...

It wasn't that the angle had increased; it had *changed.* The sides of the buildings no longer formed an upside down V, but rather an extended D or a bow, with his own block forming the bow and the other the string. The top had been pushed back towards its original position, while the middle now bellied out towards the west. If you measured with a plumb line now, you wouldn't notice anything.

From the point of view of balance, it was no doubt better, but... there was something deeply unsettling about a structure made of concrete and steel behaving as if it were made of rubber. Particularly when you lived in it.

He took the subway to Vällingby and managed to suppress his worries during the day. After all, Lasse had said there were often problems in blocks like his; perhaps fluctuations in the angle of inclination were part of the normal pattern.

The only time the anxiety pushed its way through was when a customer came in to buy a reinforcing bar for a tool shed he was building at his summer cottage. The customer weighed the bar in his hand, his expression sceptical.

'Will this really be strong enough?' he asked.

'Definitely,' Joel replied.

The customer did a quick sketch on a piece of paper to show what he was planning to do.

'You see what I mean? All the weight will be resting on the bar from directly above.'

Joel hesitated briefly, then went to check the product catalogue just to be on the safe side. As he ran his finger over the figures showing the strength of the various dimensions, he thought: *I wouldn't have done this yesterday. Yesterday I would just have guaranteed that it would hold.*

He showed the figures to the customer.

'It will tolerate a load of three tonnes. If you're planning on putting a Sherman tank in the shed it might not hold, but otherwise...'

The customer laughed, shook his head.

'No, it's just the lawn mower, that kind of thing.'

'In that case it'll be strong enough, no problem.'

When the customer had left Joel stood at the counter looking at the columns of impressive figures. The strongest flat bars they sold would bear seven tonnes. They were as thick as a broom handle.

How much does an apartment block weigh?

He had been out a couple of times to look at projects Lasse was working on. It was fascinating to think that the steel structure that looked so fragile from a distance would carry the lives and walls of hundreds of people, but you could hardly get both arms around those girders, and they were arranged in a self-bearing triangular system.

Lasse had pointed to the crane that was as tall as the building they were constructing, and said, 'Buildings are nothing. But the crane—now *there's* the miracle! Just thin metal struts, as if it were made out of your matchsticks. If it was built in rectangles, it wouldn't even be able to lift an elephant. It would collapse. But the triangles...everything presses on everything else, so all the weight goes down into the ground. Unbelievable. It's hardly surprising that Pythagoras was religious.'

Joel closed the catalogue and thought about the World Trade Center. The buildings hadn't collapsed, they hadn't even bent after the planes crashed into them. It was the fire that had done for them. The power that was needed to bring down a tall building.

He finished work at three and caught the subway home. He wasn't keen on going back to his apartment, so instead he went up the steps leading to the square, intending to go to the pizzeria, have a couple of beers and read the papers. He had hardly got through the door before Berra shot up from his table, holding out his hand. Joel took it, shaking his head enquiringly.

'Congratulations,' said Berra. 'You're three thousand kronor richer. Three thousand two hundred and sixty-one, to be precise.'

'We won?'

'We certainly did. Six right, thirteen thousand and forty-four kronor. Come and sit down.'

Joel sat down with the regulars and ordered a beer. They were all a bit bleary-eyed, having started the celebrations a couple of hours earlier. The winning coupon was in the place of honour in the middle of the table. Joel got his beer, took a swig and looked at the coupon where certain numbers were circled.

'Was it...Black Riddle?' he asked.

'Oh no,' said Berra. 'That bag of bones bolted after two hundred metres and was disqualified. If we'd gone with Morgan's nag we'd have had four hundred and twenty thousand between us.'

Joel looked at Morgan, who pulled a face, finished off his beer and stood up. Despite the fact that he was in his sixties he was wearing a denim jacket over a Hawaiian shirt. His thinning hair was slicked back with something that was presumably Brylcreem. He picked up a battered cowboy hat from the back of his chair and plonked it on his head.

'No,' he said. 'I've had enough of this. Hard to celebrate three thousand when it could have been a hundred.'

'Don't be like that,' said Berra.

'I tried, I tried,' said Morgan, pointing to his empty glass. 'I just can't bring myself to feel really happy. Sorry. See you.'

He went out and headed across the square with his hands pushed deep in his pockets.

'The thing is,' said Berra by way of explanation, 'life hasn't been all that easy for Morgan. Cheers, Joel.'

Joel stayed for an hour, chatting to Berra and Östen who both, unlike Morgan, regarded Joel as a lucky mascot. They hadn't won anything for over a year; along came Joel, and hey presto—their biggest win since they started picking numbers together. He was welcome to join them in future, as long as he left the actual selection to them.

'That Black Riddle,' said Berra. 'It's practically a hamburger factory on legs.'

Joel didn't really think he should have a share of the winnings; he suggested they should just give him back his hundred kronor, but they wouldn't hear of it. They had already collected the money and Berra counted out Joel's share on the table, down to the last krona.

They parted with slightly drunken protestations of friendship. The beer swilling gently around their stomachs, the comforting sense of companionship and the lingering feeling of happiness made Joel less than keen to deal with the Problem, and he didn't even look up as he walked down the hill. The apartment block was still there, anyway.

He rang Anita's doorbell, and when no one answered he pushed open the letterbox and peered in. There were letters and junk mail lying on the floor behind the door. He took out her key and stood there deliberating for a moment. Anita worked part time as a cleaner down at the hospital, and…a course? What kind of bloody course would she be on? New cleaning products?

But still he put the key back in his pocket. He only had it for safekeeping, really. Just in case she locked herself out. He had no right to come and go in her apartment as he wished. He stood motionless outside her door, listening.

It might have been his imagination, but he thought the building was…vibrating. His heart rate increased and he had the urge to hurl himself out of the main door before the whole place collapsed on top of him. The moment passed. The block was still standing. He went over to the list of names.

He should have had something to eat at the pizzeria instead of just drinking beer. When he looked at the white plastic letters that were a representation of the apartment block in miniature, he thought they too were tilting, twisting. Sanchez bent down towards Lundin, seeking contact. He placed his hand on the concrete wall. Nothing was moving. And yet it was as if a creeping horror was crawling up his back. He swung around. He felt as if someone was looking at him. As if someone was *here*.

But the hallway was empty. He looked at the list of names again and was seized by a sense of loss. He wished he could speak to these people who were only names, his fellow inhabitants of the village on the hill. If there had been more of them, they could have compared experiences with each other, talked. Formed a village council.

Instead he took the lift up to his apartment, alone. However, when he reached the top floor he decided to defy the taboo that prohibited contact, and rang the bell of Lundberg's apartment opposite. But no one answered. He could already feel the tilt out here on the landing.

Why doesn't anybody say anything? Why doesn't anybody do anything?

For the same reason that he wasn't saying or doing anything. People didn't want to seem difficult, awkward. He unlocked his door and made a decision: if Lasse said that what was happening to the building wasn't normal, he would ring the company that owned it the very next morning. They could say what they liked, he didn't care.

For once, the very first thing he did was to scoop a couple of glasses of wine out of the container. There was no water in the toilet bowl. When he flushed it water poured in and stayed there. He didn't need to wait for Lasse's verdict: there was something wrong here, and it needed sorting out.

He was number twelve in the queue when he rang the company. After ten minutes he had reached number eleven, and hung up. No doubt people all over the building were on the phone right now, hence the queue. The problem would be sorted.

He couldn't shake off the feeling that had come over him downstairs, the feeling that he was being watched. It wasn't until he had drunk the wine that he started to chill out and stop worrying. He lay down on the sofa and felt the movements of the building, which might well have existed only inside his own head.

At a quarter past seven the doorbell rang; Lasse was standing outside with a DVD in his hand.

'Evening,' he said, and gave a start when he saw Joel. 'How are you?'

'Not too bad,' said Joel, running a hand over his face. 'Did you bring some of your...kit?'

'Sure. Left it downstairs. I see what you mean.'

'The building's listing?'

'Yes. I mean, there's nothing to worry about. But it does seem quite pronounced. Shall we have a look at it straightaway?'

They went down in the lift and Joel felt as if he was moving through a sloping shaft. Lasse took up virtually no room. He wasn't a rough builder with hairy armpits, but the small sinewy type. He said, 'As I mentioned before, it's nothing unusual, but I thought you said it was listing towards the east. It just seemed to me to be more… well, bowed.'

'It was listing yesterday.'

Lasse looked at him and grinned. 'Maybe tomorrow it will have turned around.'

Joel didn't crack a smile. 'Yesterday it was listing, and today it's bowed.'

'Yes, yes,' said Lasse in a tone of voice that suggested Joel's judgment might not be entirely reliable.

They went outside and Lasse mounted a theodolite on a stand; it was calibrated by turning small wheels.

'We've got digital versions nowadays, but I prefer these.' He patted the theodolite and looked through the lens. Joel kept his eyes fixed on the façade of the apartment block. Windows in darkness, windows with the lights on. They were trying to tell him something, but he couldn't grasp it. Anita's apartment was still in darkness.

Lasse puffed and turned the wheels. He took a step away from the theodolite, stood beside Joel and looked at the apartment block.

'Well,' he said. 'That's quite something. It's like a bow. Incredible. As I said before: the building isn't about to fall down, it's a long way from that, but I think you should be prepared to move out quite soon. This will have to be sorted out, and I wouldn't be surprised if they have to knock the whole lot down. I've never seen anything like it.'

Windows in darkness, windows with the lights on. What does it mean?

Joel turned his attention back to Lasse and asked, 'How could this have happened?'

Lasse scratched his head.

'To be honest, I don't know. The thing is, it's just as if something is…pulling at the building from below. But that level of strength, that torsion…no, I don't know. Maybe they cut some corners when they were building the middle section.'

'It was listing yesterday.'

'Well, in that case I have no idea what's going on. That means the power has shifted, you see. Yesterday it was on the left-hand side, today it's on the right. But that pressure…no. If you could imagine an invisible spaceship the same size as the building, sitting up on the roof altering its position, then yes. By the way, they didn't have the film I was talking about, so I got *Armageddon* instead—is that OK?'

'Yes, sure.'

'Shall we go back inside?'

'You go. I'll be there in a minute.'

Lasse folded up the stand and took it inside with him. Joel stayed where he was, gazing up at the windows and squinting as if he were trying to make out blurred handwriting. Suddenly he saw it. Just as if two pictures had been placed on top of one another, he saw it: the pattern of dark and illuminated windows was exactly the same as the previous evening.

Did that necessarily mean anything? People have their routines, after all. His own lights had been on at this time yesterday, and they were on now. Besides, there was one difference: the bathroom light was on in the apartment below his. It hadn't been on yesterday.

He suddenly felt very frightened. He hurried back inside and unlocked Anita's door without hesitation. He switched on the hall light and saw junk mail and bills strewn across the floor. He pulled a face as he recognised the rent demand from the company that owned the building.

They shouldn't be asking for money. They should be paying.

He placed the post on the hall stand and stood hesitating for a moment; he was waiting for something, but he didn't know what it was. Of course—Anita's cat, Trisse. He was waiting for Trisse to come rubbing round his legs as usual. He peered into the cat basket in the hall where Trisse usually lay relaxing. It was empty.

'Hello? Anita?'

There's nothing intrinsically unpleasant about an empty apartment. But shouting for someone you know ought to be there is unpleasant. Because that means the person is lying dead somewhere, and you don't know where. That's just the way it is. Joel clenched his fists and steeled himself. The outdoor clothes and shoes Anita usually wore were in the hallway. Her keys were hanging on the hook just inside the door. She was here.

Anita, Anita...

His eyes were pricking and his heart contracted. He didn't want Anita to be dead. In fact, if he thought about it, he would rather be dead himself. He put his hands to his mouth, staring at the cat basket, and tears blurred his vision. He hadn't realised how important she was to him. Now he knew. He would rather be dead himself, if he had the choice. That's how important she was.

But Trisse wasn't here. If Anita was lying dead, a hungry Trisse should have come running to meet him. It was only two days since Joel was last here—the cat couldn't have starved to death in that time.

But the coat, the shoes, the keys...

He took a tentative step forward. In an attempt to suppress the fear threatening to take over his body, he started to sing quietly:

'The water is wide...'

The living room. He switched on the light. On the coffee table there was a pile of magazines that Anita got from a colleague at the hospital, because she enjoyed doing the crosswords. One lay open next to a half-full ashtray. It was the same crossword that had been lying there two days ago. She had asked him a question: 'Mooring, seven letters, starts with C and ends with N', and he had answered, 'Capstan'. No new words had been filled in since he last saw the crossword.

'I cannot get over...'

His legs didn't want to move. He forced them to walk to the kitchen, poised to close his eyes if it was horrible. The dirty dishes were in the sink, just as before. There was one additional item. A half-full coffee cup on the kitchen table. The coffee machine was switched on. The jug crackled as he picked it up and looked at the hot, burnt crust in the bottom.

'And neither have I wings to fly...'

He knew her morning routine. She put the coffee on as soon as she got up. Then she read the paper until the coffee was ready. The paper lay open on the table. When she had drunk half a cup of coffee and smoked her first cigarette of the day, she needed a pee and went to the bathroom.

'Build me a boat that will carry two...'

He actually started to feel ill as he left the kitchen and headed for the bathroom, raising his voice.

'And both shall row...'

Whatever had taken place, it had happened in the morning after he left her at about seven-thirty, and before she went to work at nine. The bathroom door was closed but not locked. His heart was pounding in his head and he felt as he if was about to faint as he placed his hand on the door handle and sang as loud as he could, *'MY LOVE AND I...'*

He yanked open the door. The bathroom was empty. In the light from the living room he could see something glinting on the floor. The pressure in his head eased, he started breathing again and sang quietly, *'There is a ship that sails the sea...'*

He switched on the bathroom light. Whatever it was must have happened in the morning, because all the lights were off. In the mornings the daylight was enough in the apartment. He went over to the object on the floor and picked it up. Anita's glasses. She never went anywhere without her reading glasses. When she wasn't using them she pushed them up on top of her head, her hair holding them in place. He looked around the bathroom.

'*It's loaded deep—*'

His jaws stiffened, stuck fast. The lid of the toilet was open. The inside of the bowl was streaked with red, as if someone had been pissing blood. Down at the bottom was a dark red, gooey mess moving slowly up and down, up and down. Like breathing. Rising and falling, rising and falling.

He backed out of the bathroom, still clutching Anita's glasses in his hand. When he reached the living room they snapped in half. He raised his hand, gazed at the two monocles and hurled them away.

Red rising.

The image of a thermometer flashed through his mind. The column of mercury slowly rising. He had stopped thinking. There was something he wanted to check, a suspicion he wanted to confirm. His body numb, he left the apartment and went up to the first floor as if he was walking on stilts. Opened a letter box and peered inside. Letters and junk mail.

He went up the next floor. Letters and junk mail. Third floor, fourth floor, same thing. No one was home. No one had been at home since early the previous day. There were no people in the building.

But the children, the children...

On the fifth floor the post looked different. The same advertising leaflets were uppermost, but they weren't lying on top of yesterday's paper. The residents had picked up the mail yesterday. But not today.

It's...rising.

Still stunned, he carried on up the stairs as if he was walking on stilts, or like a marionette, dangling from a string. He had to know. It wasn't until he reached the seventh floor, just below his own, that the post had been picked up. He rang the doorbell. No one answered.

He stood there with his arms dangling by his sides, the throbbing pulling at his temples, and the fear took hold of him, squeezed him. Now he understood why he had felt as if someone was watching him down in the entrance hall. He wasn't being watched, he was *enclosed* in something…alive. Something that was rising.

Lasse!

His legs jerked as if he had received an electric shock and he ran up the stairs to his own apartment. The staircase was listing, and he ran along a corridor of tunnel vision, a ghost tunnel. They had to get out of here, now. As he hurled himself through the door of his apartment he saw the thing he wanted to see least of all.

Lasse was in the toilet with the door open, just zipping himself up.

'Joel, what the hell…'

'Get away from there!' Joel yelled. 'Get out of the bathroom!'

Lasse grinned and pushed the handle to flush the toilet. There was a hollow clicking sound from the empty cistern, and Lasse said, 'Looks as if you've got a problem with—'

He got no further. A black snake shot up out of the toilet, wound itself around both his legs. Lasse shouted and threw out his arms. Joel grabbed one hand, but the strength that was pulling against him was so immense that he might as well have tried to stop a runaway train with his fingertips. He had barely got a grip when his friend's hand was wrenched free and Lasse was thrown inwards at an angle like a rag doll.

There was a cold crack as both of his kneecaps were smashed against the bowl, and the next moment both legs were in the toilet. Lasse's eyes were wide open, his mouth gaping in a silent scream. He managed to grab the wine container with one hand, but in half a second the whole of his lower body was down in the toilet, and the container tipped over, its contents surging across the floor as Lasse's body was dragged down through the impossibly small hole.

His eyes bulged out of his head with the pressure and the pain. They were looking into Joel's eyes without seeing. When his hips shattered something in the pupils was extinguished, and Lasse was no longer aware of what was happening.

Everything happened so fast that the wine container wasn't even empty by the time his chest collapsed with the sound of falling trees, breaking branches, and Lasse's head vanished out of sight below the rim.

Without knowing what he was doing—

have to look

—Joel moved over to the doorway as the wave of wine reached the threshold. He saw Lasse's head being dragged down towards the hole, but it wouldn't go through. His ears were folded back against his cheeks, and the skin on his face was such a dark shade of red that it was almost black.

The wine poured through the door and soaked Joel's shoes just as Lasse's head was torn from his body and floated a few centimetres up the bowl on a backwash of red sludge. His hair was still undisturbed. His evening coiffure, shaped with mousse, bobbed among his guts for a moment before the equilibrium was broken and the head spun around with a splash towards its heaviest point, the cranium, and the severed neck was impossible to distinguish among all the redness.

The tentacle reappeared, wound itself around the head and crushed it before emerging from the toilet once more. If there had been a nose, something recognisable as an organ of smell on the black shiny surface, it would have been obvious that it was sniffing.

Joel ran for the front door, but the snake was out of the bathroom in a second, cutting off his escape route. He carried on into the living room and out onto the balcony, slamming the door behind him.

That was no snake.

Through the balcony window he could see that the black thing making its way into the room, sniffing and taking its bearings, had no end. He moved back towards the railings.

It can't see, can it?

More of the tentacle came into the room, wriggling across the floor like a serpent. The end rose up, wrapped itself around his ship in a second like one of those old horrific pictures in which sailors are attacked by a giant octopus. It squeezed and the ship broke in half. Joel pulled himself up onto the railings, sat down and waited. His ship was in bits inside the room. Anita. Lasse. The creature swept the room, searching, knocking down the lamp and the television.

Octopus.

Not a snake. That black cable of pure muscle searching his living room was merely a runner from something bigger. Something much bigger. Something so big that it could bend an apartment block like a sapling.

No. Think about...

The balcony window shattered and Joel let himself fall backwards. He continued his chain of thought as he fell past the seventh floor, the sixth.

Think about the torsion.

His body turned in the air so that he was falling face downwards, towards a black dot at the bottom.

The torsion. You can't use your arm to bend something into a bow shape if it's not attached to your body. The creature wouldn't be able to bend the apartment block unless the thing in his living room was merely a small runner *from* something else.

Something much bigger.

The black dot was growing quickly and he was falling straight towards it. For a brief second he managed to register what it was: a drain cover. In a flash of X-ray vision he saw the entire sewerage system, the reservoirs extending beneath the whole city. The size of the body that had allowed a part of itself to penetrate the apartment block during the night of the storm, when nobody could hear.

And what if anyone had heard? If everyone had heard?

This is a village on the hill. We don't talk about that kind of thing here.

Equinox

It wasn't anybody's fault. One pebble triggers a landslide, one snow-flake starts an avalanche. Nobody's fault. Something is set in motion and it has to fulfil that movement. That's all it is.

I'm happy with my punishment.

Almost two years ago, in the autumn of 2004, Maud Pettersson rang and asked if I could keep any eye on their house while she and her husband were in the Canaries. Water the plants, feed the cat. I was a bit surprised because we hadn't really had any kind of close contact, but I saw no reason to say no. Their house is only three hundred metres from ours, just on the edge of the area where all the summer cottages are located. Playa de Nåten, as we like to call it.

I suppose it was partly because Emil had started nursery two months earlier, at the same time as Johanna started Year 3. Lasse was still working for the prison and probation service in Norrtälje, and the house was empty during the day. I could usually get my work done in two or three hours. I'm a crossword compiler. *Hemmets Journal, Allers* and *Kamratposten.*

I can work much more quickly since Göran, one of Lasse's friends, wrote a program enabling me to do the whole thing on the computer. If I really made an effort I could probably come up with something along the lines of the Sunday crossword in *Dagens Nyheter.* But that would take longer, and the weekly magazines neither demand nor want that kind of thing. I'm paid twelve hundred kronor for a crossword that takes about five hours to compile. I work three hours a day and earn marginally less than Lasse, who works seven.

Not a bad life. Quite the reverse. Almost perfect, in fact. By about twelve o'clock I've finished work. Happy if I've managed to make everything work with words that are in the Swedish Academy's dictionary, less happy if I've had to resort to 'Björn Larsson' to fit in with BL. My employers don't seem to mind; it's rare that I get any kind of response.

So from twelve o'clock the day is my own until half past three, when Johanna and Emil come home. I usually start by praying to God for a while. It goes in cycles; sometimes it's every day, sometimes I might miss a whole week. Then I have a guilty conscience.

I pray on the kitchen floor, kneeling on a cushion. I pray for the usual thing: the ability to feel love. Or perhaps that isn't the usual thing? Nowadays I know there's something wrong with me. Perhaps there was something wrong with my prayers too.

Anyway. Maud's house.

She and her husband set off for the Canaries in the morning, and in the afternoon I went over to feed the cat.

The key was where she said it would be. There was a cat flap and the cat was out, its food untouched. I put some fresh water in its bowl. When I straightened up after putting the bowl down, I felt dizzy and had to sit on a kitchen chair. I sat there for a while looking around their kitchen. Then I stood up.

There was nothing special in the top drawer. Cutlery. The other drawers also contained various kitchen utensils. Except the bottom one. In there I found a number of bundles of sheets made of a material that most closely resembled papier-mâché, except that it was stiff, shiny. I held a sheet up to the light and saw a spider's web pattern of fibres.

I couldn't for the life of me work out what it was or what it might be used for. Perhaps I wouldn't have reacted if there had been just one sheet—something for baking a particular kind of biscuit?—but there were bundles. There must have been a hundred sheets made of this unfamiliar material.

As I crouched there by the drawer I heard a sound, and felt a little shock that ran all the way up from the base of my spine. But it was only the cat. It came in through the cat flap and stood there looking at me. I suppose it was wondering who I was, what I was doing there. Stupidly, I blushed.

I left the kitchen and investigated the utility room. There were eight pairs of Bestpoint men's underpants, the kind you get at the Flygfyren shopping centre. No other brands. Lasse has lots of different brands of underpants, but this man had found the one he liked and he was sticking to it. I don't remember his name. I want to say Guran, but that's not a name, is it?

During the rest of the week I examined every single corner of the house. I went through the bills they'd paid. Found a whole lot of payments to something called Royal Court. Several thousand kronor over the years. I've looked on the internet, but I can't find a company with that name; all I get are links to royal families in various countries.

I found a gold ring underneath a bundle of cables behind the TV. I couldn't leave it out on the table, so I tucked it under the rug where there was more chance of them finding it. They must have been surprised even so. It's the sort of thing you tell your friends:

'Just imagine…the ring had been missing for four years, then one day I was just going to shake out the rugs…'

They had an impressive collection of razors in the bathroom. Five different kinds, if I remember rightly.

OK. I think you get it. I was being nosey. It gave me great satisfaction while I was doing it. When I got home I didn't feel quite so good. I promised myself I wouldn't do it again. On the first day I also promised God that I wouldn't do it again. Then I did it anyway, and stopped making promises. I also stopped praying that week.

It might sound as if this is something I've always done, and to a certain extent I suppose it is. I take the opportunity to read people's letters and diaries on the sly, check what's in their bathroom cabinets.

It's bad. I know it's bad. It involves breaking a spoken or unspoken trust. It's a violation. I know. I curse myself for doing it. I've asked God for help, but he doesn't help me. Perhaps I'm not really interested in people's secrets. Perhaps it's the actual violation I'm after. That's probably worse.

After that week it was a couple of months before anything happened on that front. Johanna was bullied by some older girls at school, and I prayed to God that it would stop. It stopped.

Perhaps I would have started on—what shall I call it?—phase two earlier if Lasse hadn't been working nights for a couple of months. That meant he was at home during the day, and could keep an eye on me.

It's only in the light of what happened later that such terminology is justified: 'keep an eye on me'. Things were good between us, me and Lasse. You couldn't wish for a better husband. He's sensitive, fun, and insists that we share the housework equally. I probably do slightly more anyway, because I have more time. But in principle. He's not good looking, not at all. But then neither am I, as I've been told.

I could have been happy with Lasse during those months. Sometimes we'd make love during the day. I closed my eyes. He has a pot belly and a lot of hair on his body, particularly around his navel. I closed my eyes and thought of the summer cottages. All those lives just waiting to be discovered, within walking distance.

It's difficult to describe how I felt during that week in Maud's house as I opened cupboards and drawers. It gave me peace while it was going on, perhaps the peace that comes with the awareness of absolute power. Of course I enjoyed giving my imagination free rein (Royal Court, what could that be? That wax paper, what was it used for?), but I won't pretend. I think it's about power.

The problem with the summer cottages was that I didn't have keys. The first time I headed over there with trembling knees, I had no clear idea of what I was going to do. Perhaps that would have been the end of it, if I hadn't immediately found the key to the first cottage I visited. In the guttering.

It was only five houses later that I found another key. I broke into the intervening four. If a spatula in the lock doesn't work, you can usually manage to undo one of the windows from the outside.

The summer cottages were less rewarding than Maud's house. Apart from the occasions when I found photographs, I didn't know what the people looked like, and had no faces to which I could attach whatever I found. Besides which, you don't leave as many clues in a summer cottage. It's cleaned from top to bottom every year, and many personal items are removed.

But you don't need much to spin a tale, if you have the gift. I find an ugly souvenir from Corsica, a Bible with various passages underlined and a high-visibility jacket from the national organisation responsible for road maintenance. The picture is clear in my mind.

It happened in January, after the Christmas break. By that time I had been inside perhaps twenty-five houses. If anyone caught me, I would say that the owners had called me and asked me to turn off the water so that the pipes wouldn't freeze. If the owners caught me it would have been slightly more difficult. But it never happened.

Christmas wasn't all that enjoyable. I'd become dependent on my breaking and entering, and the children's Christmas holidays meant I couldn't get away. Oh, it was a lovely Christmas in every way, but I just wasn't really there, I think. Lasse asked me one day, 'Veronica, what is it you're thinking about all the time?'

'Nothing in particular.'

'It's as if you're not here.'

I don't know. Perhaps looking at all these unfamiliar objects had alienated me from my own life. I looked at my own things, my own loved ones in the same way: a puzzle to be solved, a reality to bring together. Thought about how I would analyse the objects we would leave behind.

It was a relief when normal everyday life returned. On the first day I was alone in the house I neglected my work so that I could go out straight away. I chose a house that looked as if it had been lived in over Christmas, because the paths had been cleared. However, there was a thin covering of snow, so the residents must have gone home.

It was one of the better cottages. The owner had knocked the old house down and built a new one, fairly recently. Picture windows looking out over the garden, and a patio door that was quite easy to force. I moved quickly through the living room, since the large windows meant I could be seen from the road. I just had time to notice that everything in the house looked expensive. Huge sofa, coffee table with interiors magazines aesthetically arranged.

I went into the kitchen. Tiled floor, presumably with under-floor heating. Central island. Drinks shelf with every imaginable kind of liqueur, Cognac, whisky and so on. I sat down and poured myself a small whisky, then rinsed and dried the glass before putting it away.

The house was a mystery. Everything looked as if it came straight from the pages of *Homes and Gardens*. Without doubt they had employed an interior designer, and there was *nothing* personal. Steel utensils hung on hooks above the fan-forced oven with its ceramic hob, and every single thing was in the right place. Even the black granite saltcellar lying on its side looked as though it had been placed like that in order to achieve a certain effect.

I started to get excited as I sat there at the kitchen table. Finally, a decent nut to crack. The life these people lived was so markedly different from mine that I would have to carry out detailed research to build up a picture.

I decided to start with the bedroom. The bedside table is revealing. That's where you find the last things a person puts down before they go to sleep, and the first things they need when they wake up. Along with the bathroom cabinet, it's number one.

However, the bedroom door was locked.

Of all the houses I had gone through, this was the first time I had come across a locked door *inside* the house. That was the first clue: they locked their bedroom door when they went away. But why?

Of course this made me even more determined to get into the room. By this time my hands were frozen. It was colder inside the house than outside, and my breath formed clouds of vapour. I fumbled with my provisional lock-picking equipment, and bizarrely, couldn't get it open. It should have been a piece of cake. An internal door!

However. The solution was simple. As in many houses, all the doors had been put in at the same time, and I found a key in the kitchen door that fitted the bedroom. I unlocked it.

The only thing I saw was the outline of a double bed and a bundled up duvet. The blinds were drawn and the room lay in darkness. I risked switching on the light.

It wasn't a duvet lying on the bed. It was a man.

I jerked back and almost stumbled in the doorway, but grabbed hold of the frame and regained my balance. I realised at once that the man was dead. His body was chalk white, naked, completely motionless. His penis hung limply between his legs and something red was sticking up out of his chest.

My immediate impulse was to run away. But I stayed where I was. I'm quite a sensible person, in spite of everything. I realised I couldn't call the police. At least not until I found a phone box and could make an anonymous call. The closest was in Norrtälje.

I approached the bed cautiously. Stopped. I was in the process of destroying evidence that the forensic technicians might be able to find. And what about me? Were my fingerprints on the glass I'd used, for example, or on the door handle?

Strange how death alters the way we look at things. The body on the bed was worthless, and yet it defined the room around it; the entire house. This was a house that contained death. I crept closer, alert to any possible movement. But the man didn't move. His eyes were closed, his eyelids had a bluish tinge. One arm dangled over the side of the bed, the other was by his side.

I reached out with one index finger and poked his big toe. It had virtually no elasticity. It was as if the body was deep frozen. I could now see that the object sticking out of his chest, directly over the heart, was the handle of a clasp knife. The word Equinox was written on the handle. Equinox is the time of year when day and night are of equal length. I like the word, but have never had the opportunity to use it. Q and X.

I stood there motionless with my arms by my sides, as if standing to attention before the dead man, and tried to work out what was wrong. Something was wrong, something didn't fit. The red, soft rectangle sticking up from the chest was beautiful in some way. An anatomical arrow pointing at the heart, into the heart. It was a beautiful corpse. No blood.

That was it. Exactly. The knife was sticking straight into the heart, but no blood had run down the chest. I checked the sheet at the side. Just as if it had been a fairy tale, there was *one* drop of blood, just one. It was impossible to understand how that could have happened. Someone must have wiped him clean after...after it had happened.

The man was about my own age. Around thirty-five. He looked like one of those handsome guys at high school who kind of lived in a different world. If you ever danced with them, their eyes were always somewhere else.

His hair was very soft, as if it were freshly washed.

I didn't know how long he had been dead, but the cold had preserved the body intact. I thought about Snow White. The knife was the red apple. The only thing missing was a glass coffin. I laughed out loud. So I must be the handsome prince, in my dark grey padded jacket.

I pulled on my gloves and opened the drawer in the bedside table. It was empty. I opened the wardrobe. Empty except for a couple of blankets.

Where are his clothes?

The alarm clock next to the bed had stopped at twenty past eleven. I pulled a chair up to the bed, sat down and let my gaze wander over the body.

I have to say it again: he was almost perfect. Muscular, but not over the top. A body moving in H_2O, seven letters: swimmer. His jaw-line was well defined, casting a black shadow over his throat in the electric light. His lips could have convinced me that he was alive. Pale and bloodless, yes, but not sunken; they were full, pouting as if he were waiting for the kiss of life. His brow was high and smooth and his blond, medium-length hair was swept back. He was very handsome.

The only thing that spoiled the impression was the hair on his chest. Blond, almost white hair curling down towards his abdomen.

Not too much, but enough to be disturbing. And then there was the penis. The idea was new to me, I've never seen a dead body before, but is there anything more pathetic than a dead man's penis? So utterly, so mercilessly...unnecessary.

I took one of the blankets out of the wardrobe and spread it over his lower abdomen. I suppose I really should have covered his face as well—something to do with respect.

But I didn't feel any respect. No. Now the initial shock had subsided I felt only...excitement.

'Hi there, you,' I said.

He didn't reply. I would have liked to know his name, so that I could use it. For the time being I decided to call him You. I wasn't scared at all. Perhaps it was the absence of blood, the undisturbed condition of the body that made the whole thing unreal.

I sat with him for a good while. When I left, after checking that there was no one in sight on the road, I left the patio door on the latch.

By the mailboxes I counted back and forth between the houses I knew, and worked out that the man's mailbox was number 354. There was a name too. Svensson. I found it so comical that the man was called Svensson that I started to laugh. I had imagined something along the lines of, oh, I don't know, Delafour, Sander, anything at all, but not *Svensson*.

Of course there was nothing to indicate that the man on the bed was the owner of the house. I had never seen him before. As I walked home I tried out the name: 'Svensson...Svensson.'

Oh well. It wasn't too bad after all. Could be anybody.

I remember those days, those first days. Wonderful days. Blissful expectation running through my body, like honey. Lasse noticed the change in me, he said it was as if there was light all around me. Or as if the darkness had ebbed away—same thing, really. I played with the children, I cooked delicious meals. In the evenings, while we were watching TV, I curled up in Lasse's arms. I loved him because he was simple and imperfect, dirty like me. Another person.

And I was longing to be somewhere else. All the time.

I was afraid of two things: that the people who owned the house would come back, and that the weather would get warmer, begin the thaw.

However, my reasoning was this: either the man on the bed is the person who owns the house, or the people who own the house have something to do with his death. Neither of these alternatives would lead to the man being moved. I know, I know, it wasn't exactly watertight, but that's the way I reasoned in order to calm myself down.

With regard to my other fear, there was nothing to worry about. The weather forecast promised that the cold spell would continue.

So I curled up in Lasse's arms and smiled at the weatherman as he pointed to his minus signs and his snow flurries. Everything was as it should be.

As soon as the children had gone back to school and Lasse back to work, I headed over to the house. I was wearing several layers of thin woollen sweaters so that I could cope with remaining still for a long time without suffering too much.

What did I do once I was in there?

It's hard to describe, really. You could call it a confession. I told you everything, and you listened. I looked at you as I talked. You were so good to look at. Like a Greek statue. I caressed you.

No. Not like *that*. It was pointless, of course, and perhaps that was actually part of the point. I could caress you without it meaning *that*. I could caress you because you were beautiful, like a statue. I told you how beautiful I thought you were, and that you were mine and mine alone.

Is that sick?

Well yes, I suppose it is. I knew that while I was doing it. I knew I was doing something ugly, something bad. But I said to myself: what crime am I committing? I suppose the closest thing is desecrating a corpse. But how can it be desecration: talking to someone, caressing someone, telling that person how beautiful he is? If that's desecration, then what is love?

Before everything changed there was really only one thing I did that you could regard as overstepping the mark. On the third day I took Lasse's shaving things with me and shaved off your pubic hair and the hair on your chest. It bothered me so much, all that hair. I call it overstepping the mark, because it's something you would hardly have agreed to, given the option.

But you weren't a person. You were a dead thing, I was the one who had found you, and you looked so much better without all that hair. Completely smooth. No longer almost perfect, but totally perfect.

The knife?

You might think that would spoil the picture, the red handle sticking up out of your chest and breaking the surface of the skin. Equinox. Quite the reverse, in my opinion. It acted like a beauty spot, six letters: mouche. It was all about a fixed point, somewhere for the eye to focus before it moved on to the rest of your beauty.

And, if I'm truthful, I was afraid to pull it out. I mean, I've read the fairy tales. The sword is pulled out of the dead king's body. He turns to stone, crumbles to dust and is gone. So I made a virtue of necessity, called it a mouche and left it where it was.

Your eyes were closed, and I told you everything. I told you things I didn't even know I felt before I met you, found you. The constant sense of unreality, the veil between me and the world. How I would suddenly feel as if Emil and Johanna were dolls, and not mine at all. How I would be able to see Lasse in bed with X-ray vision, and realise that he consisted of minced beef packed into a bag of skin. A hundred kilos of mince. How I would have to close my eyes.

You lay naked before me. You were beautiful and you listened. If only things had stayed that way.

It started on the sixth day, a Monday.

I had been forced to leave you alone over the weekend for family reasons. I don't remember what I did that weekend. I think I baked a big batch of vanilla cakes. Emil and I watched Astrid Lindgren's *Alla vi barn i bullerbyn*, which was being repeated for the hundredth time. You just have to grin and bear it.

I was desperate by Monday morning, when they'd all gone. Just to test myself, to discipline myself, I chopped a couple of armfuls of wood and filled up the basket by the fire before I set off. I almost ran to your house, hardly bothering to look around. My heart was beating fast, I think I was blushing.

As always I was afraid something might have changed during my absence. But the snow that had fallen during the weekend lay undisturbed on the drive and there were no marks on the porch. I went inside.

When I walked into your room I stood motionless in the doorway for several minutes. You were lying there with the blanket pulled up to the knife handle. The contours of your body were clearly visible beneath the thin woollen fabric.

A new kind of beauty, but not created by my hand. I was one hundred per cent certain: I had left you naked. On the rare occasions when I had covered you with the blanket, I had placed it over your lower abdomen. I had never covered your whole body. But now the blanket was draped halfway up your chest.

I stood there motionless, listening. There had been no marks in the snow, so there must be someone else inside the house. Someone who had been there all the time.

No point in pretending otherwise: I was scared. Scared and embarrassed. There was someone in the house, someone who had known about my comings and goings, perhaps listened to my confessions. Someone knew more about me than I would wish any living person to know.

I took a carving knife from the magnetic holder in the kitchen and spent over an hour searching the entire house. I opened every cupboard, every wardrobe, every drawer, even if it was actually too small for anyone to hide in. I found nothing, and the impression I had gained on the first day was reinforced: apart from the tipped-over saltcellar, there was nothing to indicate that the house had ever been lived in.

I went back to you and sat down.

'How did you get the blanket over you?'

That was the first question I asked you. My monologues had never taken the form of questions; I had no interest in speculating about your life among the living. You were simply here.

During the search I had grown hot and sweaty in all my layers. It was as if an extinguishing material, two words, six letters: dry ice had been injected directly into my muscles as you parted your blue lips and uttered three words:

'I was cold.'

Your voice was weak, hollow, as if it came from far away. My body was suddenly ice cold, I was frozen to the chair. Your lips closed. You had parted them just far enough to allow the words to escape. It was a long time before my vocal cords thawed out sufficiently for me to speak:

'You can't be cold. You're dead.'

Did I see the faintest twitch at the corner of your mouth? The hint of a smile? Your lips opened again, a little further this time. You said, 'You're dead too. You're wearing sweaters.'

'I'm not dead.'

'You're not alive.'

Only now did it strike me as odd that you knew I was wearing sweaters. But then my gaze slid up to your eyes. They were open. Only a fraction, a slightly denser shadow below the eyelid. Like someone having a pleasurable experience, or about to fall asleep. Or someone who has just woken up. I couldn't see your eyes.

A person's ability to deal with new situations is a strange thing. You were talking to me. I hadn't imagined that you would be able to talk to me. But when you did, I accepted it. What else could I do? *You've made your bed, and now you must lie in it.* That's what my mother used to say. I hated that expression. When I hear myself saying it to my own children I am seized by the urge to punch myself on the nose. But that's the way it is.

I think you were looking at me from beneath those almost-closed eyelids. I asked, 'Would you like another blanket?'

'Yes.'

I fetched the other blanket from the wardrobe and spread it over you. When I had done that, I folded my arms and said, 'I have no intention of becoming some kind of nursemaid, you know.'

Your head moved slowly from side to side and you said, 'I don't need anything.' Your voice was very weak. I had to strain to hear the words. There was something cheeky, eleven letters: impertinent about the way you said you didn't need anything. A kind of smugness. I looked at you. Under the blankets you looked more like a normal sick person.

I removed the blankets.

'In that case you won't be needing these either.'

I carefully folded the blankets and put them back in the wardrobe. You didn't object. When I turned back to face you again, everything was as it should be. Your naked, shaved body stretched out on the bed, just the way I wanted it. Perhaps by way of apology I said it again:

'You can't be cold. You're dead.'

'I understand.'

'What do you understand?'

'Nothing.'

'Come on, tell me. I'm curious about what you understand when you're dead.'

You didn't reply. I gave your shoulder a push, just a little one.

'Tell me.'

No reply. Your eyelids were closed once more. I sat beside you for a while longer. You were so beautiful to look at. It wasn't the time for any more confessions. When I got up to leave, you said something I didn't hear, so I bent down and put my ear close to your mouth.

'What did you say?'

The lips parted. I was aware of a faint aroma of something like frozen berries. You said, 'I don't want you to come here anymore.'

I straightened up.

'I'm sorry,' I said. 'But that's not actually your decision to make.'

Your face was so rigid that it was impossible to pick up any kind of reaction. I waited a few seconds for a futile protest. When it didn't come, I left the house for that day.

From now on I am going to omit all my reaction and speculation on the fact that a dead man was talking to me. Of course I turned the problem over in my head, many many times. You weren't really dead (of course you were dead. You had spent at least six days lying in a room where the temperature was below freezing), I was mad (I wasn't mad, there was nothing in my behaviour to suggest that I was mad), I was imagining the whole thing, and so on and so on.

But it was a fact. From now on we will take that as read.

When I got home, earlier than usual despite the hour I had spent searching the house, I was disappointed. Sad. In spite of my hard attitude, your last remark had hurt me. I cried for a while. Then I tried to do some work on a crossword. I had a deadline to meet. It didn't go well, so I sent an old one from *Hemmets Journal* to *Allers*, and vice versa. The one for *Kamratposten* wasn't so urgent.

I knew it wasn't a good thing to do. The crosswords I sent were no more than four years old. The editor wouldn't notice a thing, but I could guarantee some old bag in Småland or somewhere like that would complain. People with photographic memories enjoy doing crosswords, or so I've heard.

Your body was all I could see during the hour I spent sitting at the computer, trying to come up with new combinations of words, witty little secondary meanings. Only your body, your perfect face. You no longer belonged to me. You had taken yourself away from me.

What right did you have to do that?

Yes, the disappointment slowly changed to anger. Anger because I wasn't good enough for you. Because you preferred to lie dead and alone in that bare room rather than to have me by your side. My secrets and my musings on life weren't good enough for you, *Svensson*.

My anger spilled out onto the family, I must admit. Not in the form of outbursts of rage, but rather a simmering discontent, a constant state of irritability. I could be forgiven to some extent because my period was due. That was what Lasse thought, anyway.

I was perfectly clear about one thing: I would never, ever tell anyone about you. You might well have distanced yourself from me, but you were still my secret, and mine alone.

The following morning I put some make-up on. Oh, it makes my cheeks flame as I tell you this, but I don't want to hide anything. I put some make-up on, made myself look good. The biggest problem with my face is that it's so flat. My nose is small, with a slight downturn, my lips are thin. The space between my eyes and eyebrows is shallow. My eyes are almost completely devoid of any oval shaping which, combined with the shallowness of the socket, means that they have no depth. And the colour is a watery blue, on top of everything else.

But the value of make-up cannot be overestimated, if it's done properly. I brought out my cheekbones with blusher, deepened my eyes with shadow and kohl, made my lips look fuller with a lip pencil and lipstick. Covered the spots on my forehead with foundation. I'm not claiming to be some kind of expert but what I do, I do well.

If I were to make an objective assessment, I would say that the make-up made me look twice as good or half as ugly.

I set off.

Halfway to your house I took out my pocket mirror and checked one last time, touched up my lipstick. What was I trying to achieve? I don't know. Not exactly. If I say it was an attempt to make the situation *more sacred* it sounds as though I'm dressing things up, nine letters: euphemism, but I think that's the closest thing to the truth. Like wearing a white blouse to church, making sure the back of your neck is clean.

The first thing I noticed when I got inside was that the bedroom door was open. I had left it closed, but not locked. When I looked in you were lying on the bed with both blankets over you. I took a walk around the house, and you didn't seem to have done anything.

Hang on a minute. Of course.

The saltcellar was upright.

I laughed out loud when I thought about how the dead rise from their graves to avenge an injustice, to put right something that was wrong when they died. So this was your motivation, the thing you needed to put right: a saltcellar. For the first time I thought you might just be the corpse of a pretty pathetic person.

Your eyes were closed, as before. I sat down at the side of your bed.

'So you've been up and about,' I said.

After a minute with no response, I got up and removed the blankets. You made a movement with your arm as if to stop me, but it was slow and weak. I bundled up the blankets and chucked them in the wardrobe.

Then you opened your eyes. A little more than the previous day. I could see a glimpse of something not unlike a jellyfish that had been washed ashore beneath your eyelids. Dried slime.

'You've got make-up on,' you said.

'Yes,' I said. 'I've got make-up on.'

'Why?'

'Because I felt like it, that's all.'

A twitch of the mouth. I didn't like that twitch; it made your face change.

'Share the joke,' I said.

'*Shit is shit and snuff is snuff, in golden tins as well.*'

I waited. The long sentence had clearly taken it out of you, because it was quite a while before you finished off with, 'An eastern European whore. That's what you look like.'

'What do you know about whores?'

'I know a great deal about whores.'

Call me prudish, call me prim, call me any synonym you like, but I don't like people talking that way. I really didn't like it when you talked that way. I didn't mind you being pathetic, but this wasn't acceptable.

I took out my make-up bag and as I painted your lips I said, '*Even*. It's "even in golden tins". It destroys the rhythm if you say "as well". Can't you hear it? There are few things I detest more than people misquoting poetry.'

You had closed your eyes again, and I put a thick layer of pale blue eye shadow on your slightly blue, shimmering eyelids. As I drew my kohl pencil along the edges, if could feel that the eyes beneath really were dried up, hard.

'Fröding must be turning in his grave. That's what annoys me so much, you see. Poetry is hard work. A poet can struggle for days, weeks to find the right word. To misquote is to completely discredit his work. It shows a lack of respect towards the writer, a lack of respect towards the language itself. You have no respect. That's your problem.'

I finished off by slapping far too much orange-tinted blusher on your cheeks. The whole thing was way over the top. You looked like a clown. I took a step back, folded my arms and contemplated my handiwork. You really did look funny. Like a man in a dress, twelve letters: transvestite, only without the dress. I laughed.

'You have no respect,' I said. 'I don't want to know, but I'm convinced your death has something to do with that fact, in one way or another.'

You didn't reply. You just lay there like an unsuccessful shop-window dummy.

'Think about it,' I said, and turned on my heel.

When I got home I took out the biggest pitcher we had and positioned myself in the middle of the kitchen. I hurled the jug on the floor with all my strength. Then I spent the rest of the afternoon removing fragments of glass from the kitchen. Tiny splinters had ended up in the most unlikely places: in the fruit bowl, behind the radiator, in the little gap between the oven and the cooktop. I had to squint and twist my head at different angles to catch their reflections in the cold sunshine. I tracked down every single one, and removed them. I didn't cry. I didn't even have a lump in my throat.

Then I made a really special meal for my family. Coq au vin, but

with chicken. You can't get hold of cockerel. We had a nice evening.
Very nice, actually.

I slept badly that night. Our bedroom is upstairs, and when the wind takes hold of the tin sheets on the roof and bangs them against each other, the vibrations run right through the entire bed frame. It sounded as if someone was trying to get in. I sat up in the armchair with the little reading lamp switched on and tried to concentrate on a biography of Frida Kahlo. The wind didn't begin to drop until about three o'clock in the morning, and I managed to get a few hours' sleep.

Lasse and the children had already flown the nest when I got up. I sat in the kitchen with my coffee, feeling a great sense of loss. Lasse had written me a note, as he sometimes did when we didn't see one another in the morning. 'See you this afternoon. Thinking of you. xxx L.' I sat there turning the note over and over in my fingers. I could see his fingers laboriously printing the letters with the thick point of the pencil. He's dyslexic. That's funny, isn't it? Married to me, and he's dyslexic. He'll never be able to solve my crosswords.

But the note was spelled correctly.

I went into Emil's room. Bamse the Bear comics strewn all over the floor, drawings of dinosaurs on the desk, and that smell of a small child that still surrounded his body, permeating his sheets and the air.

Johanna's room: pictures of Darin cut out of *Frida* and pinned up on the wall. Maria Gripe's *Tordyveln flyger i skymningen* neatly placed on the bedside table, a bookmark with a heart on it sticking out somewhere around the middle.

I sat down on the bed.

A couple of days earlier over dinner Emil had talked about some major project they were going to be doing in school. I couldn't remember what it was. I hadn't been listening.

I wished they were with me now. All of them. That they were telling me something, holding me tight, shaking me. That I could look into their eyes and recognise them, that they knew I was their mum, wife.

I got dressed and went down to the sea.

The wind during the night had blown the pack ice into jagged mounds, irregular patterns in the inlet. The tender from Domarö was on its way in, making for the steamboat jetty and passing a flock of tufted ducks paddling by the edge of the ice. There was no more than a faint breeze now, but it was still so cold that it pinched at my nose and cheeks. Perhaps the ice would stay this year. Perhaps we would be able to buy cross-country skis and head off beyond Domarö and Gåvasten. Light a camp fire on some distant island and grill sausages, far away from everything and everyone else.

I walked up towards your house. This would have to be the last time. I really just wanted to explain to you that you were a nasty piece of work who didn't deserve my care and attention. Then I would leave you to rot until the spring.

I had a premonition. It turned out to be correct.

Before I even turned off the road I could see there were footprints on the drive leading up to your house. I kept on walking. Sweat broke out along my hairline. Itching beneath my woolly hat.

Did I leave anything inside? The make-up…

But there was no way anyone could link the make-up to me. They would realise someone had been in the house, but was there any way they could know it was me? Had anyone seen me?

No. I didn't think so.

I carried on around the bend in the road so that I could see the back of the house. The footprints led up to the patio door. Only now did it occur to me that it was strange that there were no tyre tracks. If they had come to pick you up, surely they would have had some kind of vehicle?

Besides which, it had been very windy during the night, and yet the tracks were perfectly clear. That meant they must have come at some point between three o'clock in the morning and now. It was just after ten.

I turned and went back, constantly on the lookout for some movement, some glimpse of activity inside the house. But there was nothing. When I reached the tracks I slowed down. And stopped.

The tracks had been made by bare feet. The soles were clearly visible in the snow, which was about three centimetres deep. They were your footprints. I took a few steps along the drive, following them with my eyes. They went in both directions, but the ones leading to the road were much less clear. You had been out, then gone back home.

I stood staring at the tracks for a long time, glancing frantically over towards the road, until a thought struck me. I ran back to my house. Our house. Lasse's and my house. Lasse's and Emil's and Johanna's and my house. My family's house.

They began halfway up the path leading to the front door. They ran along the side of the house. I crouched down. These were tracks made when you were *leaving*, the heels were facing the house. But next to them was a series of faint indentations in the snow. The footprints you left on the way in, which had been filled in by the wind.

I followed the tracks, flattening them down and rubbing them out with my boots. They stopped below my bedroom window, ending with two feet side by side, clearer than the rest. You stood here. For a long time. Stood in the cold wind during the night below my window, as I sat in the chair unable to sleep.

It could have been romantic.

I fetched the straw broom and swept the entire area. I really had to scrub and bang to obliterate the last two impressions. The ones where you had stood.

'How did you know where I live?'

Few things are as unpleasant as getting hot and sweaty, then standing in the cold as the sweat dries on your skin, with your clothes still wet. My breath was coming out of my mouth in dense clouds, saturated with moisture.

You were lying on the bed as usual. The make-up was smeared across your face, the blanket stained where you had used it to scrub at your skin. I ripped the blanket off your body.

'Answer me!'

I no longer thought you were beautiful. You were nothing more than a lump of frozen meat, lying there weighing down a bed. That ridiculous sausage between your legs, your messy face. And that knife in your chest. I yanked it out. I threw it at the wall. You didn't move a muscle. A viscous, brownish bubble rose from the wound and stopped. Your lips parted and you whispered, 'You are dead.'

My stomach contracted in painful cramps, and I could feel the menstrual blood seeping out to compensate for the blood you were not bleeding. Everything went red before my eyes and I screamed, 'I am not dead, you're the one who's dead you disgusting bastard and you can lie here and rot as far as I'm concerned, I don't care about you anymore, so what have you got to say about that?'

My face was burning, and I didn't hear your answer. I leaned closer. Every word you said, every breath carried with it the stench of jam that has been left in the freezer for too long. 'Everything you told me. Indicates. That you are not. Alive.'

At first I didn't understand what was happening. It was as if the light had changed, as if the room had begun to tilt and my body was being twisted into a position where it did not want to be. A great weight fell through the air. My eyes pricked and the tears welled up.

'It's possible. But I...I...'

I cracked. An abscess of tears burst in my throat, and although I didn't want it to happen, although I didn't want to humiliate myself like that, my anger turned to sobs and my voice trembled as if in prayer when I spoke.

'I'll be better. I promise I'll be better. Leave me in peace. Don't come to me. Leave me alone.'

The fury ebbed away. The room was silent. There was only the sound of my sobs, the warm tickling feeling down my inner thigh as the blood overflowed. You opened your eyes, wider than you had ever done before, and looked at me. Two lumps of grey slime. You were smiling. This time you really were smiling. You said, 'I'm sorry. But that's not actually your decision to make.'

I don't remember how I got home, how I found the tools in the shed, how I got back. The images all flow into one. Suddenly I'm standing there again, in your bedroom. But this time I've got a hammer, nails and staples.

I forced your hand down towards the frame of the bed. I hammered two nails through the hand itself, then a staple around each finger. The sharp ends peeled away the skin, but the hoops clamped the skeleton firmly. The hand was securely fastened. You couldn't go anywhere.

All this is logical. A reasonable course of action. I had nailed you down so that you couldn't come and threaten my family, my children. I did what had to be done.

But as I stood there looking at you and panting, you smiled that smile again, the smile that said you had the upper hand because you knew my most fragile secrets, while I didn't even know your name. The smile that said I was worth nothing, a little grey, flat woman whispering and worshipping by your side.

I undid my trousers and took out my sodden sanitary towel. I painted you red. Chest, arms, legs. To finish off I tried to force the towel into your mouth, but it was too tightly closed. I placed it over your eyes instead.

Then I left.

I took a long, hot shower, then I crawled into bed and wrapped myself in a cocoon of warmth and darkness. I closed my eyes and tried to persuade my body that none of this had actually happened.

I said I was ill, that I had a temperature. Perhaps I did. The combination of sweating and getting cold. I felt wretched, shivering fits running beneath my skin, and my body felt sick, sick, sick in a way that no thermometer could measure.

They brought me food. Spaghetti bolognese. Lasse sat down by my bed and asked what I'd been doing during the day. Emil came up and told me about his project again. It was to do with a farm. They were building a farm out of cardboard and making animals out of clay. Next week they were going to visit a farmer. It sounded terrific. I just wanted to cry. I managed to control myself.

When I was alone again, I crawled onto the floor. I lay down on the wooden floorboards and lifted up my hair, exposing the back of my neck.

Seize me. Stab me.

Nothing. I wanted it to happen. There was no prayer so heartfelt or so eloquent that it could match my need. There was only one thing to say: *Punish me. Or forgive me.*

Perhaps God would punish me later. Perhaps he would allow Emil to drown. From now on, every terrible thing that befell my family was my fault. It was a dreadful thought. The alternative was that he might forgive me. Yes. It was possible. But I didn't believe it. If our picture of God is a projection of what we ourselves are, then there is no forgiveness. Not for me. Never. Everything remains as it is.

Evening came, then night. When Lasse came to bed he asked me how I was, how things really were. I said I felt sad. I wanted to tell him everything, but I said I felt sad, then I rolled over with my back to him and asked him to hold me. He did as I asked and it was nice, but it wasn't enough. He would have had to be ten times bigger. A hundred times bigger. I would have needed to lie in the palm of his hand.

So the night came, and the minutes. They were long. Lasse's breathing was warm and whispering against the back of my neck. The minutes crawled on spider's legs through pine resin. I slid out of Lasse's arms and got up. Stood for a long time in the middle of the floor listening to the wind in the tin roof. Bang. Bang. Bang bang.

I will stand here. All night. As a penance.

It was the first thought I had had all day that made me…well, not happy. But contented. It was a good thought. Stand motionless in the middle of the floor all night. See if I could do it. Perhaps God would notice me then.

I had been standing there for maybe half an hour when the urge to do what I *shouldn't* do began to make itself felt: to go over to the window, peek through the blind and see if you were standing out there. I pinched my earlobe. Hard. Lasse turned over in bed. A relief. If he opened his eyes now he wouldn't be able to see me.

Ten minutes passed. My knees were beginning to ache. The urge came over me again. I stared at the blind, tried to stare straight through it. Pinched my earlobe again. Harder this time, I almost squealed out loud.

Bang. Bang bang.

Loud bangs. I thought: if the front door opens, I won't be able to hear it.

I made my body stiff and straight, like a plank of wood. Nailed myself to the floor. I was the one who usually locked the front door at night. Had Lasse done it tonight? He had once said it made him feel as if he was at work, at the prison, if he had to lock the front door. He wanted to feel relaxed at home.

My stomach was churning. The torments of the night would be even worse if I stood here not knowing.

Anyone who really wants to get in will get in anyway, Lasse had said on that occasion.

I pinched my earlobe again. It didn't help. I had to check the door. On feet that tingled from standing still, I crept over to the door, opened it cautiously and peered down the stairs.

The air. What's different about...the air...

The air outside the bedroom was fresh and cold. Not only was the front door unlocked, it was standing wide open, with the night wind blowing through the hallway. My heart leapt in my breast, and just as I reached the top of the stairs I heard Emil scream.

Not scream. Roar. Nothing on earth is worse than hearing a child roar like that, from the depths of his body, with horror, pain, when it's your own child roaring. Nothing. Nothing.

I almost fell down the stairs as I hurled myself forward and my body was an open wound, Emil's roar was a red-hot poker being thrust into the wound. I reached the landing and saw you coming out of Emil's room.

You were naked. Your body was smeared with my blood and you were holding the clasp knife in your hand. The blade was open. Your hand reached out towards my face and Emil kept on roaring and somewhere right at the back of my mind a voice was whispering:

He's yelling. He's alive.

And the hand reaching out towards my face was not a hand but merely a ragged combination of bits of skin and skeleton left over when you tore it free of the nails and staples. You hit me across the cheek. My head jerked to one side and I fell.

As you walked out through the front door I crawled towards Emil's room. I wanted to be sick. I didn't want to see. I could see the soles of Emil's feet drumming against the mattress as if he were running up towards the ceiling ridiculously fast. I dragged myself to my feet.

Emil was stretched out on the bed, dressed only in his underpants. The quilt had been thrown to one side. The whole of his little body was shaking and jumping with the jerking of his legs as they ran and ran. His mouth was wide open, a gaping hole letting out that roar.

The wound was directly over his heart. I fell on him, I wrapped him in my arms and his roaring deafened me.

'Don't die, don't die...'

The sensible part of my brain, the cold, clear sense somewhere behind the fear was whispering:

Stop the bleeding. Help him.

I obeyed. With shaking hands I switched on the bedside light and looked at the wound, ready to tear strips off the quilt cover, tear strips off myself.

It was only a scratch. Making a point. Emil carried on screaming.

At last I heard Lasse's footsteps on the stairs. Three long strides, loud thuds and he came running into the room.

'What is it? What's happened?'

What I said couldn't have made any sense to him, couldn't possibly have seemed like the right reaction to what he could see before his eyes. I ran my hand over the wound, got a tiny drop of blood on my fingers, and I whispered, 'It's only a scratch...just a little scratch...'

It took two minutes before Lasse grasped what had happened. A man had come into his house and marked his son, frightened him out of his wits. Lasse went out to look for the man. Someone from the mental institution, no doubt.

I sat with Emil. Johanna came to join us. We sat with Emil. The fear shone from his eyes, he couldn't speak. I thought:

Thank you, Lord. Thank you for letting him live.

Lasse came back after a quarter of an hour. He hadn't found the man, so he called the police. Emil was no longer screaming, he was just panting. I asked Johanna to stay with him, then I got up and went outside. Lasse was busy on the phone.

I went to the woodshed and fetched the axe.

Nobody knew you had been dead from the start. It wasn't even possible to identify you from the remains. But there were other mitigating circumstances. Several.

I'm happy with my punishment.

Can't see it! It doesn't exist!

Frank Johansson is waiting for the picture that will change his life.

He is sitting in an elm tree, six metres above the ground. In order to avoid chafing, he has wrapped two layers of foam rubber around the branch on which he is sitting. Since he began his surveillance two days ago, he has drunk fifteen litres of water. His back is killing him.

It is summer. A fat, Swedish summer. The sun is blazing down through the foliage and the sweat is pouring off him. The only breeze comes from the wing beats of fate. This is his last chance. It's the picture or the abyss. Well, bankruptcy anyway.

One million.

The picture will bring him a million, as a ballpark figure. He's worked it out, he's checked. The *Sun* alone is willing to cough up fifty thousand pounds for the rights. Then minor royalties from others, later.

A million will solve all his problems.

1/250th of a second is all he needs. The shutter opens, exposes the film to the Picture, closes again, stores it in the darkness of the camera and Frank is a rich man.

His palms are sweaty; he wipes them on his trouser legs and grips the camera with both hands, points the lens at the pool and sees the same thing he has been seeing for two days now:

Blue water. Two wooden deckchairs beneath a large white parasol. A table between the chairs. A book on the table. With his 300 millimetre lens he can zoom in so close that he can read the title: *Lord of the Flies*.

The surface of the water is like a mirror. Nothing is moving.

It would take less than this to drive a person crazy.

Frank zooms out, allowing the surface of the pool to fill his viewfinder. A cloud drifts across the sky, making deeper shades of blue flicker across the water. His head is boiling. If only he could slide down into that water, allow himself to be embraced, cooled.

He takes a swig of water warmed by the sun from his bottle.

One million.

Someone has been here. Someone has sat on the deckchair, read *Lord of the Flies* and put it down. Amanda. It has to be Amanda. Roberto—can he even read?

All they have to do is walk out through that door—Frank tracks their route with his finger—walk over to the edge of the pool and… kiss. One kiss, one simple little kiss and Frank will be saved.

But they don't appear, they don't want to save Frank, and he hates them. As the scalding sweat pours down into his eyes and his back is agonising crystal and weariness gnaws at his soul, he keeps himself busy by dreaming and hating.

Wouldn't you?

Someone can save you with a kiss, but refuses to oblige. Perhaps that was all Judas wanted: a kiss. When he didn't get it, he responded with his own. Thirty pieces of silver, what was he going to do with those? He had responded. Then he went and hanged himself.

Frank stares at a thick branch above his head. He pictures a rope and feels himself falling, hears the sound as his neck is broken—*chapack* as the connection between body and soul is severed and you are as free as a little blue bird in a night without end.

Blue, blue...the surface of the pool lies at his feet and his thoughts begin to wander. Minutes pass, hours. A mosquito lands on his forearm and he watches it with interest as it sucks his blood. Paparazzi. They say Fellini came up with the name because it reminded him of an irritating mosquito. Paparazzi, paparazzi.

As the sated mosquito withdraws its proboscis and prepares to take off, Frank kills it. It turns into a smear on his skin; he raises his arm to eye level, studies the remains of the mosquito. Black spider-web legs dotted among the red blood, like some calligraphic symbol.

The sun drags itself across the sky, displacing the reflections on the surface of the pool and dazzling him. He shades his eyes with his hand and moves a few centimetres. He hears a creaking sound. A hammer slams into the bottom of his back and pain shoots up from his tailbone, explodes inside his head. He cries out, almost falls forward but manages to grab hold of the branch above.

The camera slips off his knee, the old strap around his neck jerks and then breaks. Through a yellow mist Frank sees the camera drift towards the ground in slow motion, hears the delicate crunch as the lens shatters. He squeezes his eyes tight shut and hugs the branch. The tears well up, forcing their way out beneath his compressed eyelids.

No, no, no, no, no...it's not fair.

He sobs, his body hunched over. His tears follow the camera's route through the air, landing on the dry grass. He's reached rock bottom. He screws this fact through his body, rotation by rotation, and continues to weep. Eventually it becomes a form of enjoyment. He opens his eyes and sees the surface of the pool through his tears, a billowing rectangle.

The reflections of the sun lift from the surface, turn into stars floating towards him. He waves his hand wearily to keep them away, but they penetrate his head like burning needles.

'Aaaaaah…'

He bangs his head with the palm of his hand, but the needles are already inside, moving around as if they are searching for something. They puncture his brain, scratching and cutting, and he feels as if he's going to be sick. He is being dissected alive.

———————

The reflections of the sun are resting on the surface of the water. His back is aching. Carefully, one branch at a time, he clambers down from the tree and crouches beside the camera like a little boy grieving for his dead pet. He unscrews the lens and shakes it. Something is irredeemably broken inside.

You've taken your last picture, my friend.

Fifteen years together. He carries the lens to the house, places it in his bag and takes out the Sigma lens. Not the same thing at all.

The camera itself seems to have survived, so he screws the Sigma in place and attaches the strap from his back-up camera. Then he fills up his water bottle and eats a couple of slices of cold pizza. His jaws move mechanically, up and down, up and down. His head is empty. He looks around the exclusively decorated room; his eyes fasten on the Bruno Liljefors hanging above the open fireplace. A picture of the sea.

I thought he only painted foxes.

Frank allows himself to flop back on the sofa, closes his eyes and falls asleep.

He is in darkness in the depths of the sea, sinking. A pinpoint of light appears, far away. He swims towards it. If he can just reach that point everything will be all right. If he doesn't make it, he will carry on sinking. He swims. His strokes are slow, sluggish, as if the water were syrup.

The pinpoint is not getting any bigger.

But he gets there. The patch of light quivers before his eyes. He reaches out to touch it.

Then he sees the mouth opening wide beyond the light. It's one of those fish. He's read about them. They live at the bottom of the sea where the sunlight never reaches them. They lure small fish with a little lantern. When the fish get there...

A door slams shut and Frank is wide away. Marcus is standing in front of him, grinning.

'Hi there, Frankie boy. How's life in the bushes?'

'It's...' Frank blinks a couple of times, frees himself from the darkness, '...not great.'

'Why not?'

'They haven't turned up.'

Marcus opens his eyes wide, his expression one of exaggerated surprise. His eyes are bloodshot and he appears to be under the influence of something or other. Perhaps the big gestures are all he can manage. He flops down into an armchair and points at the remains of the pizza. 'May I...?'

'Help yourself.'

Frank gets up and gathers his things together. When he reaches the door, Marcus clears his throat.

'The thing is, Frankie boy, one or two complications have arisen.' Frank waits, without turning around. 'It's...well, the purely financial aspect of our rental agreement doesn't seem to me to be entirely satisfactory.'

'Rental agreement.'

'Yes. The tree. The rent for the bloody tree.'

Now Frank does turn around, looks at Marcus sitting in the

armchair licking the grease off his fingers. He's wearing linen trousers with turn-ups, loafers and a white shirt worn loose. A rich man's son. Parents on holiday. Short of pocket money.

'You've had ten thousand.'

'Yep,' says Marcus. 'I have. And I've spent it. So now...I think our rental agreement will have to be torn up. Unless it can be renegotiated, of course.'

Just as when you stub your toe and wait a moment, knowing that now...now the pain will come, Frank waits for the rage to surge up inside him. But it doesn't happen.

Calmly he asks, 'How much?'

'Don't know. Five?'

'And if I refuse? If I sit there without...paying rent?'

Marcus pretends to look shocked.

'But that would be trespassing! I would have no choice but to ring the police!'

Frank nods and says, 'Tomorrow.'

He has no cards to play against Marcus. His father probably wouldn't be very happy that his son has rented out their tree to a tabloid press photographer, but there's no proof.

'Tomorrow, fine by me,' says Marcus, getting to his feet. 'Off to bed. Good luck.'

The light is perfect when Frank returns to the tree. Afternoon sun and soft shadows. Not a cloud in the sky. Like a koala he scrambles up the trunk, makes his way out onto his branch and prepares to chew on the eucalyptus leaves of the minutes for a couple of hours.

The pool shimmers temptingly. The air is warm and caressing, and the deckchairs, the parasol form a stage that is not shouting, but only whispering to its actors.

Come along...come now...

Frank adjusts his position on the branch and takes another swig of his water, which is still cold. It goes down the wrong way as he sees Amanda emerge from the villa, and he presses the crook of his arm to his mouth so that he won't make a sound, a sound that could be heard down below.

He coughs into his arm and his eyes fill with tears as he watches Amanda stroll slowly along by the edge of the pool. She is wearing a red bikini with yellow polka dots. Frank has seen a bikini like that before, but he can't remember where. Panting, he picks up his binoculars and gazes at her.

The same studied, graceful movements as when she is accepting an Oscar for best female actress in a supporting role. For some reason Frank thinks she's unhappy. Trapped in a role from which she cannot escape.

The irritation in his throat subsides by the time Roberto comes out. He walks up to Amanda, strokes her long hair. Frank picks up the camera, focuses, presses the button and captures Roberto's hand just as it passes over Amanda's cheek.

Maybe that's enough.

There has been no photographic evidence of the romance. Now there is. A hand passing over a cheek. But the hand continues down towards the waist and stops there. Frank clicks away, holding his breath.

Go on, go on...

And...yes. Roberto moves his face closer to the woman's, and all the hours Frank has spent hating him—this homemade Latin lover from Sundbyberg with his number-one hits and his English with a fake Spanish accent—are just blown away.

Good boy.

Their lips meet, the shutter flies up and down as Frank keeps his finger on the button, taking picture after picture until the film runs out. He trembles with impatience as the film rewinds automatically, promising himself that he will get a digital camera after this. He rips out the exposed film and quickly inserts a new one. His fingers are sweaty, but he manages to get it in and they're still kissing; Roberto runs his hands over Amanda's body and Frank's chest fizzes with happiness as he clicks, clicks again. He lowers the camera for a few seconds and rubs his eyes.

The couple by the pool turn into two little dolls performing a pantomime. Frank sniggers. They are moving so stiffly, so robotically; Amanda would never have won an Oscar if she had played out this love scene on film.

Frank looks through the viewfinder again. The couple's faces are oddly expressionless, as if they were playing a scene with no idea of how they ought to behave. And who is their audience?

I am.

Frank carries on snapping away, and what he hadn't even dared to hope for actually happens. Roberto gently removes Amanda's bikini and tosses it into the pool. Yellow polka dots on a red background. After a few seconds it begins to sink.

Amanda leans on the table and Roberto pushes into her from behind. The angle is perfect, so is the light. On top of everything else, the photos will be so good that no one will think they're paparazzi pictures. He'll be able to ask more than a million for them.

A million, that was for a kiss. But this…

By the time Frank has run out of film, the couple have changed position twice. Roberto on a deckchair with Amanda on top. Missionary on the tiles. Frank lowers the camera. A drop of sweat runs down from the viewfinder onto his damp palm. He is suddenly terrified. Of losing the films, the camera, whatever. Of something going wrong.

Yellow polka dots on a red background…

A pointless thought in this situation, but where has he seen that pattern before? He can't remember.

His hands are slippery with sweat, his skull a balloon because he has been holding his breath for what seems like several minutes. He feels dizzy. With slow, controlled movements he climbs down from the tree. The lovers have disappeared, gone back into the house. At the bottom of the tree are the four empty plastic containers he tossed aside as he took out new films. He leaves them where they are.

He doesn't need to bother about Marcus any longer. Doesn't need to bother about anyone.

The camera bag is lying on the seat next to him. He glances at it from time to time to reassure himself that it's still there. He is driving more slowly and carefully than he has done for years. He hasn't been all that particular about his life, but what's in the bag...

He pats it, strokes it.

He won't just be able to make the payments on the apartment, he'll be able to pay off the entire loan. Using the steering wheel as a drum he sings, 'If you don't want my kisses, then you can't have my money...'

He is so happy.

The smell of stale fixer hits his nostrils as he opens the apartment door. The low-lying sun is shining on the kitchen window, showing up the dirty marks and inviting the dust motes to dance.

He takes the rolls of film out of his camera bag, lines them up on the kitchen table, takes a painkiller for his back, then sits down and simply looks at the five small metal containers.

Now it's a matter of being careful, meticulous. He daren't give these films in to be developed—what if something goes wrong? He intends to develop the negatives himself, at least.

After a quarter of an hour's dreaming, when the painkiller has started to take effect and his back is pleasantly numb, he sets to work. He starts by cleaning: rinsing out the plastic troughs for the various fluid baths, the negative spools and the developing tray. He wipes down the kitchen table and the enlarging apparatus.

The five containers stand there, waiting.

He takes his time. When he has finished he takes a shower, puts on clean clothes. It's that kind of occasion.

When he returns to the kitchen the sun has sunk below the treetops on the other side of Gärdet, and the sky is red. The metal containers cast a lattice of faint shadows across the surface of the table.

Yellow polka dots on a red background...

He closes his eyes, tries to remember. The pattern flickers across the inside of his eyelids. Bikini. Pool.

Ah.

The swimming baths at Bällsta. He was fourteen. She was fifteen. Or so she said. The first girl to show any kind of erotic interest in him. Ma...ria? Yes, Maria. They snogged behind the changing rooms. Nothing more. She was wearing a red bikini with yellow polka dots.

That was it. Why had it seemed so significant?

Maria. Frank smiles. The hard-on inside his trunks, going home and jerking off until he was exhausted. The picture of her pounding inside his head. Oh yes. Now he remembers. She occupied his every thought for a whole summer.

He closes the kitchen door, pulls down the blackout blinds. A scrap of light seeps in through the door hinges, and he seals them with parcel tape. Nothing can go wrong. He unscrews the bulb in the fridge just in case he happens to bump into the door. You can't be too careful.

The room is pitch dark. He gropes his way over to the table.

He breaks open the first roll of film, winds it onto a spool. Then the next, and the next. When the films have been placed inside the drum he switches on the light and measures out the developing fluid with military precision.

He turns the drum once every thirty seconds precisely. He makes a huge effort to control himself, to maintain this meticulous approach. Something within him wants to rush things, get it all done as quickly as possible.

When the stopwatch beeps he sets the films to rinse. Now they are negatives, irrevocable. He bites his nails. What if he's done something wrong without realising? Used the wrong fluid. What if the negatives are blank when he takes them out of the drum?

With trembling hands he switches on the light box and unrolls the first reel of negatives.

The film is not blank.

It shows the pool, the chairs, the table, the house.

And nothing else.

He unrolls the entire film, looks at every single picture, and every single picture shows the same thing. The surface of the pool, yellow on the negatives, black deckchairs and a grey house. No people.

Frank slumps down on a chair and hardly even feels the throb of pain in his back. It's something that's happening far away.

How the hell...

He takes the other reels out of the bath and unrolls them on the light box without bothering to dry them.

The same thing in every picture. The same subject, in different degrees of enlargement. On one film he is able to follow the sequence of events, remembers zooming in and out.

That's where Roberto was lying on the chair. That's where I zoomed in as she climbed on top of him.

But Roberto is not on the chair. And there is no Amanda riding him. There is only a chair, and a table with a book on it.

Frank has one hundred and eighty pictures of a patio with a pool in Djursholm. Nothing else.

He hangs the negatives up to dry and stands there with his arms dangling limply by his side. Has he gone mad, imagined the whole thing? No. He saw what he saw. Somehow the camera has been deceived.

I'm not having this.

By the time the negatives are dry he has set up the processor, and prints twenty pictures, four from each film, on 10 × 15 paper.

As the photographs emerge in the bath of fluid, they still show the same thing as the negatives, but he refuses to accept it.

There must be something there.

He wasn't hallucinating. Roberto and Amanda were there, just as clear whether he was looking through the lens or with the naked eye. What kind of illusion can tolerate all those changes of focus, go on for so long and be so detailed?

He examines the pictures closely. Nothing. In his agitation he has been careless with the exposure time: everything blue is a couple of nuances too pale. The sky is almost white. The surface of the pool...

Hang on, what's this...

He looks from one picture to the next. Takes out a magnifying glass and examines them even more closely. He had hoped to find some kind of...trace left by Roberto and the woman. That is not what he finds. But there is a difference between the pictures. He studies them carefully, one after the other, with the magnifying glass.

Of course it could be due to carelessness during the developing process, but in several of the pictures there is a faint shadow at the bottom of the pool. What has captured his attention is that the shadow moves. Changes shape. In some of the pictures it is no bigger than a football, in others it takes up a significant portion of the pool.

The shadow of a cloud...

Yes. If there had been any clouds.

At half past ten Frank is back in the car. There is a hole in the exhaust, and the engine roars throatily as he drives out towards Djursholm. A few hours earlier, when he was driving in the opposite direction, he was sitting here wondering what kind of new car he should buy when he had sold the pictures.

Almost amusing.

There are no pictures, no millions. He is able to accept it now. For some incomprehensible reason the subject was not captured on film. Terrible but true. OK. What he cannot accept is the idea that the subject never even *existed.* That he is—to put it bluntly—ready for the funny farm.

And there is, after all, something that can prove he isn't crazy. Yellow polka dots on a red background: the bikini that was thrown in the pool. If it's still lying on the bottom, then he saw what he saw. If it isn't…well, somebody might have removed it.

Or something.

He stops at the 7-Eleven on Sveavägen, buys a bar of chocolate and the evening papers, and stuffs the chocolate in his mouth on the way out.

The houses belonging to the multimillionaires sparkle like wedding cakes in the summer evening, and a faint aroma of barbecued meat drifts in through the open car window as he pulls up outside the house where he has spent the last few days sitting in the garden. The gates are closed, and the bass beat from some dance hit is pulsating out into the garden. Through the panorama windows Frank can see bodies moving. Marcus is having a party.

He sits there, uncertain what to do. The party could go on for hours, should he wait until it's finished? Or go in right away? He hasn't got the five thousand to give to Marcus, and he'll have all his cronies behind him, high as kites, yelling abuse as Frank climbs the tree…

No.

He picks up one of the evening papers, turning the pages distractedly, and suddenly stiffens. On the entertainment pages is a picture of Roberto and Amanda. They are standing side by side at what must be an airport. A heart surrounds their faces.

'LOVE IS IN THE AIR IN MEXICO'

Frank reads the caption. It says that the picture was taken the previous day at the airport in Cancun.

The couple have kept their relationship secret for a long time…a week's relaxation at a secret location in Mexico…future film project…new album…left Sweden the day before yesterday…

Frank looks up from the paper, stares at the gates of the house with the pool. 'It's all lies,' he murmurs, without knowing exactly what he means.

Wrong. Something else is…wrong.

He looks at the picture in the paper. He sees it now. Amanda has short hair. She's had her hair cut since the last time he saw her on TV, at the Oscars ceremony. But the Amanda he saw by the pool a few hours ago had long hair.

He sits there in the car, trying to make sense of it: Amanda's long hair. The couple's stiff, unnatural movements.

The fact that they didn't appear on the film ought to be the most significant thing. And yet it didn't feel that way. The most important thing of all is the bikini, the red one with the yellow polka dots.

He closes his eyes, tries to picture it. The curve of Amanda's hips, Roberto's hand caressing the broad strip of elastic fabric. The big yellow polka dots. Then Maria: those sweaty moments behind the white wooden building where every single knot had been poked out to make peepholes.

It's…the same.

Yes. The appearance of swimsuits has changed over the thirty years since he and Maria were kissing behind the changing rooms, but the bikini Amanda was wearing not only had the same pattern, it was *exactly the same.*

And now it's lying at the bottom of the pool.

The lights in the house are switched off, only the floodlights over the pool are shining. Frank looks around and tries the gate. It isn't locked. He slips through, walks up four stone steps and stands by the edge of the pool.

There is the fresh smell of chlorine. The artificial light on the tiles and the still water give the whole experience a dreamlike character. Blue tiles make the water blue, make his skin blue. He ought to be nervous—breaking and entering isn't his thing, his place is just outside the property boundaries—but he feels strangely calm. As if he is anticipating a revelation.

He walks to the edge and looks down into the water.

The bikini is lying on the bottom, undulating slowly like an aquatic plant in the current of circulating water. In the blue light the yellow dots are green. Frank closes his eyes and rubs them hard.

So who were the people who were here?

While he is still massaging his eyelids, the feeling from earlier in the day returns. Something is piercing his head. Thin needles are being forced through his skin, his skull, penetrating deeper and deeper, moving around, searching. He wants to press his eyes tight shut against the pain, but instead he opens them.

At the very second his eyes open, the pressure disappears from his head, but he just has time to see. A number of threads, as fine as cobwebs, are floating between his head and the surface of the water. He just has time to see them before they melt away, or become invisible.

He blinks, fumbles in the air with his hand outstretched, but the threads are gone and the surface of the water...the surface of the water is covered in notes. He drops to his knees. Hundreds of thousand-kronor notes cover the entire pool like a lid. He shuffles forward.

The notes are real. Just a real as the picture he was waiting for, the bikini he was searching for. Frank puts his hands on his knees and laughs. Now he understands.

It's all in my mind.

He laughs, shakes his head and sobs out loud. Because it's tragic at the same time. The fact that his dream, the thing he wants most in the whole world, comes down to this. Pieces of paper.

Perhaps he knows exactly what he's doing, perhaps not. He reaches down towards the water to pick up a note. As soon as his fingers touch the surface of the water, the notes disappear. Something clamps onto his skin, and in a reflex movement he tries to pull back his hand, but it is impossible. His hand, his arm are slowly sucked down into the water, and Frank follows. When his face is just a couple of centimetres from the surface, he catches a glimpse of the thing that is pulling him.

It's one of those creatures that lives down at the bottom. In front of its mouth dangles something that looks like a precious stone, shimmering in every colour imaginable.

Finally the will to live takes over. Frank screams, braces himself with his free arm and tries to haul himself out of the water. The creature offers stubborn resistance, but Frank is fighting for his life, and he is stronger. One centimetre at a time he regains his arm. The creature has vanished, become one with the water again. Only the precious stone, the rainbow spot is still visible. It is pulsating.

'Frank?'

She clings to his arm. Maria. She is wearing her polka-dot bikini. He had forgotten how pretty she was. How could she ever have been interested in him?

'Frank, come on...'

Frank relaxes, opens his mouth to say that she doesn't exist. That she is just one of a series of dreams that never came true. Before he has time to speak she gives a start and he loses his balance, falls into the warm water.

The creature resumes its proper form and swallows him.

———·———

When the pool man arrives in the morning to carry out his weekly cleaning duties, he sees something on the bottom and fishes it out with his net.

A mobile phone.

He shakes the water out of it and tries switching it on. Doesn't work. He throws it in the bin and checks the water in the pool. It really is filthy. Full of fibres and fluff, discoloured. He makes several sweeps with the net, brings up scraps of fabric and…nails.

What the hell have they been doing?

The water still looks terrible. He decides to change the lot, and opens the valve. The water in the pool slowly runs away. After half an hour, it's empty.

The water continues on its way down to the purification plant. After passing through a number of filters and cleansing processes, it slips back out into the sea via enormous pipes. There it disperses, merges with the greater water and remains the same.

Substitute

When Matte rang me it was the first time I'd heard from him in twenty-two years. It's a strange feeling, picking up the phone and there on the other end is a person you assumed was…well, maybe not dead, but gone. A person you will never bump into again. Gone.

'Hi. It's Mats. Mats Hellberg.'

'Matte?'

'Yes. How are you?'

'Fine. Fine. What about you?'

A three-second pause. During that time a number of different scenarios flickered through my mind. I knew something had gone wrong in the autumn of 1982. Something that meant Matte couldn't come back to school. That was the last I heard. Something had gone wrong, and presumably it was still a problem. So the pause made me feel uncomfortable.

'There's something I have to tell you. Can we meet?'

'I don't know…'

'Please. It's important. You're the only one I could call.'

'So what's it all about?'

Another pause. I looked at the clock. *Six Feet Under* was due to start in two minutes, the last episode of the season, and I didn't want to miss a second.

'Have you never wondered what happened?'

'What?'

'To me.'

'Well yes, but—'

'It's not what you think. It's not even close to anything you might think. Can we meet?'

In the autumn of '82 there had been a great deal of speculation in my class about what had really happened. Matte had killed someone, Matte had gone completely crazy and was in some loony bin. After Christmas he was as good as forgotten. Life went on. I suppose I thought about him from time to time because I was the person who'd been closest to him, as far as it was possible to be close to someone like Matte. But even I forgot about him. As you do, I told myself.

And yet my conscience was pricking me. Not because of what I did or didn't do when we were thirteen, but because I hadn't thought about him. So I said, 'Yes, OK. When and where?'

'Can you come over here tomorrow? To my place?'

'Where do you live?'

He gave me the address of an apartment in Råcksta. I immediately thought it must be something the hospital had organised for him, and it turned out I was right.

It was exactly twenty past nine, and I would only be missing the title sequence. But before I managed to hang up, Matte asked, 'Listen, have you still got the class photo?'

'Which one?'

'The last one. Year 6.'

'I don't know. Maybe.'

'Could you have a look and bring it with you? It's important.'

'OK.'

We said goodbye and hung up.

David and Claire were smoking hash, Nate was due to have an operation and I couldn't stop thinking about the class photo. Firstly, where was it, and did I actually still have it? And secondly, what was special about it?

As soon as the program was over I went down into the cellar and started rummaging through the archive of my life: three banana boxes full of photos, letters, magazines, tapes and all the other stuff you end up collecting if you're that type, which I am.

I got hung up for a while on a concert program from Depeche Mode's Black Celebration tour. Page after page of meaningless icons that I'd copied into my school books. A picture of Martin Gore, who'd been my role model. If only I'd had curly hair. But that was around 1985–86. I burrowed deeper.

I stayed down there for a good hour. I found what I was looking for and took the photograph back up to the apartment, where I sat down at the kitchen table to study it.

There was nothing strange about the picture. I paid particular attention to Mats. He was wearing an Iron Maiden sweatshirt and had longer hair than anyone else in the class, including the girls. A studded bracelet around one wrist. If you looked at the picture without knowing anything else, you would say he had to be the class hard man.

In a way it was true. In another way it wasn't true at all.

He was hard in that he was impregnable. Nobody gave him any crap. Not because he could fight; he was as skinny and spindly as a ten-year-old, but it was as if there was an aura surrounding him, a sense that he wouldn't hesitate to rip out your eyes if you messed with him.

He had nothing to lose.

When the picture was taken it was two years since his mother and older brother had been killed in a car accident. Mats had had so much time off school that he had been forced to repeat a year, and that was how he ended up in our class. His style, the clothes he wore, all of it really belonged to his brother, Conny. His father hadn't cleared out Conny's room, he just couldn't bring himself to do it, and Matte just helped himself to whatever he fancied.

His father went downhill after the accident. I didn't go round to Matte's place very often, and I just remember his dad as something sitting in an armchair. Something grey. I once asked Matte, 'What does your dad actually do?'

'Nothing. He does nothing. He just sits at home.'

I didn't ask any more questions. But mainly I remember Matte's dad as a ghost with a physical form. A weight, nothing more. I suppose they must have got by somehow, but I didn't ask. You're not really interested in that kind of thing when you're twelve.

I looked at the class photo. We were all standing close together on the patch of grass next to the flagpole. I didn't know what had happened to any of them. I remembered all their names. Except the teacher. She was a substitute teacher who'd only been there for two weeks, and she was standing slightly apart from the class, not wanting to look as if she belonged.

All those names. Pointlessly etched into the back of my brain, never to be forgotten. As if we still lived in villages, when the names of the people we went to school with became the names of the people we worked with, hunted with, ended up marrying. But that's not the case now. Now they're just names.

Ulrika Berggren, Andreas Milton, Tomas Karlsson, Anita Köhli.

Moved away, dispersed to the four winds, forgotten. Only the names remaining. There's nothing to say about it. That's how things are these days: everything must move aside to make room for the new, all the time.

And that's the bottom layer in old boxes: melancholy, an indefinable sense of loss. You dig around and it comes swirling up to the top.

The following day was a Friday. We had decided that I would go round to Matte's place at six, and I wasn't planning to stay long. Laban was due at nine o'clock on Saturday morning. Laban is my son, he's ten years old, and he stays with me every other weekend.

That was one of the reasons why I wasn't all that keen on seeing Matte on a Friday. I try to make sure I'm cheerful on Fridays, that I don't start feeling down. No booze, no gloomy thoughts. On Saturday mornings I want to be in top form, to be as good as any every-second-weekend dad can be. I think I'm doing a pretty good job. But I could sense that Matte was weighed down by something, something I could easily get tangled up in, and I didn't want that. I've got enough with my own problems.

Anyway, I took the subway to Råcksta and wandered around among the apartment blocks before I found the right address. Even at that stage the weight started dragging at my feet. There's something depressing about a minor collection of apartment blocks. An immense area like Rissne is one thing, there's something grandiose about the insanity, a world of its own. But a clump like the one in Råcksta—that's just ugly.

There were two Hellbergs on the board down by the main door, but I guessed that Matte was the one whose name was made up of the newest letters. Brand new, they looked. He couldn't have been living here for long.

My suspicions were confirmed when I reached the fifth floor in the lift. There were no letters fixed on the letter box, just a handwritten note. Two notes, to be precise. The other one said 'No junk mail'. I rang the bell and the door opened immediately, as if he had been standing waiting just inside.

I had thought he would look like his dad. That there would be dust reaching all the way back from his eyes. But Matte had gone into his decline—if in fact it was a decline—the opposite way. He looked as if he had been blasted clean in a furnace.

He had actually grown a few centimetres since we were at school, but he was still short. And slim, really slim. His eyes were deep-set, his cheekbones were prominent and he had no hair on his head. That description doesn't really convey the fact that he looked pretty good, in a haggard kind of way. If I say Michael Stipe, the lead singer with REM, perhaps that will help. But make the eyes smaller and the chin more rounded.

On his upper body hung a snow-white shirt. I say *hung* because that was what it looked like. The shirt and the black jeans looked as if they had been placed there, kind of, like one of those cut-out dolls. A powerful smell of soap powder.

'Hello.'

'Hello.'

He held out his hand and I took it. His grip was firm and dry.

'Come in.'

His apartment was like his clothes. There was furniture and there were lamps and everything you might need, but none of it looked right, if you know what I mean. I lived in Kista for a while, and was invited to visit a family in my block who were refugees from Bosnia. They had been given a temporary apartment and that very temporariness was a little oppressive. The furniture had been given to them, or found, or bought cheap. Placed in position. Clean and tidy, but without any life. Just a place to wait. Same thing with Matte's apartment.

'Would you like a cup of tea?'

'Tea would be very nice.'

'What kind?'

'Oh, I don't know. Just ordinary tea.'

'Would that be Earl Grey?'

'I don't drink all that much tea, so I don't...'

'Hibiscus? Is that all right?'

'I expect so.'

Matte disappeared into the kitchen, a little corner where everything shone. I looked around the living room, unable to shake off the feeling that—how shall I put it?—that Matte hadn't invited me round to his place at all, but had set this apartment up specifically for the occasion.

There were no photographs on the walls, just pictures of American Indians and wolves at sunset, that kind of thing. The contents of the bookcase looked as if they had come straight from a Salvation Army shop. *The Family Moskat* by Singer, *The Da Vinci Code* by Dan Brown...the books that are always there. Something in the background of an interior design suggestion from Ikea. Nothing was in alphabetical order, and the impression was reinforced when I found another copy of *The Family Moskat* on a shelf lower down.

When Matte came in with a teapot and cups on a tray, I couldn't help asking, 'Have you read these?'

Matte put the tray down on the coffee table and looked at the bookcase as if he'd only just discovered that it was there.

'No. But I thought I would. Eventually.'

The tea looked peculiar, bright red. It smelled peculiar too. And it tasted peculiar. Bitter and flowery at the same time. Matte watched me as I lifted the cup to my lips, and I thought: *He's trying to poison me.*

'Have you got any sugar? It's slightly bitter.'

'Sugar, no. Sorry. No sugar.'

I put down the poisoned chalice and leaned back in the armchair. There was something about Matte that didn't inspire small talk, so I said, 'So what was it you wanted to tell me?'

'Did you find the photograph?'

I fetched the photo from my coat pocket in the hallway, put it down on the coffee table. Matte bent over it and nodded. Then he sat there staring at it for a while. I sat down again. When I thought the silence had gone on for long enough, I said, 'What did we look like, eh?'

'Mm.' Matte pointed at the teacher. 'Do you remember her?'

'No, not really. She was a substitute, I think.'

'A substitute teacher, yes.'

Matte got up and went over to the stereo unit, one of those towers of plastic, knobs and diodes that everyone had in the eighties; you can pick them up for a hundred kronor at flea markets all over the place these days. No CD player. Out of a drawer he took a magnifying glass, then came and sat down again. He passed the magnifying glass over the photograph, making small noises to himself.

Two thoughts:

One, he did actually have something in the drawers, it wasn't all just set dressing.

Two, there was still something badly wrong with him.

I sipped my tea, which didn't actually taste too bad once you got over the initial surprise. Matte put down the magnifying glass.

'OK. The thing I wanted to tell you is about her.' Matte pointed to the substitute teacher. 'Do you remember her name?'

'No. All I remember is…she played us some music, didn't she?'

Matte suddenly laughed. A brief, joyless laugh. It struck me that his slow movements, social ineptitude and quiet, almost whispering voice were down to the fact that he was institutionalised, or whatever it's called. He'd been locked up for quite a long time, that was all.

'Her name was Vera and the music she played us was *The Wall*. You know, *The Wall*. Pink Floyd.'

'Oh yes. Now you come to mention it. *The Wall*. That was it.'

Matte looked me in the eye.

'You do remember this? You're not just saying that because I said it?'

'No, I do remember. I thought that business of not needing an education was a bit odd, a teacher playing something like that. But what about it?'

'Do you remember her?'

I slid the photograph towards me and stared at the woman in the picture. Her face was no bigger than the nail on my little finger, and I made a movement to take the magnifying glass, but Matte stopped me.

'No. Not yet. Wait till I've told you.'

I understood nothing, but I just had to let it go. I peered at the picture. The woman, Vera, had a round face that could have been really pretty if every element of it hadn't been too small. Thin lips, small eyes and a straight, slender nose. As if everything had been pushed in towards the middle by a small but critical amount, giving her the expression of a skilfully painted balloon. The dark brown hair sat on her head like a helmet. Yes. A German helmet from the Second World War, the ends of her hair curling outwards a fraction to complete the resemblance.

The image came to life in my memory, and I recalled an unpleasant feeling. There had been some kind of disagreeable aura surrounding the woman who had come in when our usual teacher was on maternity leave.

'Do you remember?'

'Yes. I remember. There was something kind of unpleasant about her, as I recall.'

Matte nodded.

'Yes, although I didn't feel that way. At the time. As you might remember, things weren't going too well for me just then. Dad's dead, by the way. Killed himself six months after I...disappeared.'

'I'm sorry to hear that.'

'It's a long time ago. I could...understand it in a way. The car, the vacuum-cleaner hose. It wasn't really something that touched me. It was just part of everything that was going on. Everything will disappear. Anyway. This substitute teacher. Vera. When she arrived I didn't take much notice. I sat at the back most of the time eating Refreshers, those chewy sweets with sherbet inside. But then she did that thing, if you remember. It was only her second day, and she brought in a ghetto blaster and said she wanted to play something to us.'

'*The Wall.*'

'Yes. *The Wall.* And when she pressed Play...as soon as those first chords, the sound of the guitar, those thin chords on the guitar, a fragile echo as if they were playing in a big room...you know the song? 'Hey You'? Those chords at the beginning? Something got to me right from the start. It was something about the tone. And when he started singing...'

Matte looked at me, cleared his throat and started to sing. 'Hey you...'

Now I remembered the song. Matte actually sounded better than the original, and the hairs stood up on my arms: *Must get that album.*

Matte went on, 'It was perfect, somehow. Love at first sound, as it were. Iron Maiden and all that crap, it was just...that's another story, but I never really liked it. This, on the other hand. This hit the mark right away. The lyrics, of course, but I think it was mostly the atmosphere. The way it sounded. It was *me*, if you know what I mean. It was the sound of my life.'

'The soundtrack of our lives.'

'What?'

'Nothing. Go on.'

'And it was as if she was playing it for me. Maybe she was, I don't know. But it did for me completely. And then when the next one started, 'Is there anybody out there?', it was just…it was perfect.'

Matte leaned back in the armchair and closed his eyes. I couldn't work out where this was going, but listening was OK. Things I thought had gone forever suddenly twitched and came to life again. I could see the light from the window falling on Ulrika's hair as she sat in front of me. A hair slide in the shape of…a ladybird. Yes. A ladybird. The smell of scented erasers. Matte opened his eyes.

'I wanted to borrow it. But I was scared to ask. It was as if… looking back, I think I didn't want to expose myself in that way. Ask for something. I didn't like asking for anything.'

'No. You were pretty much…closed up.'

Matte ignored my comment.

'But the next day something happened that meant I could ask.' He gestured towards the picture. 'You remember she had a finger missing?'

Stupidly I looked at the picture to check his assertion, but Vera had her hands behind her back. Anyway, I remembered. The little finger on one hand was missing. We talked about it, but nobody asked her what had happened. Perhaps it was more exciting that way.

I nodded.

'OK. The following day she asked me to come to the blackboard. I think she wanted me to spell some word in English. I was pretty good at English, and maybe she wanted to encourage me, or…' Matte shook his head. 'No, I mustn't think in those terms. Not as far as she's concerned. But that was what I thought at the time. Anyway. When I came up to the board and she handed me the chalk, I dropped it and we both bent down at the same time to pick it up. And when I saw that she was on her way down too, I looked up. And then I saw…I mean, her hair lay really flat against her head, but when she bent down and I was looking from a particular angle…I could see that she had no ear. On one side.'

'No ear.'

'No. There was just skin where the ear should have been. I didn't have time to see whether there was a hole...whether the actual auditory canal was still there, but at any rate I could clearly see that the ear wasn't there.'

'You never said.'

'No. I felt as if...it was my secret. Or hers and mine, if you like. At the end of the day I went and asked if I could borrow the tape. *The Wall*. The thing about her ear meant I could ask. I know why, I've thought about this a lot, I've had plenty of time to think about it, but it's not important. Besides which, I think you understand.'

'More or less.'

Matte looked at me and something changed in his eyes.

'How are things with you, anyway? What's life done to you?'

I shrugged and told him, keeping it short. The jobs, the drifting around, the travelling, the years with Helena, Laban. I summarised it like this: 'A feeling that everything is kind of temporary, somehow. As if things never really get started. Or that it's already over, and I haven't noticed. But I'm still alive, and there's Laban after all.'

'And what about later on?'

'Later on?'

'When Laban's grown up?'

'I...I don't know. Video games are getting better and better.'

'That doesn't sound like much of a future.'

'It's perfectly OK. Many people are in a much worse position.'

Matte looked at me for such a long time that I started to feel uncomfortable, and hid my face behind the teacup. The tea was cold, and tasted better than when it was hot.

'Good,' he said eventually. 'In that case I think...I think you'll be able to understand.'

'Understand what?'

'What I'm going to tell you.'

Matte folded his hands on his knee and gazed at a point beyond the walls or behind his eyes. I waited. A sorrow so great surrounded Matte that you couldn't even call it sorrow. It was more of a condition, the element in which he lived, like a deep sea fish in his black cave.

'I took the tape home and listened to it, over and over again. I had one of those bean bags, you know, filled with plastic beads, and I lay on it for hour after hour, only getting up to turn the tape over. That initial feeling never came back, but instead I really started to love the music. I just got the whole story. *The Wall* is about society and what it does to people, but above all I saw it as a requiem for a life that had ended before it had even begun.'

'That was my line.'

'Yes, and my way of thinking probably wasn't quite so advanced at the time, but…loss. It's about loss. And the form is in perfect harmony with the content…Anyway. Forget that. The following day I took the tape back to school, said I thought it was…I can't remember which word I used, but anyway I was allowed to keep it. As I had hoped. So I spent another evening on the bean bag. My dad was completely out of it in those days, I don't know if you remember. When I was hungry I just used to take money out of his wallet and go out and buy something.

'That evening I poured myself a decent measure of whisky too, topped it up with Coke and drank it while I listened to the tape. It was…I thought it made the music even better. I went to the bathroom and threw up. Then I carried on listening.'

'What a life. For a thirteen-year-old.'

'Yes, but you know, while it was going on…I just felt…cool. I thought I understood so much that you kids couldn't even begin to grasp. Tragic, absolutely, but I was also old enough to kind of play the role to myself, if you know what I mean. I could see myself from the outside. Anyway, kids drink at thirteen these days.'

'Not on their own.'

'No, that's true. But it's not my tragic upbringing we're talking about here. The following day it was school again, and I felt like shit.'

'Sorry, Matte, I just have to ask. Have you been in a psychiatric hospital?'

'A psychiatric hospital, yes. Various kinds. For a long time.'

'But I don't get it...I'm sorry to come out with this, but...I kind of thought you'd be a bit...simple, if I can put it that way. But it's obvious you're more lucid than I am.'

'Plenty of people in institutions are lucid. When it comes to certain things. And completely useless when it comes to others. Living, for example. And I'm on medication. Very strong medication.'

'So this business about the ear...'

Matte frowned and looked annoyed.

'It's got nothing to do with that. The ear was gone. Or...it had never been there. I'll get to that. Can I go on?'

'Of course. Sorry.'

'OK. So in English the same thing happens again: she calls me up to the board to spell "conscious" while the rest of you are working in your books. And I pick up the chalk to write, and I remember this because it was...I knew the word "unconscious" and I was going to ask her if it was the same word without "un", you see. And of course it is, but my head was full of cotton wool that day, which is probably why I...instead of asking her, I prodded her in the back. I mean, you don't normally do that to a teacher, but...I prodded her in the back to get her to turn around. And do you know what happened?'

'No.'

'Nothing.'

'What do you mean, nothing?'

'Nothing. I prodded her in the back and she didn't react. So I prodded a bit harder. Nothing.'

'Maybe she—'

'That's what I thought too. That she was making a point.'

Matte glanced at the photo.

'You said before that you thought she was...what did you say... kind of disagreeable. Can you remember why you felt that way?'

'No, it was just a feeling, I suppose.'

'She never touched us. Never. Normally, if a child is sitting working on a task, if the teacher comes to help...she might put a hand on the child's shoulder, stroke his arm or hair, something. But she never touched us, do you remember?'

I thought about it. It was true, I supposed: I couldn't recall a single occasion when Vera had touched me, but when I thought back I couldn't remember any other teacher touching me either. Except when Sundgren, the music master, grabbed me by the back of the neck when I was plucking the strings inside the piano. But that was something else altogether.

I shook my head, but my expression must have betrayed my thoughts to Matte.

'I know. You don't remember. But I noticed it because when she said I could borrow the tape, I tried to be a bit grown-up. So I held out my hand to shake hers and say thank you. But she didn't take it. She just made a gesture kind of like this...'

'Maybe it was because of her missing finger.'

'Yes, but that was on her left hand.'

'What a memory.'

'I've done nothing but remember her over the past few years. OK. When she didn't react the second time I prodded her, I did this...'

Matte made a jerky, prodding movement with his finger.

'Tap-tap-tap, and you know what...her skin. It was all hard. Didn't give at all, no matter how hard I prodded. Hard, yet not solid. Do you understand what I mean? You can feel it, if you tap on...a statue, for example, as opposed to a sheet of plywood. It's not exactly easy to explain what the difference is, but it's sort of like a…a vibration in a thinner material.'

'And this was…a thinner material?'

'Yes.'

'So what kind of material was it?'

'Plastic.'

'Plastic?'

Matte snorted. The corners of his mouth turned up in a grin.

'I'm joking. I've no idea what kind of bloody material it was. Just that it was hard, and thin.'

Silence fell. I could hear the subway rumbling past somewhere down below. The room had grown darker. Only Matte's white shirt was clearly visible. I tried to picture it: a human being made of a hard, thin material. I saw metal.

'You mean she was some kind of robot?'

Matte shook his head, got up and went into the kitchen. When he came back he was carrying a lit candle in a holder, and he looked like an illustration from some ghost story. He placed the candle on the table.

'Classic paranoia, eh? Everyone is a robot except me. No, that's not what it's about. I understand, of course I do, you have to picture things in your mind. But delete robot. Can we come back to this? I'll finish telling you the story, and it might all become clearer. Or not. OK?'

'OK. Yes.'

'Eventually I got her to turn around. I waved my hand in front of her eyes like this, and she…she gave me a really funny look. I wrote the word on the board, and that was that. Oh. One more thing. Do you remember what she used to shout when she was calling us in? From the corridor?'

I shook my head.

'Come on. It would be good if you could remember this yourself.

She'd come out of the classroom, and we'd all be there mucking about, and she'd raise her arm and shout...can you remember what she used to shout?'

I closed my eyes and tried to picture the scene. Yes. There we were. And she came out. She was wearing some kind of brightly coloured blouse with big leaves on it, and she had...

For fuck's sake, we only had her for a week and she...

I opened my eyes.

'She never changed her clothes. It just struck me. She wore the same clothes for the whole week she was there. Didn't she?'

Matte smiled. Or whatever you might call that thing he was doing with his mouth.

'You're getting there. And do you remember what she used to shout?'

I closed my eyes again. The big leaves...hair like a helmet...she raised her hand, she shouted...

All you children...all you children...come in...

'I've got it. All you children! Come in! Welcome!'

'Exactly.'

'Yes. That was it. So?'

'I'm getting there. That day I followed her when school was over. Tailed her. From a distance. She didn't live far from the school. Up in those old apartment blocks on Holbergsgatan, behind the centre. You know the ones I mean? Anyway. I saw her go in through a door, so I sat down on a bench by the children's playground and waited.'

'What were you waiting for?'

'How should I know? Nothing better to do, I suppose. When I'd been sitting there for a while she came out onto the balcony. And where I was sitting...there was a tree between us, closer to me. So I could see her, but she couldn't see me. She stood there on the balcony for a few minutes. Then she went inside, and I stayed where I was.

I don't know, I suppose I was in the middle of some fantasy about a stakeout. You know, that I was…'

'Cup of coffee and a doughnut.'

'Exactly.'

'Why didn't you talk to me?'

Matte raised his eyebrows. For some reason I sounded really upset. I waved it away, told him to carry on. He leaned forward.

'I asked you. I asked you if you wanted to come with me to tail the substitute teacher, I said there was something shady about her, but you had indoor hockey training or something.'

'Handball.'

'Handball. And it was probably just as well. When I'd been sitting there for a quarter of an hour she left the apartment and went off somewhere, and I climbed up to her balcony. Up the drainpipe.'

'You're kidding?'

'No. And fortunately…or however you want to put it, she'd left the balcony door open, so I could get inside. And at this point I have to ask permission to repeat myself, because do you know what was in there?'

'No.'

'Nothing.'

'Nothing?'

'Nothing.'

'What do you mean, nothing?'

'Nothing. Not a single ornament. Nothing.'

'You mean…but she had furniture and—'

'No. She had nothing. It was completely empty. No sofa, no rugs, no tables, no telephone, no TV. Not a thing. Just like when you see pictures of brand-new apartments. Nothing.'

'A bed, then…'

'No bed. Empty walls, empty floors, empty space in between. I went into the bedroom, what would have been the bedroom, and opened the fitted wardrobes. Empty.'

Silence. I tried to imagine how a person could live in an apartment that was completely empty. It was impossible.

'But maybe she was just checking out an apartment she was thinking of buying, or something.'

'It's a possibility. But I wasn't thinking that at the time.'

'So what were you thinking?'

'Nothing.'

'There's a lot of nothing going on here.'

'Yes. But as I stood there in the bedroom I heard the key in the front door and I...just froze. I couldn't move. I just stood there. Heard the front door open, close. I somehow realised there were no explanations or excuses, but...my brain was completely empty. So I just stood there. The door to the living room was open...'

Matte stopped and looked around his own living room.

'It feels strange to be talking about living rooms and bedrooms when there was no furniture. Without furniture they're just spaces, aren't they? Kitchen, bathroom, that's different, there are things that are part of the fittings, but other rooms become what they are because of the furniture we put in them.

'So when I say *the door between the bedroom and the living room*, I mean *the door between the smaller and the larger space*. But you understand that.'

There was a short silence, until I asked, 'What happened then?'

'Guess.'

'Nothing?'

'Nothing. She came into the living room. She was wearing that blouse with the big leaves on it. She went and stood in the middle of the living room with her back to me and...just stood there. In the middle of the floor. And I stood in the bedroom, not moving a muscle, looking at her back. Felt the sweat from my armpits trickling down past my waist. I was scared shitless. I don't know why, but I felt as if there was a scream stuck in my throat that just wanted to force its way out. There was something so horrible about her back, no, not her back. But the idea that she might slowly turn around and look me in the eye. I couldn't interpret her back, you see, the way she was just standing there, the only way I could make sense of it was to think that she knew I was there, and she was simply... playing with me.

'And that scream...I was sure it would come out if she turned around, because as I stood there, I don't know why, but I became more and more convinced that if...if she turned around...she wouldn't have a face.

'We stood there. This was late summer, so...I don't know how much time passed, but it started to get dark outside. The lights outside came on, and still we stood there. I couldn't move. Every muscle in my body was numb, and the longer I stood there, the more certain I became that I would never be able to move, and my thoughts...my thoughts...got weaker and weaker too. If you imagine your thoughts like someone talking inside your head, it was as if the person who was talking...was sinking. Or disappearing. Sinking down into something. Being suffocated.

'And when you stop thinking. That's when it gets dangerous.'

For the last few minutes Matte's gaze had been fixed on something far away, or deep inside himself. Now he brought it back and looked at me.

'Do you know what happens if you stop thinking? If there's nothing to take in from the outside? Do you know what comes instead?'

I thought about it for a few seconds. Then I said, 'Life?'

Matte slapped his thigh, smacking it with such vigour that I jumped. He leapt up out of the armchair and grabbed hold of my face with both hands.

'Brilliant! Bloody brilliant!'

I didn't understand what was so brilliant, but Matte was absolutely beside himself for a moment. He shook my head back and forth, staring into my eyes. Then he suddenly seemed to become aware of what he was doing; he let go of me, took a step backwards and ran a hand over his face.

'Sorry. I didn't mean to...I was just so...pleased. That you understand.'

'Well, I don't know about...'

'You don't see the same thing as me, you're not me, but just the fact that you said it, that that's what you said when I...Life, yes. When there's nothing to see, when there are no thoughts, life comes instead. Naked. And you know, as I stood there in that room...you know what my life was like at the time. My mother drove into a rock face with my brother, you know.'

'But that was an accident, right?'

'I don't think so. I won't go into details, but...I don't think so. In the middle of the day, no oncoming traffic, just straight into the rock face...no. I don't think so.'

'Fucking hell, Matte.'

'Yes. Fucking hell, Matte. Although you know how it is when you're young...you want to live. You keep yourself busy, you find stuff. Like I did with *The Wall*. But as I stood in that room staring at her back, when I'd been standing like that for a long time...it came. Like a horrible black darkness, slowly being poured into my body. It started in my stomach. The weight. And it just kept on pouring in until it filled my head as well. My life...there wasn't just a wall between me and other people, I *lived inside* that black wall, I...it's impossible to describe it. But it was black. Completely black. That was actually when I really lost the plot. The other stuff, that was just...a consequence.'

'What other stuff?'

'Well, eventually I managed to move. One step at a time. Went over to her. But slowly, I was moving inside that wall, you see, and my progress was...slow.'

Matte held a hand out in the air as if he were putting on the brakes, then he went over to the stereo and switched it on. Several red diodes began to glow.

'I set this up before you came. To fit in with my lecture. Do you know what track four on *The Wall* part two is called?'

'No.'

'It's called "Vera".'

'Just like—'

'Yes. Just like. Now listen carefully.'

Matte pressed Play on the tape deck and a lonely note emerged from the speakers. Then, in the distance, a voice that sounded like something on short wave radio...a few words were called out in the background...more radio voices...a machine gun or something like that... a voice calling something...an explosion, then the vocal started.

Matte stopped the tape. 'Did you hear it?'

I shook my head. 'What am I supposed to hear? Vera Lynn? Was her name Lynn too?'

Matte rewound the tape, turned up the volume and pressed Play again. I leaned closer to the speakers and closed my eyes.

The note...the radio voices...the words being called out and...

I sat bolt upright on the sofa and looked at Matte. He pressed Stop.

'Did you hear?'

'Play it again.'

Matte rewound a few seconds, pressed Play.

The radio voices...the words...

I could hear it clearly this time. I was able to make out the words. The voice shouting in the background was calling: *'All you children! Come in! Welcome!'*

Matte stopped the tape, pressed the eject button, took out the tape and showed it to me.

'This is the tape I got from her. The same one.'

'But...what does it mean?'

Matte came and sat down in the armchair again, placing the tape on the table next to the photograph. He sat there for a while with his hands on his knees, not speaking. Then he pointed at the photograph.

'I'd hoped that would confirm what I've been thinking. And it has.'

I leaned forward, but Matte placed his hand over the photograph.

'Wait. One thing at a time. So eventually I reached her. And as I said: I no longer had any thoughts. So I prodded her in the back. And the same thing happened as in school. No reaction. But I wasn't afraid anymore, I was...nothing. So I walked around her and looked at her face. She had a face, but...how can I put this...she wasn't in it. She wasn't there. It was quite dark in the room by this stage, just the lights from outside shining in, but I looked at her eyes and it was as if they were made of glass. Open. But empty. And then...I don't know why I did it, but it was probably for the same reason as a dog licks its balls.'

'Which is?'

'Because it can. So...I unbuttoned her blouse to...to see what she looked like. Or to get a reaction. I don't know. I was pretty much out of it.'

Matte pointed to several spots on his chest, his stomach.

'There were holes. Spread irregularly all over this part of her body. Twelve holes, as deep and wide as...I could get two fingers inside.'

'Matte. For God's sake, that's...'

'I know. I know. Do you think I don't know? But there's nothing I can do about it. That's the way it was. I examined her head. There were a couple of holes there too. There were probably more, but by that stage I'd lost it completely. What happened next...I don't remember at all.'

Matte hadn't drunk any tea. Now he filled his cup with the tepid liquid in the pot and knocked it back in one go. I noticed that his hand was shaking. He pointed at the photograph.

'Now you can look. Use the magnifying glass. Look at her feet. Hang on.'

He got up and switched on the main light, then stood with his arms folded, looking at me encouragingly. I picked up the magnifying glass and studied the photograph.

She was wearing the blouse with the big leaves on it. The only odd things I could remember about her were that vaguely unpleasant feeling, and the fact that she always wore the same clothes. And then of course there was the business with the tape, but then that was...

It's possible to rig that kind of thing, of course. If you want to. But why?

I looked at her feet. There was nothing strange about her feet. Ordinary feet in a pair of white trainers. Matte's gaze was burning into the back of my neck.

I realised he was crazy, one way or another. He'd got some kind of fixed idea, had—what's it called?—rationalised something he'd done, whatever it might be. Created a reason.

I shook my head slowly.

'Matte, I—'

'Look at the grass. Underneath her feet.'

I looked at the grass underneath her feet. Then I looked at the grass under Ulrika's, Kenneth's, Staffan's and my own feet. Then I looked at the grass under her feet again.

It was standing up.

The grass underneath our feet was flattened down, of course.

Underneath hers it was standing up. As if she weighed nothing.

Something round and sticky descended through my throat and landed in my stomach. This was my photograph. It had been down in my cellar. There wasn't a cat in hell's chance that anyone could have tampered with it, as someone could have tampered with the tape.

As if he had read my thoughts, Matte picked up the tape and shook it demonstratively.

'You could take this to anyone who's an expert in that kind of thing, and he'd tell you nobody has done anything to this tape in twenty years.'

'But…is that voice…her voice on the original?'

My own voice sounded weird, as if I were speaking through a piece of fabric. Matte shook his head.

'No. I've checked. The other sounds are there, the other voices, but that particular voice…on the original it's a man's voice. But the interesting thing, the really interesting thing…you saw the grass?'

I nodded and whispered, 'What did you do?'

Matte waved the question away.

'I'm getting to the interesting bit. I've got a theory, you know. As you've perhaps realised I've spent that last twenty years in different…places. In order to become whole, or whatever it is you're supposed to become. Functioning. I saw the way you looked at my apartment when you arrived, and no, I haven't a clue. I've just tried to… simulate a life.

'But I've met a lot of people in the places where I've been. And Vera isn't the only one, let me tell you. I think she was quite special because of her extreme…incompleteness. But they're everywhere. People who are lacking something. Or a lot of things. And I don't even know if they are people, they might be something else.

'In fact, they probably are something else. They're here instead of someone else, they slip in through that gap and…I'm not sure, but I think there are more and more of them around.

'I checked with the school last week, by the way. It took a while and they weren't exactly thrilled about it, but they dug out lists of everyone who's worked there since the place was built. Teachers, substitute teachers, the lot. Salary records. And apart from a head-mistress at the end of the fifties, no one called Vera has ever worked in that school. Not even for one day.

'I presume they'd forgotten to book a substitute teacher for us, and she slipped in through the gap. That's what I think.'

I picked up the magnifying glass again, looked at the photograph. There was no doubt about it. Now that I knew, it just looked insane: the grass standing up under her feet, the shadows falling differently around her.

I just couldn't take it in. I scrubbed my face hard with my hands, as if to rub away a sticky crust.

'What do you mean? What do you mean, more and more of them? Why are there more and more of them?'

'Why does a dog lick its balls?'

'Because it can.'

'Yes.'

Matte gestured towards the window.

'Because they can. Out there…You'll have to excuse me. I'm so used to thinking about the world in general as *out there*. But out there, everything is based on the idea that things are interchange-able, isn't it? Temporary staff, short-term relationships, substitutes, substitutes, substitutes. I'm not moralising, it's just a fact. Someone disappears, someone else turns up instead. All the time. Spaces appear, gaps, and then…then they just slide in. But do you know what the worst thing is? They themselves don't know.'

'Don't know what?'

'That they're substitutes. They think they're people. Of course they're not usually missing a finger or an ear, it's usually something else. Something else is missing. Something is lacking. Less obvious than a finger, but equally perceptible. So we take our medication, we try—'

'We?'

'Yes, we. What's to say that you and I aren't substitutes too? How much is left of us? My illness, my so-called illness…'

Matte sighed and sank down in the armchair. He looked so small. It was as if the armchair threatened to swallow him up. If he let go the black, worn imitation leather would wrap itself around him. I felt the same thing, and straightened up. If I stayed where I was I would disappear. Before I had time to get to my feet, Matte said, 'Mental illness is about not being able to see the world as it is. My illness… the root of my illness, the reason I take medication, the experience I have to suppress, is that it's already happened.'

'What's already happened?'

'The substitutes have already taken over. There are no people left anymore. And if you look at life in that way, it becomes pretty… pointless. There will be nothing left.'

I stood up. I couldn't listen to this any longer.

'Matte. I have to go home. My son is coming tomorrow, and it's…I've got a few things to sort out.'

'I understand. Thanks for coming.'

I wanted to turn around, go into the hallway, pick up my coat and then walk or run to the subway station. But it wasn't finished. My feet refused to move. When Matte noticed that I was still standing there, he looked up at me, and his face was utterly naked. He asked, 'Do you believe me?'

The answer wouldn't come. There was both a yes and a no, in fact, and neither of them wanted to come out. Instead the question came again.

'What did you do?'

Matte shook his head slowly, and the shadow of a smile passed over his lips.

'It doesn't matter. I must have…destroyed it in some way. With a cupboard door, perhaps. From the kitchen. I remember the edges against the palms of my hands, unhooking a cupboard door. Yellow. A yellow cupboard door, although it looked more like…orange in the darkness. I remember that. There was nothing there, you see. So I unhooked a kitchen door. I remember that. Then nothing. But I think I must have destroyed it…her in some way. The way they treated me afterwards would suggest that's what happened. And then she moved in there.'

Matte waved in the direction of the table.

'Moved in where?'

'Into the music. Sorry. I didn't say, did I. That tape…I listened to it several times before…before this happened. And her voice wasn't there then. It was only afterwards, after I'd…done it that she moved in. That her voice appeared.'

Matte picked up the tape, twisting it between his fingers and looking at it as if he were contemplating the only memento of a much-loved relative.

'That's what was left. Of her.'

There was nothing more to say. As I stood in the hallway putting on my coat, Matte came up to me with the photograph in his hand.

'Can I keep this?'

I looked at the photograph, at Matte. In spite of everything, it was the only souvenir I had of that particular year, and as I said: I'm a collector. Matte was looking intently at me, and I gazed into two deep shafts.

'Please?'

I nodded. Not really because I wanted to be kind, but because I just wanted to get out of there. I nodded and held out my hand to say goodbye. Matte clasped the photograph to his heart with his left hand, held out his right. We said goodbye.

When I got out onto the street I stood for a long time looking up at Matte's window. One apartment among twenty-four others in the same block, one apartment block among several others. A space with temporary objects arranged in it. A shudder passed through my body and I hurried off towards the warmth and movement of the subway.

On the platform the cold fluorescent light poured down on a man here, a woman there, another man over there, waiting with his hands pushed deep in his pockets. The men were standing still, the woman walking the short distance back and forth, back and forth.

The train arrived. Six blue carriages pulled in alongside the platform. Stopped.

The people inside the carriages were gazing into space or looking down at their newspapers or out into the blackness beyond the window. No one was moving.

Eternal / Love

Death is just walking out of a door
leaving a room full of light
in a pair of eyes.

Mia Ajvide

Anna and Josef really loved each other. Eight years they had been together, and all the indications were that things would stay that way until death parted them. If they had to be apart for a day or more because of work or other circumstances, they both had the feeling they were in the wrong place. Life became insubstantial, unreal.

They had both grown up in Stockholm, and before they met they had each had quite an intense social life—bars, clubs, short-term relationships. Two years into their own relationship they went through their address books. Half the names they couldn't even put a face to; nine out of every ten phone numbers were redundant. They wrote the important ones in a new book and threw away the old ones.

In November the following year Josef's father had a heart attack when he jumped into the sea from the jetty after a sauna. When the grief had stopped sprawling and stabbing and settled in his chest, his father's summer cottage, made warm and cosy for winter use, was waiting there like an opportunity. No loans, no rent.

Most of what they needed they found in each other, so why would they need Stockholm? And in any case, Sågviken was only a hundred kilometres from the capital if they were in the mood for a change.

They had a farewell party, inviting the remaining ten per cent of the names in their address book, said *You must come and see us* and *I mean it's not as if we're moving to a different part of the world*, in spite of the fact that they knew that was exactly what they were doing.

After a couple of years, things were going well. Josef, who was a qualified childcare worker, had found a job at a nursery in Norrtälje, and Anna had converted the garage into a studio where she worked during the day. One week she painted motifs from the archipelago on driftwood which she could sell to summer visitors, the next she painted pictures she couldn't sell to anyone, as she put it herself.

In the evenings they read aloud to each other, drank wine. Watched TV. Or sat and talked. They rarely had visitors, but when it did happen they thought it was great when the visitors arrived and lovely when they left.

Naturally they quarrelled and had their darker moments. Like when they were due to attend a family party at Anna's parents' house. Josef took himself off in his boat with his fishing rod, returning half an hour after the time they had planned to leave. When he got in the car he stank of fish guts. They sat in silence for fifty kilometres. Anna made a point of pushing the old Toyota to a hundred and forty on the motorway; it rattled and roared as if they were inside a tumble dryer. Then they ran out of petrol. Anna had been so tense she had forgotten to fill up.

They sat there at the side of the road with their arms tightly folded. Neither of them wanted to start, because once they did start it was going to take a long time. Anna's family, Josef's reluctance. How he hated feeling forced into things. How she hated having to force him. And so on. Both of them were very angry: messy black clouds in their heads. Both of them were thinking: *I want a divorce. This isn't how it should be.* Neither of them meant it. Everything was bloody awful and really difficult, but this was where they were meant to be. They would bicker over it all and sort things out yet again. There was no alternative.

They started quarrelling as they set off to fetch some petrol, carried on afterwards. Fifty kilometres, a hundred kilometres. Outside Norrköping came the first laughter. In Linköping they bought new trousers for Josef. They arrived at the party three hours late, and as usual everybody commented on how happy they seemed together. Anna said seriously, 'It's because we're both on the same antidepressants,' and only Josef laughed.

Their love is so big and strong, but there is still room to fear two things: the child and death.

Sometimes they lie in bed, gazing into each other's eyes and thinking: *My happiness is complete. I want things to stay just like this forever.* They haven't just fallen in love, they know what it's all about. 'I want things to stay like this' pretty much sums it up: a life filled with hard work, sometimes boring, sometimes joyous. And they lie there, four eyes fixed on each other, sounding each other's depths, and they try to think: *This moment is eternity. This moment is forever.*

But we grow older, things change. A time will come when illness and frailty ravage their bodies. Senility, weakness, teeth falling out, a wheelchair ramp up the porch. Perhaps then they will look back on their happy life and feel contented.

But that isn't what they want! No! They want what they have *now* to last forever! It's not fair that love should be subject to the same limitations as our frail bodies. That it should wither and die along with our flesh.

Of course some people believe in heaven. But not Anna and Josef. Unfortunately.

And The Child? It must have capital letters, it has assumed such proportions. At family parties everyone asks, 'Don't you think it's getting time? I mean, everything's going so well for you, and Josef is so good with children, and you'll be such a wonderful mother, Anna.'

Everything seems to tend in its favour. But they're afraid.

The greatest cathedrals are finely balanced. Move a few stones from the foundations of the Globe Arena, and it will roll away. Maybe. You never know. And isn't the basic premise of love a mutual freedom? The fact that you *can* leave?

Neither of them wants to leave, not for all the tea in China, but the possibility should be there. The idea that you choose each other, not because you have to and not because you have children or a house to consider, but because that's what you want, every day.

But a child. A child...

They can't decide, so they allow chance, fate to determine what happens; their only form of contraception is to make love during Anna's safe periods. If it happens anyway, well, it happens. To tell the truth, they're not all that careful about the dates either.

And it does happen.

Anna misses a period, Josef picks up a pregnancy test on the way home from work. Anna pees on the stick, they put it on the kitchen table and stand there for three minutes, hugging each other, eyes closed. The world all around them is silent, holding its breath.

When they look there is a pale blue line showing: the child's first sign of life.

They neither laugh nor cry. The little line fills them with trepidation, leaves them dumbstruck. When one of them finally speaks, it's Anna who says in a fake falsetto voice, 'I want ice cream!'

Josef laughs. They take a litre out of the freezer, put it on the table next to the pregnancy test, get two spoons and eat the whole lot. His tongue stiff with cold, Josef asks, 'How does it feel?'

'It feels good. How about you?'

'Yes. Good. It'll be quite something.'

'Yes. Probably.'

She licks ice cream off his lips and carries on into his mouth. This is going to be good. They'll just be happy in a slightly different way. Hand in hand they go to bed, despite the fact that it's Anna's unsafe period. After all, it doesn't matter anymore.

A week went by. It would be an exaggeration to say that they drifted apart, but they were lost in their own thoughts. Perhaps it's as Pascal says: we are incapable of living in the present, it's only the past and the future that have the capacity to occupy our minds.

The future had changed shape. It took a while to get used to the idea. Anna painted gulls flying over salt-spattered cliffs, even though it was the wrong week. She had a lot to think about, and she could paint the gulls on autopilot, as it were. It was the end of September now, and most of her stock had been sold at the markets over the summer.

She stopped with the brush poised over the crest of a wave just as she was about to dab it with flake white to make the surf. Next summer. Would they be struggling around the markets with...a buggy? Reins? Could they carry on living like this? How much would they need to change?

Josef finished work early and cycled home from the bus stop because the car was out of action. Something to do with the carburettor. After they'd eaten he set off in the boat with his fishing rod to catch a few autumn perch. Anna stood at the kitchen window watching him go, and a shiver of apprehension that began in her womb fluttered through her body. The thought of never seeing him again. Bravely she went back to her seagulls, spent a couple of hours applying colour.

When she came out of the garage the wind had got up, and dusk fell quickly. Josef hadn't come home. She went down to the jetty, gazing out across the dirty grey water. After a quarter of an hour she was frozen stiff.

She went inside and made herself a cup of coffee, sat down by the kitchen window.

Come on Josef, don't do this...

But he didn't come. When it was so dark that she could no longer see the jetty she rang the emergency services and was put through to the coastguard. The receiver shook in her hand as she spoke to a man on a motor launch at Refsnäs jetty, via a crackling mobile link.

'Do you have any idea what area he might be in?'

'Yes, roughly. It's by...hang on...let me just...'

The names of the islands around the area where Josef usually fished had disappeared. She stood up to fetch the chart and her legs gave way. Her heart was pounding so much she could hardly breathe. On all fours she crawled to the bookcase, grabbed the chart and opened it out.

There were holes in the cover along the folds, and the map was stained or worn in those places. She tried to focus, but the letters were crawling like maggots over the grey vomit of the archipelago. He was out there somewhere. A little voice called, 'Hello, are you there?' from the receiver. She swallowed, rubbed her eyes and picked it up.

'I think there are some small islands east, no north of Gisslingö where he usually...the map's torn...Josef.'

'Sorry?'

'Josef. That's his name.'

'Right. So somewhere around Fjärdskäret, then?'

She looked at the map for confirmation. It was illegible, worn in that particular area. She could see her Josef there, floating in the black waves in a place that didn't exist, a hole in the world. She started to cry. On the other end of the line she heard an engine start up.

'Don't worry. I'm sure he's just got some mechanical problem with the boat. We'll go out and take a look.'

'Thank you. He's…he's going to be a father.'

A pause. A small sigh. Then: 'We'll be in touch as soon as we know anything.'

She gave them her number and hung up. In the silence that small sigh grew into an ominous, cold wind. She wrapped a blanket around her, leaned her forehead against the windowpane and stared out into the darkness. She was alone.

After a few minutes her legs started to move. She tried doing the washing-up to keep calm, but it was impossible. She walked around and around the house, but found no peace anywhere.

They must be there by now. They'll be searching now.

Searchlights sweeping across the surface of the water. Her legs kept on walking and walking. In the end she understood what they wanted: they wanted to go down to the jetty, position themselves right at the very end on the border between land and sea and wait there as women have waited for their men to come home from the sea for thousands of years. It was the only thing to do. But she lived in the twenty-first century, and her place was by the telephone.

They would get a mobile. When Josef got home they would get a mobile phone at long last, and he could take it with him when he went out. Who was it who hadn't wanted a mobile? It was Anna. If he'd had a mobile now…it was all her fault.

After two hours without any news, a black madness began to creep up on her. She fell to her knees on the kitchen floor with the blanket over her, joined her hands together, pressed them to her forehead and mumbled, 'Dear Lord, please let him come back. You can have anything you want. Anything. take the house, all my things, take...yes, take my child. I don't want it. You can have it, if you'll just let Josef come back. As long as I can spend my life with Josef. *Take it now.*'

The telephone rang.

She flung off the blanket, hurled herself at the phone. Her hands were sweaty from the warmth of her cocoon, and at first she couldn't grasp the receiver. Even before it reached her ear she could hear the crackling. Her heart expanded, filling her chest.

'Hello?'

'Hello, Magnus Jansson from the coastguard here. We've got him. He's alive.'

'Is he...'

'Suffering from severe hypothermia. We found him in the water. You live in Sågviken, is that right?'

'Yes...'

'We'll be at Refsnäs in ten minutes. An ambulance is on its way; if you can get down there you can go in with him.'

'In?'

'Yes, he'll be going to the hospital in Norrtälje just to be on the safe side. Don't worry, he'll be fine, but he was in the water for quite a long time, so...just to be on the safe side.'

After she'd hung up she ran into the hallway and pulled on a jacket. Fortunately Josef had pumped up the tyres on the bike that morning, and she raced off across the gravel with the dynamo whining.

On many occasions she had seen death notices in the local paper, *Norrtelje Tidning*, asking for donations to the coastguard in memory of the deceased. Only now did she understand. Her happiness and relief crystallised into a love for the coastguard that was so immense she wanted to sing them a hymn, paint them a picture; she would do anything for them.

'Coastguards!' she yelled. 'I love you all!'

She reached the main road, and after a hundred metres the ambulance overtook her. She changed to third gear and stood up on the pedals. The signs showed that the speed limit was 50 kph. It felt as if she was travelling faster.

On the hill leading down to the jetty she stopped pedalling. The ambulance was standing on the quayside with its blue light silently flashing as the motor launch bobbed on the waves. The sea beyond it was black. The machinery and the resources that exist to safeguard two fragile hearts. She braked next to the ambulance. A middle-aged man in an orange jacket came over to her.

'Hi...Anna?'

'Yes, I'm...'

'Magnus. We spoke on the—'

The bell on her bicycle pinged as she dropped the bike and threw her arms around Magnus. His jacket stuck to her sweaty cheek and she whispered 'thank you' into his shoulder. He patted her on the back and said, 'It's all right, it's all right.'

'Where is he?'

'We were just going to...come with me.'

The deck swayed beneath her feet as she climbed on board after Magnus, who headed along by the gunwale towards an open iron door. She started to follow him, but her field of vision suddenly shrank, leaving only a small peephole in the middle where she could see the grey, shiny deck, although that too was threatening to disappear.

She stopped and leaned on the gunwale to stop herself falling. Closed her eyes and clutched the metal rail. For a moment she felt as if she was going to throw up. The boat was rocking in time with her guts, bringing them up into her throat. She heard Magnus's voice out of the darkness: 'Are you all right?'

She ran a hand over her face, continuing the movement to encompass the boat, the night, the sea, death.

'Sorry, it's just...it's all so big.'

Magnus looked up at the masthead light and nodded.

'We've only had it for a couple of years.'

She didn't understand what he meant, but the swell in her stomach had subsided. Her field of vision expanded. A door stood open. Beside it there was a metal sign with the words Sick Bay. She walked over and stepped over the high threshold.

She almost didn't recognise him. The man sitting on the bunk wrapped in a thick blanket had wet, tousled hair and a bluish, swollen face. Apart from his forehead, which was dark red. Every feature had sunk in towards the centre, almost obliterated by the swelling. But the eyes were the same as those that had looked at her from the jetty only four hours earlier.

'Josef!'

She flew into his arms and his body was cold and stiff beneath the blanket, but she would warm him. His gaze was far away, but she would bring it home. She hugged him, rubbed his skin and whispered, 'Josef, Josef, don't ever do that again...'

After a couple of minutes Magnus cleared his throat and said they'd better make a move. Together they helped Josef into the ambulance, and it set off for the hospital in Norrtälje. Anna blew Magnus a kiss through the rear window.

During the trip Josef told her what had happened.

Just a few hundred metres before he reached his destination, the outboard motor had stopped. The usual thing: the fuel pipe inside the engine had jumped out. He pushed it back, pumped up more petrol and pulled the starter cord.

But he had forgotten to put the engine in neutral. When the twenty horsepower roared into life at full throttle, the boat shot forward and Josef was thrown over the stern.

It might not have been too bad. He got a soaking and cursed his own stupidity, but he was only a hundred metres from land, and he was wearing a lifejacket after all. The problem was that while he was still coughing up salt water and wiping his hair out of his eyes, no one was steering the boat, which had gone around in a tight circle.

The last thing Josef remembered was turning his head towards the sound of an approaching engine, thinking something along the lines of: 'Am I being rescued already?', then everything went black.

When he opened his eyes it was dark all around him and he could no longer hear the engine. The wind had begun to get up. His head was throbbing with pain and he had no feeling in his body, no idea where he was or how long he had been out.

He floated there until the coastguard arrived. They picked him up almost one nautical mile east of the spot where he had fallen in, on his way out towards the Åland Sea.

Anna tried asking questions. What had he been thinking as he lay there in the water, how had he felt? But Josef's eyes slid away, he rubbed his forehead and said he was in pain and didn't want to talk about it now. Later.

They had to sit and wait for tests. Josef's hands and feet, which had been horribly white, started to regain their colour, but as a consequence they were so itchy that he said it was better when he couldn't feel them. Anna fetched him a cup of hot chocolate from a machine and he drank it quickly, then sat studying the pattern on the paper cup, caressing it with his finger. After a while a smile spread across his face and he held the cup out to Anna.

'Isn't it a beautiful pattern?'

Anna looked at the yellow shapes on a brown background; the pattern reminded her of an abstract wallpaper design from the seventies, and she shrugged her shoulders.

'Not particularly.'

She looked from the cup to Josef, back to the cup, back to Josef. His face radiated a quiet rapture.

'You're alive,' she said.

Without taking his eyes off the cup, Josef said slowly and clearly, 'Anna. I know how we can live forever.'

She heard exactly what he said, but she still had to ask. 'What did you say?'

Josef caught her eye, put down the cup, and placed his hands on her cheeks. His hands were still warm from the blanket.

'I know. What to do. So that we don't have to die. Ever.'

She covered his hands with hers and whispered, 'Not so loud. If the doctors hear you, they'll kill you. They'll be out of work.'

Josef didn't appreciate the joke. He pulled his hands away. She caught them before he managed to tuck them under the blanket, gave them a squeeze.

'Sorry. But it does sound a bit odd, you know.'

Josef sat like a statue for a few seconds. Then he nodded. 'Yes. But it's true. We can live forever, if we want to.'

A nurse appeared and called out his name. With Anna's help he got to his feet and together they went into the cubicle. Anna watched as they stuck needles into him, listened to his heart and felt at him. All the time a quiet happiness shone from his eyes.

Later a doctor came to look at Josef's results. He was almost two metres tall, with thick black eyebrows; he frowned with concern as he read through the notes.

'We need to keep you in overnight. At least,' he said, handing the folder back to the nurse. 'So we can keep you under observation.'

His deep bass voice brooked no disagreement, but Josef still dared to question the necessity of staying in hospital. He felt fine, apart from the itching in his hands and feet, a slight headache.

The doctor stopped in the doorway, looked at the nurse as if seeking confirmation that he had heard correctly, then took two long strides back to Josef and leaned over him.

'Your body temperature when they fished you out was twenty-two degrees.' He paused to let this sink in. When Josef didn't react, he went on, 'Do you know what that means? It mean a person is dead. Very dead indeed. So one night in hospital might not be too bad, in the scheme of things. If you consider the alternative.'

Anna placed her hands on Josef's shoulders as if to protect him. The gesture seemed to appease the doctor. He took the notes back from the nurse, looked at them again and shook his head.

'You've been...' he glanced at Anna, changed it to: 'You've *both* been incredibly lucky.' He nodded at this pronouncement, let it hang in the air and took his leave with the words, 'I'll see you tomorrow,' and hurried away.

Josef was allocated a bed and Anna had to push him up to the ward herself. There was an unusually high number of emergency patients this evening, and staff shortages were noticeable. Anna was told which lift to use and which floor she needed, and off they went.

As they reached the lifts, a door slid open.

Out of the lift came a bed, pushed by a tall, white-haired woman in a floral blouse. She could have been any age between seventy and ninety. In the bed lay a man, or the remnant of a man. He was lying on his side in the foetal position underneath a blue sheet, staring vacantly into space. His body had been eaten up by illness and lying in bed, and all that was left was a skeleton covered in skin, the vertebrae making sharp folds in the sheet.

The woman nodded to them, smiled and pushed the bed out of

the lift. She was wearing rubber boots, and set off with a sure tread. On the way to some kind of test, presumably.

'Anna!'

The lift doors were closing. She moved forward quickly, placed her hand between them and they slid open. She pushed Josef inside and pressed four. They didn't speak as the lift rose.

The Emergency Department had been busy but there was plenty of room on the ward, and Josef was allocated a private room. An extra bed was brought in for Anna, and a nurse explained that she would have to pay the relatives' rate for breakfast. When they were alone Anna moved her chair closer to the bed and leaned her arms on the rail.

'What you said before—what was that all about?'

Josef remained silent for a few seconds, then asked; 'Do you really want to know? I want you to want to know, but...do you?'

'Of course I do.'

'It's...' Josef's gaze searched the room, as if looking for a clue as to where to start. 'It's quite...what's the word...quite overwhelming.'

Anna said nothing. Josef leaned back on the bed, closed his eyes.

'You asked me before what I was thinking about as I lay there in the darkness. I don't believe I was thinking very much at all. I was very calm. Strange. I'd imagined a situation like that would be the worst thing that could happen to me. Having plenty of time to contemplate the fact that you're going to die. The panic, the terror, all that kind of stuff.

'But it wasn't like that. I thought about you, of course. About how happy we've been. I was sorry that you would be unhappy when I died. That was what hurt, I think. The idea that you would be unhappy. The image of myself. The thought that I might be... mutilated. I couldn't feel my body at all.'

Josef laughed.

'For a while I thought maybe my head was just floating around on its own. But I managed to bend my head like this, heard the life jacket rasping against my stubble. Couldn't feel it though. I could kind of hear it inside my head, because apart from that I couldn't hear anything at all. As if everything was frozen, right down inside my ears. The only diversion was when water splashed up into my eyes from time to time. Apart from that, I could just as easily have been in outer space.

'But what tormented me was the thought that perhaps I looked horrible, that they would eventually find me and you'd have to come and identify me. And at the same time I hoped I *would* be found so that you wouldn't...'

A sob juddered through Anna's body as she breathed out. Josef placed his hand on her head. 'I'm sorry. I realise it must have been...I mean, I can imagine how I'd feel if you...'

Anna shook her head, wiped the tears from her eyes. 'It's just... go on.'

Josef sighed. 'So anyway, I was very calm apart from that. No fear of death, nothing like that. And after a while, when I was thinking about those insect traps I used to make when I was little... a glass jar, buried in the ground. How they could be improved. Then...'

Josef's hand reached for Anna's. She took it and squeezed it. The skin was still hot, dry, and his hand was shaking. She looked up at him. His eyes were wide open, staring at the wall opposite the bed.

'...then death came.'

Josef screwed up his eyes, opened them again. 'This is really hard to explain. It was as if I was a glove, and death...was putting me on. It came into me, slowly and...'

Josef fell silent and let go of Anna's hand. His eyes were still gazing unseeingly at the wall, or through it, out towards the sea far away. Anna asked, 'Did you start to feel warm?'

He shook his head. 'On the contrary. I could no longer feel the cold from the sea, but death came like a more intense cold inside me. I think it found its way in under my toenails and moved...upwards.'

Josef coughed. Breathed in and choked, coughed even more. He leaned forward, retching, and Anna stroked his back as he waved his hand and said, '...I'm fine...' between coughs.

When the coughing abated and Josef was leaning back on the pillows with tears in his eyes from the exertion, Anna said, 'Well, this isn't so strange. I can understand it must have been, what did you say, overwhelming, but...'

He cleared his throat. 'It's not that. I'm absolutely convinced that it wasn't coming from my own body. When I said I was like a glove that death was putting on, that's exactly what I meant. Do you understand?'

'Yes, I suppose it would probably feel like that.'

Josef shook his head.

'It didn't "feel like that". It *was* like that. Death is something that comes from outside. A big parasite that enters the body, stays there for a while, gathers what it needs, then leaves the body. Then you're dead. That's the way it is.'

Josef nodded slowly to himself, rubbing a corner of the sheet between his fingers. Suddenly he said, almost defiantly, 'It's colourless. It changes shape. At least when it's in the water. It can think. It has a language. You can talk to it.'

'Did you talk to it?'

Josef gazed searchingly into Anna's eyes, looking for any sign that she might be making fun of him. He found none. He shook his head. 'No. It's heard everything. There's nothing to say. In that situation.' He sucked at the corner of the sheet and went on, 'We human beings are just...material to them.'

Tentatively Anna asked, 'What do you mean, *them*?'

Josef looked at her, glanced shiftily to the side as if she'd asked an unusually stupid question, then said, 'Well, there are lots of them, of course.' He snorted. 'It's a big planet, after all.'

He seemed to be on the point of saying something else, but stopped himself and said instead, 'I'm sorry. This is hard to believe. I understand that. Sorry.' He took her hand again, said imploringly, 'But listen…that's how it *is*. I'm absolutely certain. Death, Anna, is a creature capable of thought. There are ways of…negotiating with it.'

Anna nodded and got to her feet. For a while she had been aware of a clicking sound from Josef's tongue when he was speaking. 'Would you like a drink of water?' she asked. 'Or…?'

Josef smiled.

'It's all right, I'm not afraid it's going to leap out of the tap or anything, it's not like that. Yes please.'

Anna gave a slightly forced laugh and went over to the washbasin, filled a paper cup and gave it to Josef, who knocked it back in one. His movements suddenly seemed easier, his expression clearer. The happiness was there again. Anna would have preferred to talk about pleasant things, forget all this. But still she said; 'But you're alive. You're sitting here.'

Josef nodded. 'Yes. I was rescued before it had finished. It left me. When the boat came…when I saw the boat and thought, *I'm going to live after all*, it withdrew. Slowly. Like when…like when we've made love and I pull out really slowly so that it won't hurt. Like that.'

That thought gave birth to the next one. He glanced at Anna's belly and asked, 'And how are *you* feeling?'

Anna stroked her stomach absentmindedly. Somewhere deep inside there was a life, as small as a dust mote, like a tick.

'I don't know. I feel…empty. Empty and happy.'

They didn't sleep much during the night. The unfamiliar surroundings and the itching in Josef's hands and feet kept them awake. They lay close together in Josef's narrow bed, made up a story together and played twenty questions. In the morning Josef was discharged from the hospital.

Anna was not by nature a sceptic. Gabriella, the only friend from art school she still saw, once told her that she almost fell in front of a subway train. At the very last moment a great hand had caught her and pushed her back up onto the platform. Gabriella believed it was her guardian angel. Anna didn't contradict her. Personally, she didn't believe in angels and that kind of thing, but you couldn't rule out the possibility.

What worried her about Josef's vision was the business of not dying, of living forever. That was a little bit more serious than seeing a ghost, for example.

They would talk about it in due course. Josef had experienced something that had come between them. It would take several evenings of conversation before they got back in step. But they would. They had to.

One day passed. Two, three. The supervisor at the nursery realised that Josef needed time to recover, and suggested he sign himself off for a week at least.

He stayed at home during the day, and Anna had no real contact with him. He did little jobs in the garden, brought up seaweed and spread it around the shrubs and on the vegetable patch. He got the boat back from the coastguard and tried to fix the engine. When he couldn't do it himself, he took it over to the marina to be repaired. He spent a lot of time down on the jetty, gazing out to sea.

On the fourth day a fat envelope arrived. It was full of drawings from the children at the nursery: 'GET WELL SOON' and 'HOP YOU SOON FEEL BETER', written, by those who could, in spidery letters. Most of the drawings were the usual red cottages with the sun and a tree. A couple showed a matchstick man lying in a billowing sea. The children had obviously been told what had happened.

Anna was making an omelette for lunch. Suddenly she heard Josef laughing out loud, the first real laughter she had heard from him in four days. She switched off the hotplate and went over to him. He was still laughing as he held out a drawing.

The picture, which must have been done by one of the older children, showed a person floating in the water. The child had talent; the figure was more than a matchstick man, and you could tell that it was supposed to be Josef from the medium-length brown hair.

The surface of the water was represented by blue wavy strokes that crossed the figure at approximately chest height. On the left-hand side a boat was on its way into the picture. Nothing remarkable there. The funny part was what was beneath the figure. A shark. An enormous shark with its mouth wide open, heading for the figure's feet. A speech bubble coming out of the man's mouth contained one word: 'HELPHELP'.

Josef doubled up with laughter. Anna smiled and placed her hand on the back of his neck. He looked up at her with tears in his eyes. Pointed at the drawing, said, 'helphelp', and started laughing again.

He rocked back and forth, clutching his stomach. The laughter slipped into a long drawn-out howl that was hacked to pieces, became a sob. Anna fell to her knees next to Josef's chair and put her arms around him. After a while the sobbing subsided, he extracted his arms from her embrace and hugged her back. Everything went quiet. Anna stroked his back, said, 'You're alive. You're alive. You're here. With me.'

'It's too much. I can't.'

'Josef. You nearly died. It's going to take time.'

He shook his head vigorously as if to chase away an unpleasant thought. 'It's not that. It's just that I know…what to do.'

'What to do?'

'To avoid dying. Ever. It's driving me crazy.'

Anna took a deep breath. Many times over the past few days she had asked him how he was feeling, tried to get him to talk about the accident, but he had avoided the topic, answered in monosyllables or said he didn't want to talk about it at the moment.

But here it was in all its simplicity: Josef still thought he had discovered the key to the secret mankind had been seeking for thousands of years, and Anna knew this was impossible. A wall between them.

Knew?

She knew nothing.

With an imperceptible effort she cleared her brain of all preconceptions and prepared to listen to him, to believe him if possible. Quietly she said, 'OK. Tell me.'

'You won't believe me.'

'We'll see. If it's as you say, and I can believe it, then we'll talk about what we're going to do. Together.'

Josef shook his head mechanically for a long time, then said, 'I can't talk about it. There's only one thing I want to know: do you want to live with me? Forever?'

The question was posed in such a way that there was no room for manoeuvre. Anna was silent for a moment, then said the only thing she could say. She said: 'Yes.'

Josef gave a brief nod. 'OK.' His gaze returned to the drawing. Anna took it away.

'Josef, I can't cope with this. You have to tell me what's going on.'

'If I tell you, you won't believe me. Not until you've seen it.'

'Seen *what*?'

Josef reached out his hand; she thought he was going to caress her cheek, and was about to move back—she didn't want to be patted like a child who understood nothing. But his hand kept on moving downwards, to the drawing in her hand. Pointed at the shark. His index finger right in the middle of its mouth.

'That.'

———

Autumn was turning into winter.

The summer visitors no longer came out to their cottages. The jetties in the bay stretched out into the grey sea like frozen fingers, robbed of the boats that clothed them. The larger ones had been taken to Gräddö Marina to be stored over the winter, while the smaller ones had been taken out of the water and lay along the shoreline, turned upside down and as helpless as a beetle on its back.

The first snow came one night in the middle of November.

When Anna went for a morning walk through the area where the summer cottages were, she could see tracks—hare, deer, maybe foxes—crossing the deserted gardens. She smiled at a set of hare tracks heading into a garden where something, presumably garden furniture, was piled up and hidden beneath a tarpaulin. The tracks reached the artificial hillock, then disappeared. But on the thin layer of snow covering the tarpaulin there were skid marks. As if the hare had tried to clamber up. Or played at sliding down. At night, when there was no one to see.

Anna liked the idea that in winter the animals reclaimed this place, where man had pushed his way in only fifty years earlier with his holiday dreams. In fact, she liked the whole area better in winter. In the summer there was a kind of desperate relaxation cult, with barbecues sizzling, glasses clinking, games of Jenga tumbling down, and shrieks of joy or frustration slicing through the air day and night.

In the winter the houses regained their souls. Oh, not

extraordinary haunted-house souls, just little section-built-cottage souls, but still. Covered in snow, guarding their empty gardens, the cottages had a kind of dignity they lacked in the summer. They looked as if they were capable of thought.

When Anna got home she lit the paraffin heater in the garage. Soon it would be too cold to work in there, and she would have to move her paintings into the cottage for a couple of months. Even now she needed to wear fingerless gloves to stop her hands seizing up. She made herself a cup of camomile tea with honey, sat down and looked at her current project.

Current?

She had been working on it for three years; nobody could accuse her of losing faith just because it was a lost cause.

Persistent, that's what she was. Or stupid, she thought sometimes.

It had begun as a practice piece and turned into the only thing she worked on in her free time, her seagull-free time.

She called the series Adjectives; it now comprised some fifty canvases. She just began with an adjective; among others she had already painted *Round*, *Hard*, *Yellow* and *Sad*. The simple words, the basic words that exist in every language in one form or another.

She remembered she had thought it would be *easy*, a little exercise while she was waiting for inspiration. It wasn't. The majority of the paintings, particularly those from the first year, no longer had anything to say to her. She was very pleased with a few of the recent ones, but no doubt she would change her mind.

When she was in despair she often thought of Claude Monet and how he painted that bloody lily pond over and over again for five years. But there was a difference: Claude Monet was a great artist; Anna Bergvall had held *one* exhibition, with some of her contemporaries from art school, and the only thing she had managed to sell to an outsider was *Open*.

The woman with the big earrings and severe lips who bought the painting said she liked its powerful erotic charge. Anna had accepted the two thousand-kronor notes and nodded in agreement. When the woman had gone and Anna was finally able to attach the red dot indicating that the painting was sold, she had scrutinised it carefully to try and fathom out what the hell the woman was talking about.

In a fiery blue landscape stood a mountain pool, in the middle of which the outline of a door was just visible. Fir trees half-hidden in the mist stood guard around the pool, their branches outspread. Where was the erotic charge the woman could see?

When she told Josef and described the woman, he said he wasn't at all surprised. The woman had tried to come on to him at the private view, and no doubt she saw an erotic charge in *everything*.

Anna put down her cup and contemplated the painting on which she was working. It was called *Vanished*, and there was a lot of white. The idea was that the person looking at the picture would get the impression that something *had* been there, but was no longer there, something that had…

'Vanished,' she said to herself out loud. With fingers that were already frozen she squeezed a blob of zinc white onto her palette, sighed and tried to get down to work.

Josef came home later than usual. Later than he used to *before*, that is. These days it could sometimes be two hours or more between the time he finished work and the time she heard the Toyota's gloomy roar in the driveway.

Anna was standing at the bedroom window. In the glow of the outside light she saw him get out of the car, pick up a carrier bag from the front passenger seat, plug in the heating cable and set off towards the house. She felt nervous, but couldn't quite put her finger on it. It was as if she needed to arrange her expression. Greet him in the right way. Despite the fact that it was only Josef, her nearest and dearest.

But he had changed. The laughter was no longer quite so close to the surface these days. More often than in the past he got caught up in a thought, and remained there. She had hinted that perhaps he ought to let someone help him work through the accident, but Josef wouldn't hear of it. He was doing fine on his own.

And perhaps he was. Anna hoped so.

When the front door opened she went into the hallway and welcomed him home with a kiss. He returned her kiss, caressed her cheek. 'Hi, how's things?'

Anna shrugged her shoulders. 'Wasted a bit of paint, made some reasonable cakes, waited around a bit. That's it, really. What have you been up to?'

Josef hung up his outdoor clothes and shook the bag he was carrying. 'Library.'

Anna nodded. That was where he was when he didn't come home. In the library. It the living room there were piles of books by Bertrand Russell, Schopenhauer, Nietzsche and Simone Weil. Among others. Josef had started reading philosophy, or rather he had *started borrowing books about philosophy.* He never actually read them. They just sat there.

He took a couple of books by Wittgenstein out of the bag to add to his collection. They had already had a couple of reminders about books he hadn't read, and the piles were growing.

He placed a hand over her belly. 'How's the tummy feeling?'

'It feels good. Unreal still, but it feels good.'

'I'm looking forward to seeing it grow.'

'Are you?'

'Yes, of course.'

He took his hand away, and Anna replaced it with hers.

The winter came to nothing. The coldest days had been in November, and Anna was able to continue working in the garage after Christmas and New Year.

They spent Christmas with Anna's parents, but came home on Boxing Day when Josef couldn't stand it any longer. Anna didn't mind. The family's solicitousness around her pregnancy almost suffocated her.

The snow that fell at the beginning of January quickly melted away, and Josef didn't need to take the boat out of the water this year as there was no risk of ice.

Anna had begun to show. She didn't have a real baby bump yet, but it was there, and a few days into the new year she felt the first movement. A little fish jumping.

The heavy atmosphere around Josef had lightened somewhat, and now that Anna no longer needed to be the cheerful one, she took the opportunity to have a crisis. Perhaps it was the growing child that put things in a different perspective: what the hell was she actually doing?

One Monday morning in the middle of January she was standing in front of her paintings, seriously thinking that the best thing would be to set fire to the lot. Stop trying. Stop thinking. Just paint seabirds on bits of wood, look after her children and bake bread.

She wandered around the house doing bits and pieces for a couple of hours. Towards midday she was overcome by a sense of melancholy and isolation. She had been a sociable person in Stockholm, with lots of friends and acquaintances. Now she was sitting in a miserable little cottage, and in five months she would give birth to a child and be stuck for ever. *This is your life.*

Panic threatened to overwhelm her, and the only thing she could think of to suppress it was to take a trip to Norrtälje. See a few people. Go to the library, perhaps. Wait for Josef there, see what was on at the cinema.

Yes. That would have to do.

She walked up to the bus stop and stood there moping with her hands in her pockets, thinking that she ought to take up smoking again. The landscape around her made her feel that way. Mist in the air, sodden fir trees surrounded by dirty snowdrifts, traversed by a grey road with the white lines in the centre worn away. Next to her there was a notice board, but the bus timetable had been ripped down. Somebody had scrawled 'BASTARD VISITORS GO HOME' on the wall of the shelter. Perfect for a smoke. Unfortunately she had given up five years ago, and while taking up the habit again during pregnancy would be an original idea, it wasn't very clever.

The bus came, cheerily red. She felt slightly better as she sat down by a window and looked out at more sodden fir trees, more dirty snow. At least she was on the move now.

In Norrtälje she wandered around the shops for a while. Spent some time in H&M fingering a little snowsuit with stars and moons on it, which she couldn't buy because they didn't have much money and because the family had given them bags full of baby stuff over Christmas and because if you assume that everything is going to be fine it will probably all go wrong and anyway the snowsuit was probably made by an Asian child with a chain around its ankle and fuck it all.

She went to the off-licence on the other side of the street and bought a small bottle of whisky instead. Shoved the bag into her coat pocket.

I am a bad person, she thought as she walked up to the library. It felt like a relief.

It was only half past three; Josef probably hadn't arrived yet. She stopped outside the library and looked at an old poster informing her that one of the more famous battles from the American Civil War would be re-created in a field outside the town one weekend in

August. Hot dogs and stalls. All welcome.

This is your—

Then she caught sight of Josef in the café next door to the library. She was about to raise her arm and wave, but stopped. He hadn't seen her, because he was completely absorbed in conversation with the person opposite him. The paper bag in her pocket rustled as Anna squeezed it. The person was a woman: slim, long-haired and with slender hands that moved slowly in the air as she spoke.

Josef looked up and spotted her. When their eyes met, Anna just wanted to run away. He looked as if he had been *caught out*. So what she had imagined in her darkest hours was true.

The future exploded into a thousand pieces.

The other person turned to face the window. It wasn't a woman. It was a man who looked like seven years of famine and seven years even worse than that. A face so hollow that it was impossible to tell how old he was. His hair, she could see now, was unwashed and hung down in lank strands over ridiculously sunken cheeks. Big, shining eyes.

But Anna had *thought* it was a woman.

We've drifted apart.

She went inside. Josef met her in the doorway, gave her a hug. 'Hi. What are you doing here?'

Anna let go first. 'I'm just…just having a little wander round. Couldn't cope with being at home.' She nodded in the direction of the table. 'Who's that?'

Josef glanced over his shoulder. 'Oh, just…just a friend.'

Anna made a vague noise, as if it was perfectly natural for Josef to have friends she'd never heard of. As if they had that kind of relationship.

Josef made no move to let her in, so she pushed past and went over to the table, her hand outstretched.

'Hello, I'm Anna—Josef's…'

The man looked up at her, and Anna recoiled.

At close quarters his face carried the mark of death. Nothing but bones and pale skin, hanging loose with no flesh to adhere to. Narrow, chapped lips, and above them a nose that would have been comically large in the disappearing face, if the whole thing hadn't looked so dreadful. The eyes, burning bright, were looking at her. He didn't take her hand, but whispered, 'Sorry. Bit of a cold, better not...' He nodded in the direction of her stomach. 'With the baby and everything.'

Josef came over to the table, wringing his hands nervously. As if he were introducing his boss to his wife, he said, 'This is Karl-Axel.'

Anna managed to produce a smile. 'Karl-Axel.'

The man made a small sound of disagreement and said, 'Kaxe.'

'Sorry?'

'Kaxe. That's what I'm usually called.'

'Kaxe?'

'Mmm.'

Anna nodded. Kaxe nodded. Josef nodded. Anyone watching through the window would have thought they were all in perfect agreement.

An uncomfortable silence. Anna looked around. Three men with a southern European appearance were sitting by the newspaper section, absorbed in old news from their homelands. She didn't know what to say, so gesturing towards the street outside she asked, 'So do you live here?'

Without the slightest hint of a smile Kaxe replied, 'No, I just come in here for a cup of tea.'

I can't do this.

On another day she might have been able to make an effort in order to penetrate the barriers of hostility between her and Kaxe, but not today. So instead she said, with exaggerated briskness, 'Anyway,

I must…get on.' She glanced at Josef and added, 'Have a nice time,' and turned to leave.

Kaxe raised his hand.

'Sail in peace, sister.'

She got out into the street and had no idea where to go. Nothing had actually *happened*. Except that everything was…wrong.

As she had expected, Josef came hurrying after her.

'Anna…Anna?' he said.

'Hi.'

'Don't you want to come in?'

'No, it all felt a bit too…difficult.'

Josef looked down at the ground, chewing his lower lip. 'I was thinking…of inviting him round one day?'

'Right. Yes. Fine.'

This approval didn't make Josef any happier. He folded his arms, kept moving his feet up and down. Anna waited. She was well aware that he was on the point of telling her what this was all about, and she was equally well aware when the impulse left him. He put his face close to hers and said, 'Trust me.'

She threw her hands wide. 'Josef, I don't understand.'

'You will. I promise.'

'Josef, this isn't good. You talking like this, the fact that we… that we can't…'

Josef clamped his lips together.

'I know, I know, I know. It's for our sake, OK? I promise. I love you. I love you.'

A sense of grief swept through Anna. Something had been lost here, on the steps outside Norrtälje library. But still she said, 'I love you too. What *are* you up to?'

Josef looked slightly relieved.

'Soon,' he said with a grin. 'It's a kind of surprise for your birthday.' He laughed. 'When it's ready I'll tell you everything. OK?'

Anna nodded, even though it wasn't OK at all. She went into the library and browsed listlessly through the CDs for a while. Then Josef came in and they went home in the car together.

He asked how her work had gone, and she said it was crap. It was pointless, all of it. He tried to console her, telling her that she'd done so much that was really good, maybe it was to do with the child, things were bound to improve. He did it mechanically. His mind was elsewhere.

While Anna was in the library, it had been decided that Kaxe would come to visit them on Thursday.

Those days, those days between Christmas and New Year...

Josef was somehow transformed once again. Before he went to work on Tuesday he laid out her breakfast and wrote her a little note: he would be lost without her, she meant everything to him. When he got home he was full of affection, stroking her arm, her back, the nape of her neck at every opportunity. He wanted to get close to her again, wanted to get back in. But he wanted it *now*, he wanted it *quickly*, and it was like carrying out an archaeological dig with a great big mechanical digger. Things got broken along the way.

She spent the mornings staring at her paintings and searching her heart and mind. She ruined a beautiful piece of driftwood by painting Kulkan from Dungeons and Dragons on it, complete with grazing sheep. But she made the sheep into skeletons, grazing in a meadow where the grass was fingers, the sun a grinning skull.

When she took a step back and looked at the painting as a whole, she felt happy with something she'd done for the first time in a couple of months. The combination of tourist kitsch and romantic horror had something. The fact that the picture had been dashed off quickly didn't matter at all; the blurred lines gave it a dreamlike quality.

For the rest of the day she felt happier than she had for a long time. She did bits and pieces around the house, listening to her body. The child was there. Even when it wasn't kicking or moving she could feel its presence like a faintly perceived tickling sensation, another person in the room. There were two of them now.

When Josef got home she showed him the driftwood picture and he laughed until he cried. Said he would happily have coughed up two thousand for it if he'd been a visitor. She gave it to him. He said he was going to hang it in the staffroom at the nursery, perhaps with a little sign saying SMOKING KILLS.

'Sheep don't usually smoke, Josef.'

'No, but these did, and look what happened.'

That evening Josef talked about Kaxe. He was a philosopher, or at least a student of philosophy. He had read through the history of philosophy and had come out on the other side feeling totally disillusioned. He was the most depressing person Josef had ever met. As if to prove the idea that inner emptiness leads to disease, he had contracted leukaemia and had only a year to live at the most.

While Josef was telling her this, he kept biting his nails. Anna gently took his hand and moved it away from his mouth.

'Josef, what *is* it?'

'Nothing, I just...I feel sorry for him.'

Anna took a deep breath. 'This business with...with Kaxe. Does it have anything to do with your accident?'

Josef's little finger found its way back to his teeth. He nibbled on the nail for a while, then said, 'He wants to die.'

Anna waited for the next bit, but nothing came. In the silence the words still hung in the air. *He wants to die.* She opened her mouth to get him to continue, but Josef got there first. 'What were you thinking of doing on Thursday?'

'On Thursday?'

'Yes. When he comes round.'

It hadn't occurred to her to do anything special on Thursday. She laughed. 'You mean…what am I going to wear when I'm serving the food? Fishnet stockings, maybe?'

Josef turned up the corners of his mouth, turned them down again. 'No, I thought…maybe you'd prefer not to be here.'

'Don't you want me to be here?'

He didn't say anything. Which answered the question. She felt a sudden surge of fury: at his bloody secrecy, his nail biting, at the fact that he didn't give a damn how she was feeling, and why was she showing such exaggerated consideration just because he'd been involved in an accident *almost four months ago, for fuck's sake*, and she said, 'Well, I was thinking of putting the heater on in the garage soon anyway, so I can do that on Thursday. I can sit out there and have a lovely time by the fire all on my own while you two…do whatever the fuck you're going to do.'

She got up from the sofa, picked up the book on top of the pile on the coffee table—Leibniz' *Pre-established Harmony*—and hurled it on his knee when he tried to get to his feet.

'Sit down. Read a fucking book. I can go and see Gabriella on Thursday. What time am I allowed to come back?'

Josef looked tormented. He clasped his hands and held them out in front of him, pleading.

'Anna…please. Don't be like that. I…' He closed his mouth abruptly. Then answered her last question as if she had meant it seriously.

'It would be best if…if you came home on Thursday night.'

'So I don't need to stay over? Thanks very much.'

Josef sighed. 'Please, Anna, if you could just…'

'Thursday night. Right. Fine. That's sorted then.'

She left him and went off to bed.

Wednesday passed in mutual silence. Anna started sketching out a new piece, a small island with a single, huge tree on it. From one of the tree's branches dangled a woman, hanging from a rope. But her body was drawn so that roots were emerging from her feet, working their way down into the ground beneath the tree, and her skin was turning into bark.

She didn't bother transferring it to a piece of wood. She realised nobody would buy it, because it didn't have the black humour of the skeleton sheep. It was the kind of picture that might make the neighbours look away if they met her by chance by the mailboxes: *And she always seemed so nice.*

She rang Gabriella who of course said fantastic brilliant really looking forward to seeing you on Thursday evening kiss kiss.

Josef came home and they avoided an argument, kept out of each other's way. He went down to the jetty and messed around with the boat. When she heard the engine start up her heart missed a beat. She ran to the kitchen window with a feeling that *he's leaving me... he's disappearing...*

But the boat was still moored by the jetty, and Josef was standing on board revving the engine. When he had finished she quickly moved back so that he wouldn't see her watching. After all, she didn't care about him.

In the evening they watched some stupid film with Jim Carrey in it, where he and another guy ran around being idiots. In a couple of places she noted, 'I could have laughed here', but didn't.

When the film was over there was nothing to add, so they went to bed. Anna could feel Josef's anger coming from his side of the bed like an electric cloud, but she took no notice. She'd tried. Enough was enough.

Instead she lay awake with her hands resting on her stomach. She could feel sleepy, fumbling movements from inside, and she pressed her hands down gently in response.

She had almost fallen asleep when Josef got out of bed and crept into the kitchen. The light went on, the fridge was opened. After a while she could hear the crunch as he ate a piece of crispbread. She drew up her legs, pressed her hands between her thighs. She wasn't just angry. She was afraid too.

She wanted to go to Josef, sit beside him and talk, talk, talk until dawn. Sort things out, find some transparency. But she didn't dare. Didn't want to see his expression when she appeared in the doorway. His face might close down, rejecting her. Pushing her away yet again.

She would rather lie here and embrace the only thing she was sure of.

She fell asleep before Josef came back.

When she woke up on Thursday morning Josef had already gone, taking an early bus so that she could have the car. There was a note on the kitchen table.

Darling Anna.
It's two o'clock in the morning and I'm going to bed in a minute to see if I can get some sleep.
I know I've been strange and difficult to be with lately, but from tomorrow everything will be better. Much better. I promise.
Can you come back around 11 or 12 tonight? Please. It's important.
And remember I love you. Always and forever.
Your
Josef

Later Anna would wish she had followed her instinct and stayed at home. Grabbed Josef's head, threatened him with divorce and forced him to tell her what he was up to. But she didn't have the strength. She wanted to see Gabriella, talk to somebody outside the situation about how things were. She was wandering around in a porridge of pregnancy, darkness and slush. She needed some distance. So with a chorus of warning bells ringing in her ears she got in the car just after one o'clock and left Josef to his fate. She ended up in a convoy of trucks from Kapellskär that dragged her along with them all the way to Stockholm.

Gabriella's one-room apartment was a time machine. Twenty-seven square metres in Midsommarkransen, cluttered with finished and half-finished canvases, photographs, flyers about exhibitions, pictures downloaded and printed from the internet, clothes. Anna caught herself thinking *For God's sake, grow up.*

They were both thirty-one, and Gabriella was still in exactly the same place Anna had been eight years earlier. A sub-let apartment, no long-term relationship, no job. She probably read Nemi.

Maybe I'm just jealous?

Gabriella had made crêpes, which they ate in the tiny kitchen with a view of the carpark while Gabriella talked about her latest application to the University College of Art and Design, samples of her work, hassle with some Hungarian she'd met at a private view, how she'd started pinching stuff from shops as a protest. Anna sang the first line of 'Shoplifters of the World Unite' and Gabriella joined in for a few bars. She put down her cutlery and rested her chin on her hands.

'And how are things with you two?'

Anna shrugged. 'Fine.'

When Gabriella didn't say anything, she added, 'I'm not really in the mood for work, but that could be to do with the baby. Do you remember that series I started...'

They went back to talking about art. Anna didn't feel like talking about her life. She knew what Gabriella would say. *You can't let your life be ruled by his nightmares. Set yourself free, for God's sake.* Easy to say when you've never been faithful to the same person for longer than a year. Easy to say when you're not pregnant and you live in a one-room apartment in Midsommarkransen. Easy to say when you've never loved, expecting it to last forever. So they talked about art.

In the evening they went into the city and headed for Pelikan, their regular haunt from the old days. Perhaps that was a mistake; there they sat, the same people in the same place as before. It became painfully obvious that they *weren't* the same people anymore. At least, Anna wasn't.

They reminisced about school, talked about what had become of old friends. When the conversation flagged they both started looking elsewhere: Gabriella flirted with a guy with dreadlocks, Anna eyed up the clock above the bar. When it finally reached nine-thirty, she said, 'Sorry. There's something I have to do at home. I think I'd better make a move.'

Gabriella finished off her third beer. 'No surprise there.'

Anna got up with a mixture of relief and a guilty conscience. It hadn't turned out the way she expected at all; she hadn't said a word about her real problems. It felt like a betrayal of their friendship.

Fuck it all. As long as she got home.

They kissed and hugged and said they must get together again soon and it was all lies and as Anna hurried out of the bar she saw the dreadlock guy heading over to take her place and be much better company.

She almost ran the five blocks to the car. She would be home too early, but now she'd made the decision it felt more as if she would be home too late, whatever that might mean.

He wants to die.

She scraped the car in front with her bumper as she jolted out of her tiny parking space and headed across the city towards Roslagstull. Sweat trickled down her back from the running and her growing anxiety.

Right now Josef was sitting in their house with a man who wanted to die. She could see a possible connection, and hoped to God she was wrong.

When she turned into their drive her head was spinning after an hour listening to the din of the Toyota doing 140. The silence was intense when she switched off the engine and got out of the car. The outside light shone with a welcoming glow, and everything looked just the way it always did. She walked towards the house, thinking that if everything was OK she would…withdraw, somehow. Go and sit in the garage, perhaps.

What's become of us?

The silence was just as palpable as she walked up the steps to the porch. No talking, no laughter. She opened the front door. The light was on in the hallway, and in the kitchen. On the kitchen table stood a half-full bottle of whisky and two glasses. A bag of ice cubes in a little puddle of water.

'Hello?'

She looked out of the kitchen window. Impenetrable darkness.

From the magnetic holder above the sink she took the carbon steel knife they had invested in last winter, sharp as a razor blade. No reason, it just felt good to have it in her hand. In the bottom drawer she found the torch. She went back outside. Down towards the jetty.

The beam of the torch made the familiar somehow alien and threatening. She lit her way across the rocks, slippery with slush, saw the slimy backs of whales, an eye opening in a crevice. She went on, out onto the jetty, treading carefully on the wet planks. She shone the torch over the edge, and it was as she feared.

The boat was gone.

There wasn't a sound to be heard out in the bay. There was only the lighthouse on Fårholm reef, sending out its monotonous, silent light signal, which made the darkness in between even darker.

She sat down on the jetty, feeling the dampness soaking through her trousers. Switched off the torch.

When she had been sitting there for maybe ten minutes, she heard the engine of a boat start up. She couldn't judge how far away it was, perhaps five hundred metres. It sounded like their boat. The sound came closer. Her heart began to beat faster and she got up, fingering the torch. But she didn't switch it on for fear of...frightening him away.

What's become of us?

All of this could still be...normal. Josef had taken Kaxe out for a little trip to show him the boat. Or something. They were drunk and happy and felt like a little outing in the dark.

And I'm Claude Monet.

After a couple of minutes she was able to make out the boat as a vague white dot which grew in size and clarity. There was something ominous about the sound of the approaching engine across the dark waters. A monster making its way ashore from the seas. And yet she remained on the jetty, erect, almost standing to attention. The knife lay at her feet, and instead she clutched the reassuring weight of the old torch.

There was something wrong about the way the boat was coming in. It was moving too fast. The engine was switched off and the boat crashed into the jetty, which juddered beneath her feet.

'Fucking hell...'

Josef's voice. A slapping sound as his hand found the jetty. She could hear him panting in the darkness. She took a step forward, said, 'Hi...'

Josef screamed. There was a dull thud as he lost his grip on the jetty and fell backwards into the boat; he screamed again, this time with pain. She switched on the torch. Josef was lying in the central well with his head against the gunwale. He looked like a terrified animal, paralysed by the headlights of a car. His hand shot up instinctively to shade his eyes from the light. Anna switched off the torch again, said, 'Sorr—'

Before she got the word out of her mouth her brain had managed to register what her eyes had seen during those brief seconds of light. Next to Josef lay Karl-Axel with his mouth open, his eyes open, and an almost...ecstatic expression on his face. Pupils blown. Dead.

'For fuck's sake, you frightened the life out of me.'

Josef got to his feet and grabbed hold of the jetty once more. Anna shook her head. This couldn't be happening. They were Josef and Anna who suited each other so well and had a house by the sea and were having a baby and this couldn't be happening.

Josef crawled onto the jetty and made the boat fast. Anna was still shaking her head. As long as she kept on doing that, it wasn't real. She whispered, 'What have you done...what have you done?'

He came up to her, grabbed her by the shoulders and hugged her. She pushed him away because his body was in the way; it stopped her shaking her head.

'Anna, this is what he wanted. I just helped him.'

'You...you killed him.'

'No.' His hand squeezed her shoulder as if to emphasise the point. 'I helped him to die. There's a huge difference. Anna...'

'But...why? Why? You'll end up...it's...'

Josef took hold of her face, forced her head to stop moving. Then he said, 'Death is in him. It's there. Now.'

'Death...'

'Yes. It's in his body. It can't get out. It's ours.'

He pushed her gently downwards until they were both sitting on the jetty, facing one another.

A damp wind blew in off the sea, flicking a strand of her hair across her cheek. She grabbed it, wound it around her forefinger—a lifeline back to what was familiar. She pulled it; pain in the skin on her scalp.

She took a deep breath of the salt-laden night air, and it might have been the effect of the adrenaline pumping through her body, or it might just have been a final defence against madness, but she opened her arms as if to embrace the night, the sea, and suddenly experienced a limitless freedom.

What Josef said couldn't possibly be true, but the very fact that they were sitting here together on the jetty in the cold night air, with a dead body just a few metres away...this was the end of everything, wasn't it? Nothing would ever be the same again, nothing would be the way she had thought it would be. At that point all responsibility fell from her shoulders and she was...free.

Josef's hand on her knee.

'Do you want to know?'

'I want to know.'

Her voice was clear, composed. She was simply here, now.

Josef said, 'This is what we'd decided. He came to the house. We drank a little whisky to...well, to celebrate. Then we went out to the perch reef, you know, south of Tjockö. The water's only three or four metres deep there. I tied the anchor rope around him and he jumped in. We said...what did we say? Goodbye...see you again... thanks for this...thanks for the whisky.'

He snorted; it was almost a laugh.

'The atmosphere was...funny. I suppose we were scared, both of us. Each in our own way. Then he said I should throw the anchor overboard; I asked if he was sure and he said, "No, but throw it in anyway." So I did. He disappeared beneath the surface, the rope played out a few metres, and then I sat there. Looked at the light-house. Counted the flashes.'

He cleared his throat. Anna could see the pale backs of his hands as he ran them over his face, could hear the soft rasping of stubble against his palms.

'He was just below me. I could have pulled him up if I'd wanted to.'

'But that wasn't what he wanted,' said Anna. 'Was it?'

Josef's voice had changed when he said, 'After one minute, maybe. Eight flashes. Then the rope began to...play out.'

They sat there without saying anything for a long time. Eventually Anna said, 'He was trying to pull himself up.'

'Yes.' Josef's voice broke slightly as he added: 'But I had plenty of rope. Thirty metres. And still...still he managed to use up the whole lot.'

Josef was weeping. Anna couldn't bring herself to console him. She was cold inside, hard. The child in her stomach moved a hand or a foot, and it was as if it was happening to someone else.

'What did you do?'

'Nothing. Nothing. He couldn't pull himself up. After a while it...went slack. I waited another minute. Then I pulled him up.'

Afterwards Anna found it difficult to grasp that she did what she did. It was even more difficult to understand why she felt excited while it was going on. As if they were engaged in some spine-tingling party game. Sitting around a ouija board or something. It was the only explanation she could come up with. The fact that the whole thing was unreal.

And that—*God forgive me*—she and Josef were doing something together again, were fellow conspirators in the name of love as they had always said they were in the days when everything was good between them.

They carried Kaxe up to the house. His clothes were dripping wet, and Anna found herself mopping up with a dishcloth while Josef laid out some black plastic sacks on which to lay the body.

It wasn't until they were standing side by side with their arms folded contemplating their efforts that repudiation sank its claws into her.

'Josef. We can't do this. We have to call the police. Or something. Someone who can...'

Josef shook his head and crouched down next to the dead body. He said, 'Show yourself.'

Anna's eyes widened. He really had gone mad. The here-and-now feeling evaporated, replaced by a succession of days as a single mother, explaining to her child that Daddy's in a place where they're looking after him. Josef was totally focused on the dead body. She was alone. A lonely accessory to a crime.

Silent tears began to flow when Josef kicked the body and shouted, 'I'm going to bury you, understand? You'll never be able to come back if you don't show yourself to her. She's in this too, understand? I promise. I'll burn you down on the rocks. Don't you believe me? I'll put you in the boat, pour petrol over you and...'

Anna stood there paralysed as Josef rained down curses on the corpse, threatening something that could no longer be threatened.

What...

Fluid began to trickle from one of the corpse's hands.

Her lower jaw was trembling as she crouched down beside Josef.

From the gaps beneath the fingernails, fluid was running onto the floor. No, not running. Finding its way out. It didn't spread across the floor like water, but curled into a stream that moved down towards the corpse's feet, curved around them. A snake of water, the thickness of a forearm, continued to pour out from the fingers while its other end worked its way up towards the other hand.

It then split into a delta of five thinner streams that forced their way underneath the fingernails, while at the same time the flow from the other hand ceased.

Anna put her hand to her mouth, whimpering slightly while the water snake grew shorter and shorter as it disappeared back into the body. A few glittering droplets remained on the tips of the fingers, until they too disappeared. It had gone.

She no longer saw a person in front of her. She saw...a shell. A cold burrow where death lived. If the corpse's belly had swollen up when death crept back into its lair, the picture would have been complete.

When the telephone rang she got up on stiff legs, went over and picked up the receiver. It was completely natural. An explanation would be forthcoming: some authority or power would inform them about the new situation. These days it used the telephone.

'Hello, Anna speaking.'

Clattering, voices in the background.

'Hi, it's Gabriella. Just wanted to check that you got home OK, you seemed so...Is everything all right?'

Anna looked over at the blackness of the windowpane. Outside there was a mirror image of herself and the room in which she was standing. Behind her, Josef straightened up and went into the kitchen. The corpse was lying motionless on the plastic sacks, which looked like a black hole in the reflection, creating the illusion that the body was hovering in space. She reached out and touched the glass.

'Hello, are you there?'

Anna nodded. A voice speaking in her ear. In front of her a shadow world. The voice said, 'For fuck's sake...Anna? Are you there?'

'Yes. Yes, I'm here. Here I am.'

'Is everything OK, you sound so...'

'Everything's fine.'

'OK. Listen, that guy, the one with the dreads, he...'

Anna was no longer listening. Gabriella's voice droned on in her ear, but Anna was caught up in the reflection. If she opened the window she would be able to step into that world, just like Alice in Wonderland. She moved her hand, waved. The other Anna waved. In the background Josef reappeared.

She turned around. Josef was holding one hand as if he had something in it. She couldn't see what it was. With the other hand he gestured towards the phone, telling her to hang up.

Gabriella was still talking. Anna said, 'Sorry, I haven't got time right now. Talk to you soon,' and hung up.

'Who was that?'

'Gabriella.'

'What did she want?'

Anna dabbed at her lips with her fingers, said 'I don't know', then moved her fingers in the direction of the corpse. 'This...this... is very...is very...'

'Overwhelming?'

'No...it's not that...' Her voice sounded distant, as if she was talking to herself on the phone, long distance. '...I'd say, without... that this is absolutely...disgusting. This is absolutely disgusting. I think it's absolutely disgusting. This.'

'But do you believe me now?'

'Yes. Yes. But the idea...the idea that I would want us to...Josef. There's...there's a snake inside him. In our house. Now.'

Josef shook his head.

'It isn't a snake anymore. It's spread right through his body. As it did with me.'

'Yes. But...' The words just wouldn't come to her. She sat down on the sofa, avoided looking at the corpse. 'Don't you think...this is disgusting?'

Josef sat down beside her. She could see now that the thing he was holding in his hand was a needle. He put his arm around her shoulders. Anna could hear the creaking of the boat against the jetty, the sea whispering outside the window. The sea. The snake's home. All those times she had dived, swum in that sea.

She leaned against Josef. 'We were happy as we were. Weren't we?'

Josef nodded. 'Yes. And we're going to be happy. But I couldn't just...once I knew about this...I...'

'No. I understand.' Anna thought for a moment. 'I do understand. Yes, I do.'

'Do you?'

'Yes.'

Suddenly Josef fell on her. He burrowed his head in between her breasts. She stroked his head and looked up, gazing at the corpse lying on their living room floor. She understood. If you've survived once, you want to go on. Perhaps he couldn't have done anything else. Perhaps she would have done the same thing. If she'd known.

Josef's hair was damp and stuck to her fingers as she ran them through it. It was several years since the world outside the two of them had any significance. They had talked about this.

If I die, if I go crazy, what will you do?

I'll die too, I'll go crazy too.

That was what they had said, and they had said it as if they really meant it. Time to see if it was true.

She lifted Josef's head between her hands.

'So what do we do now?'

Josef blinked, wiped the tears from his eyes. 'I...sorry, it's just so...Anna, you know I...'

'I know. What do we do now?'

Josef straightened up, sat close beside her on the sofa. 'Don't ask me how I know all this, I just...know.' He held up the needle. 'We have to give it a little blood. Then it will recognise us, and it will know that it's not allowed to touch us. It's like a...pact.'

They carried on talking. About what eternal life really meant. About whether they would cease to age, whether they might have to move from time to time in order to avoid arousing suspicion. About the fact that no one would believe them if they told their story.

When it came down to it, this was a risky enterprise. What

frightened them most was that they didn't know on behalf of what or whom the creature might be acting.

In the end Anna said, 'We either do it, or we forget about it.'

Josef took her hands. 'Do you want to do it?'

'Do you?'

'Yes.'

'Then let's do it.'

They got up from the sofa and approached the body. Perhaps it was her imagination, but Anna thought she could see small twitching movements, tics on its skin. Perhaps the creature was impatient to be set free, to return to its element.

They crouched down by the head and looked into each other's eyes. Even though they had now reached the nub of the whole thing, Josef's expression was calm. Perhaps because he no longer had to carry the entire burden of the decision. Anna felt numb, hypnotised. As if she really had stepped through the window and was now in the looking-glass world where the rules are different. Where the only transgression is to question.

Josef had warned her in advance: the creature could manipulate the dead body. On the way back in the boat it had used Kaxe's voice to conduct a conversation. So there was nothing to be afraid of if it made some kind of movement. Anna didn't think she would be afraid. She was beyond such things.

Josef held out the needle. 'You or me first?'

Anna looked at the sliver of silver in his hand and giggled. A few lines flashed through her mind: *The junkies' wedding: a shared needle,* and she said, 'And we're not even married.'

Josef smiled. 'We will be now.'

'Yes. You first.'

The muscles in his jaw tensed slightly. Then he stuck the needle into his right index finger. A bead of blood appeared. He pressed his finger until the bead was so big that it almost burst. Then he held his finger to the corpse's mouth.

Anna wasn't quite as far gone as she had thought.

When Josef's finger touched the dead mouth, the body raised its head and closed its lips around the finger.

She screamed. Josef jerked his finger away.

A flower of revulsion blossomed in her stomach as a bluish tongue emerged from the corpse's mouth and licked the juice of life from its lips.

I'm not going to throw up I'm not going to throw up...

And she didn't. Josef put his arm around her shoulders. His whole body was shaking, he was almost bouncing up and down. His voice was hoarse with excitement. 'It's done, it's over...'

Anna shook herself free. She too was shaking, her teeth were chattering and the room was billowing violently as she dropped to her knees, searching for the needle.

Want to do it, going to do it, have to do it...

Because something else had happened, something beyond what the eye could see. At the moment when the creature licked the blood from its lips, a change had taken place in the room. Something shifted, and even though Josef was sitting beside her speaking in her own language, she was the only person here. There was no other way of describing it. Josef had become something else, even if he was still in human form.

The balance had been upset. Perhaps it was only in her head, but it was as if everything around her was protesting because death had been cheated. The corners of the room bent up towards the ceiling, the floor bellied.

The needle was lying next to Josef's foot. As he kept gasping, 'It's happened, I can feel it, it's in my whole body...' she tried to pick it up. Her fingers groped their way over the round, shiny surface, and just as she got her nails underneath the needle and managed to lift it, she saw a movement from the corner of her eye.

She sat up with the needle in her hand. The corpse had turned its head towards her, and pale blue eyes were looking straight through her, straight into her. There was a rushing noise inside her head, like hundreds of seabirds taking off, and the crazy motion of the room almost made her lose her balance. She stabbed at her finger.

Nothing happened. She looked at her finger, at the needle. She had used the wrong end. When she tried to turn the needle around, it slipped out of her sweaty grasp.

'You...'

A blast of rotting seaweed as the corpse's mouth opened and uttered that one single word.

Enough.

Out out out have to get out

She yelled, 'Josef! I can't, I don't want to, I...'

The corpse's hand shot out and grabbed her between the legs, squeezing hard. She tried to pull away in a panic, but lost her balance and fell flat on the floor.

'Josef, it...'

She couldn't get another word out, because at that moment she felt a wet, icy chill spreading across her belly, her thighs, and in a second it passed through her trousers and carried on moving inwards.

Josef hurled himself forward and tore away the corpse's hand, but it was too late. Death was already inside. Anna's womb turned to ice. A cloud of living cold occupied her belly, which swelled up to double its normal size as she screamed with pain, and because she knew, knew what was happening.

The balance was restored.

'Anna, Anna, Anna...'

The flight of the seabirds. Through the rushing of their wings his voice was the last thing she heard before the wings became visible, came closer, filled her field of vision and everything became white darkness.

With shaking hands Josef managed to pull off her trousers, her underpants without any idea of what he was going to do; there was just one clear thought pulsating through his head: *Got to get it out, got to get rid of it...*

Perhaps he would have done something horrendous in his confusion if Death hadn't left her at that point. Anna's belly collapsed as what had been inside it came pouring out. A cascade of pink fluid gushed out onto the floor in a fan shape, soaking his knees, and soon he was sitting like an island in a pink sea as the fluid continued to pour out.

In the end the foetus came too.

It was about the size of a tern, already fully human and attached by the umbilical cord to the placenta that followed it, a dark red clump of pure life. Something that had been life.

Josef shuffled backwards on his knees, banged into the coffee table, couldn't take his eyes off what would have been his child. Its foetal sac had burst with the pressure, it had drowned in salt water.

He screamed until his vocal cords were on fire. He kept on screaming when his scream was nothing more than a hoarse bark, when he saw the blood from Anna's womb growing darker as Death removed itself. In the end there was only a foetus lying in a pool of blood. Two bodies on the floor. And a pool of water.

The pool of water retracted, forming itself into a thin, transparent rope.

Josef stopped screaming and stood there open-mouthed.

It could be outside...

The rope began to move towards the door. He laughed, but no sound came; he began to stamp on the rope. It split it two, ran across his foot, kept on going. He laughed, sobbed, kept on stamping, jumping on the rope, but it simply slipped away, reformed.

When it reached the door it slid out between the hinges.

He tried to grab it. It slipped out of his hands. He opened the door, ran after it down towards the sea. Just as the front end of the rope reached the water and slid in, he stumbled on the treacherous rocks and fell forwards.

He heard a crunching noise inside his head as some of his teeth smashed, and his mouth filled with blood.

He lay face down on the rocks until the dawn came.

———

What else is there to tell?

Anna survived. After a few days in hospital her physical recovery was complete. She didn't even need a D and C. Death had done its job meticulously. She would never be able to have children.

The case featured in the papers for a week or so, and Josef got four years for contributing to the death of another person. A psychiatrist who had been working with Kaxe was able to confirm that he had strong suicidal tendencies, and that Josef's version of events was not at all unlikely.

There was no mention of Death, which lives in the sea.

Anna visited Josef in prison a few times, but their relationship was untenable after what had happened. She said he shouldn't blame himself, that it had been her own choice, but it didn't help much. Josef was lost to the world.

After a couple of years Anna started painting again, taking up the thread she had begun in the days before the thing that had happened, but without the comic element. Things went well for her. She was never happy again, but she kept going.

When Josef came out of prison he went back to the house. Spent a few months sorting it out.

In prison he had had plenty of time to consider his impressions from the hours spent in the company of Death. In spite of the fact that he had striven for eternal life, it came as a relief when he realised that the immortality given to him through the pact applied only to death by water.

He would age, like other people. He could take his own life if he wanted to. But he would never drown.

The years passed. Josef was unable to return to any kind of work. At the age of thirty-eight he was an old man, sitting in his cottage and living on benefits, drinking as much as he could.

The locals avoided him. They knew who he was, what he'd done. Perhaps their attitude might have mellowed over the years if he hadn't also stopped washing, stopped eating more than was absolutely necessary to stay alive.

One evening as he sat there, mercifully drunk, staring out at the lighthouse sending its flashes of light across the water as it had always done, he realised with a bitter laugh that he was becoming exactly like Kaxe.

Life lost more and more of its meaning. He was incapable of enjoying anything any longer. Even the booze didn't help. In this desert the importance of his only oasis grew and grew, the reason why things had turned out like this, the only gift he had been given. The fact that he couldn't drown.

One October day he fetched an anchor with a chain from the boathouse, heaved it into the boat and set off. He sailed to the same spot where he had sunk Kaxe. There he fastened the chain tightly around his waist with a lockable split pin so that he would be able to open it again once he was convinced.

When he threw himself into the water with the anchor, he felt a kind of happiness.

The water was cold. He quickly sank three metres below the surface, stopped. Floated. His ears popped and he equalised the pressure by holding his nose and breathing out with his lips pressed together. Above him he could see the silhouette of the underside of the boat, highlighted against the sky. Thought he had been stupid not to fasten himself to the boat as well. It would drift away.

He floated on the spot. After a minute or so he was no longer able to hold his breath. He opened his mouth and breathed in.

Whatever might come, let it come.

The water poured into his lungs, chilling him completely in just a few seconds. A moment of panic, the panic that always clings to life. But nothing happened. He was no longer breathing, but he was fully conscious.

He floated there for a long time. Saw the boat drift out of sight. Saw the sky begin to darken. He no longer had any feeling anywhere, he was merely a floating consciousness, a thinking jellyfish.

The full significance of this did not become clear to him until he had had enough. When he began to long for the cottage in spite of everything, for a few leisurely glasses of schnapps to thaw his body out slowly. For TV.

He had no feeling. He couldn't move.

Therefore he couldn't open the split pin.

A few hours into the night, as the billowing stars shone through the surface of the water just three metres above him, his mind gave up. A soft, sparkling madness closed around him.

But he was alive. And he would remain alive.

Forever.

Let the old dreams die

(For Mia. Still.)

I want to tell you a story about a great love.

Unfortunately the story isn't about me, but I am part of it, and now it's all over I want to bear witness for Stefan and Karin.

Bear witness. That sounds a bit grand, I know. Perhaps I am creating exaggerated expectations about a story that is not in any way sensational, but miracles are so few and far between in this world that you have to do your best to make the most of them when they do appear.

I regard the love between Stefan and Karin as a miracle, and it is to this miracle that I want to bear witness. You can call it an everyday miracle or a conventional one, I don't care. Through getting to know them I was privileged to be part of something that goes beyond our earthbound constraints. Which makes it a miracle. That's all.

First of all, a little about me. Have patience.

I am part of the original population of Blackeberg. The cement was still drying when my parents and I moved to Sigrid Undsets gata in 1951. I was seven years old at the time, and all I really remember is that we had to trudge all the way down to Islandstorget to catch the tram if we wanted to go into town. The subway came the following year. I followed the building of the station's ticket hall, designed by none other than Peter Celsing, which is still a source of pride for many of us old Blackeberg residents.

I mention this because I actually spent a considerable portion of my life in this very station. In 1969 I began work as a ticket collector, and I stayed there until I retired two years ago. So apart from odd periods spent filling in for colleagues who were off sick from other stations along the green line, I have spent thirty-nine years of my working life inside Celsing's creation.

There are plenty of stories I could tell, and it's not that I haven't thought about doing so. I enjoy writing, and a modest little autobiography of a ticket collector might well find an audience. But this is not the appropriate forum. I just wanted to tell you a little bit about myself, so that you know who's telling the story. The anecdotes can wait.

I've heard it said that I am a person who lacks ambition. In a way this is true, if by 'ambition' you mean a desire to climb the career ladder or the staircase of status or whatever you want to call it. But ambition can be so many things. My ambition, for example, has been to live a quiet, dignified life, and I believe I have succeeded.

I would probably have fitted in much better in Athens about two thousand five hundred years ago. I would have made an excellent Stoic, and much of the attitude to life I have been able to understand from the writings of Plato fits me like a glove. Perhaps I would have been regarded as a wise man in those days. Nowadays I tend to be regarded as a bore. That's life, as Vonnegut says.

I have dedicated my life to selling and punching tickets, and to reading. There's plenty of time to read when you work in the ticket office, particularly when you work nights as I have often done. Dostoevsky and Beckett are probably my favourites because both of them, although in very different ways, attempt to reach a point of—

Sorry, there I go again. 'Stillness', I was going to say, but this is not the place to expand on my literary preferences. Enough about me, and over to Stefan and Karin.

Oh, but there must be just one more little diversion. Perhaps after all I was a little too ambitious in the conventional sense when I said I'd like to write my autobiography. I seem to find it difficult to organise my material. Oh well. You'll just have to put up with it, because I need to say a few words about Oskar Eriksson.

I don't know if you remember the case, but it attracted a great deal of attention and an enormous amount was written about it at the time, particularly out here to the west of the city. It's twenty-eight years ago now, and thank goodness nothing so tragic and violent has happened in Blackeberg since then.

A lunatic in the guise of a vampire killed three children in the old swimming baths—which is now a pre-school—and then abducted this Oskar Eriksson. The newspapers wallowed in what had happened for weeks and weeks, and many of those who were around at the time can barely hear the word 'Blackeberg' without thinking of vampires and mass murder. What do you think of when I say 'Sjöbo'? Integration and tolerance? No, I thought not. Places acquire a stigma, which then sits there like a nail stuck in your foot for years on end.

A lunatic in the guise of a vampire, I wrote, because I wanted to remind you of the image that was prevalent. However, I have had good reason to revise the account of what took place, but we'll get to that eventually.

What does this have to do with Stefan and Karin?

Well, the reason they moved to Blackeberg was that Karin was a police officer, and one of those responsible for the investigation into what was known as 'the Swimming Pool Massacre in Blackeberg'. To be more specific, she was actually involved in the section working on Oskar Eriksson's disappearance. Her enquiries meant that she spent a great deal of time in Blackeberg and she became very fond of the place, in spite of everything.

When she and her husband Stefan were looking for somewhere new to live a couple of years after the investigation had been put on the back burner, they came to Blackeberg, and so it was that they ended up moving into an apartment two doors down from me on Holbergsgatan in June 1987.

Under normal circumstances people come and go in the apartment blocks near me without my taking any notice at all. Even though I've lived here a long time, I'm not one of those who keeps an eye on things. But that summer I spent a lot of time on my balcony—I was ploughing through Proust's *In Search of Lost Time*—and I noticed the new arrivals for one very simple reason: they held hands with each other.

I estimated that the man was about my own age, and the woman a few years older—so well past the stage where most couples abandon that kind of physical closeness in public. There are exceptions, of course, but these days it seems as if not even young people bother holding hands any longer, at least not if they're over the age of ten.

But as soon as this middle-aged couple set foot outside the door they took each other by the hand, as if it were the most natural thing in the world. Sometimes of course they were alone, and they didn't always hold hands when they were walking together, but almost always. It made me feel happy, somehow, and I caught myself looking up from my book as soon as I heard their door open.

Perhaps it's a drawback of my profession, but I am in the habit of studying people, trying to guess who they are and putting two and two together from the various occasions on which I have the opportunity to observe them from my ticket booth.

Since the couple spent a great deal of time on their ground floor balcony that summer, I had plenty of chances to gather facts in order to draw my conclusions.

They often read aloud to one another, a virtually obsolete form of entertainment. The distance prevented me from hearing what they were reading, and I had to stop myself from fetching my binoculars when they left a book on the table. There is a difference between observation and spying. When a pair of binoculars enters the picture, that line has been crossed. So no binoculars.

They drank a fair amount of red wine, and they both smoked. One of them would roll a cigarette while the other was reading. Sometimes they stayed up quite late with a cassette player on the table between them. From what I could hear, they played mainly popular old songs. Siw Malmquist, Östen Warnerbring, Gunnar Wiklund. That kind of thing. And Abba. Lots of Abba.

Occasionally they would dance together for a little while in the limited space available, but when that happened I would look away and busy myself with my own affairs, because it felt as if that was *private* in a way I can't really explain.

OK. Let me tell you what conclusions I drew before I got to know them. I thought the man worked in some kind of service industry, and the woman was a librarian. I decided they had met at a mature age, and this was their first apartment together. I felt they had both had their own dreams, but now those dreams had been put on ice so that they could invest their energy in their relationship, their love.

Not bad, as you will see.

I was completely wrong on just one point, as you already know.

The woman was a police officer, not a librarian. If someone had asked me to describe my idea of a female police officer, I would probably have said something about short black hair, prominent cheekbones and sinewy muscles. Karin didn't look like that. She had thick, fair hair that hung right down her back; she was comparatively short and very pretty in an appealing way, with lots of laughter lines. Just the kind of person you would happily ask for advice about which book to read next, in fact.

You could ask Karin that question, of course, but if she were really to be on home ground you would have to ask her about the development of scar tissue, the psychology of murderers and the density of ammunition in handguns. Her area of particular expertise was interrogating witnesses and the verbal collection of information, but she was also well versed in ballistics and blood-spatter analysis. 'Although that's mainly just as a hobby,' as she once explained.

I found out what Stefan did for a living at the same time as our embryonic friendship began.

After the Proust I turned to a biography of Edvard Munch. I had just finished it when my holiday started at the end of July, and I decided to take a trip to Oslo to visit the Munch museum. That's one of the advantages of being alone. You get an idea, and the very next day you can put it into practice.

I took the morning train so as to arrive in the afternoon, and when the ticket collector came along, who should I see decked out in his cap and full uniform but my new neighbour? So we had more or less the same profession. A profession that definitely counts as part of a *service industry*, wouldn't you say?

As I held out my ticket he frowned and looked at me as if he were searching for something. I helped him out.

'We're neighbours,' I said. 'And I'm on the ticket barrier at the station. In Blackeberg.'

'That's it,' he said, punching my ticket. 'Thanks for telling me.

I'd have been wondering all day otherwise.'

There was a brief silence. I felt as if I wanted to say something more, but I couldn't come up with anything that wouldn't seem intrusive. I could hardly ask what books they read, or which was his favourite Abba track. He came to my rescue with the only neutral fact available at the time.

'So,' he said. 'You're off to Oslo?'

'Yes. I thought I'd go and have a look round the Munch museum. I've never been.'

He nodded to himself, and I wondered if I should have specified *Edvard*. Perhaps he had no interest in art. So it came as a bit of surprise when he asked, '*The Kiss*. Have you seen that one?'

'Yes. But not the real thing.'

'That's in the museum.'

He looked as if he were about to say something else, but the passenger in front of me was waving his ticket. The man I would later come to know as Stefan clicked his hole punch a couple of times in the air and said, 'It's a wonderful museum. Enjoy yourself,' then carried on with his rounds.

When I visited the museum the following day I couldn't avoid paying particular attention to *The Kiss*, especially as it was already one of my favourites. As I have already said I have a tendency to speculate, and it was impossible not to interpret the painting in the light of what I thought I knew about my hand-holding neighbours.

It's more a matter of two bodies *melting together*, rather than a kiss. On the one hand the painting depicts the kiss above all other kisses, the union that makes two drift together and become one. On the other hand the painting is very dark, and there is something tortured about the position of the bodies, as if we are witnessing something inexorable and painful. Whatever it's about, it shows two people who are completely absorbed in one another and who have ceased to exist as separate individuals.

I thought I had learned something about my neighbours, but at the same time I told myself not to read too much into it. After all, even I had liked the picture, and I was all alone.

One amusing detail I would like to mention, in the light of what happened later: I spent a long time standing in front of the painting entitled *Vampire*. Here again we have a kind of kiss, bodies melting together. But is this about consolation, or a fatal bite? Is the woman's red hair enveloping the man in oblivion and forgiveness, or is it actually blood flowing? At any rate, we see the same faceless individuals as in *The Kiss*, the same blind and tortured symbiosis.

A few days after my return from Oslo, I passed the balcony where Stefan was sitting reading Dostoevsky's *The Idiot*. It would have been impolite not to speak, so I said something and he said something about Dostoevsky and I said something about Munch and he asked if I'd like a cup of coffee and that was how it started. To cut a long story short, there were more cups of coffee on other days, and in September I was invited to dinner.

I must apologise for this lengthy detour to Oslo with the sole aim of explaining how our friendship started, but as I said: with hindsight it doesn't seem to me to be entirely without significance. The end was already encapsulated in the beginning, so to speak.

It was easy to spend time with Stefan and Karin. We had similar interests, and more importantly the same sense of humour. Like me they enjoyed turning ideas and orthodoxies inside out, and for example we could spend a considerable amount of time speculating on what would happen if islands weren't fixed, but just floated around. How those in power would formulate their immigration policy, and so on and so on.

One evening when we were sitting on the balcony sharing a bottle of wine, I asked how they had met. They suddenly looked quite secretive, and glanced at one another with an expression that suggested they might be sharing a private joke. Eventually Karin said, 'We met...during the course of the investigation.'

'What investigation?'

'The one in Blackeberg.'

'The swimming pool...incident?'

'Yes. Stefan was a witness and I interviewed him.'

'A witness?' I looked at Stefan. 'But you weren't living here then, were you?'

Stefan glanced at Karin as if he was requesting permission to talk about an ongoing investigation, and she gave a brief nod.

'Oskar Eriksson,' said Stefan. 'I punched his ticket. On the train. The day after it all happened. So I was kind of the last person who definitely saw him.'

'Were there other people who saw him?'

'You'd have to ask Karin about that.'

'Sorry,' said Karin, pouring more wine into my glass by way of compensation. 'It's an ongoing investigation and I can't...you understand.'

'But I mean it's...what is it...five years ago?'

'It's an ongoing investigation.'

And that was the end of that. For the time being.

This was an unusually striking example, because it was to do with a professional code of conduct, but I noticed that in general terms there were clear delineations with both of them when it came to boundaries. What they were prepared to say and what they were not prepared to say, particularly in matters to do with their relationship. During the twenty-three years of our friendship I never asked a question about their sex life, for example. The way they touched one another, the looks and the snatched kisses indicated that they probably had quite an active one, but I instinctively knew it wasn't something they wished to discuss with other people.

I have never met a couple with such integrity, such closeness as those two. They comprised their own little universe. I won't deny that I sometimes felt quite sad in their company, especially if we'd had a few glasses of wine. We would sit there having a lovely time, chatting and laughing, but I was the one who had to get up and go home alone at some point. However much we all liked each other, I was on the outside.

They weren't perfect by any means. More than once I thought that part of the reason they valued my company was that they wanted a witness. Someone who would gaze appreciatively at their love and confer the seal of approval. They lapped it up like cats when I said something about how terrific they were together, what a miracle it was that two people...and so on. A kind of vanity. Look how wonderful we are together.

But that's just a footnote. The love was there, and it was a great and true love, and even love can be permitted a certain amount of conceit, after all.

The years passed and we grew closer. They didn't spend much time with other people; they seemed perfectly content in each other's company, and I think I can say with confidence that I was the only one they let into their life to any extent.

In 1994 Karin retired. I apologise if that comes as something of a shock, but I felt the same when I found out about the age difference between them. Stefan was born in 1945, which meant he was a year younger than me, while Karin was born in 1929. My initial impression was that there were perhaps seven or eight years between them. But in fact it was sixteen. The combination of her bright eyes and long blonde hair had misled me, coupled with the fact that Stefan had something of the old man about him.

So Karin retired while Stefan carried on travelling around on the trains, principally the route from Stockholm to Oslo and back. As I said I worked mainly evenings and nights, so I had quite a bit of spare time during the day. Karin and I weren't quite as easy with each other when it was just the two of us as Stefan and I were, but after a year or so and a number of shared coffee breaks, we had reached a level with which we were both comfortable.

In fact it was while we were having coffee one day that she told me the Oskar Eriksson case was still occupying her mind, in spite of the fact that it was no longer her job. Perhaps because she had retired she felt able to disclose a little more.

'It's not true at all,' she said. 'The official version, it's not true at all.'

'What do you mean?' I asked tentatively, anxious not to break the atmosphere that had led her to bring up the subject.

'First of all, there was blood on the ceiling in the swimming pool. On the *ceiling*. And it was directly above the water. Five metres above the water. Given the way it had spurted, someone would have had to climb up a ladder to splash it on the ceiling. A ladder that was standing in the actual pool. The blood came from the victim whose head was torn off.'

'Chopped off, you mean?'

'No. Torn off. And you can't imagine the strength it would take to do that. Try pulling apart a Christmas ham with your bare hands—and you don't even have a skeleton to contend with in that case. You know the old custom of executing people by getting horses to pull them apart?'

'Yes.'

'That's just a form of torture. Horses aren't capable of pulling off even an arm or a leg. You have to help out by chopping. And that's *horses*.'

'Which are very strong animals.'

'Yes. Elephants can do it. But not horses. And most definitely not people.'

'So what did happen, then?'

Karin sat without speaking for a long time, gazing out of the window as if she was trying to use X-ray vision to penetrate the buildings that prevented her from looking into the boarded-up swimming pool four hundred metres away.

'There was a blow, a cut,' she said eventually. 'Which allowed the tearing-off process to begin, so to speak. But it wasn't done by a knife. We also found another victim, an elderly man, in an apartment...' The latter remarks were made mostly to herself, and she blinked a couple of times as if she were waking up. She looked at me. 'Oskar Eriksson. You saw him once, didn't you?'

'Several times. He used to travel on the subway like everybody else.'

'But there was one night...'

I had told Stefan and Karin about the incident several years ago when we had been chatting in general terms about the massacre in the swimming pool. I had been sitting by the ticket barrier at two o'clock in the morning reading Kafka's *Metamorphosis* when Oskar Eriksson came up from the subway. Some drunk over by the door was singing a song about Fritiof Andersson, and the boy...I told the story again.

'It was as if a great feeling of happiness suddenly came over him as he stood there. I had been on the point of asking if he was OK, what such a young lad was doing out so late at night, but as he stood there with the drunk singing, it was as if...he started to smile with his whole face and then he *rushed* out of the building as if he was in a tremendous hurry to get to whatever was making him so happy. And then the drunk started pissing in a rubbish bin and—'

'So what was it? What made him so happy?'

'No idea. And I wouldn't have given it a thought if he hadn't hit the headlines a couple of weeks later.'

'What could make a twelve-year-old boy so happy?'

'I don't know. I was pretty gloomy at that age. Are you still working on this?'

'I think I always will be.'

During the years that followed Karin would occasionally let slip some further snippet of information. For example, Oskar Eriksson had lived next door to the person who took him away from the swimming pool, and there was also evidence which indicated that Oskar had been in this person's apartment on at least one occasion.

Some of the odd characters Karin had questioned at the time, the ones who still hung out in the Chinese restaurant or pizzeria as they had done in those days, had said that the dead man who was found in the apartment next door to Oskar had been looking for a child, a youngster who he insisted had killed his best friend. Who was in fact the same man who had been cut out of the ice down below the hospital with a tremendous amount of commotion.

It was a hell of a mess, and the more Karin dug around and puzzled over the case, the more connections she found to other unsolved and inexplicable murders and in the end, just before she retired, she had put forward the only theory that made all the pieces fit: 'What if it really was a vampire?'

The Chief of Police had tilted his head to one side and asked, 'What do you mean?'

'Exactly what I say. That the perpetrator really was a creature with supernatural strength, a creature that needs to drink blood in order to survive. It's the only thing that makes everything fit.'

'I still don't understand what you mean.'

Karin had given up at that point. Of course she didn't believe in the existence of vampires any more than anyone else did, it was just that...it would explain everything. On the other hand, there were plenty of unsolved cases that could be neatly tied up if you just accepted the idea of a supernatural perpetrator. Police work didn't sit well with superstition.

During Karin's final weeks at work she began to think that the counterargument was weak. The reason why so many complex cases could be solved if a mythological figure was the perpetrator could simply be because *that was exactly what had happened.*

She didn't breathe a word of this to her colleagues or her superiors. However, the Chief of Police had a certain amount of trouble keeping things to himself, and when Karin retired she thought she sensed an air of relief through the celebratory drinks and speeches at the thought of getting rid of somebody who had gone a bit soft in the head in her old age, and sure enough some bastard made a comment about making sure she ate plenty of garlic.

During her last few years at work she had been allowed to spend time on the Oskar Eriksson case only as a concession. When she retired it was regarded as done and dusted, something of a hobby for Karin and nothing more. She would still ring her former colleagues from time to time just to check if anything new had come in, but it never had. The case was dead. Or so everyone thought.

My friendship with Stefan and Karin took a new direction in 1998, when Stefan's father died. At the age of seventy-eight he had gone out in his skiff to lay nets, fallen in the water and been unable to get out. Stefan inherited a cosy house and a summer cottage in Östernäs on Rådmansö.

The summer cottage had been available to rent for next to nothing, and Stefan and Karin decided to sell it. The cottage was in a very pretty spot up on the cliffs overlooking a cove, and the bidding went mad. Stefan ended up with just under three million kronor.

They told me all this during one of our evenings on the balcony, and then they dropped a bombshell: they were planning to move to Östernäs. I muttered something about Stefan's job and the difficulty of commuting, but they had worked it all out and come to the conclusion that the inheritance and Karin's pension would be enough to keep them afloat for as long as they wanted to stay afloat.

That same autumn I helped them load up the removal van. Then I stood at my window and watched them drive away, feeling as if an era of my life was at an end. Of course we had parted with promises to meet up often, it was only a hundred kilometres after all, there was always a place for me to stay and so on. It was a nice thought, but nothing would be the same from now on.

However, my worst fears came to nothing. Their open invitation really was exactly that, and about once a month I would go over to visit them, staying overnight and travelling back the next day. Sometimes, particularly in the summer, I thought it wasn't too bad having friends with a veranda overlooking the sea where you could sit drinking wine and chatting into the small hours. It could have been worse. I could have had no friends at all.

Their apartment on Holbergsgatan was taken over by a man from Norrland who had a big dog. I assume he was from Norrland, because that's what his dialect sounded like when he talked to the dog, which he did quite often. He never spoke to me, nor I to him.

By the time Stefan and Karin had been living on Rådmansö for a couple of years, everything was more or less chugging along as it had always done, by which I mean as it had done before they moved to Blackeberg in 1987. In 2000 I was fifty-six years old, and as I worked my way through *In Search of Lost Time* once more, it struck me that the title of the book doesn't chime with my perception of time at all.

Time neither flies nor flows nor crawls along. Time stands completely still. We are the ones who move around time, like the apes around the monolith in the film *2001*. Time is black, hard and immovable. We circle around it, and eventually we are sucked into it. I don't really know what I mean, but that's how it feels, and you may or may not believe this, but it's an uplifting feeling.

Speaking of *2001*, I celebrated the millennium with Stefan and Karin. The much-vaunted computer chaos didn't happen, and time gazed blindly at us as we entered a new millennium. Age had begun to take its toll on Karin. She suffered from dizzy spells, and the least exertion wore her out. When she fetched champagne from the cellar she had to sit down and recover for a long time before she was able to come out onto the veranda with us to drink a toast as fireworks lit up the winter sky.

In spite of the fact that I fear neither time nor the ageing process—as befits a stoic—it was somewhat painful to see the change in Karin. To me she had always been the very picture of how to grow old attractively, and it cut me to the heart to see her leaning against the oven or bending over the table to recover after doing something as simple as putting more wood on the fire.

If Stefan found it painful too, he never showed it. He would take over some task as if in passing when Karin faltered, and would put his arm around her waist as if in fun, supporting her without making a fuss about it. I left with a good feeling in my heart in spite of everything.

Oh, that heart.

A month later Stefan rang to tell me that Karin had suffered a heart attack. They had spent three days at the hospital in Danderyd, and Karin was due to have an operation a couple of hours later. The coronary arteries were severely affected by atherosclerosis and she needed a major bypass, which was by no means guaranteed to succeed.

'What do you mean?' I asked. 'What do you mean, not guaranteed to succeed?'

Stefan took a deep breath, and I could tell he was forcing himself not to cry. 'There's a risk that she could die. If the operation fails, then...Karin will die.'

'Do you want me to come?'

'Yes. Please.'

I made a few calls and called in a couple of favours to cover my shift that evening and the next, if it should prove necessary. Then I took the subway. As I sat alone in a block of four seats I felt empty-handed. At first I thought it was because I hadn't got a present with me, but when I changed at Central Station and took the red line I realised the feeling went deeper than that.

I was empty-handed because I had nothing with me that could help or save Karin. I *should* have had something. Stefan had called me, and I had immediately rushed to his rescue. I should be the one who came along with the solution, the one who made everything all right. And I had nothing. Nothing. My own impotence made my lungs ache.

I found my way through the immense hospital complex and found Stefan sitting alone in a waiting room on the third floor. A green linoleum floor with metal-framed chairs and tables dotted around. Our fate is determined in rooms that must be easy to clean. Stefan was slumped over the arm of a two-seater sofa. When I sat down beside him I could see that his skin was grey and his hands were shaking.

'Thanks for coming,' he whispered.

I rubbed his back and took his hand, which was dry and unnaturally hot. We sat like that and after a minute or so Stefan started to stroke the back of my hand with the fingers of his other hand. I don't think he was aware of what he was doing, or whose hand he was holding, because he suddenly stiffened in mid-movement, squeezed my hand and then let go of it.

'That's how Karin and I met,' he said. 'We were holding hands.'

There was a faint hint of something more cheerful in Stefan's voice, and I tried to play along. 'People usually hold hands *after* they've met.'

'Yes. But that's how it was. It happened when we were holding hands.'

'Tell me.'

Stefan straightened up, and the ghost of a smile flitted across his lips.

'It was during the investigation. Into the Oskar Eriksson case. The police called me in, and Karin was conducting the interview. I think I can say that as soon as I sat down in that room, opposite this woman, I...'

Stefan's gaze wandered to some closed double doors at the end of the corridor, and I sensed that somewhere behind those doors the doctors were trying to save the life of the woman he was talking about.

'I had information, you see. That's what she wanted, and I was under no illusions about anything else. Or...I don't know. Karin has said that she felt something too when I walked into the room. But it wasn't until we held hands that it...blossomed.'

'I still don't understand. Why were you holding hands? It's not usually part of a police interview, as far as I know.'

Stefan gave a snort and a little of the greyness in his skin disappeared; there was a slight pinkness in his cheeks.

'No, sorry. I'll have to tell you the story. The story I told Karin at the time.'

Stefan had punched the boy's ticket and wondered about his luggage, but hadn't given the matter any more thought because the boy had told him he would have help later on. Stefan had finished his shift in Karlstad and spent an hour or so in the staffroom at the station while he waited for the train back to Stockholm.

Fifteen minutes before the train was due he went for a stroll around the station to get some air in his lungs in the chilly November evening before spending several hours in the stale air on the train.

That's when he spotted the boy again. Next to the station there was a small grove, an open space surrounded by deciduous shrubs where people could wait for the train in the summer. The grove was illuminated by a single floodlight, and Stefan saw Oskar Eriksson sitting on the trunk he had had with him on the train. A girl with black hair was sitting beside him.

'And of course I reacted because the girl was only wearing a T-shirt, even though it was well below freezing. The boy, Oskar, was fully dressed in a jacket and everything. But they were sitting side by side on that trunk. And they were holding hands. Like this.'

Stefan held up his right hand, then gently took my left wrist and raised my hand to his, weaving our fingers together and rubbing our palms together before letting go.

'It was when I was telling Karin about the children sitting there holding hands. She didn't understand what I meant. So I had to show her, just as I showed you. And that was when it happened. As we sat there with our hands joined just like the children, that was when... we looked into each other's eyes and that was when...it started.'

Stefan's voice had grown weaker and weaker, and as he uttered the final words he collapsed and began to weep. He bent over his knees, the sobs tearing his body apart as he whispered, 'Karin, Karin, Karin. My darling, darling Karin, please don't die...'

My hands were empty, and all I could do with them was to stroke his back as he continued to whisper his prayer beneath the cold, indifferent fluorescent light. There should be storm-lashed rocks or the hall of the Mountain King. But our lives are weighed in cold, white light, and is it even possible to imagine that anyone hears our prayers?

The doors at the end of the corridor opened and a man of about our age dressed in a white T-shirt and green scrubs came towards us. Stefan didn't see him, and I tried to read the man's expression to work out what Stefan could expect. It was completely neutral, and I couldn't prepare myself one way or the other.

The man nodded to me and said, 'Larsson? Stefan Larsson?'

Stefan gave a start and turned his tear-stained face to the man, who smiled at long last.

'I just wanted to tell you that the operation went extremely well. No complications, and I think I can promise that your wife will experience a considerable improvement in her quality of life once she gets through the rehabilitation stage.'

I put my arm around Stefan's shoulders, but his mouth was hanging open and he didn't seem to understand what he had been told.

'It went...well?'

'As I said, it went extremely well. The blood vessels we took from your wife's leg to replace those that were damaged were of a surprisingly high quality for a woman of her age. In all probability her heart will work much better in a couple of months than it did before.' The doctor held up a warning finger. 'But the smoking. The smoking...'

Stefan leapt to his feet and looked as if he might be on the point of giving the doctor a hug, but he came to his senses and merely grabbed his upper arms.

'She's not going to so much as look at a cigarette packet from now on, and neither am I! Thank you, doctor! Thank you! Thank you!'

The doctor gave a brief nod and said, 'She's in the recovery room at the moment, but you can see her in a couple of hours. We'll be keeping her in for a few days.'

'You can keep her for a month as long as she gets better.'

'She's going to be fine.'

The doctor's predictions were correct. Two days after the operation Karin was allowed to go home, and after only three weeks she was able to go for walks in a way that had been impossible for her for years. It wasn't so much the weakness of her heart as the pain from the scars on her legs that prevented her from going even further, but after another month those too had healed.

Walking became a new passion for both of them. Karin started walking with Nordic poles, Stefan beside her. Sometimes he would read aloud from a poetry anthology as they walked. Both of them gave up smoking, apart from the odd evening on the veranda when they might smoke *one* cigarette each if for some reason the atmosphere was particularly festive.

This story is beginning to draw to its conclusion. I began by saying that I was going to tell you about a great love, and I don't know whether you think I have fulfilled that promise. Perhaps you are disappointed? Perhaps you were expecting something more dramatic?

All I can say in response is that for one thing you haven't heard the end of my story yet, and for another I feel that I have carried out my duty to bear witness, as I promised to do.

Because how do you picture a great love?

Perhaps it's something along the lines of *Gone with the Wind* or *Titanic* that immediately springs to mind. But those aren't really about love as such, they are about the context. Everything seems grander when it happens against the background of a civil war, a shipwreck or a natural disaster. But that's like judging a painting by its frame. Like saying the *Mona Lisa* is a masterpiece mainly because of the ornate carvings surrounding it.

Love is love. In those dramatic stories the main characters are willing to give up their life for the other person on a purely practical level, but that's exactly what happens in an everyday love story that is also a great love. You give your lives to one another all the way, every day, unto death.

Perhaps it's true that we recognise great love by the fact that the people involved could easily have been actors in some major drama, if only the circumstances had been different. If Stefan had been a Montague from Ibsengatan and Karin a Capulet from Holbergsgatan, perhaps they might have woven their escape plans behind my ticket booth. To run away means life, to linger means certain death. I'm sorry, I'm losing the plot here. But I think you know what I mean.

Love is love. The way it is expressed changes.

I thought a lot about what Stefan had told me at the hospital, picturing the situation. The two of them in a bare, sterile interview room—at least that was how I imagined it. Gripping each other's hands to re-create the scene between the two children in Karlstad, something that would last their whole lives beginning in that moment.

It was a pleasant thought, but Stefan had been interrupted in his narrative, and it would be some years before I was given the full picture.

Perhaps that was a contributing factor in Karin's refusal to give up on her investigation into what happened to Oskar Eriksson—it was this case that had brought her and Stefan together. Perhaps it had a special place in her heart, which was now functioning perfectly.

When we celebrated Karin's seventy-fifth birthday in April 2004, she told me that at the very beginning of the investigation the police had received a great deal of information, mainly from people claiming to have seen Oskar Eriksson in various places in Sweden and even abroad. His picture had been all over the press, and in a case like that it was normal for people to see the missing person in every conceivable place. But none of the leads had produced any results.

It was on a number of these loose threads that Karin was still working some twenty-two years later. She rang people in the places where Oskar had allegedly been seen, carefully read photocopies of old newspapers. But nobody knew anything, and if they had known anything, they'd forgotten it.

Karin sighed and shook her head as we sat on the patio beneath the infra-red heaters, took a decent swig of her wine—good for the circulation—and said, 'I think it might be time to give up. Start doing crosswords or something instead.'

'You already do crosswords,' said Stefan.

'Do more crosswords, then.'

That evening I had the opportunity to look around Karin's study properly. She had kitted out a spare room upstairs with bookshelves and a desk. Dozens of files were lined up on the shelves, and the desk was piled high with papers, maps and printouts. Karin waved her hand and said, 'The nerve centre. All this to investigate *one* case, and do you know what the only practical result of the whole lot has been?'

'No.'

'The fact that Stefan and I met.'

Stefan walked over and weighed a bundle of papers in his hand; he shook his head gloomily and said, 'A singles night for the more mature individual would have been simpler, there's no denying that.'

'True,' said Karin. 'But then neither of us would ever have gone to such a thing.'

'No. You're right. So it was all worth it, wasn't it?'

They gave each other one of those looks that still had the ability to send a pang of sorrow through my heart, even after all these years. If I had been different, if life had been different. If anyone had ever looked at me that way.

Then the stoic in me took over. Socrates was able to stand on guard in the bitter cold for hours on end without uttering one word of complaint, and he emptied his cup of hemlock in one draught. He took his place within me, and the sorrow abated.

The following year Karin devoted no time to the investigation, apart from making one phone call to police headquarters every six months to check if there was anything new. There wasn't.

The final phase in my story begins in the summer of 2007. I had noticed that Stefan was sitting in an odd position when we were out on the veranda, as if he couldn't get comfortable. When we rowed out in the skiff to lay some nets, he pulled a face when he grabbed the oars, and allowed me to take over for once.

'Are you OK?' I asked as we headed out towards Ladholmen. 'Are you in pain?'

'My back hurts,' he said. 'And my stomach. It's as if there's something…I don't know…inside. Don't say anything to Karin.'

'But she's bound to notice.'

'I know. But I want to tell her myself. I think it's something… that's not good news.'

Stefan and I had once talked about the age difference between him and Karin, about the fact that statistically she was likely to die several years before him, and about his feelings. As Stefan doesn't exactly have the same controlled attitude to life as I do, and tends to get worked up about things or to sink into a trough of despair, his answer surprised me.

'That's just the way it is,' he said. 'She's my life, she's my story. If part of the story is that I end up alone for a few years at the end, then so be it. There's no alternative. And when there's no alternative, there's no point in brooding on things. That's just the way it is.'

I imagine I would have said something similar if I had been in Stefan's shoes, and we ended the conversation with some jokey comment on how he and I could always sit around throwing bread to the pigeons until the grim reaper put a stop to our activities.

But that's not how things turned out.

Stefan's pains grew worse over the next few days, and Karin drove him to the hospital in Norrtälje, which referred him to Karolinska Hospital in Stockholm. After a series of tests it was established that Stefan was suffering from pancreatic cancer. I remember with perfect clarity the day Karin rang to tell me.

I stood there with the phone in my hand, looking out of my window at what used to be their apartment. The flowerbeds were magnificent in shades of green and pink. Some children were sitting on the climbing frame with their heads close together and everything was summer and life as Karin uttered the words: 'Cancer. Of the pancreas.'

I knew. I'd read enough books and was generally well-informed enough to know. But I asked the question anyway: 'What are they going to do?'

'There's nothing they can do. They can slow it down slightly with radiotherapy and so on. But there's no cure.'

I couldn't form the words. 'How...how...?'

'In the worst case scenario a few months. At best a year. No longer.'

There wasn't much more to say. I put the phone down and looked over at what I still thought of as their balcony, their door. I remembered how I had noticed them because they held hands, the pop music they used to play, the faint sound of their voices on distant summer evenings. In search of lost time.

The tumour in Stefan's pancreas had spread to his liver, and barely responded to the radiotherapy. When I visited them in October he had been given a morphine pump so that he could administer his own pain relief. I had thought that he would look terrible, but sitting there on the veranda with a blanket over his legs, he looked healthier and more at ease than he had done in August.

When I mentioned this to him he gave a wry smile and clicked the pump a couple of times. 'It's just because the pain has gone. I actually feel OK. But it's gnawing away inside me, I know that. It's a matter of months now.'

'It seems so bloody unnecessary. Looking at you today.'

'Yes. We've both said the same. But there's nothing that can be done. That's just the way it is.'

Karin was sitting next to him, and he reached for her hand. They sat there holding hands and gazing out to sea. I had two years left to my retirement, and I couldn't remember when I last cried. But I cried then.

Silently I wept, and when Stefan and Karin noticed they put their arms around me to console me, absurdly enough. That made me cry even more. For them. For myself. For everything.

Stefan's liver could no longer cope with alcohol, but as we sat on the veranda that evening he made up for it by smoking more than ever. Karin drank wine and smoked, since it no longer mattered. We talked about what had happened when Karin had her heart attack, how she had felt ever since that she was living on borrowed time. She sighed and stroked Stefan's arm. 'I just never thought it would have to be paid back.'

'Don't think like that,' said Stefan. 'I could have been dead twenty-five years ago if what you believe is true.'

'What do you mean?' I asked.

And that was when I was given the final piece of the information available on Oskar Eriksson. Stefan went back to what he had told me at the hospital, about the two children holding hands, which in turn had become the beginning of Stefan and Karin's story.

'But that wasn't quite all. The girl was about to kill me.' He stole a glance at his wife. 'According to Karin.'

'It's just a theory,' she said. 'Which very few people would subscribe to.'

'Anyway,' said Stefan. 'The children were sitting on the trunk rubbing their hands against each other's. I was on my way over to say something, since the girl was so inadequately dressed, and then… she turned to face me.'

Stefan grimaced with pain and clicked the morphine pump a couple of times; he took a deep breath and slowly let it out again, closing his eyes. A couple of minutes passed without anyone saying anything; the only sound was the lapping of the waves on the shore and the faint ticking of the infra-red heater. I had started to think he wasn't going to say any more when Stefan exhaled once again and went on:

'So. I know this sounds strange. She was a child of perhaps twelve, thirteen, but when our eyes met I felt two things, as clear as a revelation: firstly that she intended to kill me, and secondly that she was capable of doing so. Because I had disturbed them. When she jumped off the trunk and I saw that she had a knife in her hand, the feeling didn't exactly diminish. We were standing a couple of metres apart. I looked at her and the boy, saw what they were up to. The girl looked as if she was on the point of hurling herself at me when the guard shouted that my train had arrived. I think that saved me. I backed away, and she stayed where she was with the knife in her hand.'

Stefan lit a cigarette and sighed with pleasure as he inhaled deeply. He looked at the cigarette and shook his head. 'Being able to smoke again. It's almost worth it.'

Karin thumped him on the shoulder. 'Don't say that, silly.'

'So what were they up to?' I asked. 'The children?'

Stefan ran his index finger down his palm.

'She'd cut her hand. So that it bled. He'd done the same. They were sitting there mixing their blood. That was why they were holding hands like that. And that's why Karin has her theory. Which isn't exactly popular with the police.'

'We know so little, we human beings,' said Karin. 'We know almost nothing.'

We gazed out over the sea and considered this while Stefan sucked on his cigarette. When he had stubbed it out he said, 'Do you know what the worst thing is? It's not the fact that I'm going to die. It's all the dreams I had. Which have to die. Which will never be fulfilled. On the other hand...' Stefan looked at Karin's hand, which was resting on the table. 'On the other hand there are so many that have been fulfilled. So perhaps it doesn't really matter.'

I don't remember what else was said that evening, but it was to be the last time I saw Stefan and Karin. At that stage Stefan's condition had been critical but stable, and the doctors believed he had at least a few months left, so when we said goodbye there was nothing to suggest that it would be forever.

But something intervened.

When I rang on the Monday a couple of weeks later, no one answered the phone. When there was no answer the following day either, I started to worry. On the Wednesday I received a card with a Stockholm postmark. It was a picture of Arlanda airport, and on the back it said, 'Let the old dreams die. We are dreaming new ones. Thank you for everything, dearest friend. Stefan and Karin.'

I turned the postcard over and over, but I was none the wiser. Arlanda? Let the old dreams...had they gone abroad? Was there some new treatment available elsewhere? It seemed highly unlikely. After all, that was why I had taken the news so hard; I knew as well as they did that pancreatic cancer was untreatable. Anywhere.

I was free on the Saturday and caught the bus to Östernäs. I had a spare key to their house and permission to use the place whenever they were away. However, I still felt uncomfortable as I unlocked the front door and called out, 'Hello? Anyone home?' As if I were barging into something private. But I had to find out.

The house had recently been cleaned, and a faint smell of detergent lingered in the wooden floor. There wasn't a sound, and it was obvious that no one was at home. But still I crept through the hallway as if I were afraid of disturbing some delicate balance.

The fridge had been emptied and the water heater switched off. No radiators were on, and it was quite cold inside the house. When I opened Stefan's wardrobe to borrow a sweater, I saw that quite a lot of his clothes were missing. They had gone away, that much was clear. I pulled on a yellow woollen cardigan with big buttons that Stefan loathed; he had kept it only because I used to borrow it when we were sitting on the veranda.

I went through the house and found more signs of a well-organised but definitive departure. The few photograph albums they owned were gone, along with a number of favourite albums from the CD rack. Eventually I found myself standing outside Karin's study. If the answer wasn't in there, then there was no answer to be found. I cautiously opened the door.

Yes, I might as well admit it. With every door I opened I was afraid I would find the two of them in a deathly embrace, in the best-case scenario achieved with an overdose of Stefan's morphine, in the worst-case with more obvious means.

But there were no beautiful corpses in Karin's study either. There was, however, a printout of a receipt, along with an envelope containing a photograph. Both were neatly laid out on the desk, as if they had been placed there so that I would find them.

The receipt was for plane tickets. Two one-way tickets to Barcelona, four days earlier. So far so good. They had gone to Spain. The photograph, however, made no sense at all. It showed a group of people who were presumably a family. Mother, father and two children standing on a street at night, brightly lit by the camera's flashbulb. The signs around them were in Spanish and Catalan, so it wasn't a great stretch to assume they were in Barcelona.

I looked at the envelope. It had been sent by the National Police Board a week earlier, and was addressed to Karin. Right down in the bottom corner someone had written 'Something for you, maybe?' and drawn a smiley. When I looked inside the envelope again I found a short letter from someone who lived in Blackeberg and had known Oskar Eriksson very well. He apologised for wasting police time, said the whole thing was completely crazy of course, but he asked them to look carefully at the enclosed photograph.

I did as the letter asked, and took a closer look at the picture. I thought I knew what he meant, but looked around on the desk for a magnifying glass. Instead I found an enlargement of the relevant part of the picture, which Karin had presumably printed out herself.

There was no doubt. Once I had seen the enlargement, it was as clear as day on the first picture too. To one side behind the family were two people who happened to have been caught in the camera flash. One was Oskar Eriksson, and the other was a slender girl with long, black hair. In spite of the fact that the photograph must have been taken immediately after his disappearance, Oskar had changed his hairstyle; it was cut short in a way that was more fashionable among young people today.

I remembered him as a chubby child, but the boy in the picture was considerably slimmer, and as he had been caught on the run, so to speak, he actually looked quite athletic. I looked at the enlargement again, and Stefan's story about what had happened in Karlstad came back to me. There was something vaguely menacing about the way the two children were moving behind the smiling, unsuspecting family. Like predators.

Then I spotted something that made me gasp. The father of the family was holding a mobile phone, and not just any mobile phone, but an iPhone. How long had they been around? A year? Two years?

I turned the photograph over and read the words in the bottom right-hand corner.

Barcelona, September 2008.

The photograph had been taken barely a month ago.

I sat at Karin's desk for a long time, looking from the receipt for the plane tickets to the photograph of Oskar Eriksson and the girl with black hair, moving through the night. And I thought about how the end can be encapsulated in the beginning, and I thought about Stefan and Karin, my dearest friends.

It's been two years now. I haven't heard if they're alive, but nor have I heard that they're dead.

Let the old dreams die. We are dreaming new ones.

I hope they found what they were looking for.

To hold you while the music plays

I want you to understand something. Are you listening? Yes. I want you to understand…it's important to me that you understand…I'm not doing this because I enjoy it. Can you understand that? I'm not going to enjoy this. This is going to hurt me as much as it hurts you.

You're laughing. Yes, OK.

But you understand…the whole point is that it will hurt me too. That's the whole point. Can you understand that?

Of course you're not as au fait with these matters as I am. But if you were. If you had devoted an entire lifetime. To trying to…grasp. These issues. Then I think…

[---]

Did everything work out OK with the money?

Good.

I mean, it hasn't been all that easy for me to…stage this, as you perhaps realise. Neither when it comes to you, nor to those who will be here in ten minutes. You don't exactly belong to…my normal circle of friends, if I can put it that way. It's dead, incidentally.

My normal circle of friends. Is dead. Nothing strange about that. It's time. Of those who attended the seminary with me, only I and one other are still alive.

The seminary. That's where you train. That's what it's called. The seminary for priests.

I don't want you to drink any more now.

Good.

[---]

I remember when I was...yes, even when I was only...thirteen or fourteen. I started thinking about these things.

What it was really like.

The actual experience. It's much more central than we are really prepared to admit, in fact. Here in Sweden, at any rate.

What?

Yes, they'll get half of what you get. Their task is also quite... unpleasant, after all.

There is one thing I'm wondering about.

Do you find any form of...how shall I put it...moral satisfaction in this?

No. I don't mean it like that.

I mean...

When you're a child. And you're pretending to be someone else. You're pretending to be...Robin Hood. And while you're that person, you can...

No. That's a different matter.

Have you never wondered?

No. Most people don't, after all. Not even in my profession.

You must understand that this is something that has preoccupied me all through my life. In a way which is perhaps...unhealthy. But there's nothing I can do about that. We are how we are.

Some people are driven down into the depths of the sea. Others up to the peaks of mountains. Some study the stars. All their lives. In order to understand. Whatever that means.

For my part...

I saw a man pierced by a scythe when I was eleven years old. In through his stomach and out through his back.

I mean, you might think that would be...enough.

But he died immediately.

What?

No, it wasn't anybody I knew.

[---]

Do you have anyone...particularly close?

Why is that, then?

No, I suppose it's these...what are they called...pimples, in that case. Otherwise I think you have a nice face.

No, don't drink any more.

[---]

This project...

Right. It's seven o'clock. The others will be here at any moment.

This project has been on my mind for quite a while.

The fact is, I wish I had done it a long time ago.

As things stand now...

Well, it will be more like a last wish.

Not something from which I will be able to...gain any benefit.

And I suppose that's how it should be, in some way.

[---]

It's a bell-headed nail. It's used for fixing tin roofs, normally.

Nails with the kind of head you really need for this...you can't buy them. Not any more.

There. That was the doorbell. It's time.

Can you go and answer it, I can't get up.

I think it's best if you...don't get to know each other.

Majken

My friendship with Majken began with a telephone call.

I'd been annoyed with the Konsum supermarket chain for a long time; they make such a big thing out of being environmentally friendly, but they wrap their turnips in plastic. I can understand them doing that with peppers, or Spanish cauliflowers. But to wrap plastic around whole local turnips and then to call themselves 'Green Konsum' just isn't acceptable. It's hypocrisy, and nothing less.

I'm no expert when it comes to dealing with vegetables, but one thing I do know: turnips keep just as well as potatoes if you treat them the right way. And they don't use plastic on potatoes. So every time I came home with a turnip and had to peel off a layer of thin plastic film before I could use it, I got annoyed.

The earth's finite resources, fossil fuels, oil, plastic. You know all that stuff. I always have a couple of cotton bags with me when I go shopping. Little things, insignificant you might say. But many drops make a huge river, and a few tonnes of plastic will undeniably turn into a mountain eventually. A mountain of plastic. And what do we do with that?

So I made a phone call.

We really want to hear what you think, it says on their blue and white packaging. KF customer services, and the telephone number.

'Majken,' replied a voice on the other end.

I explained why I was ringing, expecting cool approval, an assurance that we are working to make our stores more environmentally friendly, thank you for ringing, your views are important to us. Something along those lines. I've done this before.

But Majken did more than agree with me. She chimed in. Did I know that Konsum spent more money on marketing its environmental policy than on implementing it? Did I know that a significant proportion of the goods labelled 'ecological' are actually produced by workers earning starvation wages, and using methods that would never be accepted in Sweden?

Well yes, I had read something about that, but now I was getting the information from the inside, so to speak, it had a different kind of credibility.

We talked about where all the money goes. Where the profits actually go. I said I always tried to shop at Konsum, because I believe in the idea of a co-operative, even though it's gone a bit off course in recent years.

Majken laughed. 'Gone a bit off course? You could say that. You could also say it's been flayed alive, ripped to shreds and thrown on the rubbish dump. Do you know what the bosses at KF earn?'

I didn't. She told me.

As the conversation went on I got a strange, sinking feeling in my stomach. Majken was the last person I would have expected to talk like this. I mean, she was the face of the company—or rather its voice—as far as the public was concerned, and her job was to deodorise and sanitise anything shady rather than highlighting it. I asked her why she was so critical.

'Is there any other way to be?' she asked. 'I know how things are, and I can't just sit here and lie to you, can I?'

I had also expected the conversation to be short. A couple of minutes at the most. But I think we talked for over half an hour. I ended up telling her quite a lot about my life and my job as well. Twenty years as a cleaner and five as a carer for my husband, Börje.

'How much do you earn?' asked Majken.

'Ten seven.'

'After tax?'

'No. Before.'

A long sigh.

'Can you manage on that?'

'Yes and no,' I said. 'It's…well, that's why I buy turnips. As I said. Some months are a bit tight. If it weren't for Börje's disability pension, I don't know what we'd do.'

There was a brief silence.

'Why don't you do a bit of shoplifting?'

The feeling in the pit of my stomach, which had disappeared while we were talking about other things, came back again. But still I answered, quietly, 'I do.'

Majken laughed again, and a doubtless foolish smile spread across my lips. It was an appreciative laugh.

'I'm pleased to hear it,' she said. 'Shoplifting is the only reasonable answer.'

'Hm,' I said. 'But what was the question?'

I really liked her laugh. It came so easily, bubbling out. Her voice was an old person's, if women of my age are old, but her laugh was something different, it came from a different source. The picture of her I had in my mind grew younger. I saw big blue eyes, a sparkle.

'The question every store, every aspect of the consumer society asks us,' she said. '*Have you earned this?*'

'Oh,' I said. 'That one.'

'Sorry,' said Majken. 'Am I getting confused, or didn't I get your name?'

'You don't sound confused to me. My name is Dolly.'

'Goodness. After Dolly Parton?'

Now it was my turn to laugh. 'I'm not that young, ' I said. 'It says Dolores on my birth certificate.'

'That means sorrows.'

'It does.'

It was only now, as the conversation was drawing to an end, that I realised how much I wanted it to continue. I wanted her to ask me how I came to be called Dolly, anything at all. At the same time a rational voice told me that it was Konsum customer services on the other end of the line and not an old friend, even if it felt that way. She must have lots of calls waiting.

Does she talk to everybody like this? I wondered, but I just said, 'Anyway, thanks for the chat. I enjoyed it.'

'Me too,' said Majken.

There was silence for a few seconds. I studied the pattern on the rag rug in the hallway, let my gaze wander along to the front door, battered from all the bumps with Börje's wheelchair. Let my thoughts carry on out into the silence of the stairwell. The silence everywhere that would return when I put the phone down.

Majken said, 'Maybe we could do it again.'

'Yes,' I said. A little too eagerly, perhaps, but goodness me, we were two mature ladies, not shy teenagers. Our integrity might grow over the years, but we can do without superficial prestige. I was very lonely and Majken was a little breath of life. No point in pretending otherwise.

'In that case I'll give you a ring one day, if that's OK,' said Majken.

'Yes. My phone number—'

'I've got it here on my monitor.'

'Right. Of course, yes.'

I still haven't got used to the technological advances when it comes to communications. I find it difficult to speak to an answering machine.

I got her private number too, one of those that begins with 070, which I have learned means it's a mobile phone. Majken was obviously more modern than me. We exchanged farewell phrases and hung up.

The silence wasn't as deafening as I had feared; it was as if there was a little song inside my head. Which one? Oh, maybe one of those Svante Thuresson hits from the sixties. The ones that paint pictures in pastel shades, giving you the feeling that the world has just been created.

Do you know what I mean?

A couple of months ago there was an exhibition of photographs up in the library here in Blackeberg. It was about the first ten years, 1954–64. A lot of the pictures were black and white, but when it came to the colour photos you could kind of hear 'You're a Spring Breeze in April' playing as background music.

The sensibly arranged shops, the subway station. People in the square: women in plain coats, men in hats. A kind of freshness mixed with emptiness, as if the people had just discovered that this place existed, were trying to get their bearings. In some ways that's exactly how it was, I'm sure.

I remember those days. We came here before they'd even finished building. Our place on Björnsonsgatan was ready, but the earthmovers were still working further up the street. It was a good time. Lots of children. There was a sense of expectation in the air: We're going to live our lives in this place!

Lena was six, and Tomas was born six months after we moved

to Blackeberg. They had plenty of friends to play with, and the forest was just behind our building. It should have been a good childhood.

Perhaps it's no coincidence that the exhibition focused on those particular years. The idyllic years, the ones you can go back to in order to reflect on what went wrong. One thing I do know: it was after this period that my own life started to go in a different direction from the one I had hoped for.

Talking of Svante Thuresson.

I put the piece of paper with Majken's phone number on it in the drawer under the phone and went in to see Börje. He was sitting on the sofa as usual, staring at the wall. It was only an hour since I had helped him to the toilet, and he'd had a good breakfast that morning, so for the moment there was nothing I could do for him.

Talk to him, you might well be saying. Get out and about.

He stopped talking three years ago. I don't know if he understands what I say; he gives no indication that he does. He moves only if he absolutely has to, and then with great difficulty, so perhaps you can understand that the opportunities for getting out and about are limited.

In fact he shut himself off thirty years ago, when Lena died. But he kept functioning on a mechanical level. Carried on working as a ticket collector, came to the cinema, met up with friends. But the spark, the soul or whatever you want to call it—that had gone out. We were invited to visit other people less and less often, he lost interest in films. In the end his part-time job as a ticket collector was his only contact with the outside world.

That was when I started cleaning. Tomas was eighteen and perfectly capable of taking care of himself—after Lena, Börje had lost interest in him too, and from the age of fifteen Tomas essentially had no father—and we needed the money.

I'll be honest with you: when Börje started sinking into this final catatonic state five years ago, I had to choose between putting him in a home, or giving up my job to look after him. I very nearly went for the first option. It might sound heartless, but I'd had enough. Frankly, if Börje hadn't withdrawn into his shell so completely, I would probably have asked for a divorce.

I don't know. Maybe he knew I felt that way, maybe it contributed to his decision to cut himself off from the world. Because I believe it was a decision. I still think he could talk if he *wanted* to. But to be honest I prefer this care package sitting on the sofa to the shadow of a human being who used to move from room to room under his own steam.

So I stayed. Or *I kept him*, I suppose you could say.

Am I talking too much?

You must forgive me, but I think all this is necessary if you want to understand. And I hope you do. For your own sake.

What do I mean by that?

You'll see.

That afternoon drifted by like many others. When dusk started to fall I took a stroll down to the eco-cottage to see if anyone had thrown away anything I could use.

Ha ha, no, I don't mean *food*. We haven't got to that stage yet. I just mean something that might come in useful. A breadbin or a rug or a better vacuum cleaner than the one we've got.

It's incredible what people throw away. Stuff that's practically new. Although I suppose the really incredible thing isn't so much the fact that they've thrown away an electric mixer that works perfectly well, but that they've bought a new one even though they had the old one. What do I know; maybe they suddenly decided to chuck out the mixer without buying a new one. But I don't think so.

The only thing I found that afternoon was five brand-new plastic storage boxes for the freezer. I took them home.

In the evening we watched the news as usual. I'm not much of a one for TV, but I suppose that's the only time of the day when Börje and I sit together. I mean, otherwise it's impossible. Just sitting there staring at nothing.

When the news was over I went and lay down and read *The Idiot*. You can never really understand that book. Börje stayed put, watching some comedy or other. He's OK on his own, he can get to the toilet and so on. It's only when we're going out I have to get the wheelchair, and we don't do that so often in the winter when it's icy.

Towards ten o'clock I went in to have a look at him. He looked tired and I asked him if he wanted to go to bed. Sometimes I get an almost imperceptible nod in response.

I tried to get him to bed, but he resisted as he sometimes does. When that happens I usually make up a bed for him on the sofa. You could say that's the only expression of will he ever shows these days: refusal. Refusal to eat, refusal to go to the toilet, refusal to go to bed. So I respect it.

In any case, there was some film on TV with soldiers running around shooting at one another. He likes that kind of thing, always has done. The last film we saw at the cinema together was called *Platoon*, and I thought it was horrific. Although I suppose it's regarded as good.

Perhaps I don't need to tell you any more about all that. I look after my husband, and that's all there is to say. One day at a time. We sit in our tomb and nod to one another.

I don't know what would happen if he died. I mean, the absurd thing is that I'm dependent on him. The amount I'm paid for looking after him, along with his meagre disability pension, keeps us afloat.

I am sixty-seven years old, which means I can't get another job. My pension will be...well, will it be anything at all by the time they've finished speculating? I might end up owing the state money instead—what do you think?

So there we are. Each dependent on the other in our own way. Tomas rings sometimes, but he's got enough to think about. I don't blame him.

Anyway, let's move on.

The following day I went into town in the morning. Perhaps you could say the road that has led me here began that morning in the cheese department in Åhlén's department store.

I've been shoplifting for several years. Got caught twice. The second time I was fined. Fifteen hundred kronor. Perhaps that should have put me off doing it again, but it didn't.

I mean, you have to think in economic terms these days, in which case shoplifting is extremely rational. I've stolen goods worth far more than the amount I was fined. Ten times more, perhaps. What puts most people off doing the calculation is the fear of being caught. The shame.

Oh yes, I've felt that way too. But there have been times when I just had to shoplift. We have enough money for basics, but then I smoke, and...well yes, I could stop buying books. But I don't want to. So I take the risk, even if it's felt like a low thing to do at times. Being a thief.

But on this particular day, as I stood there looking at the various blue cheeses and the parmesan at twenty kronor for a hundred grams, the words Majken had said were running through my mind: 'Have you earned this?'

Have I earned this?

Put like that, the answer was quite simple:

Yes.

A weight fell from my heart. I remembered seeing a documentary on TV about the Swedish national cookery team. A banquet, a load of celebrities sitting there eating dishes with unbelievable names. The King was there.

The King. In what way has he *earned* (that's the key word) the right to travel around eating gourmet food in different places every day? How has this person and that person *earned* the right to sit there with their mouths open, waiting for lamb chops and parsley-scented potato croquettes to just pop in?

Have they worn out their shoulders carrying buckets of water, burned the skin on their hands with cleaning fluids, or sat in a tomb with a zombie, saving society enormous amounts of money?

Have you earned this?

I slipped a Danish blue cheese in one coat pocket, two hundred grams of parmesan in the other. Then I went up to the clothes department and dropped three pairs of expensive tights in my handbag. For the first time I didn't feel the slightest bit worried. I looked around and spotted a wonderful nightdress made of silk. I looked at the price ticket. Nine hundred kronor.

Have you?

Yes. I have. Many times over. But there was a magnetic tag on the nightdress. I don't suppose it's all that difficult to take them off, but unfortunately I don't know how to do it. So I had to leave it. I went down to the book department instead.

I must emphasise one thing at this point. Regardless of what I've earned or not earned, I would never, ever, ever steal anything from a small bookshop or—God forbid—a library.

As you know, the limit for shoplifting rather than theft is one thousand kronor. The tights were one hundred and fifty kronor a pair, the cheeses about a hundred altogether, so I had four hundred kronor left before I reached the limit. With the new reduced sales tax on books, it was enough for Kerstin Ekman's latest two novels;

I've been wanting to read them for ages, but they're always out when I go to the library. They also fitted in my handbag. It's quite a big handbag.

Perhaps you're surprised that I haven't been caught more often?

I think it's got something to do with attitude. Routine. Sometimes I've simply walked out of department stores with goods in my hands. It's a matter of not hesitating. Not giving the slightest indication that you might be doing something illegal. Sometimes I see other shoplifters who might as well have a sign hanging round their necks. Eyes all over the place, uncertain movements.

Once I even went over to a boy who was about to pinch a bar of chocolate. I walked past him and said quietly, 'Don't do it. There's a store detective watching you'.

I actually know who the plain clothes store detectives are in most of the big shops. They might as well be wearing a sign too. The boy left the chocolate bar and scurried off. I thought of pulling a face at the store detective, but there's no point in attracting attention unnecessarily.

After I left Åhlén's I went to the City Library. My shoulders and my back might be worn out, but there's nothing wrong with my legs. Sometimes I get off at Ängbyplan and walk the last two stops to Blackeberg.

OK, it's a way of putting off my return home to the tomb, but I believe in exercise. As long as you can stretch your legs and walk, you're not completely past it. Not completely.

If an angel came to me and asked, 'Would you like to die right now, with no pain?' I would answer yes, but I've never been anywhere near the practicalities of suicide. Sleeping pills combined with a plastic bag over the head is supposed to be the most effective method, but…no.

Isn't the City Library a beautiful building? Just the experience of all those books in a *circle*. As if it's never-ending. I cleaned there for six months in the eighties. Unfortunately I was only filling in for somebody else; I would have liked to stay longer.

At night, when you walk around these silent spaces, you feel like...a custodian. Like someone out of a story by Borges. Do you know Borges? No? That's a shame. When my time was up I tried to explain to them that I loved the place, that they'd never find another cleaner who was so happy in her work as me. Perhaps they would contact me if a job came up?

They never got in touch. It all goes out to contract now.

Anyway. Let's move on.

I took out a couple of books by Joyce Carol Oates. One of those authors you've heard of, intended to read for ages, but never got round to. I probably wouldn't get round to it this time either, I thought, with my Kerstin Ekmans in my bag.

That's it. Something happened there.

When I got to the loans desk there was a woman standing there already. As you do, I had a look at the books she was borrowing. I remember exactly. Maria-Pia Boëthius. Geir Kjetsaas' biography of Dostoevsky. An anthology of poems by Thomas Tidholm. And the real clincher: *Gravity and Grace* by Simone Weil.

Apart from *Gravity and Grace*, they're not exactly the books I'd take with me to a desert island, but they come pretty close.

I glanced at the woman who was taking the books out. She was in her thirties, looked perfectly ordinary. One of those thick tops they make out of plastic bottles or whatever, fastened right up to the top. Hair caught up in a loose pony tail. Nothing like me when I was her age, and yet she was borrowing *my* books, so to speak.

When I got outside I followed her. She went into the McDonald's just past the library, stood looking at the menu above the counter for a while, then came out again. She walked slowly, gazing around as if she was looking for something. I stayed ten paces behind her.

I don't know. It was as if I was waiting for her to...drop

something. A glove, perhaps. I would pick it up, go over to her and we would start talking. No. Not like that. I just wanted to follow her and see what she got up to. What she did.

When we reached the subway station on Rådmansgatan she stopped and looked at the noticeboard outside. One funny thing about her was that she was holding her bag from the library in her arms, like this. I've never done that. She looked at the noticeboard. I looked at her. A kind of—what shall I call it?—solace came over me. There was a little warm feeling in my stomach. When she suddenly turned away and set off along Sveavägen, I stayed where I was. Enjoyed the warm feeling. Then I headed down to the subway and went home.

I could hear the phone ringing as I walked up the stairs. I unlocked the door quickly so I would get there before it stopped. It doesn't ring often, so you have to make the most of it, ha ha.

It was Majken.

I presume she could tell from the way I spoke, because the first thing she asked was, 'Were you out?'

Well yes, I was. I don't know why, but I told her in some considerable detail about my raid on Åhlén's. Majken laughed and laughed when I told her about the reduction in the sales tax on books which meant I could take both novels.

'I've never thought of it in that way,' she said.

We talked for a while about Kerstin Ekman. Oddly enough, Majken's favourite was *Make Me Alive Again*. Personally I find it too fragmented, disjointed, but Majken thought that Ekman's finest characterisations are to be found in that book. She also maintained that it had a completely different resonance if you were familiar with Eyvind Johnson's Krilon Suite. I had to admit I hadn't read a word of it.

'Listen,' I said. 'What you said to me yesterday: "Have I earned this?" I've been giving it some thought today.'

'Oh yes? Did it make a difference?'

'A huge difference. I can't help it, I've always felt a bit dirty when I've been pinching stuff, but today—'

'Pinching stuff!'

'Yes.'

'That's not a very nice way of putting it.'

'Well, when I've been shoplifting then,' I said, slightly offended. 'You know what I mean.'

'I do. Perhaps we could agree on "picked up"?'

'Picked up? I've been to Åhlén's and...*picked up* a few things today?'

'Yes.'

I let the words roll around inside my head, caressed them. Picked up.

Majken went on, 'I mean, that's what we do. We pick up things that are really ours.'

'So you...pick things up as well?'

Majken laughed. 'Yes, Dolly,' she said. 'Yes, I do.'

I didn't understand what was so funny, but it was a relief to be in the same boat.

'What kind of things do you pick up, then?' I asked.

'Oh, all sorts. Clothes. Lots of clothes.'

'But how? They've got security tags on them.'

'There are ways.'

I told her about the nightdress I'd seen in Åhlén's. Majken said she thought she knew the one I meant, that it was beautiful but not quite her style.

'What kind of ways?' I asked.

I didn't think she was going to answer; there was something kind of secretive about her, but she started to go through them: 'Tools to unlock the tag, diversionary tactics. Setting off the alarm before you leave the shop—'

'Hang on,' I said. 'You sound like an expert in all this. What's a girl like you doing working for Konsum customer services?'

More laughter. I liked it when she laughed.

'Dolly,' she said. 'Would you do me a favour?'

'Just say the word,' I replied.

I don't know how to describe it. A kind of playful flirtation had quickly sprung up between us. As if we were trying to impress each other, charm each other. In spite of the fact that she was slightly mysterious, or perhaps for that very reason, I felt a strong, instinctive closeness to her. Maybe I was just starving, how should I know.

'It's nothing major,' she said. 'It's just picking up a bag.'

'I can pick up a bag,' I said. 'As long as I know where it is and where it's going.'

I listened carefully to her description and wrote it down on a piece of paper. The bag would be in the right-hand Armani fitting room in the women's department at NK. It was to be picked up at 14.00 the following day. Outside the store I was to hand it to a woman wearing a pale blue scarf.

'Is that you, the woman with the scarf?' I asked.

'No. She's another member.'

'Member?'

'Yes. We'll get to that.'

I couldn't get any more out of her. When we'd said 'speak to you soon' and hung up, I read what I'd written on the piece of paper:

NK. Armani. Right-hand fitting room. 14.00. Blue scarf.

It was like being in a Graham Greene novel. The detail of the blue scarf in particular was classic. Perhaps that was the intention. I have to confess that at this point I thought Majken was slightly crazy. Of course there would be no bag, no woman in a blue scarf.

But I liked the game. The fact is that I started sketching out a scenario of my own right there and then. I imagined speaking to Majken the following day, telling her that the mission was accomplished and giving her one of my own. A man sitting on a bench in the park at Humlegården. She was to give him a carton of milk that I'd left in the reading room at the Royal Library.

Or something like that. I don't remember exactly.

I went and saw to Börje. He was sitting on the sofa as usual. I felt underneath him to check that he hadn't wet himself. He hadn't. Which meant he'd managed to get himself to the toilet. I heated up some vegetable soup and spent half an hour feeding him. It was a slow process, even though he'd eaten next to nothing all day. I think he's in the final phase of simply fading away. I don't know what I'm going to do.

Perhaps I ought to put him in a home after all. If things carry on like this, he's going to need a drip in order to get any nutrition at all. But if I let him go, his pension will be used to pay for the care home, and I will lose the money.

It sounds crass and terrible, but what do people in my situation do?

Of course I'll make sure he gets help in the best possible way if it does become necessary, but until then…I'm intending to keep him. And he is company of a kind, in spite of everything. Another person's eyes, even if they are empty.

He carries my life within him, if you know what I mean. He is my only witness. When he disappears, there will only be me and a few old photo albums to prove that I ever existed.

Tomas, of course. But he rings so rarely.

It was that film that really broke Börje. *They Call Us Mods.* Lena's in it, you see. It's only a short scene. Kenta and Stoffe are talking to some friends in the square in Vällingby. One of them is Lena.

She died just a couple of weeks after they'd filmed it. An overdose. Börje had never really accepted what she was up to. When she came home and wanted to sleep and looked completely wrecked, when she borrowed money. To the very end he refused to believe things were as bad as they actually were.

The film came out about six months after she died, and Börje heard she was in it. I didn't want to see it, stupid of me perhaps, but he went.

And he saw the world she'd lived in. He took it very badly. He came home shaking his head, and said, 'My little girl, my little girl...' It hurt him so much. Perhaps I wasn't as understanding as I should have been, but I had my hands full trying to stop the same thing happening to Tomas. He was well on his way, and Börje was even more in denial than he had been with Lena. He just didn't want to see.

So...there are things I should perhaps have done differently. But Tomas made it. He's a vet now. In Södertälje.

Anyway, let's move on.

At ten to two the following day I was standing outside the NK department store.

I'd never pinched or picked up anything in there before. Why not? Well, it's certainly not because NK doesn't deserve to have things stolen. Quite the reverse, if anything.

No, it's just a feeling. I always feel a bit insecure in NK. I feel as if I don't fit in there, as if there's a kind of warning glow around me. It *could* be to do with the fact that security is tighter there. But it's probably a question of class, if you understand what I mean. The aroma in NK is different from the one in Åhlén's. Perhaps it's the absence of sweat.

I remember an advert for NK a couple of Christmases ago. *This year's perfect gifts*. One of them was a duck press for twelve thousand. I don't think it ended up under many Christmas trees in Blackeberg. Do you know what a duck press is? Me neither. But people who shop at NK know.

At two o'clock precisely I was upstairs in the women's

department and spotted the shop with Armani Collezione on a sign above the entrance. I walked past but didn't go in. It looked exclusive, to put it mildly. More like a temple than a shop, a sacred space dedicated to style. The security alarms discreetly embedded in black blocks of wood. Two assistants standing with their hands behind their backs, looking both elegant and indifferent. No customers.

I took a stroll past the other franchises as the sweat broke out on my scalp. I have never felt less well dressed, more likely to arouse suspicion. I had no business going into Armani Collezione, and I felt guilty even though I hadn't done anything, even though it was all a game.

I stood outside Gants, keeping an eye on things. When one of the Armani assistants went out, and then a customer went in a couple of minutes later, I took my chance. Without glancing to either side I walked straight into the holy place and headed for the right-hand fitting room.

It will soon be over, I thought as I pushed open a door so tall it almost reached the ceiling. When I walked into the spartan room I gasped out loud. There was a bag on the floor. A plastic Konsum carrier bag.

This changed everything, of course, as you can imagine. No carton of milk in the Royal Library; this was serious. Like when Palme got shot. You didn't believe it at first, it just sounded too unlikely. Then you went to Sveavägen and saw all the flowers and candles, caught a glimpse of the blood. Then you understood. Well, I say understood. You *accepted* it. Irrespective of what had happened or what hadn't happened, you just had to adjust to the situation. Same thing when Lena—

Well.

Of course I couldn't help looking inside the bag. There was a bundle of clothes in there, neatly folded and piled up. I pressed them down with my hand, felt around and couldn't find a single security tag. So all I had to do was pick up the bag and walk out.

My back was sweaty. I took a couple of deep breaths, picked up the bag and walked out of the fitting room. I hadn't looked at the price tags, but I was still certain that the value of what was in the bag was way over the limit for shoplifting. I had felt that from the quality. With my eyes firmly fixed on the escalators, I walked through the security check. No alarm went off, no one stopped me. I carried on down to the ground floor.

Despite a little sweat and hesitancy, I think I conducted myself pretty well. Routine, as I said. Once you've embarked on a task all you have to do is switch off, disconnect the fear and the uncertainty. And besides.

Have I earned this?

Yes. Yes. Although the question was formulated slightly differently:

Have we earned this?

Who 'we' were I didn't know at the time. It was what Majken had said about 'another member'. I had already begun to form a vague picture of what this was all about.

I was wrong, but we'll come to that.

When I got outside I stopped for the first time, pretending to look for something along the street while at the same time sneaking a glance at the entrance to see if anyone was following me. I wouldn't normally have done that, because I've got no chance of getting away in any case if someone young and fit is after me. But this time my role was different: in a way I didn't understand, I was a link in a chain.

No one was following me, and the sweat on my back cooled as I headed for the meeting point at the junction of Regeringsgatan and Hamngatan.

I laughed out loud when I caught sight of the scarf. It was so blue it wasn't even attractive. And worn with a blue coat, may I add. Brr.

I don't know, perhaps I'd expected some kind of...style. I have a romantic streak. Otherwise I don't suppose I'd be sitting here.

The woman was about my age. Grey, semi-permed hair, glasses that were slightly too big and mended with tape on one side. The coat she was wearing looked expensive, much too expensive. You know what I mean. A checkout assistant who's had a winning scratch card.

As I approached her I thought she looked boring. Dreary. Like me, probably. But just before I handed over the carrier bag our eyes met, and my impression of her altered.

Her eyes were blue. Their colour was probably intensified by the scarf, but for a brief moment it was like looking into a welding flame. I don't mean to exaggerate, but there was a *light* in them that the context couldn't explain. It came from within, and it was so powerful that I gave a start, hesitating with the bag half-raised.

She nodded briefly, took the bag, handed me a package and walked away.

I suppose I'd vaguely thought that *if* things turned out as Majken had said, I would follow the woman, but it just didn't happen. I simply stood there like an idiot with the gift-wrapped package in my hand, staring after her.

After a minute or so I put the package in my handbag and went down to the subway.

I couldn't wait. Since there was no one else near the disabled seat I'd chosen, I dared to open the package on the train. What was there to worry about, after all? I don't know, it was as if I'd got mixed up in something that demanded watchfulness, secrecy.

The woman's eyes still hovered before me, as a light does for a few seconds after you've switched it off. Why hadn't I said anything to her? It hadn't seemed appropriate, that's all. And I had been stunned by those eyes.

The package contained the nightdress I had seen in Åhlén's

the previous day, along with a note.

Hope it's the right size. Talk to you soon. M.

I looked around and unfolded the nightdress. It was wonderful. Black, with tiny, tiny red roses, not too close together, not too sparse. Fine silk. And the right size.

I folded it up again, wrapped the paper around it and tucked it in my bag. The train was just emerging from the darkness at Thorildsplan. The Dagens Nyheter building sparkled in the sunlight. A woman on the platform smiled at me.

I had almost expected the phone to be ringing as it had done the previous day, before I got through the door. It wasn't. But I only just had time to go to the toilet, wash my hands and see to Börje before it began to ring.

I went into the hallway, reached for the receiver and stopped myself. It rang twice, three times, four times. On the fifth ring I grabbed the receiver, but let go before I picked it up. It kept on ringing. Six, seven, eight times. It became more and more impossible to pick up the receiver. I went into the kitchen and stared out of the window. Some children were playing down by the eco-cottage. One of them had climbed up onto the roof. The telephone kept on ringing.

I had stopped counting. Presumably I must have dozed off somehow. When I came round, there were no children by the eco-cottage, but the phone was still ringing. I could be wrong, but the sky might have grown darker too.

Börje was sitting motionless in the semi-twilight of the living room, his expression unchanged—just as if a constantly ringing telephone was part of his everyday life. I don't know why, but I felt a sudden stab in my stomach and I started to cry. It was something to do with the desolate sound of the telephone ringing, echoing between the walls like someone drowning, dying, screaming and screaming with no one there to respond.

I pressed my hands to my head, staring at the telephone and trying to get it to stop. I was the telephone. I was the one calling out. It was so horrifically sad that I couldn't bear it. The salty tears ran down into my mouth, and suddenly a totally clear thought flashed through my mind:

You're wrong. It's the other way round. Someone else is calling out, and I am the one who isn't responding!

I wiped away the tears and picked up the phone.

'Dolly speaking.' There was silence at the other end. 'Hello? Majken?'

No one answered. But the line wasn't dead; I could hear that the receiver at the other end was off the hook, and that it was probably a public phone because I could hear the roar of traffic.

'Majken?' I said again, a little louder this time.

Nothing. I pressed the receiver to my ear and—now don't laugh—tried to guess from the sounds where the phone box might be. Cars, footsteps. A bus or truck drove past. Someone shouted something. It sounded like: 'Roooger!' A street appeared in my mind's eye, but which street? No idea. I was just about to put the phone down when there was a clattering sound and a man's voice in my ear.

'Hello?' it said. 'Is there anyone there?'

I slammed the phone down and everything went red before my eyes. For a moment I thought I was going to faint. My heart expanded, pushing the blood up into my head.

I'm getting worked up for no reason, I tried to tell myself. *I'm making things up.*

And yet I still felt afraid. Of what? I don't know. A feeling that I'd got mixed up in something I didn't...I don't know. Anyway, I went in to see Börje, sat down beside him and took his hand in mine.

'Börje,' I said. 'Help me.'

He didn't help me. That is the curse of the strong: when a strong person does fall, everyone is so surprised it doesn't occur to them to hold out their arms to receive her. I'm not just talking about this situation, about Börje. I mean, he's…incapable. Always has been, really.

And I've been hard. Yes, I have.

When Lena died…I said before that I wasn't as understanding as I should have been.

You see, what a memory. You don't actually need to record this, I can repeat it word for word, ha ha.

Not as understanding as I should have been? No, I was hard. He tried to reach me, wanted to share the grief. But I couldn't do it. Couldn't grieve like him. I probably pushed him away many, many times. Physically pushed him away, sometimes.

Perhaps I can't grieve. Perhaps I'm incapable of accepting things that are terrible. Yes, incapable. There's that word again. But in my defence I must say that I had Tomas to look after. If I had buried myself the way Börje did, I don't know how things would have turned out.

So it's no surprise that Börje didn't rush to my aid when the weakness came over me. So I just sat there beside him as twilight fell. It was some small consolation.

When the telephone rang again I got up calmly, went into the hallway and picked up the receiver. It was Majken.

'Was it you who rang before?' I asked. 'About half an hour ago?'

'Yes.'

'Where were you? I answered, but there was no one there.'

'No,' said Majken. 'I had to go. You did well today.'

'Thank you. It wasn't too difficult. Thanks for the present.'

'Does it fit?'

'I haven't tried it on yet. But it's my size, so I'm sure it will.'

'Good.'

There was a brief silence.

'Majken,' I said. 'As you probably realise, I'm wondering about a lot of things.'

'Yes,' she said. 'Of course. I just want to ask you to do me one more favour, then we can talk and I'll tell you everything.'

I don't need to bore you with the details of how hesitant I was, and how I went along with it in the end. The task was exactly the same as before, except that the bag was to be picked up at eleven-thirty the following day.

Actually, no. There were two other things as well. First of all, I had a good look inside the bag this time before taking it with me. My suspicions were well founded. There wasn't a single item of clothing in the bag with a price ticket showing less than three thousand. The total value was around thirty-five thousand.

I remember thinking something along the lines that the clothes seemed to have been chosen purely on the basis that they should be as small and thin as possible, and as expensive as possible. On that point I would turn out to be absolutely right.

Secondly, it was a different woman when I handed over the bag. The same type of woman, if you know what I mean, but this one had brown eyes. And the light was there, but it didn't burn quite so fiercely. Perhaps the blue scarf didn't intensify the colour of her eyes in quite the same way.

I had decided not to say anything, not to ask any questions, and I didn't. I went home and waited for Majken to call.

One thing is bothering me. If I'm going to be stuck in here for a long time, what's going to happen to Börje?

Could you possibly ring for someone to call round and see to him? You just have to ring the home care service on Brommaplan, and they'll send someone.

The key, yes. I'll just get...

I haven't got it. It's downstairs, in the handbag they took off me when I...could you? Oh, thank you. There are only three keys on the ring—the front door, the deadlock and the eco-cottage. The one for the front door—

Yes, of course you'll sort it out. Sorry. I've always been a bit of a fusspot.

Anyway. How's this going to work out?

Could I have another glass of water, please?

Where was I?

Oh yes, Majken. She rang a little while after I got home. It occurred to me that the first time she rang, if you remember—that perhaps the phone had been ringing for a long time before I arrived home and heard it. I once read about some celebrity or other. Some major celebrity, it was, not here in Sweden.

And this...man, I think it was, his number was in the phone book. So of course people rang up all the time. So he had the ring tone switched off. And as soon as he felt like talking to someone, if he was feeling a bit lonely, he just picked up the phone. There was always someone there.

Sorry. That's got nothing to do with this. Did you ring about Börje? Oh, good. Thank you.

I'd been given a present this time too, I forgot to mention that. A bottle of good Cognac. Majken and I had joked about it on the phone the previous day: I was very fond of Cognac, but it's difficult to shoplift in the state-owned liquor outlets, because all the bottles are kept behind the counter.

So now I had my Cognac. I told Majken straightaway that I wanted to know what all this was about.

'Did you like the Cognac?' she asked.

'I'm sure I will,' I replied. 'But right now I want you to tell me what's going on.'

She took a deep breath and asked, 'Dolly. Do you think life has treated you fairly?'

'It depends what you mean by fairly.'

'Let's not split hairs. Life, society, people, whatever you want to call it. Has it or have they given you what you deserve? Have you been able to shape your life in the way you wanted, or have you lived under a constant pressure that basically involves earning money for *other people*?'

If I'm honest, this was delivered in a tone of voice that sounded rather too rehearsed for my liking. It smacked of rhetoric to a certain extent, if you know what I mean. It wasn't what I'd expected.

'Majken,' I said. 'I'm not a fool. You don't need to talk to me like some kind of evangelist.'

I had expected her to be offended. Instead she burst out laughing so loudly that I had to hold the receiver away from my ear.

'Sorry,' she said when she'd finished laughing.

'No problem.'

'Sometimes we call ourselves shoplifters united, as a joke. Perhaps we ought to rename ourselves the church of the latter day shoplifters instead.' I didn't say anything, and she went on, 'Anyway, that's what it's about. We help each other to pick things up. Sometimes there are two or three of us working together, sometimes more.'

I waited for her to continue. When she didn't, I asked, 'Why?'

'Why? Well, because it's so much more effective if you work in a group. Diversionary tactics, all the things I mentioned. There is no so-called criminal who is as exposed as a shoplifter. Alone, unarmed, working in broad daylight surrounded by other people. And if we get caught, there's no one to support us. We've changed all that. One for all and all for one.'

'That wasn't what I meant,' I said. 'I wondered why you do this at all.'

'But Dolly, surely that's obvious?'

'Is it?'

'Hm. I thought you just said you were no fool. Look around you. I'm not going to preach, but do you think anyone loves us? All the members are women between the ages of...sixty-three, I think Eva is, and eighty-four. Ragna, you'll be meeting her, she's...special. We've got the whole gamut: divorced, injured at work, taken early retirement, dependent on medication, ordinary pensioners and so on and so on. And I think that's our greatest common denominator: nobody loves us. We've built up society, and now we're all used up, worthless. Of course we could get involved in the national pensioners' movement, but that wouldn't fit in with our aims.'

'And what would those be?'

'I thought you might ask that. Revenge, pure and simple. Revenge. To make ourselves feel a little bit better by harming whatever has hurt us. Perfectly straightforward.'

'So is it the department stores that have hurt us?'

'Among others. They'll do. It works. Didn't you feel it yourself?'

Yes, I did. Apart from the sheer satisfaction of walking out of a department store with something you hadn't paid for, the relief at having got away with it, there was also that bitter gratification at having swindled the giant out of a little bit of his hoard. At the thought that you had gone up against him and won.

'But what about all the stuff?' I asked. 'What do you do with it all? I looked in the bag today, and I mean it was all really expensive stuff. What do you do with it?'

'Some of it we sell. To cover running costs. Most of it we burn.'

'You're joking.'

'No. Don't you understand? That's the whole point. One of our members, Eva-Britt, has a place in the country up near Sigtuna. We meet there once a month and burn almost everything we've picked up. It's our little ceremony, our...service. If there's something special someone wants to keep, that's fine, but by and large most of it ends up reduced to ashes.'

I actually fell silent for a little while then, if I remember rightly. Majken didn't say anything else. When I had gathered my thoughts, I asked, 'Isn't that a terrible waste?'

'For God's sake, Dolly...'

'I don't mean that. I mean: couldn't you just as easily sell the stuff and give the money to...oh, Save the Children or something? The effect on the department stores would be the same, after all.'

'The idea has been discussed. But think about it.'

I tried. I got nowhere, and I told her so.

'Well,' said Majken. 'If we did that, we'd start to think in a different way. We've got a hundred thousand, right? Perhaps we should invest it so that it can grow a bit before we give it away. Who's going to be in charge of the investment? Who's going to be the cashier? Who's in charge? One of us gets a ten-thousand-kronor electricity bill, shouldn't we be able to...and then there's...you see? It all turns into money. It would just end up like everything else.'

'But it would be more like the right thing to do.'

'Very possibly. But this isn't about doing the right thing or doing good. This is about revenge, nothing else. Well, maybe a bit of fun along the way. It's not meant to be pretty. And besides...'

'Yes?'

'We wouldn't have our bonfire.'

We carried on arguing for a little while. I abandoned my attempts to get Majken to change her mind. I could see the point in what she was saying, even if it still seemed a bit...wasteful to me.

'You'll change your mind,' she said. 'When you've been up to Sigtuna with us and watched the fire burn.'

'Yes,' I said. 'Maybe.'

'Back to work. Would you like to be involved in a slightly bigger event tomorrow? You and I could meet as well.'

'What does "a slightly bigger event" involve?'

'There are more of us. Various roles to play. Ragna will be there, and she's...' Majken laughed. 'She's the star, you could say. Do you want to come along?'

'Tell me what to do.'

She told me.

Once again I had to resort to pen and paper, and this time there was a lot to note down. Times, places, movements. When Majken had gone through the whole plan, I had no choice but to say yes. I just had to be there to see if it worked.

We said, 'See you tomorrow,' and hung up.

I sat there for a long time staring at the piece of paper, shaking my head and laughing to myself.

Such ideas.

Then I did some cleaning. Partly because I couldn't sit still, partly because it needed doing. If my account of these days is a bit messy, it's because that's how it was. Messy. It might seem clear and lucid when I'm talking about Majken, but in between there are...gaps.

For example, I had left some food out, and the apartment smelled horrible, to be honest. The home care service were due to call the following day, and there was no way I could let them see things in that state. I mean, we didn't want to end up being monitored, ha ha.

So I cleaned. All afternoon and all evening. I cleaned in every single corner, underneath all the chairs. Cleaned the oven and polished the mirror until it no longer existed, it was merely an opening. Börje lay on the sofa watching me work. For once the television wasn't on. It was like a...spur, I don't know. A small amount of contact. I carried on until late in the evening.

With hindsight, of course, I understand why I cleaned like that. I was getting ready to move out, although I didn't know it at the time.

My decision the following day was quite unexpected, and yet I had clearly prepared for it in my subconscious. By cleaning. I mean, you want to leave the place nice and tidy.

I don't know. Time disappears from this part of my story too. I could well have gone on cleaning all night. I can see myself opening the kitchen drawers, emptying them, wiping them out. I can see myself scrubbing behind the radiators with a bottle brush. Yes. I must have been at it for a long time. Perhaps I didn't sleep at all that night. Now I come to think of it, it was light outside when I was doing my last job, wiping down the phone with Ajax.

I made some sandwiches for Börje, put them on the coffee table with a glass of milk. Then I sat with him for quite a long time. If I'd been able to say to him, 'Börje, I'm off now,' would it have made any difference? Would he have said something, something along the lines of, 'Dolly, I want you to know I've always…'?

I doubt it. And of course at the time I didn't know I was leaving. I just knew I was going into town to take part in an 'event', and that the home care service would come round while I was out to give me a few hours' respite.

But I just sat there beside him. Looked at the same spot on the wall as he was looking at. Perhaps I said something, perhaps I said, 'Forgive me,' perhaps—

Anyway. Let's move on.

The only things I took with me were the piece of paper with my instructions, and my handbag. My beloved handbag. As the subway trains are so often late, I was out in plenty of time, and in position half an hour before it was due to start. Before I was due to start it.

The envelope was where Majken had said it would be, taped to the bottom of a rubbish bin on the way out of the subway station. It contained only two security tags and a note: 'Good luck! M.'

I suddenly felt nervous. I didn't understand why Majken had given the most important aspect of the plan to me. OK, this Ragna had more to do, but if I didn't play my role correctly, there was a risk that the whole thing would go wrong.

Perhaps it was another test. Or…I laughed to myself. Perhaps it was a favour. After all, I was the only one who wouldn't be doing something punishable by law.

I looked at the people passing by on the street. Lots of people. My anxiety subsided slightly. I thought that all these people, all these strangers are also involved in secret contexts unknown to me. They all have their roles to play in businesses, clubs, love and friendship. They all stand outside a closed door or an open door sometimes, palms sweating, not knowing how to begin.

I was not alone. And unlike most of them, I had a script to follow.

I had synchronised my watch with the speaking clock before I left the apartment, in accordance with Majken's instructions. At nineteen minutes past eleven I began to walk towards the main entrance of the NK department store. I weaved my way through people who were rushing around in their lunch break and reached the door at exactly twenty past. Without hesitating I walked in through the magnetic security readers.

The alarm went off, triggered by the security tag in my pocket. I stopped for a moment to let the security guards see me. When one of them came over to me and said, 'Excuse me,' I turned to face him.

'Why is the alarm going off?' I asked.

'Well,' he said, 'it appears you have something that…'

'That's the most ridiculous thing I've ever heard,' I said, heading away from him into the store. 'I've only just walked in.'

The guard followed me. The alarm carried on beeping. When I had lured him perhaps twenty metres into the store, the woman who must be Ragna came towards me. I bumped into her and she fell, slowly and deliberately, clutching her chest.

I carried on into the store with the security guard following me.

Ragna let out a scream, then lay there like a dead person. The other guard left his post to help her. All the shop assistants were looking in Ragna's direction. The alarm was still going off.

Of course I couldn't see what happened next by the doors. Nobody could see, because everyone's attention was focused on Ragna. But I know that four women with big bags and boxes left the building at that moment. The items they were carrying would have set off the alarm, if it hadn't already been going off, and no one had thought to turn it off amid the general hullabaloo.

I stopped by the escalators and let the guard catch up with me. I threw my hands wide open, then reached into my pockets where, much to my surprise I found the security tag and held it out to him.

'What kind of stupid joke is this?' I asked.

The alarm was switched off. The security guard took the tag, turning it over and over again as if he'd never seen anything like it.

'Why have you got this?'

'You tell me,' I said. 'Somebody must have put it in my pocket. What kind of a place is this, anyway?'

The guard stood there with the tag in his hand, wondering what to make of the situation. I walked back towards the doors.

The other guard and three shop assistants were gathered around Ragna, who was lying on her side looking in my direction. Our eyes met for a second, then two of the assistants helped her to her feet. I waited for a moment until the third assistant had given Ragna her big bag, then I walked out. The alarm went off again.

Ragna waved goodbye to the people who had helped her, then carried her bag out through the beeping magnetic barriers. My guard came hurrying towards me, still carrying the first security tag in his hand. I walked back into the store, put down my handbag and spread out my arms as if to say, 'Go on, search me!'

The alarm was switched off, the other tag was found in my other pocket, and the two guards held a brief conference in subdued voices.

I waited, an irritated expression on my face. The sweat was pouring down my back. The conference ended with no agreement on what I could possibly be accused of. My guard shook his head and said, 'OK, you're free to leave'.

I almost pushed my luck by saying something about reporting them and so on, but decided to leave it. My guard already looked more than suspicious. So I left. This time the alarm remained silent. It struck me that I could probably have taken something with me. If the alarm went off again, would they have stopped me? Maybe, maybe not.

I would like to have tried.

From NK I walked slowly down to the meeting point on Biblioteksgatan. The fear, which I had kept well hidden while I was in the store, began to subside, replaced by the usual sense of relief, but greater than usual. It felt as if my entire rib cage was filled with helium, my hands as light as birds. I laughed, applauded myself. I had played my role to perfection. Majken would be pleased with me.

From a distance it looked quite funny: five women of a certain age gathered around a silver VW Beetle with the bonnet open. Just the way men sometimes stand, discussing carburettors and points. All it needed was for one of them to start kicking the tyres.

As I got closer I could see that the engine had been replaced by NK bags. Then I remembered that the engine is at the back in a Beetle, and the boot is at the front. I recognised Ragna and the first woman, the one who gave me the nightdress in exchange for the Armani bag.

So here they were. Shoplifters united. Gathered around a silver Beetle full of stolen goods. A woman I hadn't seen before turned towards me as I approached. I realised straightaway that it was Majken.

How should I describe her?

Let me put it like this: there are two ways of ageing. In some cases, age distorts the appearance, the face we had when we were twenty or thirty. It puffs up, becomes wrinkled or slack. When you see a face like that, you can just about imagine what the person once looked like, but now she is spoiled, ruined.

In other cases people look as if they were always meant to be that age and to have that appearance, however old they might be. There are wrinkles and grey hair, but it's *just as it should be*, if you know what I mean.

As you have perhaps worked out, Majken belonged to the latter category. She wasn't exactly beautiful in the classical sense. Her hair was peppered with black and white, swept back. A square face with prominent cheekbones, a bit like one of those Inuit. An Eskimo. I don't know; I thought she looked like someone who had spent her whole life living on a little island. Although she hadn't, of course.

She was tall, the tallest of the group, as tall as me. There was nothing sweet about her. When she caught sight of me her thin lips broke into a smile, and she came to meet me.

'Dolores!' she said. 'Welcome to the gang!'

We hugged briefly and I could feel that her limbs lacked any sign of an old woman's frailty. Her eyes were dark brown, almost black; her nose was big, curved like a beak. Oh, now I've got it. Sorry, but I've been trying to find this picture, and it's just come to me.

The way you picture those women in Greek tragedies: Antigone, Medea, do you know what I mean? No. Well. But that's what she looked like, anyway. She introduced me to the others. I don't need to make up any names.

Well, what did you expect?

Of course Ragna isn't called Ragna, what do you take me for? Did you think I was going to give you a list?

Majken was called Majken, but I assume you know that by this stage. It doesn't matter anymore. She has gone to her rest among her mothers, to misrepresent the Greeks. Mis-rep-re-sent. Good grief, what do you learn at the police academy these days, ha ha. To misquote, to create a variation.

I only had nine years' basic education. I wish I'd been able to go on to some form of further education, but—

Anyway. Let's move on.

We left the others and drove out of the city. I didn't ask where we were going. There was a remarkable self-assurance about Majken; it was in her movements, in the absence of questioning glances. I leaned back in my seat and let myself be carried along.

I said before that I am strong, I've always been strong. Perhaps you can understand that there is a certain amount of relief in handing over the tiller to someone else. But this too demands strength, in fact. The strength to know that you will apply the brakes, bring things to a halt when necessary. Then you can stretch yourself to your limits. Of course you can be utterly weak too, simply give yourself up with no will of your own, but that's something else altogether.

Oh, all this is just talk. My life hasn't given me the opportunity to know anything about stretching myself to my limits. But I know a thing or two about survival. About gritting your teeth and carrying on.

Anyway, I enjoyed sitting there in Majken's car, enjoyed, in purely practical terms, the fact that someone else was driving me somewhere, and that there was a purpose to our trip. The heater wasn't working so my legs were a bit cold. Just as I started to become aware of it, Majken asked, 'Are your legs cold? There's a blanket in the back seat.'

'Are we going far?'

'Not very.'

'In that case I'll be fine.'

We drove north towards the outskirts of the city; I'd never been there. It was like an outing. It was just after twelve o'clock on a beautiful winter's day. Lakes and inlets were frozen, with just the odd swan swimming by outfalls, waiting for summer. I felt as if I was out for the first time in many years.

We turned into a gateway and drove up a steep hill to a tip, I don't remember what it was called. Majken stopped the car next to the electronic items container, and we got out and opened the bonnet. It turned out that the bags from NK contained lots of small boxes. I don't know what all that stuff is called, but it was a lot of abbreviations. CD I know, but there were other things too.

Yes, that's it. MP3, that's what it said on some of them. And DVB, maybe. Or DVD.

What?

No, there's no point whatsoever. It isn't there anymore. Or maybe it is, but Majken had two hammers in the car. One for each of us.

I'm starting to get a bit mixed up now. I think I need a little break, if that's all right. Perhaps you could talk to me instead.

I'm sorry?

What are you saying—of course he is! Börje hasn't set foot outside the apartment under his own steam in eight years.

Have they searched the whole apartment?

I don't know what to say, in that case.

Are you joking? I mean, Börje can't just have disappeared, he…

No, hang on, listen. What are we thinking? The home care service. That's it. I haven't been home for two days. They'll have taken him with them, of course.

It's the home care service, they've taken him, ha ha.

Where was I?

Oh yes. We took all those black, shiny things out of their boxes and put them in the boot. Or the front boot, if you like. Then we separated the packaging into plastic and cardboard. All neat and tidy. Majken insisted.

I'd never been to one of those places before, I thought it was fascinating. I only had the eco-cottage to compare it with, and this was the eco-cottage times a hundred. There were whole sofas and kitchen fittings in the containers. In a separate area there were hundreds of fridges all piled up; the only thing missing was a polar bear on the top. Televisions, stoves and armchairs in better condition than the ones I've got at home.

There was hardly anybody there at that time of day. A middle-aged man was unloading a trailer full of furniture. He was doing it in a mechanical way, his eyes empty. Perhaps one of his parents had died, who knows.

Anyway, eventually we got to the fun part. We picked up a few of those black machines and carried them over to the container. Majken held up a little device, no bigger than a matchbox for those long matches you use to light the fire.

'This,' she said, 'is worth about five thousand.'

'Right,' I said.

I thought it seemed strange, I mean I've seen great big brand-new televisions on sale for two thousand. But I suppose it was some kind of computer, and that makes a difference, as far as I understand it.

She held it in the palm of her hand and hit it with the hammer, not particularly hard. It split.

'And now,' she said, 'it's worth nothing.'

She threw it in the container. I held out the biggest item I'd carried from the car, and asked, 'What's this?'

Majken studied it and pressed a button. Nothing happened. She pressed another button and a little screen flipped up.

'Aha,' she said. 'It's a DVD player. Portable. Expensive.'

'How expensive?' I asked.

She shrugged her shoulders and said, 'Twelve, thirteen thousand. Maybe fifteen. I think people buy that sort of thing to keep the kids quiet in the back seat of the car.'

'Fifteen *thousand*?'

'Yes.' Majken found another button and pressed it. A little tray slid out from the side of the machine. 'You put a disk in there with a movie on it. Yes, at least fifteen. Maybe even twenty.'

I turned the object over. Twenty thousand. If for some reason I had set my mind on having one of these, I would have had to scrimp and save for at least two years, probably more. It would never have happened. It was like holding a fragment of another world in my hands.

'Majken,' I said. 'I can't, it's too…I was brought up to…'

I held out the object to Majken. She didn't take it, she said nothing. I looked at it again. It was square with rounded corners, matt black.

What was I brought up to do? I thought.

To have respect for money and the value of money. When a sheet was worn out, my mother saved it to make rag rugs. When a rag rug was worn out, she saved it to put over the potato bin in winter, to protect it from frost.

Today you can buy a sheet for thirty kronor, a rag rug for a hundred. The piece of equipment in my hand was worth twenty thousand, it was…power. Yes. I looked at the concealed buttons, the purity of the design, thought about the town hall where I was summoned after my second arrest. The same blank impenetrability, the same weight. Another world, the world of power.

I hit the little tray with the hammer. It broke and fell at my feet with a clatter. A terrified thrill shot through me. I whacked the screen and it shattered, minute shards of glass scattered across the metal. I gathered my strength and brought the hammer down in the middle so that some of the buttons were crushed before it flew out of my hand and landed on the ground. I stamped on it a couple of times, feeling it crunch under my foot.

Before I knew it I had laid into everything I had brought over with the hammer. There was a particular pleasure...I don't know how to explain it...you know that *smell* you get around things that are brand new? That's what I was dealing with. That's what I was smashing to pieces.

Majken passed on the things she had carried over, and when I had finished there was scrap metal on the ground all around me. I got up; I felt as if I had a red veil in front of my eyes. Majken looked at the rubbish, nodded and said, 'A hundred and fifty thousand, maybe. Shall we go and get some more?'

I nodded. We made a couple more trips. We both attacked the rest of the stuff. Bang bang. Majken estimated the total value at around half a million. I couldn't stop laughing. We tipped the broken glass and bits of metal into the container. There were a couple of televisions in there. I had to stop myself from attacking them. I could have carried on for much longer. One million, two, five.

I twirled the hammer around in my hands. 'If we all went into the electronics department, if we just...' I swung the hammer through the air a couple of times. 'How much do you think we could get through before they managed to stop us?'

'More,' said Majken. 'But then we'd have to pay. Our budget won't run to that. Unfortunately.'

'But what if we haven't got any money?' I said. 'Then they'd have to pay anyway, in the end.'

'No,' said Majken. 'They're insured against that kind of thing.'

'But surely that's even better. Then it's the insurance companies, the bloody insurance companies who'd...'

Majken looked at me sadly. I fell silent, thought about it. I did know how things work, actually. The department stores recoup the costs of shoplifting through increased prices. Insurance companies do the same thing. If they don't make enough profit, they raise the premiums. In the end it's the ordinary individual who has to pay.

I lowered my arms. The hammer dangled loosely in my hand. I looked at the rubbish we'd just thrown in the container.

'Why are we doing this?' I asked.

Majken placed her hand on my arm.

'Because it's fun,' she said. 'No other reason. Come on.'

We went back to the car and drove away from the tip; neither of us spoke for a while. My legs were cold, my entire body was cold now, and I took the blanket from the back seat, wrapped it around me and closed my eyes. The gentle metallic rattle of the car was soothing and I must have nodded off for a while, because when I opened my eyes we were back in the city centre.

'Shall I drive you home?' Majken asked.

I saw her profile sharply delineated in the light from the side window. Individual strands of hair glowed bright orange. I suppose she could feel me looking at her, and when she smiled a deep dimple appeared in her cheek.

'No,' I said. 'I'd rather not.'

She nodded and drove out towards Djurgården. I leaned against the window, watched the exclusive shops along Strandvägen filing past. Hopeless. Hopeless. I suddenly thought of something: 'Why weren't the others with us? At the tip, I mean.'

We crawled across the bridge and Majken turned to face me for a moment before looking back at the road.

'This was just for you,' she said.

I can't say I ever managed to work Majken out.

It's a shame; I would have liked to get to know her better. Or maybe we just weren't meant to get really close.

The only thing I don't understand is why I survived.

How many more died, do you know?

Yes, yes. Later, later.
Always later.

You'll have to forgive me, those days are all mixed up in my head. I'm not senile, I haven't got dementia or anything, but as soon as I try to think about those two days with Majken, everything kind of…dissolves. The only thing I remember really clearly is the conversation we had out at Djurgården.

We were sitting in the café by the canal, do you know the one I mean? I think it used to be a boathouse once upon a time. We were drinking hot chocolate with whipped cream. We were both coffee drinkers really, but chocolate with whipped cream seemed appropriate after our expedition to…Malsta, that's what it's called. The Malsta tip. Perhaps because the whole thing felt a bit like a game.

'Are you happy?' Majken asked when I had scooped the first spoonfuls of whipped cream off my chocolate.

'Do you mean right now? Or in general?'

'In general.'

'No, not at all. Quite the reverse. What about you?'

She shook her head. 'Too much has disappeared,' she said. 'Things you thought were going to happen, but they never did.'

'Yes.'

We took a few sips in silence. There were quite a lot of people in the café, it was the lunchtime rush, but we had found ourselves a corner where nobody came. A big red bus drove past on the street outside. For a second I saw myself lying beneath its wheels, and I burst out, 'Do you want to die?'

Majken looked at me with a strange expression on her face. She had a bit of cream on her upper lip.

'I see you're just as direct as I am.' She nodded. 'Yes. Yes, I do. But wanting to die isn't enough, or so I've heard.'

'No. They say a plastic bag and sleeping pills are the best method.'

'If you want to be considerate, yes. If that's what you want.'

'What do you mean?'

Majken wiped her mouth with a serviette, took a bite of her Danish pastry. I looked out of the window. I've never been very keen on watching people chew.

'Well,' she said, 'the only reason for using that method is because you want to spare the people who find you. You don't look as terrible as you would with the classical methods. Or so I've heard.'

'The classical methods,' I said. 'The ones the Greeks used.'

She laughed.

'Yes. The death of Socrates, that's exactly what they do in Holland.'

We talked about euthanasia; we were both in favour. Majken looked at her watch. 'Don't you have to get home? To your husband?'

I shook my head. 'That's over.'

When I said it I realised it was that simple: it was over. I'd had enough. We drank our hot chocolate, ate our Danish pastries and looked at a solitary swan as he came walking along outside the window, in the middle of the path. I've never seen a swan doing that before. I interpreted it as a sign, without knowing what it meant.

Everything was sparkling white when we left the café. A couple of ice-skaters whizzed past on the Djurgård Canal. The people standing waiting in the bus shelter looked anonymous, like names in the phone book.

'In fact,' I said, taking in the world around me, 'in fact we are absolutely free.'

'If we don't have any consideration for other people, yes,' said Majken.

'And why should we? Who's shown any consideration for us?'

Majken shrugged. 'Not many people.'

We stood with our hands in our coat pockets, looking around as if we were standing at a crossroads and had to choose between right and left. I extricated my hands, and Majken did the same. We took each other's hands. I can't say for sure who reached for the other first. For a second I had the dizzying feeling that I was looking in a mirror. I mixed my own face up with Majken's.

'Shall we do exactly what we want?' I asked. 'And forget about consideration?'

Majken pressed my hands.

'Yes,' she said. 'Let's do that.'

Hand in hand we walked past the bus stop towards the car. The people were shop dummies with clothes on.

As I said, it's difficult to sort out the rest.

But now I'd like to ask *you* something.

Do you remember the duck press, the Christmas present of the year for twelve thousand? You said before that you didn't know what it was. And yet it's your job to protect and defend the people who buy duck presses, or bottles of perfume *this small* for two thousand.

How can you do that? How can you?

That's no answer. You're not *helping* anyone, apart from those who despise you as they despise me. It's hardly surprising if we lose it eventually.

By the way, what's the actual charge?

Arson?

That's quite...lenient, I have to say. How many people died in there?

Now you're lying. You're lying. To cheer me up. But it won't work. It doesn't matter.

It was somewhere in Hammarbyhamnen, the same man, the one who bought stuff from Majken when necessary. She spoke to him and he came out with a box, about this big.

This was the following day, I think. The day after we'd been to… what was the name of the tip again? Malsta, that's it. This was the day after Malsta, I think. Yesterday, in fact.

I stayed the night at Majken's. An apartment with lots of flowers. We sat and talked all evening, all night. I think we came up with a kind of…balance sheet. For and against.

That's the end of your tape, I think. Aren't you going to change it or turn it over or whatever it is you do?

I see. I thought this was what you would be most interested in. Where we got hold of the explosive, who sold it to us, why we did it. I would hope you know *why*, after everything I've told you. I don't remember the rest. It was in Hammarbyhamnen.

But why am I still alive?

I saw everything burning around me, I saw it with my own eyes. The whole of NK. What's happened to the store? It must be closed, at least.

Yes. That's what I thought. How long will it be closed?

Is that all? But I thought…I thought the whole building would collapse. It was plastic explosive. A big white lump. Like when you make bread.

You can't make people invisible. Eventually they will demand to be seen, and then everything explodes—do you understand?

Right.

But aren't you going to…lock me up?

Where else would I go? Majken no longer exists, and…did you give me back the key, is it in my pocket? Oh yes. In that case I'll go home. Straightaway.

I thought I'd be sent to prison for life, and you're just letting me go. How does that work? Yes. I'll go home.

I expect the home care service will bring Börje back, ha ha.

'Thank you for the loan,' they'll say.

Yes, right. Goodbye.

———·———

The woman they had just interviewed was led out of the room by one of the new custody officers; Lennart could never remember his name. Something Arabic. Mattias was sitting at the opposite side of the desk, looking at him with an enquiring expression.

Lennart tore off the top page of his notepad—where he had written, among other things, Konsum customer services, Majken, silver Beetle, Malsta—and threw it in the waste paper basket.

'Why did you let her go?' asked Mattias. 'Suspected arson, normally we'd—'

'Normally, yes. What do you want to do? Lock her up in a cell?' Lennart sighed, took the tape out of the machine and added it to the collection. 'Social services will take over when she gets home.'

'But arson?' Mattias shook his head. 'No, I don't get it.'

Lennart sorted out his things on the desk. It was a mess after the long interview, because he was in the habit of fiddling with pens, paper clips, bits of paper and so on while the suspect was talking. Particularly when it was virtually a monologue, as in this case.

He looked at the young man opposite. Mattias might turn out to be good in time. Or he might turn out to be the very worst kind of pedant. At the moment things were definitely tending towards the latter.

When Lennart went out to make some phone calls, Mattias had taken over the questioning. If you listened to the tape you would probably hear that the suspect's narrative became fragmented and disjointed at that point. Mattias immediately started asking questions. Lennart's method was to gather as much information as possible *before* he started to pick holes in it. But in this case it wasn't necessary.

'Listen to me,' he said. 'We can agree that she didn't try to blow up NK, can't we?'

Mattias nodded sulkily.

'She poured ethanol onto a rug and set fire to it. OK, there was a certain amount of smoke damage and so on. But they're probably losing ten times more through having to close the store than the actual cost of the damage. No one was even slightly injured, apart from Dolores. And she hasn't got any money. She *will* be charged. But I don't see any reason to hold her in custody.'

'But what about this Majken?' asked Mattias. 'Why didn't we try to find out where she is, how she—'

Lennart held up his hand.

'I rang Konsum customer services. There are only two people working there. Neither of them is called Majken. They're both men. They've never heard of any Majken.'

Mattias snorted. 'That's nothing to go on though, is it? I mean, she could have...made that bit up. To protect Majken.'

'Yes,' said Lennart. 'That's possible. But I don't think so. I rang the home care service as well.'

'And?'

'The thing is, the detail of her story is true, but...' Lennart sighed and leaned back on his chair. 'She said something about the fact that she hadn't been able to grieve, hadn't been able to accept things, do you remember?'

'No.'

'Yes, she said...' Lennart looked at the younger man's closed expression and waved away what he had intended to say. There was no point. Mattias would have to go on a course, empathy training or something. But suddenly he thought he could see something different in Mattias' eyes. Something...supercilious, *Oh yes, you've got your ideas, but you don't really know what you're talking about.* Lennart felt a sudden rush of fury, leaned across the desk and said, 'Listen to me. There's something about interviewing suspects that you will hopefully understand in time. *Maybe.* A person has committed a crime, but insists he or she is innocent. OK. This person is not going to confess. What they might let slip, however, is an admission of a *trait within their character* that could theoretically lead to the crime being committed. We don't force that out. Sometimes it just comes out, in passing, while the person is talking about something else. If the person is cunning, it won't come out at all. But most people aren't that smart. And there we have the little thread that we can begin to pull until the whole thing unravels. Do you understand?'

Mattias shrugged his shoulders.

'Anyway,' Lennart went on. 'The home care service confirmed that they went round two days ago, and that she wasn't there. But her husband, Börje was at home, and he was dead.'

Mattias, who had folded his arms and adopted an even more sullen expression after Lennart's lecture, came to life. 'Dead?' He looked at the door through which Dolly had disappeared and reached out as if to grab her. 'But in that case she's…I mean, that's, what's it called, neglect…'

Lennart shook his head. 'He died of natural causes. Three or four days ago.'

This time Mattias had nothing to say. He sat there with his mouth open, seemed to be on the point of speaking, but closed his mouth instead.

'Yes,' said Lennart. 'Everything she told us about looking after him, sitting with him. He was dead the whole time.'

When Mattias had nothing to add, Lennart went on, 'If I were to make a guess, I'd say it was just after her husband died that she rang Majken. Who's Majken? Could be anybody; she might not even exist. Maybe she didn't phone anybody, maybe she just phoned the speaking clock. If this case was more important, we'd check her outgoing calls for that period, but I suspect she just picked up the phone and started talking.'

'So you mean she just made the whole thing up?' said Mattias.

'Not all of it. She's got a record for shoplifting. That's what she did. Went shoplifting and looked after her husband. When he died, she made the shoplifting more important. Made it into her world. Amateur psychology maybe, but you'd be surprised how often it actually is that simple.'

'But...what will happen to her now?'

'I would have preferred it if they could have picked her up right away, but they didn't have anyone available. They'll go round to her apartment later. She can't sit there all on her own.'

'God, what a mess,' said Mattias.

'Yes.' Lennart switched off the desk lamp and gathered up his things. He really wanted to get home to his wife. He had a feeling he would appreciate the mere fact of her existence more than usual this evening.

'Of course I could be wrong,' he said before leaving Mattias to his thoughts. 'Completely wrong.'

———✦———

Twilight had begun to fall when I got out onto the street. I didn't know I'd spent so long with the two police officers. My hands were still smarting from the ethanol that had burned on them for a second before I managed to put out the flames. I scooped a little snow out of a drift to cool them down.

I had said all I intended to say. Now they knew what it was about.

Gently falling snow stippled the heat in my face. It was nice to be on the move after sitting still for such a long time. Ahead of me on the street a woman in her seventies was struggling along with a shopping trolley. She was stooped, bowed, as if she were dragging all the troubles of her life along behind her.

I brushed the snow off my hands, pushed them into my coat pockets and strode off around the corner.

———————

After Lennart had gone, Mattias stayed in the interview room for a long time, pondering. He hadn't been convinced by the woman's story at all. It was incorrect, yes. They knew that. But Mattias had a nagging feeling that it wasn't because she was mentally ill, but because she was…lying.

Lying.

He wound the tapes backwards and forwards for a while, listened carefully to certain sections and just became even more convinced that he was right. For example, if she had wanted to give the impression that her husband was alive during the period when he was in fact dead, she could have simply said that she saw him get up and go to the bathroom, for example.

But she never said that. She said she sat with him, made up his bed on the sofa, that he stared at the wall. Of course. She didn't lie, she just…left out the obvious. The best way of lying is to tell it exactly as it is, but to make little changes here and there.

He rang the telephone company and asked them to check the outgoing calls from Dolly's number. It didn't take long. On the day he was interested in, six days earlier, only one call had been made. The number was 020-83 33 33.

The anxious feeling in his stomach settled slightly. It was just the kind of number you might ring if you pressed the buttons at random. However, he still asked if it was a genuine number, and if so, the name of the subscriber.

It took only three seconds for the woman on the other end to come back to him: 'ICA customer services.'

He heard a rushing sound like the beat of a huge wing pass by his head.

Small details...

His voice broke as he asked to be put through, and when a woman answered 'ICA customer services' he immediately asked, 'Would it be possible to speak to Majken, please?'

'I'm sorry,' said the woman. 'She hasn't been in for a couple of days. Is there anything I can help you with?'

'No thanks, I...I'll be in touch.'

He hung up, looked down at the desk. It was almost an hour since they had let the woman go. The best way of lying is to change small details. Or to tell it exactly as it is, *but in the wrong order.*

When the door of the interview room was flung open, he already knew what had happened.

The Beetle was illegally parked by the entrance to the carpark, but Majken was sitting in it. I brushed the snow off my coat and got in.

'How did it go?' she asked.

'Fine,' I said. 'They've closed the store, so there's no one inside.'

'And they know why?'

'Yes. If they understood. I told them everything.'

'Bravo,' said Majken as she put the car in first gear and drove out of the carpark.

We drove slowly down towards Hamngatan. I had plenty of time to go through my life. Go through. What was there to go through?

So much emptiness, years compressed into seconds and the same actions repeated over and over again. I was done with all that.

Majken reversed up to Kungsträdgården and stopped. The entrance to NK glowed like an orange in front of us. I couldn't see any people. If it hadn't been for my expedition earlier in the day, it would have been packed.

The car was across the carriageway. A bus stopped, angrily sounding its horn.

'Any last words?' asked Majken.

'No,' I said. 'What is there to say?'

She accelerated gently, headed for the entrance and aimed for the double doors in the centre. When she was sure of her target she floored the accelerator. The doors resisted for a moment before they gave way, splintered.

We were on the ground floor, inside a car. It was a weird feeling.

Majken picked up the detonator, hesitated, then gave it to me. I sat there with the little lump of metal in my hand, looking at the blue button. If years can seem like moments, there are moments that can seem like years.

Somewhere far away, someone screamed. I pressed the button.

Once again I had managed to forget that the boot is at the front on a Beetle. Therefore I just managed to be surprised, for a fraction of a second, that the annihilating blow came from the *front*. The windscreen shattered into a white blur that covered my eyes, made everything disappear. We are not invisible.

Let's move on.

Paper walls

The summer when I was nine years old, my dad came home with a cardboard box on the back of his truck. A big cardboard box. The biggest I'd ever seen. Two by two by two metres. Dad said it would hold eight thousand cartons of milk. I don't know what had been in the box. In those days my dad was working at the sawmill, so it was probably some kind of building material. Rockwool, maybe. I didn't speculate at the time. It was just a wonderful box, for me.

As soon as Dad had thrown it off the truck, I dragged the box over to the lawn and got inside. It smelled wonderful, like brand-new toys on your birthday. The double doors formed by the lid stood open, facing the garden; they framed the image and made the daylight brighter. The everyday trees and bushes became new and strange, as if I were watching a film.

I sat down on the floor and saw Dad come into the picture, on his way to the front door. He stopped, turned to face me and waved. I waved back, even though it felt wrong. You don't wave to people in a film. But I was really pleased about the box, after all.

Dad went into the house and I closed the doors of my box as best I could. However I fiddled, there was a gap about one centimetre wide that I just couldn't get rid of, and through the gap a strip of sunlight fell across the floor. It was impossible to achieve total darkness so I closed my eyes instead. Listened.

Through the thin walls I could hear birds singing, the sea lapping on the shoreline, faint voices, outboard motors. It was as if everything had been moved far away from me, out of reach. I was able to distinguish each individual sound, but the whole picture, the world, was gone and couldn't reach me.

I lay down and pretended I was in a different time. The strip of sunlight lay across my hips like a narrow belt. All around me were castles, tournaments. The voices I could hear were knights quarrelling. Soon the swords came out. If I opened the doors, my horse would be outside waiting for me. Through the roof I could see pterodactyls crossing the sky. They were circling around the box, but they couldn't get in. Perhaps they couldn't even see it, perhaps I was invisible.

There was a knock at the door, and I opened my eyes. The strip of sunlight lay across my thighs.

'Anyone home?' called my father's voice.

'Yes.'

'Dinner will be served in the main house shortly.'

I got to my knees and crawled out of the box. The afternoon sun dazzled me. The faint, electrical hum of the summer brought me back to the real world. The smell of sawdust from Dad's Fristads trousers. I wasn't aware of any smells inside the box.

'How's it going?' he asked.

'Great,' I said.

He ran his hand over the box.

'There's no room for it anywhere inside,' he said. 'If it rains, well...' He shrugged his shoulders. 'You can keep it for as long as it lasts. Or do you think we should chuck a tarpaulin over it?'

'Dunno.'

Dad nodded. 'I'll check the weather forecast.' He looked up at the sky. 'It's not going to rain for a while. Unfortunately for the potatoes.'

'Fortunately for the box,' I said.

'Yes.'

We went into the house.

When Dad had gone to work the following day, I went out to the box. The dew hadn't yet evaporated, and the cardboard surface was damp, buckled. The box looked odd standing there in the garden, like something that had been dropped from a spaceship. It made everything around it look different.

In the garden shed was an old pram that Dad had saved so that we could take the wheels off if I wanted to build a go-kart. It was difficult to get the box up onto the pram, even more difficult to get it to stay there. After several failed attempts where the box fell off after a couple of metres, I got the idea of putting a few stones in the bottom.

I had to pull the pram along behind me so that I could see where I was going. The box fell off several times. It must have taken me an hour to move it the three hundred metres to Sjöängsstigen, and when I got there things became even more tricky. The track was narrow, and the trees were so close that the branches scraped along the sides of the box, constantly threatening to knock it off.

Adults came along the track, joking with me: 'Moving out, John?' One person offered to help, but I declined. I didn't want them to know. When I got to the last part, actually going into the forest, I left the pram, tipped out the stones and pulled the box along behind me. It was easier. I had only brought the pram to give the task a kind of legitimacy. A child dragging a massive box behind him along the ground doesn't look good. I knew that.

In the forest there was no one to get in my way. I held onto one of the flaps and the box slid smoothly across the grass and the moss. As soon as I felt the slightest resistance, I stopped and checked. Pushed aside a branch or shifted the box sideways to get around a rock. The box was still completely undamaged when I reached my goal.

My old den, made of sticks and bundles of fir branches, had withered. The needles that were still attached had turned grey, and the whole thing looked like a pile of brushwood. I spent a while clearing it away and spreading it around the forest. Then I put the box in its place.

I took a few steps backwards. It was fantastic.

The box created a world within the world. Its pale brown, geometric shape in the middle of the chaos of the forest was my work. My creation, my orderly lines. The box had made me the owner of this place. My house was here. The doors were wide open, all I had to do was step inside.

I ran home with the pram, made up a bottle of squash, grabbed some biscuits and a roll of tape and ran back. Then I spent the whole afternoon in and around the box. With the tape I could close the flaps so that no daylight found its way in.

'What's happened to the box?'
'I moved it.'
'Oh?'
'Can I sleep there tonight?'
'In...in the box?'
'Yes.'
Dad peeled a boiled potato, put it on my plate. I could do it myself, but it took five times as long. He looked out of the window.

The sky was pale blue, with hardly a ripple to be seen on the water in the bay.

'Yes, I should think so,' he said. 'But in that case I want to know exactly where you are. How did you manage to move it, anyway— it's a real whopper!'

'With the pram. It's in the forest, by Sjöängen.'

'Up towards Bogefors?'

'Yes.'

'Oh, I know.' He looked at me. For a moment I thought he looked sad. Then the expression vanished. He smiled. 'I think we'd better give the sleeping bag a bit of an airing first.'

The sleeping bag, which had been packed away for a long time, was hung on the clothesline to air. Dad put new batteries in the big torch and I made myself some sandwiches and a big bottle of squash, then packed the whole lot in my rucksack along with some Tintin annuals and a pillow.

Dad was sitting on the front porch in the evening sun, reading old magazines. I stood in front of him with my bag to show him. *Here I am. All packed and ready to go.* He squinted at me, nodded.

'Right. So you're off, then.'

'Yes,' I said. 'I'm off.'

There wasn't much more to say. We always hugged each other when I came out to meet him, or when I was leaving. This wasn't one of those occasions, so I was surprised when he got up from his chair and put his arms around me.

'You take care of yourself,' he said.

'I will,' I said. 'I'll be back tomorrow morning.'

'Yes. I know.'

I set off and he sat down again; I could hear the creak of the springs behind me. I turned around one last time, waved. He waved back. His reading glasses had slipped down his nose and the sun set them on fire; the shadows made the porch look soft and warm. I'll always remember him that way.

The low sun didn't reach down as far as the box, and the glade lay in shadow. I unrolled my sleeping bag, placed the pillow at the top and arranged my provisions in the corner. Then I lay in the sleeping bag for a long time, reading Tintin and gazing out across the forest where the twilight was making the tree trunks dark. I didn't play any fantasy games; it was just the way it was.

When the light was too poor to read any longer, I closed the doors. I made a few air holes, taped the doors shut and switched on the torch.

The big difference between this and being in a tent was that nothing was moving. No canvas flapping, no hint of the shadows outside. No contact with the ground. Only the smooth walls, all exactly the same. I could have been absolutely anywhere.

I read about Tintin until my eyes started to feel gritty, then I switched off the torch and curled up in my sleeping bag. It was pitch dark. I opened and closed my eyes, couldn't see any difference.

Perhaps I slept, perhaps I didn't. If I did sleep, I was woken by a noise. Something was moving across dry twigs, through grass. It was getting closer. I felt my eyes with my fingers to check that they were open. Yes. It hurt when my nail touched the eyeball. I reached for the torch and found it, but didn't switch it on.

I held my breath. Whatever was outside stopped, started moving again, towards the box. I could hear it breathing now: it was deep and slow, I pictured a big animal. My head was spinning from the lack of oxygen and I slowly exhaled, breathed in again and stuck my fist in my mouth.

This was no horse or cow. Something that size, though. Much bigger than a person. I could hear that from its footsteps. But the thing that was moving towards my bed was walking *on two legs*. I can't tell you exactly how I knew that, but there was something about the interval between the steps, how the feet landed on the dry grass, the dry leaves.

In vain I stared at the cardboard walls in the direction from which the creature was approaching. Nothing but darkness. I screwed up my eyes and red stars began to explode. The creature was just outside now, on the other side of the wall. My heart was pounding like mad and I wanted to hurl myself at the taped-up door and run, run.

The sound of the creature's breathing was now so loud I thought I could feel the warmth of its breath on my face. The thing that was breathing was no more than half a metre away from me. Slowly, slowly I reached out my hand, until my fingers touched the cardboard wall. I kept them there, waiting.

I imagined a blow, a sudden jolt, the thin wall ripped open, and I would be sitting there face to face with the creature on two legs that was not a person. But nothing happened. Everything was quiet. I exhaled again, breathed in new air.

Then it happened. I felt it first as a faint vibration in my fingertips, then I heard the shuffling noise. The thing on the other side was running its hand over the wall. Slowly, like a caress. I felt the pressure of its hand, the wall bulged a fraction as it passed directly under my fingers. It stopped there for a moment, and then it was removed.

I sat with my fingers touching the wall, listening. Footsteps disappearing through the grass. The muscles in my legs were aching from sitting still in such a cramped position, but I didn't move until the footsteps were indistinguishable from the soughing of the treetops. Then I moved my hand away from the wall and curled up on the floor.

It had left me.

The final processing

From *Vi* magazine, August 2006

For those of you who might be interested in the phenomenon of the awakening of the dead that took place in Stockholm on August 13, 2002, there are a number of books available.

The most thorough account of the course of events is to be found in Dead or Alive? *by Sten Hammer, which was published recently. In addition to a detailed minute-by-minute analysis, this 800-page work also includes interviews with a number of key figures.*

A more critical view is prevalent in The Compound *by ETC journalist Dag Eliasson. Here the main focus is on the actions of the authorities before and after the escape from the Heath on August 17, 2002. The interview with Health Secretary Lars Härstedt, who resigned in connection with this incident, is particularly interesting.*

Much of the research that has been carried out is available only in specialist books which can be difficult to get hold of, but science journalist Karin Johannesson takes a more accessible approach in The

Revolt of the Enzymes. *The various schools of thought within what came to be known as ATPX research are presented very clearly; X stands for the mutation of co-enzyme ATP, which has not yet been mapped, and which is believed to be the cause of the phenomenon.*

Jovan Sislek's In Death's Boardroom *is a pure thriller, depicting the rise and fall of the Lifeguard pharmaceutical company. The scandal surrounding Lifeguard's much vaunted 'death vaccine', which turned out to be no more than a bluff, is highly relevant, since the trial begins in Stockholm very soon. Exciting reading.*

Very little has been written about current activities in the Heath. A tabloid journalist recently compared the Heath with North Korea. Almost nothing comes out. A small number of eye-witness accounts have been gathered together in Slaves into Death, *published by Timbro, which unfortunately has a noticeable political bias.*

It is also worth mentioning P. O. Enquist's play The Processing, *now available in the series of contemporary dramas published by Stockholm's Dramaten Theatre. The play, which had a lengthy run in the city, is based on a large number of interviews with relatives of the reliving, and is absolutely gripping.*

This is just a fraction of everything that has been written. In English alone there are another twenty books that I have chosen not to mention here.

———⸱———

Kalle Liljewall was a humper and the black sheep of the family. On his father's side, more or less everyone was a member of SACO, the trade union for academics. Except for Kalle, who lugged gear for the dance band Tropicos, and wasn't a member of a trade union at all.

Kalle couldn't do much right in his father's eyes: he was the drummer in a funk band that wasn't successful enough, his apartment was in Rinkeby, and his job had a title that didn't appear in the Swedish Academy's official list of words.

'Humper?' his father had asked, putting down his wine glass. 'And what exactly does a...humper do?'

'Drives stuff around. Carries stuff.'

His father tried to catch the eye of Kalle's sister Rebecka, who was twenty years older, to see if she could help with the interpretation. Rebecka placed her index finger over her lips and pondered for a second, then asked, 'Is it the same as a roadie?'

'No. A roadie's like...well, I do some roadie stuff as well. Plug in leads and so on, but mostly I drive stuff. And carry it in.'

'So being a roadie is a somewhat more highly qualified role than a humper?'

'I suppose you could say that, yeah.'

Rebecka nodded. It was all clear to her now. Kalle had the lowest-ranking job in the entertainment industry, and that was the end of that. Her father shook his head and sighed.

Kalle wasn't upset. That was exactly the reception he'd expected. He'd only told them about his new job to wind them up, actually. And for the satisfaction of hearing his father utter the word 'humper', of course.

He had been a neglected child in a way, the result of a brief relationship between his father and one of his students at university. Kalle had lived with his mother Monica until he was thirteen, when she committed suicide by standing in the middle of the subway track and simply waiting. His father reluctantly took over his care.

Kalle had met his half-sister only a few times while he was growing up. Just after Kalle moved in with his father in Danderyd, Rebecka gained her PhD at the University of Stockholm. With her father's help she subsequently became Sweden's youngest ever female professor of philosophy, and took up a post at the University of Lund.

In connection with the awakening of the dead in 2002 she acquired a certain level of fame, or notoriety, as an advocate of a strictly utilitarian approach to the issue. Her father was delighted. Notoriety was often a sign of academic stringency.

But Kalle...Kalle was something else.

While living with his father, Kalle was under constant pressure to strive upwards, ever upwards. The conditions in his new home could probably have been described as ideal. But not for Kalle. He just wasn't the right type.

You only have to look at the family photograph from Rebecka's doctoral graduation ceremony. There stands his father, tall, slim and angular in a perfectly cut suit. Sharp as Ockham's razor. Beside him stands Rebecka, in a simple but elegant sky-blue dress that accentuates the line between her shoulder and jaw, the line a male PhD candidate half-seriously, half in jest transformed into a logarithmic curve with the aim of extracting the equation for true beauty.

A short distance away stands Kalle, his arms dangling by his sides. He is looking into the camera as if he has just been caught doing something he shouldn't be doing. He is fourteen years old, 163 centimetres tall, and he weighs seventy kilos. He wears his suit like a prison cell into which he has been forced with an electric cattle prod. In spite of the fact that he had shaved in the morning, his face is shadowed with stubble. His hair is thick and red.

A changeling. No other possible explanation. A mix-up on the maternity ward. But a DNA test has been carried out: Kalle is the biological son of Emeritus Professor Sture Liljewall. Sometimes genetics goes out of the window and that's the end of it.

Ten years had passed since the photograph was taken; Kalle was now twenty-two centimetres taller and thirty kilos heavier. He wore his hair in dreadlocks, usually caught up in a knot at the back of his neck. He had a full beard which he trimmed with scissors to keep

it around five centimetres long. He was, to put it simply, a bear of
a man.

Kalle carried within him a great pain, contained in the space
of a hand's breadth beneath his right collarbone. No, there was no
tumour or anything lurking there, he'd had it checked out, but that
was exactly where it started to hurt when life came over him. A
black heart, pumping a feeling of powerlessness through his body.
When it happened he hammered on the drums until the sweat was
pouring off him, which usually worked. Sometimes he had to drink
a lot of beer.

Life is for living. Kalle had worked that out a couple of years ago.
It's not necessarily obvious, it wasn't obvious to Kalle, but for that
very reason he had defined it in his own mind: I want to live. There
was no need to say any more.

Kalle had been working as a humper for Tropicos for about a
year when his father rang and offered him the chance to earn a bit
on the side. He didn't put it quite like that. *The possibility of supple-
menting your income somewhat*, or something along those lines. A
few things needed moving. Technical apparatus.

'Haven't you got people who do that sort of thing?' asked Kalle.

'Do you want the job or not?'

'I was just wondering.'

'Well don't. It's a driver we need. Three hundred kronor an hour
plus expenses. Cash in hand.'

'Wow. I didn't know you were into that kind of stuff.'

'Do you want the job or not?'

'Yeah, yeah. Sure. OK.'

Kalle was given a time and place, and the conversation ended
with no fond farewells. He wasn't all that keen on working for his
father, but the money sealed the deal. He had a small monthly salary
to remain on standby for whenever Tropicos might need him, plus
he was paid for every job. Over the past few months it had been

only a couple of times a week. It was five years since the group had appeared in the Swedish charts, and although they had their circuit, there weren't many new jobs.

Kalle got by, but no more. While he was waiting for Funkface to break through—which to be perfectly honest he didn't believe would ever happen—a couple of thousand extra would go down very well.

He borrowed the small van, the one they used only for transporting equipment (he didn't think it was a good idea to turn up in the bus with the name of the band airbrushed along the side with palm trees and a sunset) and presented himself at the goods entrance to the Karolinska Institute at nine o'clock in the evening.

In the loading bay stood seven metal boxes, their surfaces a matt sheen. In contrast to Tropicos' battered sound system, these boxes looked as if they had never been used. Not a scratch. Each roughly one cubic metre.

Kalle switched off the engine and got out. A door opened and a man with small hands and small glasses emerged. He nodded to Kalle and gestured in the direction of the boxes, then folded his arms. Kalle estimated that he could probably throw the man about four metres. Tempting thought. Instead he set to work and loaded the boxes into the van. Some were light, a couple weighed in the region of eight kilos. They were so well packed that there wasn't the slightest rattle from inside as he put them down.

When everything was loaded, Kalle stood beside the van and folded his arms too. The man hopped down from the loading bay and got in the van without a word. Kalle stayed where he was for a few seconds—*two metres up in the air, smack! Head first on the tarmac*—then slid in and started the engine.

'Where are we going?'

'The Heath.'

'Where those dying people are?'

'Yes.'

'Are we actually going into the—'

'Yes.'

Kalle put the van into gear and set off with an unnecessary jolt. The man put on his seatbelt. After a couple of minutes they were on the E4, and the man didn't say a word. Kalle switched on the CD player and 'Monkey Woman' by King Kong Crew boomed out. When the man still didn't say anything, Kalle turned up the volume and they funked their way along the E4, turned off onto the E18 and eventually onto the gravel track across Järva field.

As the approached the gates of the compound, the man touched Kalle's arm and pointed first at the CD, then *dab-dab-dab* with his finger at the floor. Kalle pretended not to understand; he looked at the floor as if he were searching for something, then shook his head.

'Turn it down,' said the man.

Kalle slowed down. A guard came out of the booth next to the gates.

'What?'

'Turn it down!' said the man more loudly, looking annoyed. Kalle turned it down. He'd got a reaction. Point made. The man opened the door and got out of the van, went over to the guard. He took a piece of paper out of the inside pocket of his jacket and handed it over. The guard looked at the paper, at the van, at Kalle. He didn't seem very happy. He gestured at the man and went back into his booth. The man stayed put.

Kalle stared at the compound beyond the gates.

So this is what it looks like.

There must be hardly anyone in Sweden who hasn't heard of the Heath, but after the events of 2002 very little was known about what actually went on in there. The living dead, or the reliving as they were called, had escaped and managed to take the lives of around a hundred people before being captured and returned to the Heath in an unconstitutional joint operation between the police and the military. Since then the area had been closed to the public.

The official version was that they were undergoing rehabilitation, that the reliving were carrying out some form of therapeutic work, but for one thing no journalists were admitted to the compound, and for another public interest had waned since the situation had stabilised. The Heath had been left to its fate, and as long as the dead didn't get out, hardly anybody cared about what happened there. The relatives who complained had given up, in the majority of cases.

Kalle just found the whole thing unpleasant. If he'd known the job involved a trip to the Heath, he might well have opted out. As he lived only a couple of kilometres away, he had once taken a stroll down there to look at the fence surrounding the half-finished living accommodation; his interest didn't extend any further. But now he was here, he found he was curious after all. His heart was beating a little faster.

What does it look like in there?

The strange thing was that his companion also seemed nervous. He stood there moving his feet up and down on the spot, rubbing his hands together. A light drizzle had begun to fall, and in the floodlights the man looked trapped, alone in a deserted field.

Kalle sounded the horn and the man jumped. Oh yes, he was nervous all right. Kalle grinned as the man waved a hand to shut him up. He almost felt sorry for the jumped-up little bastard.

The guard came out and handed back the paper. Evidently everything was in order, but Kalle could tell from the guard's body language that he wasn't happy about the situation. He would have preferred to tell them to turn around. Instead he went back into his booth, and as the man got in the van the gates silently swung open.

Kalle drove through.

'Which way?'

The man pointed. 'Turn right up there.'

There wasn't a single street lamp, and the beam of the headlights swept over bare concrete walls, was reflected in lifeless window-panes. It looked like a ghost town, appropriately enough, and Kalle's foot was ready to hit the brake at any moment if a zombie should come staggering out in front of the car. He wasn't feeling too good, there was a kind of buzzing noise in his head, a cacophony of voices in a room far away.

After a couple of turns they drove into an area with floodlights mounted at regular intervals on the front of the buildings. The lights were all directed towards the centre, and a large building unlike those surrounding it. It looked more like an oversized cottage than anything else, and perhaps it had once been intended as a laundry and community centre. There was a similar place where Kalle lived, and the Kurdish Society held parties there. The party atmosphere was distinctly lacking here, though: a number of guards were positioned around the building, and the windows were covered with both shutters and bars. It looked a lot like a prison.

'Here?'

'No. Keep going.'

The guards by the entrance looked at them expressionlessly as they drove past. A couple of images that didn't belong to him flashed through Kalle's head: two children jumping into a bed, a huge tree falling into the sea.

He had heard of this: people sometimes found they had the ability to read minds in the proximity of the reliving. He realised there must be a lot of them contained inside the building. He turned to the man by his side, but the only thing he managed to pick up was some kind of series of mathematical calculations.

He's shutting me out. He's doing it on purpose.

The man turned to face him, and for the first time there was the hint of a smile on his lips. 'Yes,' he said. 'Of course.'

Even as he spoke the series of numbers continued to flow. Kalle blinked and tried to concentrate on the road. It wasn't that easy, it was like driving through a storm of whirling pine needles, but the phenomenon faded as they moved away from the building.

After a few more twists and turns they reached an area without lights, and the man beside him suddenly said, 'Here. Stop.'

Kalle looked around. The only difference between these buildings and the others they had passed was that here there were lights on in a couple of basement windows. The thought field was once again no more than a distant rushing sound.

The man got out, went over to the door and knocked. It opened and he slipped through. Kalle leaned against the steering wheel and thought things over. There was something shady about all this, that was obvious. Not completely shady, because they'd got through the gates, but a bit on the shady side.

Dad...

In what way was Sture Liljewall mixed up in all this?

His father's life and work had always been a mystery to Kalle. In one way it was very simple: he couldn't understand why it was necessary for professors of philosophy to exist. People who think. Well yes, that's all well and good, but as a profession? His father never appeared in public, and Kalle didn't have a clue what he did all day. Unlike his sister. She wrote controversial articles sometimes, articles Kalle didn't like, but at least he could get his head around them.

You bang on your drums, you clean offices, you write stupid articles. OK. But his father...

Then there was the other thing. The thing Kalle had never been able to put his finger on. He didn't like his father. Sture was stiff, cold, analytical. That's one thing. But on top of that...on top of that there was something *wrong* about him. Kalle wasn't analytical by nature, he hadn't tried to define the problem, but the feeling was there. A slight insanity.

A Trivial Pursuit question Kalle remembered for some reason:

When the poet Geijer died, what was found under his bed?

Answer: A pair of brand-new, unused ice-skates.

That feeling, only worse. That there was something under the bed that couldn't be explained. Something in the wardrobe, something in the deepest recesses of the brain. Something not right. That kind of thing.

When the basement door opened, Kalle got out of the van. He had thought things through, and he no longer felt it was strange. This place, this darkness fitted perfectly with his father, and the word for it was *depressing*.

The man who emerged from the basement was different from the one who'd been in the van. This man was dressed in a shirt and jeans, and even held out his hand.

'Hi. Are you Sture's son?'

'Yeah.'

They shook hands. Kalle gave an extra little squeeze, and the man responded. Then they unloaded the boxes together.

The basement was much bigger than it looked from the outside. The walls were brilliant white, and there was a smell of fresh paint. In one long wall there were two metal doors with round windows, which also looked brand new. The room was illuminated by a couple of portable floodlights on the floor. When they had carried the boxes in, Kalle looked around.

'What is it you do here?'

'Nothing. Yet.'

'So what will you be doing?'

The man looked at Kalle for a couple of seconds, then said, 'I don't want to be unpleasant, but you don't know about this place, OK? If anyone asks, you've never been here.'

'Like that, is it?'

'Mm.'

Kalle looked around again. With this new information, the room took on quite a different character. He smiled as he saw Q from the James Bond films walking around testing stuff.

'Do you want me to…sign anything?'

The man tilted his head to one side. 'Do you want to?'

'No, it's fine—I'll keep quiet.'

'OK. Good.'

The man held out his hand to say goodbye. Kalle took it, and this time he looked into the man's eyes. He recognised that expression.

I'm sitting at the computer. I turn around. Dad is standing there. He's looking at me.

That look. Searching. Evaluating. But here there was something more, something that belonged to this place, like a finger feeling its way across a soft membrane, trying to find a way in, into his head.

Kalle squeezed the man's hand even harder, a piece of cartilage moved and the finger inside his head jerked in pain.

'Bye,' said Kalle, and went back to the van.

He took the longer route around the outside of the compound to avoid driving past the community centre again. The security guard at the gates glanced at the van and opened up.

How the fuck do they avoid going crazy in there?

When he was perhaps a hundred metres from the gates, Kalle stopped the van and let the engine idle as he leaned back and let out a long breath. The whole expedition had taken no more than two hours, and he was completely exhausted.

Six hundred. Is it worth it?

He closed his eyes, enjoying the silence inside his head. After a couple of minutes he was calm. Just as he pressed down the clutch to put the van into gear and drive off, there was a knock on the passenger door. He let out the clutch, reached over and opened the door.

A girl was standing outside, perhaps a couple of years younger than him. Her medium-length hair lay plastered to her head with the rain.

'Hi. Can I have a lift?'

'Where are you going?'

'Rissne.'

'Jump in.'

The girl got in and closed the door behind her. Kalle glanced sideways at her. While the interior light was on he had noticed that she had red hair.

He put the van into gear. 'Is it natural? Your hair?'

'Yes,' she said. 'The one per cent club.'

'Is that all?'

'Yes. So the chances of us meeting are…one in ten thousand.'

'Are they?'

'I don't really know.'

They considered this in silence as they bounced across the field heading for the E18. Kalle thought it was a shame she wasn't going to…Bagarmossen, for example. He would have liked to drive her home.

'Do you live there? In Rissne?'

'Mm. You can drop me by the turn-off.'

'I live in Rinkeby, but I've got nothing…I could drive you home.'

'OK. Valkyriavägen 13.'

Kalle nodded. The monolithic apartment blocks of Rissne were rising ahead of him. Kalle knew Valkyriavägen, because Totto who played bass in Funkface lived on Odalvägen, which was the next road. What are the odds on that?

As they turned off for Rissne the girl asked, her eyes firmly fixed on the road ahead, 'So what were you doing out there?'

Kalle thought about the man in the shirt and jeans. *You've never been here.* But then he could hardly deny it. He shrugged.

'Moving some stuff. What about you?'

'What kind of stuff?'

Kalle sighed and glanced at her. 'I'm not really allowed to talk about it.'

'OK, who are you working for?'

'No, listen, seriously. What were you doing there?'

There was a brief silence as Kalle turned into Valkyriavägen. Number thirteen was at the far end.

'Trying to get a feeling,' she said eventually. 'About what's happening.'

'In there?'

'Yes.'

Kalle pulled up outside her door. He switched off the engine. The rain was pattering on the roof of the van. He might be a big man, but he was incredibly feeble when it came to this kind of thing, and a little bud of relief burst into flower in his breast when the girl asked, 'So have you got a phone number?'

'Yes. Have you?'

They both had phone numbers. They swapped. When the girl opened the door and the interior light came on, Kalle took the opportunity to have a good look at her. Her face was round, like his, but the bones beneath the skin were more prominent. And then there were the freckles, of course. Thin body, she probably weighed less than half as much as Kalle.

'Hang on,' he said as she was about to close the door. 'What's your name?'

'Flora. See you.'

The door slammed shut and Kalle watched her walk away with long, determined strides.

What was it called? Twin souls.

One in a million. The kind of story that keeps you going, the kind you remember. You get together, and you can never part because you have to be true to the incredible chance that led you to meet in the first place.

One in a million.

Kalle was humming to himself as he turned the van around and headed for Rinkeby, thinking that six hundred was a pretty decent amount. He would happily have done this particular trip for free.

The following day he had a job with Tropicos—the opening of a shopping centre in Norrtälje. Mario the Magician, Fame. Balloons for the kids and Tropicos for the more mature customer. They were just going to play the twenty-minute set, which meant their four chart hits plus a track from their latest album, which had come out two years ago. Tropicos weren't quite as hot as the name might suggest, but they could still charge a reasonable fee because they were…reliable.

In addition, Roland the lead singer still had a little stardust on his shoulder pads. He sometimes turned up on the odd game show on TV, and his divorce a year earlier had preoccupied the weekly gossip magazines for a month or so. That was the level of his fame.

The amplifiers and other equipment were already at the venue, so all Kalle had to do was transport the instruments and the band members who weren't driving themselves. That was the usual routine these days, and he only needed to get the big bus out of its garage in Haninge for a longer trip about once a month. There was some talk of selling it.

On this occasion he had the instruments and microphones, plus Roland and Uffe, the bass player. As usual Uffe was sitting in the back sucking on the chewing tobacco under his top lip while flicking through the sports section, while Roland sat in the front with Kalle.

It would be overstating the case to say they were friends, but Roland and Kalle had discovered a level of communication that suited them both. A month ago Funkface had opened for King Kong

Crew at Mosebacke, which meant Kalle had been unable to drive Tropicos that evening, so they had hired another driver. Roland said afterwards that it felt as if something was missing the whole time, that it wasn't as much fun without Kalle.

So they got on well together, even though they didn't exactly open their hearts to one another. For example, Kalle knew very little about the reasons behind Roland's divorce after twenty years of marriage.

Roland pointed to the mobile phone which for once Kalle had placed on the dashboard.

'Are you expecting a call?'

'Yes…no. Maybe.'

'A girl, then?'

Kalle overtook a Toyota that was moving particularly slowly and was able to confirm his prejudices once again: an old man in a flat cap.

'I don't really know.'

'You don't know if it's a girl?'

Kalle grinned and said nothing. After a while Roland asked, 'Bit of a sensitive issue?'

'Yes, I suppose it is.'

'Serious, maybe?'

'Mm.'

'OK.'

They talked about food instead; it was a mutual interest. Roland talked about the advantages of using soft drinks in cooking, particularly Trocadero, which went very well with coriander. Kalle wasn't really there, somehow. Yes, he was waiting for that call. Of course she'd asked for his number first, but maybe he could ring her?

As so often happened, he couldn't quite put his finger on it. There was something about Flora. He'd felt it as soon as she got into the van: *I like her.*

348

That didn't necessarily mean a great deal; Kalle found it easy to like people (with the exception of academics), but there was something special about her, something you didn't often find. A seriousness, perhaps. A kind of gravity. Something that responded to the call from the dark materials within Kalle's own breast.

The gig was the same as usual. Cheerful songs, good reception, applause that quickly died away among the shops. A couple of drunks dancing. A child crying because the bunny rabbit balloon Mario the Magician had given him had burst. Pack up and drive home. Not bad. Not sad. A job.

On the way home his mobile rang. Kalle's heart leapt and Roland burst out laughing when Kalle dropped the phone in his eagerness to take the call. When he managed to pick it up he could see from the display that it was his father. He sighed. 'Kalle speaking.'

'It's Daddy.'

(Kalle couldn't understand why his father persisted in using this peculiar phrase, always uttered in a regretful tone.)

'Yes?'

'Your services are needed tonight. A few things to be moved within the compound.'

'Look, I don't know...'

'What don't you know?'

'If I want to do it. Again. I just thought it was so...unpleasant.'

There was silence at the other end of the line. Kalle could picture his father chewing over his disappointment once again. Then it came: 'Let's say double, then. Six hundred. An hour.'

'That's...extremely well paid.'

'Yes.'

'What is it you want me to do?'

Kalle was to be outside the big community centre inside the compound at seven o'clock. If he showed his ID at the gate, he would be admitted.

'…and Karl, a slightly pleasanter tone on this occasion would be greatly appreciated.'

'Mm. Just one question: What's your involvement in all this?'

A brief pause. Then his father replied, 'I think the conditions that apply to this job have been explained to you—isn't that correct?'

They hung up. Kalle turned to Roland. 'Can I borrow the van again tonight? To go out to the Heath?'

'Sure. What is it you're moving?'

'Just some stuff.'

Back home in his apartment Kalle wandered around like a cat on hot bricks, waiting for the phone to ring. From time to time he picked it up and carried it around with him for a while. It was so small in his big hand, ridiculously small. All his fingers had to do was press the numbers in the right order, and it would be done.

All his fingers had to do. He had let himself be seduced by a special offer, and had ended up with a phone with such tiny buttons that he had to use his little finger to key in a number, and even then it was often wrong. Texting was out of the question.

He started to key in the number. Got it wrong. Deleted it. Put the phone down.

Why am I so nervous?

Presumably for the same reason he hadn't wanted to talk to Roland about Flora. This was serious.

Kalle closed his eyes and pressed his mobile to his heart.

Come on, ring. Buzz. Do something.

Kalle had got together with Emilie when he was fifteen. Her home and her family had been his refuge from Sture and the silence in the big house in Djursholm, and later a sanctuary of comparative orderliness when he started moving around, staying for a while with a series of friends.

It wasn't until he was twenty-one and renting his own apartment in Rinkeby that he realised what his relationship with Emilie had come to mean to him. Refuge. Sanctuary. And now he had his own. As for Emilie, she had started her university course and was tired of Kalle's lack of ambition. They parted as friends, as the saying goes, in spite of the fact that they actually had nothing to say to one another, and therefore weren't friends at all. But still. No bitterness, no recriminations.

Since then Kalle had had a couple of short-term relationships, but in the small hours when he sat alone gazing blankly at Jay Leno or *Sex and the City*, he acknowledged the truth: he had never experienced love. Therefore, the very idea terrified him.

He put some pasta on to cook, made a simple tomato sauce with fresh basil, and ate while watching an episode of *Beverly Hills*. Then he fiddled with the Portastudio for a while until it was time to leave. Funkface were putting together a demo, and a couple of the tracks would sound better with a slightly more pop beat. He couldn't find anything.

The security guard on the gate examined Kalle's ID closely as if to underline his disapproval of Kalle's presence, then let him through. There was still a scrap of daylight left in the sky and the buildings didn't look as unpleasant as on the previous evening. Rather it was as if a great sorrow was held within the walls. Something that had never quite come to pass; something that had been too late a long time ago.

It wasn't easy to find the way. Signs showing contradictory numbers reinforced the impression that he was in a place that was no more than a maze, a labyrinth leading inwards towards an empty centre. He thought he caught a glimpse of faces at some of the windows.

He gave up trying to remember the route and instead allowed himself to be guided by the strength of the hum of others' thoughts.

Eventually he turned into the right area and without understanding how, he knew that one of the guards was the same as the previous day. The one with the tree falling into the water. Right now the man was thinking of clouds changing shape.

Kalle stopped and got out of the van. The guards who came towards him were carrying a more up-to-date version of the submachine gun he had used during his military service. They checked his ID, looked closely at his face and ransacked his brain.

The man with the clouds (he was still thinking about clouds while he was talking, and Kalle didn't understand how he could do it) pointed at the doors and said, 'You gather up everything in the entrance and pack it away. That's it. OK?'

Kalle nodded, and they let him pass.

The items to be moved had been placed in a small foyer with a pair of double doors leading further into the building. There were a couple of metal hospital beds, some drip stands and a number of boxes. The lids were not sealed, and Kalle peered inside one of the boxes. He saw a large quantity of one-litre bags containing a clear liquid. He looked at the labels: glucose 10%, sodium chloride 3%. Sugar and salt, as far as he could tell. He set to work.

When he had carried out everything except the drip stands and came back for the last time to fetch them, he stopped for a moment to catch his breath. He had already begun to learn how to control the intrusive alien thoughts. He played the drums. As soon as another voice, another series of images started to take over, he laid a beat over the top of them and played it until they fell silent.

There was a small gap between the double doors leading to the next room. He walked over to it.

To have been here and not—

He put down a beat over his own thought. A bossa nova, gently seductive, which he increased in pitch and volume until it filled his head. Hopefully his own thoughts could no longer be heard. He widened the gap and looked in.

It looked like a gigantic classroom. Rows of long benches were laid out at regular intervals, and at each bench a number of people sat doing something with metal objects. Next to each person was a drip stand, with two tubes leading down into the person's arm.

People? But they're dead—

Quickly Kalle tried to recapture the bossa rhythm, but the impression he had just received was too powerful, and forced its way up to the surface. The people sitting at the benches were dead. Empty eyes or no eyes at all, dried-up flesh, bony fingers moving over the metal objects. Kalle couldn't see what they were doing, but he had no time to ponder the issue because the door behind him opened and the guard walked in. Kalle backed away from the double doors, and the guard grabbed him by the shoulder.

'You just couldn't help yourself, could you?'

Kalle didn't speak. The guard snorted and waved a hand in the direction of the drip stands. 'Get those out of here.'

Kalle gathered up the stands with the guard's eyes burning into his back and his clouds floating through his head. He felt sick, and couldn't manage to come up with a rhythm to hide the fact. When he had finished loading the van and walked around to the driver's door, the guard came over to him.

'Listen. It's fine. But you're a part of this now. With all that entails. Just so you know.'

Kalle nodded, knowing nothing about what anything entailed. He just wanted to get out of there. When the guard looked away Kalle got in the van and drove off as quickly as he dared. Somehow he managed to find the basement and unload the stuff. With a lump in his throat caused by either nausea or tears, he drove out of the compound and stopped in the same place where he had met Flora.

His thoughts were his own once more, but he didn't want them. He'd never seen a dead person before. Now he'd seen hundreds.

Perhaps it wouldn't have been so bad had it not been for the intense sorrow and impotence that poured wordlessly, blankly from the dead bodies.

This is hell.

Kalle switched off the engine and lay down across the seats. He tried to fight it, but the darkness was pumping through his body, a paralysis that began in his hands and spread inwards until he was incapable of moving. Everything was darkness, and his body was a part of it.

The memories came back to him. The man who had turned up at school and asked Kalle to accompany him to the headmaster's office. The head and the school counsellor were sitting there. The counsellor asked Kalle to sit down next to her. Then she took his hand, and Kalle knew he didn't want to hear what she was going to tell him.

An accident. Your mother has been involved in an accident. On the subway.

It wasn't until a year later that he found out from Sture what had actually happened. She had simply positioned herself in the middle of the track and waited, staring into the big eyes as they came closer. Kalle could see it in his mind's eye, all too clearly. He could see the body being hurled backwards a few metres before it ended up underneath the train. His mum. Mush. She must have turned into mush.

Kalle forced some feeling into his fingers, clenched his fists and hit himself on the chest, hard. Hit the black heart, and the pain unlocked the paralysis. He sat up and thumped his thighs, chest, head, drumming pain into his body. He was moving, he was in pain, he had a body. He was alive, and he just kept drumming.

His phone rang. His hands stopped in mid-air and he stared at the phone. Heard the sound, couldn't work out what it meant, his thoughts were somewhere else. It rang again.

Telephone. Answer.

He picked it up in one aching hand and managed to hit the reply button.

'Hello?'

'Hi, it's Flora. Do you remember me?'

Kalle blinked and looked out through the windscreen. Far away he could see the lights shining in the windows of tower blocks, the glow of the city spread across the sky. He opened his mouth to say something, but he didn't know what it was.

'Hello? Are you there?'

'Yes. Hi. Sorry. I was…hi.'

A brief pause. Then Flora asked, 'Are you upset?'

Kalle inhaled deeply, then let the air out.

'Yes. But I'm…a bit better now.'

'Do you want to come over?'

'To your place?'

'Yes.'

If a bomb fell on your house and it collapsed. If another bomb fell a couple of minutes later and rebuilt the house. You'd probably end up just standing there for a while, pondering over the incomprehensibility of life. Kalle was fumbling. He felt like a idiot, heard his previous responses replaying in his head, but there was nothing he could do. The words just wouldn't come to him.

'If you want to,' said Flora. 'If you've got time.'

'Listen, I'm just…' said Kalle. 'I'm starting the van now and I'll be there in five minutes. OK?'

'OK. Great.'

Kalle put down the phone. He'd said he was going to start the van. He started the van. He set off across the field. He was so used to driving that it was automatic. He headed for the lights in the distance.

When he parked outside Flora's apartment block he was more or less back in his body. He got out, locked the van, then stood for a while taking in the facades, the many windows around him.

So many people...

That there should be someone among all these people, that their paths should happen to cross and that now, among all these windows, he would know that...*There. That window. Behind that window, nowhere else.*

Kalle ran his hands over his face and shook his head.

Calm down. You're just making all this up. You've met a girl who seems nice, OK. Now you're going to go up and see her, have a chat. Take it easy.

But he couldn't help it; the highs and lows of the past half hour were like some reality-enhancing drug. Everything seemed so beautiful: the lights in the windows, all the people with their lives and their hearts pottering about doing little tasks almost reduced him to tears.

He went inside and realised he didn't know which floor she lived on, or what her surname was. He was just taking out his wallet so that he could find her number and phone her when a door opened on the ground floor and Flora looked out.

'Hi.'

Kalle waved his wallet. 'I didn't know where you lived, I thought I'd just—'

'I live here.'

'Yes. Right.'

Flora went back in and Kalle followed her. It was as if everything was happening five seconds in the future, and he couldn't keep up. Once he was inside the apartment and had taken off his shoes, he said, 'Listen, you'll have to forgive me, but I'm completely out of it. I've been waiting all day for you to ring me and now you have and I'm just...I'll pull myself together.'

Flora walked around him and closed the door.

'What's happened?'

'It's that place. It makes me feel really ill.'

Flora nodded and led the way into the kitchen. The apartment was sparsely furnished; things were there to fulfil a function, not because they had been chosen specially to fit in a particular spot.

In the kitchen there was a table with two chairs of one kind, two of another. A rag rug on the floor and an illuminated Christmas star in the window, even though it was September. Kalle sat down and pointed at the star.

'Are you early or late?'

Flora laughed and Kalle realised it was the first sensible thing he'd said since she rang.

'I just wanted a lamp, and it…was there. We haven't got much money.'

'We?'

'A friend and I share the rent. Can I get you anything?'

'What have you got?'

'Beer. Tea.' Flora was staring at him; he probably looked like something the cat had played with for a while then left to its fate. 'How about a beer?'

Kalle gestured in the direction of the window. 'I'm in the van.'

'Well, you could walk home. Or stay.'

Kalle no longer felt as if things were happening five seconds in the future. More like a couple of hours. He looked down at the table, patted it as if he were checking what it was made of.

'Beer would be good.'

Flora took two bottles of Tuborg out of the fridge and sat down opposite him. They both took a swig in silence. Kalle nodded appreciatively at the bottle, then looked around and asked, 'Have you lived here long?'

'No. Listen, there's something I need to say to you straightaway. It's a bit hard to put into words, but…'

Flora clamped her lips together, thought for a moment. Kalle leaned forward a fraction, expecting the worst. She had a boyfriend, she wanted him to sell drugs, all kinds of unimaginable things. Flora smoothed her hand across the table and said, 'The thing is…you don't need to worry so much about what you say. What impression you're making. I already know you're…a good person.'

'In what way?'

Flora smiled and looked shyly into his eyes for a second, then went on, 'In a very fundamental way. I know you and I fit together. And I know I want to be with you.'

Kalle sat there with his mouth open. Then he took a couple of deep swigs of his beer, put the bottle down and said, 'Wow.'

Flora nodded.

'I know this sounds…but I have to say it. I have a kind of… ability. To read people. It's not the usual kind of thing, but…I know a lot of stuff about you, for example. And it would be wrong not to tell you.'

Kalle barely heard any of this; he was still digesting the fact that he was a good person, that she wanted to be with him. That was the most important part, after all. He nodded slowly and said, 'Yes…'

Flora frowned. 'You don't think this is weird?'

'Yes. No. I don't know. What did you say?'

'That I know stuff. About you.'

'Like what?'

Flora looked into his eyes; Kalle straightened up on his chair, pushing back a couple of dreadlocks that had fallen over his face. He couldn't decide what colour her eyes were; they shifted between green and brown like the forest in early autumn.

'Someone died,' said Flora. 'Someone really important to you. You haven't been in a relationship for a long time. You play the drums. You haven't got a home.'

'I've got an apartment…'

'Yes. But you don't have a place you can call home. A place you can go back to. It's gone. Your mother died when you were…twelve, maybe. Yes, that's it. You like cooking and…' Flora glanced at Kalle's empty beer bottle and stood up, 'you like beer.'

She fetched another bottle. Kalle pressed his forehead against his hand as if to feel whether anything was visible.

'How do you know all this?'

Flora sat down. 'These are the concrete things I can see. They're not really all that important. But I know who you are, if you understand what I mean. In a way that's much more difficult to describe.'

'And you…you like what you see?'

'Yes. Very much.'

Kalle leaned back in his chair. There was a lot to take in this evening. Shouldn't he feel some kind of…unease at the fact that she could see into his mind, the same unease he had felt in the Heath? Yes. On the other hand, this was exactly what everyone dreamed of: the idea that another person would see you, understand exactly who you were…and like you anyway.

'This…' said Kalle. 'This ability of yours. Does it have anything to do with the Heath? You were there, after all.'

Flora sighed. 'Yes. And no. I have…a lot to do with the Heath. But that's a consequence of my ability. Not vice versa.'

'You had it before?'

'Yes.'

Kalle thought this was all very difficult. Why? He thought it over. Because everything was the wrong way round. Normally a relationship started with the details. What the other person did, where they lived, what kind of music they liked. Slowly you worked your way further in, found out the other stuff, the deeper perception of who this person really was. And Kalle had no corresponding information about Flora. Anything he might say or ask would be no more than trivia, scum on the surface. He sighed and scratched his head.

'I know,' said Flora. 'It's stupid, telling you this. But I have to. Otherwise it would be like…'

'Spying?'

'Yes. But I want to know all the other things too. If you want to tell me. If you want to…'

'No,' said Kalle.

Flora's eyes closed as if she had been struck by a sudden but expected pain. She nodded. 'I understand.'

'No,' Kalle went on. 'I want to hear about *you*. It seems as if we've saved a few weeks finding out about me, so we've got plenty of time left for you.'

Flora burst out laughing. She lit candles and switched off the main light. Kalle fetched more beer. Flora talked about growing up in the Söder district of Stockholm, and her parents who were both lawyers. About her grandmother Elvy, who she saw frequently. About her grandfather Tore, who was one of the dead locked up in the Heath. How she and her friend Maja, who was studying politics, had found this apartment and moved in six months ago.

For the moment Flora was getting up at five o'clock in the morning four days a week and travelling to a place in Kungsholmen where she made sandwiches that were shrink-wrapped and sold mainly in newsagents'. The rest of the time she played Nintendo games, went to gigs, read a lot of poetry.

It was after midnight and they'd run out of beer; they'd moved on to sharing a bottle of wine that really belonged to Maja. They were both slightly tipsy, and Kalle was gazing at Flora, who was in the middle of a monologue about Nintendo.

'…because the fantastic thing is there are no enemies in the Mushroom Kingdom. OK, Mario beats Bowser for the hundredth time, but suddenly he's back playing golf or go-karting. They're all friends. And there's this really weird thing in Mario Sunshine. Someone who turns out to be Bowser's son kidnaps Peach and there's this long…he says Peach is actually *his mother*. Mario's completely floored. So's Peach. She doesn't get it at all.' Flora laughed. 'Which means that Peach and Bowser must have had a sexual relationship *without Peach knowing about it!* How stupid is she? Then of course it turns out that—'

'Flora?' said Kalle.

Flora blinked and looked up. 'Yes?'

'This business with the Heath. How does that fit in?'

Flora pulled a face. 'Not now, Kalle. I'm a bit drunk, and that means…this perception of mine, it disappears. It feels so good. I'm just sitting here with a nice guy and I'm…happy. I don't want to…'

'No. OK.'

'I can't even cope with horror games anymore. I used to like them…but now I just want cute characters who are always friends. Cheers.'

'Cheers. Where's your…Maja?'

Flora knocked back the last of her wine. 'I asked her to stay away tonight.'

'I see.'

There was a brief silence. Then Kalle stood up. Flora stood up. They met in the middle of the kitchen floor. Kalle bent down, Flora stretched up. They tasted each other, quietly. Kalle held Flora's head between his hands and asked, 'What do you want to do now?'

A smile flitted across Flora's lips.

'I want to play Peach and Bowser.'

They laughed. They were a little bit scared, both of them. That's how it is. They carried on anyway, as you do when you have to. Kalle's shirt ended up on the draining board, Flora's sweater on top of the cooker. Something ended up in the hallway and something else in the living room. They spread their shells and concentrated their bodies.

It was a quarter past ten in the morning when Kalle was woken by a knock at the bedroom door. He looked around and knew where he was, who he was with and exactly what the situation was. He also knew that nothing was expected of him. He relaxed and sank back on the pillow. Flora sat up, gave him a quick smile and shouted, 'Come in'.

The girl who walked in was not unlike Flora, except that her hair was black and everything had been enlarged. She looked as if she was more or less the same height and weight as Kalle, and her facial features were small and unimportant in a broad face framed by frizzy, teased hair. He realised this was Maja, and he liked her straightaway.

Maja glanced at him in passing before coming over to the bed and saying to Flora in a serious tone of voice, 'I think we need to ring the police.'

Flora didn't look particularly worried. She rubbed her eyes and asked, 'Why?'

Maja gestured towards the apartment. 'That lunatic's been here during the night chucking clothes all over the floor. What's the matter with these people?'

Kalle glanced at Flora. Then he turned to Maja and asked, 'Does he come here often?'

Maja shook her head. 'No. This is the first time. But I think we ought to put a stop to it right now.'

'Maja,' said Flora, 'this is Kalle. Kalle, Maja.'

They shook hands and Maja gazed at Kalle for a few seconds. Then she nodded as if giving her approval. She pointed to the newspaper protruding from her jacket pocket. 'Have you read the paper, or have you been busy?'

'Maja…' said Flora.

'OK. I'll go and sort out some breakfast.'

She turned and left the room, closing the door behind her. Kalle and Flora lay in silence, as if they expected Maja to come storming back in at any second beating a tattoo. When it didn't happen, Flora laid her hand on Kalle's chest, stroked him gently and said, 'Maja is...she thinks she has to...take care of me.'

'Is that necessary?'

'She thinks so.'

'And what do you think?'

To Kalle's surprise, the answer didn't seem to be straightforward. Flora's expression was distant as she thought about the question for a few seconds. Then she said, 'I can understand why she feels that way.'

Before Kalle had time to ask any more questions, Flora got out of bed and said, 'Come on. Breakfast.'

Kalle waved a hand at his naked body. 'Fine by me, but I don't know what Maja would...'

Flora went and gathered up their clothes. They got dressed, and when they were ready Kalle put his hand on Flora's shoulder and turned her to face him.

'I just wanted to say...I think you're fantastic.'

Flora looked up at him and something grew within his breast, a sac that was gradually filled with light, pretty things. Her expression was naked and he knew with the clarity of a revelation: *I will never, ever hurt her.*

Bread, cheese, butter and milk had been put out on the table. Maja was sitting with the newspaper open in front of her. When they came in she began to read aloud:

'*The reliving are still waiting for us to solve their mystery. Since chemical and biological analysis has still failed to produce results after three years, we should now ask ourselves if it is perhaps time to take the next step.*

'*A thorough pathological investigation could solve the central issue with minimal evidence of life. On a cellular level it has been established that ATP is produced in the mitochondria...*'

Maja made a circular movement with her hand to indicate that the article continued in the same vein.

'*...a vesicular exchange that corresponds with...*blah blah... *the international research foundation is amazed at the Swedish inability to*—we've heard this before—*thousands of Swedes dying unnecessarily every year...despairing relatives...*But listen to this!'

Maja pointed to a section towards the end of the item and went on:

'*A proposed law that would allow research on living specimens has now been published for discussion. However, the Law Council has ended up in a Catch-22 situation. In order for this research to be sanctioned, results are required. These results can be obtained only by allowing the aforementioned research.*

'*The only solution is to grant permission on a temporary basis. The results can then be used as a foundation to formulate the proposed law. We must not let this opportunity slip through our fingers yet again.*'

Kalle and Flora sat down opposite her, and Flora put two slices of bread in the toaster.

'No chance,' said Flora. 'Permission on a temporary basis? It's just not going to happen.' She pointed at the paper. 'Is it her?'

Maja nodded.

'Who are you talking about?' asked Kalle.

Flora's lips were compressed into a thin line. 'Rebecka Liljewall. She's Professor of—'

'I know. She's my sister.'

Flora reacted as if Kalle had just said you could make yourself invisible by picking your nose and eating what you found in there. She stared at him with a mixture of disbelief and distaste. Eventually she managed to speak: 'So Sture Liljewall...is your father?'

'Yes.'

The silence around the table was absolute. After a couple of seconds the toast popped up and broke the deadlock. Maja tossed the slices over to Kalle and Flora with a cheerful comment: 'My, but you two have *lots* to talk about!'

Flora grabbed the newspaper and held it up in front of Kalle. 'Have you got anything to do with this?'

'I don't know.'

'You don't *know*?'

'No. I've been moving some stuff.'

'What kind of stuff?'

Kalle sighed. It was as if his family got to him whatever he did. He scraped a burnt patch off the toast and said, 'I'm not allowed to say.'

Flora's gaze felt like a physical heat burning into his cheek. Then she stood up, said 'Fuck', went back to her room and slammed the door. Kalle looked at the slice of toast, which he no longer wanted to eat, and heard Maja's voice. 'Flora hasn't told you, has she?'

'No.'

'You could say she's heavily involved in this business at the Heath. And now it seems as if you are too. On the side of the enemy.'

'I'm not involved at all. I've just moved some stuff around, and it made me feel ill.'

'But your sister and your father are right in the middle of it.'

'Yes. But they might as well be Tarzan and Jane. I don't have anything to do with them.'

Kalle looked at the picture of his sister next to the article and hated the sharp features pecking at his life. Suddenly Maja said, 'Drop the secrecy. You're just protecting something really, really bad.'

Kalle nodded and stood up, heading for Flora's room. Behind

him he heard a bark of laughter. He turned around.

'What are you laughing at?'

'Nothing, it's just…you two are like Romeo and Juliet. And I'm the nurse.'

It took a while to convince Flora how limited his involvement was. It wasn't made any easier by the fact that he felt hurt by her bitterness, and by the idea that he was somehow responsible for what his father and sister were doing, when he didn't even know what it was. Eventually, however, she kissed him on the forehead, on the cheeks, on the lips and said, 'I'm sorry. I just get so…this is important to me. It's almost…the only thing that matters.'

Kalle waited for some small correction, some acknowledgement that he was important too, or could be. Nothing. He could only cling to that *almost* and hope it covered him.

When they went back into the kitchen Maja was reading the article again. She looked up at them and assessed the situation: 'Friends?'

They both nodded.

'Good. I'm just wondering about this "thorough pathological investigation". Wondering what they mean.'

Flora and Maja looked at Kalle. He shrugged his shoulders. 'Haven't a clue.'

---

lab. 4.11
Resectio intestinalis partialis, pulmones, linalis et renes. Nil reactio. Functio cerebri immatatus.

lab. 4.12
Collum femoris extirpatio cum extremitas inferiora. Epicondylus

humeri extirpatio cum extremitas superiora. Nil reactio. Functio cerebri immatatus.

lab. 5.2
Exeres medulla oblongata (thoracalis). Paraplegia superior.

———·———

From *Ordfront Magazine*, April 2004
...among those in power who like to remain hidden, the so-called Association holds a particularly strong position. It is an organisation comprising loosely linked interest groups, which has some influence on both Parliament and the government.

The Association was originally known as Bentham's Friends. It was formed in 1908 as a discussion group centred around the ideas of Jeremy Bentham, who is regarded as the father of utilitarianism; Peter Singer is probably his best known successor.

Bentham's Friends developed strong links with the Institute of Racial Biology at the University of Uppsala. After the end of the war the group ceased to exist—on paper. These days it has no name, no headquarters and no known register of members. But it remains influential.

Utilitarianism has been called an attempt to make a religion out of practical logic. By looking at the factual effects of a decision rather than its ethical or moral content, it is claimed that society can be led to decisions that are more sensible in the long term.

For many, utilitarianism acts mainly as a kind of touchstone. It can be beneficial to measure ideas and convictions against its unsentimental logic. Few seriously believe that utilitarianism can function as the underpinning ideology of a society, since it all too often goes directly against standard morality.

However, the Association believes that it can.
[---]

———·———

Love. It changes everything.

Kalle's activities and days had acquired a direction. If he drove Tropicos to a gig, it was so that he could go home to Flora afterwards. If he worked out a new beat for Funkface, he could play it to Flora. When he found an old carton of cream right at the back of the fridge, he saw that the use-by date was before he met Flora. Therefore it could be thrown away.

Big things, small things. He thought perhaps that's exactly what love is: everything is connected to another person. To be alone is to be a pair of seeing eyes, hearing ears, registering. A meter. Nothing. To be in love is to relate to someone else, to know: *another person exists*. And life expands, acquires something resembling a meaning. That's what he thought.

When they had been together for a week, Flora took him to meet her grandmother Elvy in Täby. She had told him that her grandmother had the same ability as her, and to Kalle's relief Elvy seemed to see the same thing as Flora. He had her approval.

As they sat drinking coffee in Elvy's kitchen, the topic came up again. Elvy asked what Kalle did and he told her about Tropicos, at which point Flora chipped in and mentioned the trips to the Heath. Elvy fell silent and looked Kalle in the eye.

'You *work* there?'

Kalle sighed. Here we go again. 'I've just moved a few things in the van, that's all.'

'What kind of things?'

Kalle had realised that there was absolutely no point in being mysterious. 'Hospital stuff. They've built some kind of...clinic there.'

Elvy looked sharply at Flora, who shook her head. 'I don't know either. Something's going on. Something...terrible. I don't know what it is.'

This was news to Kalle. 'How do you know that?'

'I've been there. Outside. I can feel it.'

'Do you still go there?'

Flora looked at him, her expression uncomprehending. 'Yes. Why wouldn't I?'

Kalle had no answer to this. Without really thinking about it he had assumed that he had saved Flora from her loneliness, her obsession when he picked her up in the van that night. She hadn't mentioned the Heath much since they met, but now he realised this was perhaps out of consideration for him. He was brought back to reality by Elvy placing a hand on his arm.

'What does it look like in there?' she asked.

'Well, it's...empty. Desolate.'

'I mean the security. How tight is it?'

'There are guards more or less everywhere. Submachine guns, the lot.'

Elvy nodded and thought for a moment. Then she looked at him, her expression serious. 'If you wanted to get inside, how would you go about it?'

Kalle smiled. 'Well, I suppose I'd just drive the van in.'

'Can you take me in?'

Kalle laughed and looked at Flora. To his surprise she didn't smile back, but simply looked at him, waiting for him to answer the question. Kalle wound a dreadlock around his index finger as an unpleasant feeling grew in his stomach.

'Yeees...but why?'

'Hasn't Flora told you?'

'She's told me some things.'

Flora looked down at the table and said quietly, 'I didn't really want to drag him into it.'

Elvy folded her arms and stared at them both with the severity of an interrogator. Then she said, 'In that case I think you need to reconsider. This could be our only chance.'

Flora nodded. 'I know.'

Kalle looked from one to the other. 'Hang on, this chance you're talking about—would that be me?'

Their silence was answer enough.

A great deal was explained that afternoon. When Kalle and Flora got back to his apartment in the evening, his head was spinning. They played a few games of Mario Kart so they wouldn't have to talk or think. Kalle had bought a Gamecube so that he could practise on his own, but he still had no chance against Flora. He could win the odd round, but never a whole tournament.

He had just driven into the ravine on Rainbow Road for the third time when the phone rang. Kalle paused and looked at the caller display. It was his father. He glanced at Flora, took a deep breath and answered.

Things needed moving. *From* the compound this time. At ten o'clock tonight. Flora didn't take her eyes off him while he was talking, and the unpleasant sensation in his stomach moved up a gear. When he had hung up he stared at the TV screen for a while, where his car was just being dropped back onto the track, frozen in the air. He turned to Flora, weighing every word:

'I need to ask you something. Did you get together with me because I'm…a chance?'

'Is that what you think?'

'I don't know what to think, to be honest.'

Flora put down the handset and shook her head.

'No. But you are a chance. As well. And I have to...make the most of it. Unfortunately.'

At last Kalle had the opportunity to ask the question that had been going round and round in his head since the conversation with Elvy that afternoon. 'Why?'

Flora didn't say anything for such a long time that he thought she wasn't going to answer, but eventually she said, 'Because nobody else will do it. Nobody else can do it. I've been burdened with a terrible responsibility. Which I don't want. But I can't just run away from it. That would be...wrong of me.' She looked up at Kalle. 'To use your sister's terminology, I would be contributing to the misery of the world. By not doing anything.'

Kalle nodded, accepting what she said. He lowered the car onto the track. Flora was home before he'd even started his last run.

At half past eight they parked the van where it couldn't be seen from the Heath and walked the last few hundred metres to the fence, on the opposite side from the entrance. They sat down to practise. It would be impossible for Kalle to get away with having Flora hidden in the van unless he could mask his thoughts. The field was not as strong outside the fence as it was inside, but on the other hand Flora's ability to read thoughts was better than that of the guards.

They sat down cross-legged opposite one another. Kalle opened his hands wide.

'So what do we do?'

'Don't think about a polar bear,' said Flora.

'A polar bear?'

'Yes. Don't think about it.'

Kalle made an effort not to think about a polar bear. First of all he thought of a blackboard. A piece of chalk appeared and started to draw the outline of a polar bear. He erased the blackboard and thought about a beach with palm trees, like the one on the Tropicos' bus—an impossible location for a polar bear. A cloud drifted across the tropical sky, forming itself into a polar bear. Kalle shook his head and asked Flora, 'Are you doing this?'

'I'm not doing anything.'

'Has it got something to do with the fact that we're here?'

'No, that's just the way it is. If you tell somebody not to think about something, it's hopeless. The polar bear won't disappear until you forget about it.'

'Could you see what I was thinking?'

'Yes. Chalk. A cloud.'

'OK. Can I try again?'

'Mm. Don't think about a giraffe.'

Kalle thought about a giraffe on the savannah. It was nibbling leaves from a tall tree. Flora burst out laughing.

'Well, that's just—'

Kalle held up one hand. 'Wait.'

He started drumming over the picture. Laid down, appropriately enough, an African rhythm on top of the giraffe. The animal's legs moved as if it were dancing to the music. Then Kalle took the drumsticks that were beating out the rhythm and started to hit the picture, banging and banging until it broke into pieces and dissolved into a disjointed collection of colours. Flora stared at him, searching for the giraffe. But there was nothing but the rhythm.

She nodded. 'Say something.'

'Like what?'

'Tell me something. Not about the giraffe.'

Kalle searched beneath, behind the rhythm for words and contexts, but the fact that Flora had uttered the word made the orange and black patches on the giraffe's coat begin to take shape. He could just see the outlines of the body; he drummed louder and said at the same time, 'I've met this girl called Flora. She's got some strange hobbies. At the moment I'm sitting by a fence doing some kind of workout for the brain. I say the word giraffe without thinking about a giraffe and I really like the look on her face right now as she tries to find the giraffe that isn't there.'

It was true. Even though he'd said the word, neither the image nor the concept of a giraffe came into his head. Kalle relaxed and smiled. 'OK?'

Flora nodded and waggled her hand in the air: *so-so*.

'What? There was no giraffe.'

'No,' said Flora. 'But you weren't talking. You were singing.'

'Was I?'

'Mm. It sounded good, but the guards might think it's a bit odd if you start rapping at them.'

They carried on practising. After half an hour Kalle had learned to separate his speech from the rhythm in his head, and Flora could see no trace of the thing he wasn't allowed to think about. They went back to the van. It was a quarter to ten.

'OK,' said Kalle. 'So what's the plan?'

'There is no plan.'

'For safety reasons, or because…?'

'Because there is no plan. I'll get in the back.'

They kissed, then Flora climbed over the seats and found a cloth to hide under.

'Do you realise,' said Kalle as he started the engine, 'that you're actually lying underneath Tropicos' backdrop?'

'I'm honoured,' Flora's voice came through the fabric.

Kalle headed for the gates. Fortunately it was the same guard as last time. He merely glanced at Kalle's ID through the open window and let him in. Kalle found it more difficult to get his bearings this time, because he couldn't allow other consciousnesses through his carpet of drumming. However, he was beginning to recognise the route, and after a couple of minutes he pulled up outside the basement room.

Six metal boxes of the same type as he had seen before were stacked up outside. He went round and opened the back doors of the van. Flora peered out from under the cloth; he saw her, but didn't think about her.

Nobody answered when he knocked on the door. He looked around and opened it. The place had changed. A couple of fluorescent lights hung on chains from the ceiling, shining down on the hospital beds Kalle had brought last time. The cement floor under the beds was discoloured.

Something...disgust...it's...pain

It was the perceptions, not the words that forced their way through the rhythm which was beginning to dissolve, become uneven and

sticky

it sounded as if the drums were standing in clay, mud, there was a squelching sound with every beat and he could hear screams inside his head, beads of sweat broke out on Kalle's forehead as he strained to incorporate the screams into the rhythm, make them

Flora

He looked around. Flora was getting out of the van. He waved his hand to make her stay where she was. She remained by the van, and just as Kalle turned back into the room, one of the doors set in the wall opened.

The man he had seen before wearing a check shirt was now dressed in a white coat. He gave a start when he saw Kalle, and looked into his eyes for just a second too long before a little smile appeared on his lips.

'Hi.'

Kalle just had time to think *Flo*— before the rushing sound of static filled his head, obliterating every thought. The man must have heard it too, because he put his hand to his temple and looked around, searching. On a level that did not involve thought Kalle sensed what it was, and through the noise he said as calmly as he could, 'I've come to pick up the boxes. They're going to Karolinska, right?'

The man nodded absently; Kalle backed out through the door and closed it behind him. Flora was no longer standing by the van.

The boxes were heavy. Each one weighed around eighty kilos, and there was a difference from the boxes he had carried last time: these weren't just locked, they were welded shut. Apart from the handles on the sides, there wasn't a single gap or protrusion.

Kalle loaded them in the van as quickly as he could, grateful for the additional protection they would provide for Flora. The rushing sound had abated as soon as he closed the door, and he carried on drumming as he shifted the boxes. When he went to fetch the last one, the door opened and the man came out. He had taken off his white coat and was now wearing a check shirt in a different colour from the last time. He looked at the van. Kalle pretended not to notice him as he heaved the last box inside.

He closed the doors and the man said, 'Heavy?'

'Yeah,' said Kalle, wiping the sweat from his brow.

The man nodded. 'Sorry. I was a bit busy.'

'It's OK.'

The man was still looking at the van, and Kalle had to make a huge effort not to let any suspect thoughts break through. Whether it did any good or not, he wasn't sure. The man pointed at the van.

'It's a Toyota, isn't it?'

'Yes.'

'Good cars. Bloody good cars.'

The man looked Kalle in the eye and Kalle could feel the groping he now knew he was able to withstand. The man shrugged his shoulders, said, 'See you,' and went back inside.

Kalle was dripping with sweat by the time he started the van. He drove carefully through the compound, out through the gates and up to the spot where he had first met Flora. He switched off the engine, let go of the steering wheel and screamed as loud as he could.

Flora's arms came creeping around him.

'What's the matter?' she asked.

'It's driving me mad. Being in there makes me completely fucking mental.'

'You did really well.'

Kalle took a couple of deep breaths. Then he asked, 'That rushing sound. That was you, wasn't it?'

'Yes.'

'Thought so.'

They both fell silent. Kalle's head felt utterly exhausted, as if he'd been to the dentist, completely drained of energy by the effort of distancing himself. He turned around and looked at the boxes.

'What do you think is in them?'

'No idea.'

'You can't feel anything?'

'No.'

Kalle reached over and ran his hand over one of the boxes. The join between the lid and the box itself was uneven, bumpy with melted metal. He shook his head and looked at Flora. Her expression was distant, as if her thoughts were elsewhere.

'Are you OK?'

'In there…' said Flora. 'It was terrible in there. It hurt. Much worse than outside. The place where we were. That's where it comes from. The pain.'

'Yes.'

'Was it the same when you were there before?'

'No. It's something new.'

They sat without speaking for a while. The boxes behind Kalle felt like a burden, a threat. He turned and knocked on the nearest one. The material was unresponsive against his knuckles, nothing but thick metal. No clue as to what might be inside. His watch was showing just before eleven.

'I think we'd better make a move,' he said to Flora. 'They'll be wondering.'

Twenty minutes later they had reached the loading bay at Karolinska. When Kalle opened the van door to get out, Flora laid a hand on his arm and said, 'Don't ring the bell. Just leave them. And save one.'

'What do you mean, save?'

'Just leave five. We'll take one with us. Shall I give you a hand?'

Kalle shook his head. 'No, it's probably best if I...what the fuck do you think they're going to say?'

'Well, you could have left one behind.'

'Yeah, right. They're going to believe that, aren't they?'

'Have you got any better ideas?'

Kalle had a number of better ideas, but none of them involved finding out what was inside the boxes, so he said, 'No,' and got out of the van. He moved the boxes as quietly and carefully as he could. Luckily nobody came out to check this time.

Luckily. Absolutely. Lucky me. Just like winning the lottery. What the fuck have I got myself mixed up in?

As he put down the last box, his phone rang. He gave a start and ran back to the van to stop the noise attracting unwanted attention. He closed the door and looked at the display. ROLAND, it said.

Roland? What the hell does Roland want?

In his stressed state of mind he didn't consider the consequences, but simply answered as he started the van, the phone tucked awkwardly between his shoulder and his ear.

'Hello?'

'Kalle,' said Roland. 'My dear Kalle. The son I never had.'

Fingers wriggled their way in beneath his cheek. Flora took the phone and held it to his ear so that he could drive properly. Kalle nodded his thanks and manoeuvred out of the loading bay. Roland was obviously drunk, and when he was drunk he became solemn and sentimental.

'Hi,' said Kalle.

'Kalle, my friend. Are you in the van?'

'Yes, I'm...yes.'

'That's absolutely wonderful. Fantastic.'

'If you say so.'

Kalle headed towards the E4 and wondered where this conversation was going. Roland went on, 'The thing is, I've got myself into a bit of a situation. A delicate situation, as they used to say in the old days. I need a lift.'

'Roland, it's a bit...tricky at the moment.'

'You never spoke a truer word, my friend. I accompanied a lady home, and without going into detail I find myself standing here without any money, without...anything on some *fucking* suburban estate in Södertälje.'

'At least you've got your phone.'

'Indeed. And I'm ringing to ask you...to *beg* you to come and pick me up, Kalle.'

Kalle squeezed his eyes tight shut, then opened them again. He couldn't say no. After all, he was driving around in Roland's van.

'OK. Where are you?'

'Now there's a question.'

'Come on, Roland.'

Well, I saw Saltskog on some sign. Salty Forest, for God's sake. That's where I am. So all you have to do is...if you see a man on his own wandering around in a salty forest, that's me. You see, Kalle...'

'On my way. I'll be in touch.'

Kalle indicated that Flora should end the call. He'd been around a couple of times before when Roland was drunk, and he knew that Roland was perfectly capable of bending his ear all the way to

Södertälje if Kalle didn't put a stop to it.

Flora pressed the button and put the phone down on the dash-board. Kalle sighed.

'I have to.'

'OK.'

Kalle waved in the direction of the box. 'What are we going to do with that?'

Flora shrugged. 'We've got a box in the back of the van. So what?'

'And afterwards?'

'No idea.'

Kalle gritted his teeth and concentrated on the road. He'd put his job at risk, presumably done something illegal that would cause him considerable problems, and for what?

No idea.

They drove in silence for a long time. As they drew closer to Södertälje, Flora said, 'I don't know any more than you do. I'm just trying to do the right thing.'

'I know. It just feels a bit odd, driving around in a van thinking we're going to…actually, what is it we're going to do? Save souls? It feels really weird.'

Flora rested her chin on her hands and gazed out through the windscreen. 'Jesus probably felt the same. At first.'

Kalle grinned and looked at her. They both started to laugh.

Roland was slumped against a lamppost on the way into Saltskog, looking utterly miserable. His mobile was by his side and his hands rested limply on the tarmac. He had no jacket, and when Kalle got out of the van he could see Roland wasn't wearing any socks either.

Kalle walked over to him and held out a hand to help him to his feet. Roland looked up at him, but didn't take his hand. He waved feebly at his phone. 'I rang my wife.'

Kalle picked up the phone and put it in Roland's pocket, then slid his arms around Roland and heaved him up. Roland's face was right up against his as he spoke in the tone of someone revealing a great truth: 'Hold on to what you've got. Don't start playing around. Hold firm. There's... nothing out here.'

Roland sighed deeply and looked down at the ground.

'She said she loved me. All along. Up until the day when I said I'd met someone else. That's when it all went wrong. Everything fell apart. Everything. No way back. And I thought...I thought I'd have fun. I didn't. Instead I ended up...' Roland waved his hand to encompass the houses in darkness, the tarmac, the dirty light, '...with this.'

Kalle bundled him towards the car. 'Come on.'

Roland shook him off. 'I'm perfectly capable of walking. I'm not drunk anymore. I'm just so bloody unhappy. Playing in fucking shopping centres. Fake tan. Covering myself in fake tan. Whitening my teeth. Fuck. It's over. What have I done with my life?'

When Roland got to the van and opened the door, he saw Flora. He stopped, straightened up. It took him three seconds to retrieve his charming self, and there it was, all guns blazing. He smiled.

'And you must be...?'

'Flora.'

'Ah, the mysterious lady. Is there room for someone like me next to someone like you?'

Flora shuffled closer to the driver's seat to make room for Roland next to the door. He got in with no sign of intoxication or depression. Kalle looked around on the ground where Roland had been sitting to see if he'd left anything behind. Socks, for example. When he didn't find anything he got into the van, started the engine and said to Roland, 'I'll drive you home, OK?'

Roland flung his arms wide. 'Drive me anywhere you like. I don't care, I don't care.'

When they'd been driving for a couple of minutes, Flora suddenly said, 'I really like "You Forever".'

Roland raised his eyebrows dramatically and looked at her.

'You must forgive my preconceptions, but I wouldn't have thought you were among our target audience.'

'I've heard it on the radio a few times. I usually can't stand that kind of music, but...it's good.'

Roland nodded. 'Thank you. So...you two are out for a drive, are you?'

'Yes,' said Kalle, keeping his eyes firmly fixed on the road ahead. Roland looked around inside the van and noticed the box behind him.

'What's that?'

Kalle cursed his stupidity—why hadn't he covered it up? Flora answered for him: 'We don't really know.' Roland looked at them, waiting for someone to continue. When no one did, he looked at the box again and said, 'If I didn't know better I'd think it was a bomb. Given how guilty you two look.'

Kalle rubbed his temple, but still didn't say anything. He couldn't come up with a single lie that would explain why they were driving around with a hermetically sealed box in the back of the van. Something suddenly occurred to Roland. 'Is it from the Heath?'

Kalle glanced at Flora, who gave an almost imperceptible shrug. Kalle nodded briefly.

'And you shouldn't really have it?'

Kalle said, 'We forgot to drop it off,' and could hear that it sounded every bit as stupid as he'd expected.

'So what's in it, then?'

Kalle injected a little more strength into his voice and said, 'We don't know', hoping that Roland would drop the subject. He seemed satisfied, and for the rest of the trip to Åkersberga they talked mostly about music. Kalle learned that Flora had been a dedicated Marilyn

Manson fan until three years ago, when she had grown tired of his covers and sexist videos. When her parents wanted CDs to hang in the fruit trees at their place in the country to frighten off the deer, she'd given them her Manson CDs. The deer weren't frightened at all. Roland said it might have been more effective to play the CDs instead of hanging them up.

At half past one in the morning they were outside Roland's house in Solberga. Kalle switched off the engine, but Roland made no move to get out. He sat there chewing his lips, then said, 'I've got an oxyacetylene cutting torch in the garage. If you're interested.'

Kalle looked at Flora. She wobbled her head slightly in a way that could mean almost anything. Except for no. Roland held his hands up, palms outwards. 'I won't say a word. And I'll settle for a *little* explanation.'

Ten minutes later Roland had driven his Jaguar ('the midlife crisis', as he called it) out of the garage, and found the torch and a mask. They were standing around the box, which was in the middle of the garage floor. Roland tapped the box with the nozzle of the torch and asked, 'Could there be anything explosive inside?'

'We have no idea,' said Kalle. 'But I don't think so.'

'Might be best if you two go outside, just in case.'

'What about you?'

'Me...' Roland pulled a face to indicate how little his life mattered to him at the moment. 'It'll make a good headline, if nothing else.' He picked up a lighter and held it to the nozzle, turned a knob. Nothing happened.

'How do you start one of these things?'

Kalle could now see that the whole thing was brand new, and had never been used. There wasn't a single scratch on the welding mask. Roland smiled sheepishly.

'It was cheap at Biltema. Thought it might come in handy.'

Flora walked over to the gas tank and unscrewed a valve. A needle on the dial twitched and they heard a spurting, hissing noise. Roland nodded and held the lighter to the nozzle again. The spark caught, and the hissing became sharp and threatening as Roland adjusted the level until he had a blue flame. Kalle had to raise his voice to make himself heard.

'Roland, are you sure you—'

'One hundred per cent. Better to burn out than fade away. Out you go, kids.'

Roland pulled down the mask and approached the box. Kalle and Flora backed out of the ordinary door next to the up-and-over garage door and closed it behind them. Flora pulled Kalle towards the house. They could hear a loud whining from inside the garage, and Kalle could see a flickering blue light in the gap under the door.

Flora sat down on the bottom step, and Kalle thudded down beside her. He slowly shook his head. 'What the hell are we doing?'

'He wanted to do it,' said Flora.

'Yes, but—'

'He wanted to do it. He's enjoying himself. This is...cool. Something like this was exactly what he wanted.'

'You think so?'

'I know so.'

When five minutes had passed without the garage blowing up, they went back inside. They had to screw up their eyes to protect them from the sparks flying from the box where Roland was hunched over, holding the nozzle in a vice-like grip. The garage had a dry, electrical smell and was several degrees warmer than it had been.

Roland straightened up, pushed up the mask and let out a long breath. He caught sight of them and wiped away the perspiration that was running down his face.

Flora's right, thought Kalle. Roland looked childishly happy.

383

'Hi,' he said. 'Hot work, this.'

They moved closer to the box. Roland's cut traced an erratic, wavy line along the top edge of the box. A gap about a centimetre wide had opened up. It still wasn't possible to see what was inside, but it was clearly nothing flammable. However, it was something that stank. When the torch had been off for a while, they were all aware of the stench emanating from the box. Roland leaned forward until his mask hit the edge of the opening, then quickly jerked backwards with his hand to his mouth.

'Fucking hell,' he said between his fingers. 'That really stinks. What the hell is it? Is it...could it be...?' Roland looked at the box and licked his lips. 'If it is, the police ought to be doing this.'

'Can you get it open?' asked Flora.

'Well yes, but...' Roland wrinkled his nose and pressed his hand more firmly to his mouth. 'Fucking hell, what a stench.'

'I don't think the police would do anything,' said Flora. 'I think this is...sanctioned.' She looked at Kalle for confirmation. He nodded and walked over to Roland. 'I can finish it off.'

Roland moved the nozzle out of Kalle's reach.

'No, no. I just...I mean this is really vile, guys.'

Nobody had anything to add, so after taking a deep breath Roland flipped down the mask and carried on. Kalle and Flora looked down at the floor to avoid the glare. Flora's hand slipped into Kalle's and he squeezed it, trying to convey a confidence he didn't feel.

We open it and it's full of dead bodies and what do we do then?

And the answer, the persistent theme of the evening, came back once more:

No idea.

When Roland had cut along another side he switched off the torch and removed the mask. It was now possible to force open the lid. As the electrical smell faded, the other took over. The putrefaction. The smell of death. Roland no longer looked as if he was enjoying himself, but he straightened up, attempted a smile and said, 'Right then. Just one question: Shall we throw up now or wait until later?'

The very mention of the words 'throw up' made Kalle feel as if a finger was poking at his throat, from the inside. Flora's lips were firmly clamped together. She didn't look as if she felt quite as ill as Kalle and Roland; the expression in her eyes was one of sorrowful determination. She went over to Roland's side of the box and pulled at the lid. Roland did the same, and Kalle took the other side as they all struggled to prise it open.

The metal was hot against Kalle's fingers, but it didn't burn. It wasn't as thick as he had thought. He could probably have got the lid open by himself. It resisted stubbornly, but in just a few seconds they had managed to force it right up. They held their shirts and sweaters to their mouths and looked down.

Waste material from a slaughterhouse.

The box did not contain bodies. It contained parts of bodies. On the top lay a white spongy mass that Kalle didn't recognise as a hand at first, because the fingers had been chopped off. It was lying in a clump of something that was presumably intestines. Along the edges lay severed feet, a forearm and several hands, along with odd fingers, the nails faintly reflecting the light from the ceiling.

A couple of the fingernails still bore traces of nail varnish. A woman had made her nails beautiful many years ago. Or perhaps her nails had been painted when she was laid in her coffin. Someone had sat with a brush and painted her nails bright red, then folded her arms across her chest and said goodbye. Now her hands lay here, separated from everything else, in a pile of waste material.

Roland threw up first. He just had time to twist his body away from the box before he brought up the contents of his stomach. Kalle managed to move back a couple of paces before the sound of Roland vomiting started him off. His stomach turned itself inside out and everything went black. He threw up until there was nothing but bile left, then stood with his hands resting on his knees, listening to the sound of Roland panting for breath, echoing his own gasps.

Flora...

He looked up from the yellowish-brown puddle in front of him and saw Flora sitting on the floor in the corner. She hadn't thrown up. She didn't even look as if she felt sick, but there was a veil of dark sorrow over her face. Kalle managed to wheeze, 'Flora?' but got no reply. He wiped his mouth and staggered over to her.

'Flora, are you OK?'

She looked up. Her eyes were wet, her eyelids trembling.

'They're...taking them apart. They can't kill them, so they're... why are they doing this?' She pointed to the box. 'There are no heads.'

Kalle looked at the box, not wanting to think about how Flora had found out that particular piece of information. He thought: *I don't know her. I don't know anything about her,* but he simply said, 'Perhaps they're in a different one. A different box.'

Roland came over to them. His head was moving mechanically backwards and forwards as he whispered, 'Anyone need a drink?'

Without waiting for an answer he headed for the door leading into the house, opened it and disappeared. Kalle helped Flora to her feet and they followed him. Kalle took a last look at the nondescript metal box on the floor, and something someone had said flashed through his mind:

You're a part of this now. With all that entails.

He didn't want to know what it entailed. He wanted to drink until nothing entailed anything anymore.

Roland was sitting on his white leather sofa pouring himself a full glass of whisky when they walked in. He waved towards the drinks cupboard, the armchairs: *Help yourselves and sit down.* He knocked back half the contents of the glass in one, flopped back against the cushions and said, 'What a fucking night.'

Kalle went over to the cupboard and let his eyes roam over the neatly arranged bottles. Stopped. Stared. Let the image of the bottles sink into his head. It felt like a balm. The orderliness of the bottles versus the chaos inside his skull. Nice colours, soft light. Pretty labels. He grabbed a bottle containing a clear yellow liquid at random; he knew nothing about liqueurs.

When he turned back Flora was sitting in one of the armchairs and Roland's glass was empty; he was just pouring himself another. Without bothering to be polite and ask if Flora wanted anything, Kalle slumped down in an armchair and unscrewed the top of the bottle.

He was just raising it to his mouth when Flora said, 'Kalle?'

He paused. 'What?'

'Perhaps...perhaps you shouldn't have a drink.'

'Why not?'

'We have to drive.'

Roland cleared his throat. 'You can sleep here. Wherever you like. Drink and be merry. Smile and rejoice.'

Kalle nodded and put the bottle to his lips; he took a swig and closed his eyes. The alcohol burned his throat, which was sore from so much vomiting. Flora took the bottle from him and he opened his eyes.

'We have to go there,' said Flora.

'Go where?'

'There.'

'*Now?*'

'Yes.'

Kalle shook his head and reached for the bottle. 'No way.' Roland sat up straight, with some difficulty. The rapid intake of alcohol had exploded in his head, and he was already slurring his words when he said, 'That's good. Good. Don't let them tell you what to do. You stick up for yourself.' He wagged his finger at the bottle and at Flora. 'Don't be like that. Let the boy have a drink.'

Flora got up, still holding onto the bottle. Roland followed her movements with his mouth hanging open, and patted the sofa beside him.

'Come and sit by me. Just chill. Take a break. This has been... fucking awful. Let's just relax for a little while.'

Flora looked at Kalle with an expression that made him pull back his hand. Then she slammed the bottle down on the table in front of him.

'Go on then, have a drink. Drink, for fuck's sake. Make yourself feel better. Drink.'

Kalle looked at the bottle. The desire to have a drink no longer felt so urgent, but he hadn't the slightest inclination to drive back to the Heath. Roland leaned forward and pushed the bottle closer to Kalle.

'Do as the girl says. This is good stuff. Unfortunately I can't... pronounce the name at the moment. From Scotland.'

Flora ignored Roland. She turned to Kalle, extending her arms as if to show her unprotected body.

'Who do you think I am? Go on, tell me. Who do you think I am?'

Kalle said what he felt: 'I don't know.'

'Am I...some kind of authority figure? Am I a fucking cop? Am I some kind of official body who comes along and gives orders? Am I...the person who's in charge here?'

Kalle picked at a stain on the arm of the chair. 'Well, you're the one who sort of...drives things along.'

'Yes. And why do I do that? Do you think I'm going to get anything out of all this, do you think I'm going to be...happy? It's just that I know…I know…if you knew that maybe a thousand people were going to be murdered and you could do something to stop it, wouldn't you do it?'

'Yes. Yes. Of course. Obviously. But I mean this is…'

'This is worse. It's not just that they're murdering people, they're already dead, they can't murder them, but they're obliterating their souls. I don't know where we end up when we die, but there's a place that might be heaven, or at least a place where we're meant to end up. This thing your…your relatives are doing means that these people will end up…somewhere else. In nothingness, in a vacuum, in a place that…doesn't exist. For all eternity. Do you understand? For all eternity.'

Tears started to pour down Flora's cheeks, but she didn't bother wiping them away. She pointed in the direction of the garage.

'I've seen it. I know it. Every single one of those people, what used to be people lying in that fucking box, every single one of them has been condemned to…an eternity of nothingness, to the closest thing you can get to hell, for all I know, and I don't understand why it's being done, why those bastards are doing it, but that's what they're up to and I don't intend to let it continue if I can do even the smallest thing to stop it!'

Flora suddenly closed her mouth, snivelled and rubbed her eyes. She sat down on the armrest of her chair and put her face in her hands. Roland had listened open-mouthed to Flora's diatribe. He blinked rapidly a couple of times and said, 'Bloody hell…'

Kalle placed a hand on Flora's knee and asked, 'But what can you do?'

Flora took a deep, sobbing breath and let it out in a sigh. 'They don't know. They're scared. I can convince them. To…give themselves up.'

'To…?

'To death.'

Silence fell. The word *death* has a way of making other words seem inadequate. There isn't much to add. Roland cleared his throat as he worked himself up to speak, but Flora got in first. She looked up at Kalle, and he saw a little girl.

'Kalle, I didn't choose this. It's been laid on my shoulders. And I can't...' Flora searched for the right words, and Kalle supplied the phrase she had used before: 'Run away from it.'

'No.'

Roland cleared his throat again, and this time he managed to get it out: 'I just wanted to say that...if that's the way things are...I just wanted to say that...' He sat up straight and placed his hand over his heart. 'I'm in. I'm with you all the way.'

Flora looked at Roland as he sat there swaying on the sofa, doing his best to look solemn.

'Thank you,' she said. 'But maybe not tonight.'

'You only have to say the word. When my services are... whatever.'

Flora nodded, grimacing slightly to stop a smile from reaching her lips. Kalle ruffled his dreadlocks, rubbed his fingers against his scalp as if to erase a dark woolliness inside. It didn't help much. The problem was still there.

'How are we going to get in?' He interrupted Flora before she could answer. 'Don't tell me. Let me guess: No idea.'

Five minutes later they were sitting in the van. Kalle felt more or less as if he had been drinking all night, had two hours' sleep then climbed a mountain. The hand that reached for the ignition key, the foot that depressed the clutch were objects he could manipulate, but they didn't seem to belong to his body. If they were stopped by the police, he wouldn't have the strength to blow into the bag.

They stopped at an all-night petrol station and bought six chocolate biscuits and a cup of coffee each. Flora could only manage two biscuits, so Kalle shovelled four into his mouth in the space of five minutes, then swilled down the gooey mess with coffee. After a while the sugar hit his bloodstream and he felt better. His hands were attached to his arms once more, and the road looked more like the E20 than a video game. He said, 'If they've found out about the missing box we've had it. And they probably have.' When Flora didn't say anything, he went on, 'We could be facing prison and stuff.'

'I don't think so,' said Flora. 'I think they want to keep this outside…the system. If they can. That's what I think.'

'That's what you think?'

'Yes.'

Kalle snorted. 'Maybe we'll have the fucking secret police after us. Or something. Military intelligence, or whatever it's called. Maybe the doctors have their own secret police.'

Kalle laughed and glanced at Flora. 'That's it. We'll have the medical secret police after us.'

Things felt no less desperate. But at least it was vaguely amusing.

They stopped at the beginning of the track leading across the field. A couple of hundred metres away they could see the floodlights at the gate. Kalle leaned over the steering wheel and gazed across towards the Heath. He felt as if he were in a film. A war film rather than a horror flick. He wasn't keen on either. Screwball comedies were his thing. There were undeniably elements in all this that could be described as screwball. But comedy? No. Not really.

'Kalle,' said Flora. 'You have to make your mind up.'

'About what?'

'About whether you want to do this or not.'

'I drove here, didn't I?'

Flora shook her head. 'I mean whether you really *want* to. Not just because you're being kind to me, or doing your duty or whatever. That won't work. You have to do it because you want to. Not because I tell you to. I can't handle that.'

Kalle sat staring at the fenced-in compound. It all seemed so impossible. He asked, 'They end up in hell, you say?'

'Something similar, yes.'

Kalle tried to imagine it. He thought for a moment. Then he covered his face with his hands and kept them there for a long time. He took them away and snuffled.

'What is it?' asked Flora.

'I was just thinking about my mum. If I'd...' He broke off. 'OK. Yes. OK. It's not your responsibility. It's ours.' He looked at her. 'That's what you meant, wasn't it?'

'Yes.'

'OK. That's it then. I'm in.'

Flora leaned across and kissed him gently on the cheek. 'Thank you.'

Kalle gave a wry smile. 'If we're in this together, you can't say that.'

'I'm saying it anyway.'

Flora crawled into the back of the van; Kalle started the engine, began drumming inside his head and moved off towards the gates. The same guard as before emerged from the small booth. He looked as if he'd just woken up. Kalle wound down the window. From the way the guard was moving and the expression on his face Kalle sensed that, as he had hoped, the theft of the box hadn't been discovered. Yet.

The guard made a show of looking at his watch, then at Kalle. Kalle nodded towards the compound.

'My father called me. I left something behind.'

'Like what?'

'A box.'

Kalle couldn't come up with anything better, given that he

couldn't use his brain. The guard stroked his chin. 'What are they up to over there?'

'No idea. I just shift boxes. Big boxes, small boxes.'

The guard grinned and went back inside. The gates opened.

The worst thing about the drumming, about controlling his thoughts was the fact that he couldn't let his emotions break through. The relief and triumph Kalle felt could not be allowed to rise to the surface, and he hammered frenetically on his mental drum kit as he drove through the compound.

The lights were still on in the basement. He knew what to do. Without consulting Flora. There was only tonight, and after that...

No idea.

He switched off the engine. The thought field was weaker at this distance from the big community hall, and he risked lowering the beat as he turned to Flora.

'Come on.'

'What are we going to do?'

'We'll see.'

They got out of the van and walked over to the door. Kalle tried the handle, and the door opened. The room looked the same as it had done a few hours earlier. Kalle guessed that the doctor, or whatever he might be, was behind one of the doors in the long wall.

Flora looked around and her hand flew up to her head. She whispered, 'It *hurts*.'

Kalle squeezed his eyes tight shut. 'Yes.'

One of the doors flew open and the doctor emerged. He was wearing a white coat and his eyes were veiled, covered with a film of concentration or agitation. He was wearing latex gloves, and they were messy. When he caught sight of Kalle and Flora, he stopped dead.

'What the hell are you doing here? You're not allowed in here!'

The doctor quickly pulled off his gloves and threw them on the floor; one hand slipped into his pocket and he took out a mobile phone. Kalle reached him in two strides. He clenched his huge fist and held it in front of the doctor's face.

'Think about it,' he said.

The doctor looked up from the phone, looked at Kalle's fist. He thought about it. The he lowered the mobile and glanced from Kalle to Flora, who had just closed the door behind them.

'What do you want?'

Kalle grabbed the doctor's shoulders. They were like apples in his hands, and he squeezed hard. He leaned down towards the other man's face and said, 'You don't need to worry about that. The important thing is this: I can knock you down, or I can decide not to knock you down. What's it to be?'

'Are you threatening me?'

'Of course I am. What's it to be?'

Kalle squeezed harder and the doctor pulled a face as something made a crunching sound. He snapped, 'What the hell do you *want*?'

Kalle sighed and clenched his fist again, measuring the distance for a blow. The doctor's hands flew up to his face and he nodded quickly.

'Yes, yes, yes. So what...do you want me to do?'

Kalle looked around and spotted the bed. 'Lie down.'

As the doctor crawled onto the bed, Kalle noticed that, conveniently, there were leather straps attached to the sides. He and Flora worked together to secure the man's arms and legs. The doctor kept on shaking his head as if he just couldn't believe this was happening. His voice was dripping with scorn as he said, 'You're going to be in so much trouble. You have no idea what you're doing.'

He carried on like this as Kalle rummaged through a drawer and found several packs of disposable syringes. He read the labels.

'Pentymal?' he asked the doctor. 'What do you think? Is this any good if you want to shut someone up?'

The doctor closed his mouth. Kalle found a roll of gauze bandage; he tore off a piece, rolled it into a ball and stuffed it into the doctor's mouth, then wound a length of the material around his head. Kalle surveyed his work and said, 'Tell me if you can't breathe. Or…think it.'

Flora was standing over by the internal doors. They had bolts on the outside, but the one on the door through which the doctor had come was pushed to one side. Kalle went over to her and placed a hand on her shoulder; she was trembling. There was so much adrenaline pumping through his body that he had forgotten to be afraid. When Flora's trembling passed through his hand, he remembered exactly why they were there. He licked his lips and swallowed a lump of viscous saliva.

Flora's eyes were huge and frightened as she opened the door.

The room was bigger than it seemed from the outside—twenty square metres at least. There were no windows, just bare cement walls, and the same merciless fluorescent light as in the outer room flooded the space, illuminating the source of the scream reverberating inside both their heads.

Three beds were arranged in a row. In the corner stood a box like the one they had taken. Next to one of the beds was a trolley laden with surgical instruments: knives, forceps, saws and scalpels, gleaming in the white light. That was where the doctor had been working when they arrived.

On the first bed lay the remains of an old woman. Long, grey hair that had perhaps been beautiful once upon a time hung halfway down to the floor. The woman's eyes were cloudy blue, staring straight at them. Her arms and legs had been hacked off, leaving only greyish, dead flesh and white bone visible. The trunk was fastened to the bed with a thick leather strap.

On the second bed lay a hollow man. What had once been a big, round body was now reduced to a shell. The man still had his arms and legs, but his guts had been removed completely. Rubber straps with clamps on the end held his belly and chest cavity open, and his ribs stuck out as if he were a ship under construction. His entrails had been scraped out, removed and thrown in the box in the corner.

On the third bed, where the doctor had been working, lay a woman's head attached to a spinal column and very little else. A number of dark red strands ran from the severed neck, presumably blood vessels or nerve fibres, which had been gathered up in a knot. It hung down to one side, making the head tilt slightly. The woman was younger than the others, but it was difficult to determine her age; her face was sunken and grey, and her eyes...

Kalle had clenched his jaws together so tightly that he could hear the grinding inside his head. He was no longer capable of prising them apart, he stood there frozen as if he had cramp, and he felt, he knew:

They're alive.

He didn't know what was true and what was false when it came to the reliving, what could be called life, but the pain and fear pouring from the mutilated bodies were perfectly clear: they were alive, and were in some way aware of what was happening to them.

The grip of the cramp eased. He regained control of his body, and it let him down. His legs gave way and he collapsed. Everything went black, and the blackness was like water on a burning body. He received it with gratitude.

When he opened his eyes he couldn't make sense of what he was seeing at first, why the world looked so strange. Everything was hanging from the ceiling. He saw Flora standing by the beds, her lips moving silently. He opened his mouth to say something, but no sound came out. Wave after wave of nausea coursed through him, emerging only as tainted air.

Something's happening, something's...happening...

He blinked, tried to understand. The atmosphere in the room

had thickened. The cloying stench of stale blood had intensified, the light grew brighter, the walls seemed to be moving closer and he heard a noise. It started like a distant whisper, but quickly increased in volume to a whining, piercing howl that would have made him press his hands to his ears, had he been able to do so. As it was he just lay there gasping with his mouth open as the searing noise turned into a metal blade slicing up the air around his head.

He wanted to yell at Flora, tell her to be careful, but the sound paralysed him, and his face was slowly pushed in the opposite direction, as if by an invisible force, until he could no longer look at her. The last thing he saw was a tall, thin figure suddenly standing next to Flora, reaching out its arms towards the human remains on the beds.

Kalle closed his eyes. Squeezed them shut as tightly as he could. The noise went right through his head, bouncing around inside his skull, and he no longer knew if it was coming from inside or outside. He had no awareness of time or space, was incapable of thinking or not thinking.

Then it abated. Quickly, much more quickly that it had come, the terrible noise faded away and the room was silent. Completely silent. Kalle opened his eyes. Flora was standing alone next to the beds, her arms hanging limply by her sides.

Silent.

It was so…silent. Kalle slowly heaved himself up from the floor and looked around. He didn't want to get up, didn't want to see what was on the beds again. He got to his knees and looked around.

So silent.

Then he understood. It was the people on the beds. Their screams had fallen silent. They were no longer there. He coughed once, briefly and harshly, mostly to check that he was still alive. Flora came over to him. Strands of hair were stuck to her forehead with perspiration, and she looked exhausted. But calm. She hadn't been involved in something horrible, just something that was incredibly hard work.

Kalle asked, 'Is it...over?' and Flora nodded.

Without looking, Kalle gestured towards the beds. 'Was that... death, that thing?'

'Yes. Or...your version of it. What did you see?'

'I don't know. Something tall. Thin.'

Kalle got up. He was still taking care not to look in the direction of the beds. Instead he gazed down at Flora, who seemed transparent, fragile, as if she might break if you touched her. He stared deep into her eyes, searching for a clue. There was nothing to be found, so he asked, 'Who are you?'

The corners of her mouth twitched. 'No one special.'

She pressed herself against him, her cheek resting on his chest. He placed his hand on her head and she was an ordinary, exhausted girl. He put his arms around her, but couldn't help thinking that something alien, something...godlike was working inside that head, which was just an ordinary head that almost fitted into his hand.

I've had a responsibility bestowed upon me.

He bent down and kissed her sweaty brow.

When they came out of the room, the doctor was staring at them. Flora went over and untied the gag. As if the words had been penned in, just waiting to leap out, he started straightaway, 'What have you done! What have you done, you fucking lunatics!'

Flora did something Kalle had never expected. She slapped the doctor across the face. Hard. His mouth snapped shut. Flora hit him again. She placed her mouth close to his ear.

'Listen to Dr Mengele. Who the fuck is the lunatic around here? Do you realise what you're doing?'

Kalle just stood there open-mouthed. He had never seen Flora like this, wouldn't have believed she had it in her. But she was angry now, more than angry. Furious. The doctor turned his head towards the inner room; he too was trembling with rage.

'You've killed them. You've destroyed everything I—'

Flora hit him across the mouth with the palm of her hand, as if to block up the source of something disgusting. His lip split open and blood trickled down the doctor's chin. Kalle touched Flora's arm. She shook off his hand and bent over the doctor; a hint of fear showed in his eyes.

'You're the one who's killing them.'

'They're already—'

Flora raised her hand to deliver another blow, and the doctor didn't finish what he had been intending to say.

'I want to know…' said Flora. 'I want to know why you're doing this.'

The doctor's mouth had begun to swell, and when he tried a scornful grimace he looked more like a tragic clown.

'Because I'm so horribly evil. Why the fuck do you think? To contribute to research. To find a way of conquering death. To help humanity. I realise you two think you're the heroes around here, but—'

This time Flora simply moved her hand, and he shut up.

'I know all that,' she said. 'What I want to know is what you're trying to achieve by cutting them up. On a purely practical level.'

'That's what I'm telling you. Think about all the people who die before their time, quite unnecessarily…'

Flora sighed and turned to Kalle. 'You can hit him much harder than I can. Want to have a go?'

Kalle looked dubiously at Flora. She winked. He nodded and walked over to the bed; he rolled up his right sleeve and opened and closed his fist a couple of times. The doctor followed his movements with wide-open eyes. As Flora had hoped, the threat was enough. The doctor said, 'I'm investigating the minimum conditions necessary for life.'

'Which means?'

'Which means that…we haven't found anything at a cellular level, so now I'm investigating exactly how much one can…remove without life ceasing to exist. Which parts have a life of their own, which parts the body can't do without.'

'And how many of you are working on this?'

'Three, normally.'

'And the others will be here tomorrow?'

'Yes, but this is a total bloody disaster for our—'

'Good,' said Flora. 'In that case they'll be able to untie you.'

She took Kalle's arm and pulled him towards the door, the doctor protesting vociferously behind them. As they closed the door he started to scream. It wasn't particularly audible through the thick concrete walls, and the thought field was almost gone now the reliving had left the building. He would probably have to stay there until the morning.

They drove out of the compound. At the gates the guard asked if Kalle had found what he was looking for. Kalle said he had, and they parted with a mutual goodnight.

At half past three in the morning they were sitting in Kalle's kitchen. Kalle had drunk three beers, Flora one. There were so many questions to ask that his brain refused to work at all. After the third beer a pleasant warmth began to spread through his body at last.

'There's going to be trouble,' he said.

'Yes,' said Flora. 'Tomorrow.' She looked at the kitchen clock. 'I'm supposed to be at work in two hours. I think I might just take the day off.'

'Making sandwiches?'

'Making sandwiches.'

Something resembling a laugh emerged from Kalle's mouth,

sounding more like a weary gasp. 'First this, and then...you have to stand there making sandwiches. Ups and downs...'

Flora nodded. 'And this is just the beginning.'

'What's just the beginning?'

'What we did tonight. There are several hundred left.'

Kalle rubbed his eyes. 'How are we going to...' He threw his hands wide, let them drop. 'Tomorrow.'

'Tomorrow.'

They went to bed and made love slowly, tenderly as if through sleep. When it was over and they were satisfied, sinking down towards genuine sleep, Kalle was still unable to take the final step. Flora was lying with her head resting on his chest. He stroked her ear with his finger and asked, 'Aren't you scared?'

Flora's voice was thick, heavy with sleep. 'Of what?'

'...death?'

She didn't speak for a few seconds, then eventually she replied, 'She's not dangerous. She just...does what she has to do.'

'She?'

'Yes...'

While Kalle thought about that, Flora's breathing grew deeper and more regular. He didn't want to wake her with more questions, so he lay there gazing up into the darkness until his eyes closed of their own accord and he fell asleep.

It felt as if he had only just dozed off when he was woken by the doorbell. It was a quarter past seven in the morning. He lay there staring up at the ceiling, his brain confused with sleep. In the silence between two rings of the bell he could hear a fly struggling to reach the light outside the window.

Fly. Light. Morning.

There was the sour taste of stale beer in his mouth as he swung his legs over the side of the bed and pulled on his dressing gown. He went to the door and opened it without a single conscious thought. Only when he saw his father standing outside did the events of the previous night start to come back to him.

They stood there looking at one another for a while. Kalle was incapable of digging anything to say out of his sleep-befuddled brain, and judging by his father's expression he too was lost for words. After a few seconds Sture came to life and pushed past Kalle into the apartment.

Kalle rubbed his face hard and yawned. 'Yes?'

His father, who had made it as far as the living room, swung around and looked at him as if that was the most inappropriate thing he could possibly have said.

'*Yes*? Is that all you've got to say?'

'Noooo...' Another yawn forced its way out. It was as if he could stand here with his mouth open for ages, just yawning, yawning until this was over.

His father caught sight of the open bedroom door. He walked in and positioned himself at the end of the bed, pointing at Flora, who was still asleep.

'Is that her? Your...partner in all this?'

Kalle didn't like the idea of his father being anywhere near Flora, particularly when she was asleep.

'Listen,' he said. 'We'll talk about this later. I'd like you to leave now.'

Sture was taken aback for a moment. He couldn't believe what his son had just said. His chin dropped and then he said, with a hint of fear in his voice, 'You don't know anything.'

Kalle scratched his chest. 'No. So we've heard.'

Suddenly Sture grabbed hold of the bed and shook it furiously. He yelled at Flora, 'Wake up! Wake up!'

Kalle grabbed Sture by the shoulder and shoved him away from the bed. 'Who the hell do you think you are?'

Sture knocked his hand away, and Kalle couldn't help being impressed by the old man's stubbornness. Kalle could easily have picked him up with one hand and thrown him out. Through the window, for example.

Flora sat up in bed and Sture brushed the shoulder of his jacket as if he had got something dirty on it. Kalle said, 'Say what you have to say and get out.'

Flora's eyes were puffy. She looked from one to the other and asked Kalle, 'Your father?'

Sture leaned against the foot of the bed. He glared at Flora, who wrapped the sheet around her.

'Yes. Unfortunately. Young lady, are you aware of the extent to which you have destroyed your future? How much trouble you're both going to be in?' Neither Flora nor Kalle spoke. Sture went on, 'Illegal entry into a protected area, unauthorised interference, physical abuse, possibly also manslaughter.'

Flora looked at Sture. For a long time. Then she asked, 'Are the police involved?'

'No. Not *yet*.'

'So when will they be involved?'

Sture snorted, and something akin to a laugh escaped from him. He looked at Kalle, then at Flora. Then back at Kalle.

'Nice company you keep.'

'Yes. Have you got anything important to say, or are you just going to…keep banging on?'

Sture fell silent. His eyes widened. At first Kalle thought it was surprise once again at the incomprehensibility of their actions, but then he heard the sound Sture had picked up. There was someone in the hallway. Someone was heading towards the bedroom. Sture grabbed hold of Kalle's arm as if he were about to say something important, but before he had time to speak the visitor was in the room.

At a passing glance, Kalle would have taken the stranger for yet another suit. He was certainly wearing a suit, and a very loud tie. But the body was wrong. The first impression was that the man was fat, because a well-filled belly stretched the shirt tight, with the tie resting on it rather than hanging. However, the legs and arms were spindly, the face small and narrow, almost emaciated. A famine victim in a suit.

The eyes didn't fit either. Instead of the shiny, wide-open gaze of the starving, this man had small eyes that were so deep-set they looked as if they were burrowing into his skull.

The man folded his thin hands together, rested them on his stomach and gazed around.

'I see the entire family is gathered.'

His voice was high, like a young girl's. Kalle couldn't take his eyes off the man's face. He had a magnetic quality, and Kalle had to make an enormous effort not to move closer to him.

The man's eyes rested on Kalle's father.

'How are you, Sture? Well, I hope?'

It was rare for someone to call Sture by his first name. It was Professor Liljewall or Father or Professor. Kalle tore his eyes away from the man and glanced at his father. Sture had shrunk, and was rubbing his hands together in an almost comical fashion.

Flora wriggled back towards the bed head. The man noticed the movement, strode forward and sat down beside her on the bed.

'And you're here too.'

Flora pulled the sheet more tightly around her to form a barrier between herself and the man's body, his stomach. Something within Kalle told him he ought to intervene, but it was impossible to move. Flora whispered, 'You can't do anything to me.'

The man nodded pensively. 'No. That's true. But the number of willing bodies. At my disposal. Would surprise you.'

The man got to his feet. His movements were surprisingly supple, as if his belly weighed nothing. When he came and stood next to Kalle, that dark pull was palpable. It was like standing somewhere high up, looking down. The urge to take that step.

'I realise this may be difficult to grasp. But your actions. Are threatening great human values. We are on the verge. Of a break-through. And I will admit. That it is difficult to foresee the consequences. But in the long run. I am convinced. That this will lead to greater happiness.' The man turned to Sture. 'Isn't that right?'

Sture nodded. 'Yes. Absolutely.'

Kalle stared at the man's face. The mouth seemed to move entirely without the help of the facial muscles. As Kalle watched, a fly landed on the man's cheek. The man didn't notice, he simply carried on talking. The mouth moved and the fly, drawn by the same pull that Kalle felt, crawled inside without the man even pausing. The fly didn't return, but the words kept on coming:

'I also realise. That my direct involvement. May seem counter-productive. That it may serve only to strengthen your conviction. That you are doing the right thing. Is that correct?'

Both Flora and Kalle nodded, almost without moving their heads. There was an aura of immobility around the man that spread outwards, affected others. He went on, 'I have however discovered that logical arguments. Have no influence on your...what I might call ideological point of view. And my experience tells me. That when faced with a case like this. Fear is the only remaining means of exerting pressure. Fear almost always conquers logic.' The man turned to Sture and waved his thin hand in Kalle's direction. 'Sture, you may now punish your son.'

Sture licked his lips. 'I don't quite understand...'

'He has been disobedient, and you must do your duty as a father. Punish him.' Kalle was still incapable of any movement. The man looked him over as if seeking out his most vulnerable spot, then pointed: 'Break his nose.'

Sture shook his head. 'I can't.'

'I understand. You're not used to it.' The man walked over to the bedside table and picked up a solid glass cube that usually contained a candle and handed it to Sture. 'There.'

Sture weighed the cube in his hand and looked at Kalle. If this was about fear, then Sture was the one most at risk. His lower lip was trembling and he was frantically licking his lips. Kalle wasn't experiencing a feeling of calmness; it was more like indifference bordering on apathy. He couldn't understand how he was still on his feet.

Tears sprang into Sture's eyes. He positioned himself directly in front of Kalle and raised the glass cube. The man nodded. 'Go for it.'

'Stop,' Flora whispered from the bed. She was getting up, the sheet still wrapped around her. 'Stop.'

The man looked at her. 'Is this some kind of negotiation? Are you offering to stop if I stop?'

Flora swallowed and said, 'Yes.'

The man's eyes locked into hers. He looked deep inside her for a second, then said, 'You're lying. Get back in bed.'

Driven by a will that was not her own, Flora lay down on the bed again. Kalle heard a drumming sound. Du-du-dunk, du-du-dunk. The only thing he could move was his eyes, and he searched the room, hunting for the source of the noise.

A sparrow was sitting outside on the window ledge, pecking at the glass. The bird hopped to and fro along the ledge as if seeking a point where the glass was less solid, then pecked again. The man glanced at it, then turned his attention back to Sture.

'Let's finish this.'

Sture's arm was shaking as he raised it above his head to reach Kalle's face. The bird let loose another burst of drumming on the windowpane. Sture drew back his arm, then jerked it forward with considerable force, as if he were going to throw the cube as far as he could. The solid surface hit Kalle right in the middle of his nose. He heard a muted crunching sound, and burning heat radiated across his face like a spider web as blood poured down into his mouth.

Flora screamed, the cube fell to the floor and Sture covered his face with his hands. The man leaned closer to Kalle's face, inspecting the damage. He nodded, said, 'Good,' and turned to Sture, whose body was locked in a hunched position. 'I thought you might deal with the girl as well, but...you seem to have exhausted your strength.'

The man went over to the window and looked out. The sparrow's drumming grew more feverish.

'I must say this building is one of the most tasteless I've ever set eyes on.'

Blood was pouring down Kalle's throat, inside his dressing gown, tickling as it trickled down the sides of his stomach. His face was a receptacle for red heat that just kept on pumping and pumping. He wanted to reach up and feel how bad it was, but he didn't have permission to move.

The man turned the handle and opened the window. With a couple of rapid hops the sparrow was inside the room; it circled around Kalle's head before swooping down towards the man, who opened his mouth wide. The bird flew straight in, and it was gone.

As if he had done nothing more than take a deep breath, the man exhaled and grabbed Sture by the shoulder.

'Come along. I assume you have no interest in staying here to explain yourself.'

Sture shook his bowed head and they walked towards the door. Before he left, the man turned back to Kalle and Flora. He studied them for several long seconds, then said, 'I don't think there's much to add.'

Then he walked out, with Sture trailing behind him.

———·———

The room remained completely silent for a long time after the man had disappeared. A faint breeze wafted in through the open window, making the curtains billow. It was Flora who first managed to extricate herself from the net of impotence in which they were caught. She got out of bed on wobbly legs, went over to Kalle and said, 'Come with me...'

Kalle allowed himself to be led to the bathroom, where Flora gently washed his face with toilet paper and lukewarm water. Even his tongue felt swollen, and he had to form the words very slowly as he asked, 'What. Was that? What. Happened. There?'

As if his slurred words had opened the floodgates to the real world, where Kalle stood with a broken nose after being attacked by his father, Flora let out a single sob and clamped her lips together to stop herself from bursting into tears.

'I don't know, Kalle. I don't know.'

Kalle looked in the mirror. His nose had swollen to at least twice its normal size, and was pressed against one cheek. A fragment of bone was sticking out where the skin had split, and when he tried to breathe through his nose, it proved impossible.

Flora said, 'We need to get you to the hospital. I'll just...'

She dabbed at his cheeks, his throat and his chest with wads of paper, which she threw down the toilet when they were soaked in blood. Eventually she tore off a long length and folded it up to make a compress.

'Here. Hold this against...'

She pointed and Kalle filled in the missing words: '...what used to be my nose.'

'Nose' came out as 'dose', and Kalle thought that was funny. He tried to laugh, but it came out as no more than a jerky, whistling sound through his mouth. Flora shook her head and gave him a hug.

'You're crazy. You're laughing.'

Although it probably didn't matter, they didn't like the idea of going to Karolinska Hospital. Instead they headed out to Danderyd, where they had to wait only half an hour before Kalle was seen. His nose was straightened and a plaster dressing was applied, after which the doctor said Kalle should come back in a week for further adjustment, unless of course he wanted to end up looking like a retired boxer.

When they got out into the corridor Kalle looked at himself in a mirror and thought he looked like something out of a cartoon. The square dressing covering his nose, the long dreadlocks framing his face. The main character's dopey friend in a Disney film, the one who says weird things and never quite knows what's going on.

When they were sitting in the cafeteria, with Kalle drinking a milky coffee with some difficulty and pulling faces more than necessary just to find some humour in his situation, Flora said, 'I think you're weird. Aren't you upset? I mean after all, it was your father who did this.'

Kalle shook his head. 'No. In fact, I think it's kind of…nice, in a way. Now we know exactly where we stand. I don't need to bother about him anymore. He's out of my life.'

'But even so.'

'I've hated him for years, actually. But I've never quite been able to admit it. It's better this way.'

The cafeteria was virtually empty. A couple of tables away a very old lady sat slurping a cup of tea, her Zimmer frame by her side. A sad expression lost in the pastel-coloured walls. Kalle looked at her and thought: *I have no family either.*

But, as he had said, this was a sadness he had carried for a long time now, not something new, merely a fact and a gnawing emptiness. He took a deep breath through his mouth, let it out again and said, 'Have you given it any thought? That business this morning?'

'I didn't know it existed,' said Flora. 'I haven't seen it before.'

'What do you mean?'

Flora swept together a few sugar crystals that were scattered across the table as she tried to find the right words. When all the sugar had been gathered into a little pile, she said, 'There's a...representation of the other. An image. I thought it was only death who had one. And we both saw the same thing, didn't we? Death...she shows herself in different ways to different people, depending on the image we have of her. But this...'

'It was like a kind of magnetic pull.'

'Yes. But it's only an image. To enable us to see something. Of this...power. Or principle. It can't do anything by itself.'

'How do you know that?'

Flora gave a small shrug. 'I just do.' She reached across the table and Kalle took her hand. She looked at his square plaster and shook her head. 'I'm sorry I dragged you into all this.'

'Are you?'

'For your sake, yes. Not for mine.'

'That's all right, then.'

They sat there holding hands. Out of the corner of his eye Kalle could see that the old woman had shifted her interest from the wall to them. She was resting her chin on her hands and staring at them. Kalle leaned over to Flora.

'Are you scared?'

'Yes. You?'

'Yes.' He squeezed her hand. 'What are we going to do?'

'I think...' said Flora, 'we ought to speak to my grandmother.'

They were getting ready to go when the old woman got to her feet with some difficulty and shuffled over to them on her Zimmer frame. When she reached them she stood there for a few seconds with her toothless mouth hanging open, looking from one to the other. Then she said, 'I'm scared too.'

Kalle didn't know what to say. But Flora moved her face close to the woman's and said, 'You really don't need to be.'

The woman's eyes widened slightly. 'Don't I?'

'No,' said Flora. 'I promise.'

The woman nodded, made a few chewing movements with her mouth, then dragged herself off towards the lifts.

Elvy's friend Hagar had called round, and they were both appalled at what had happened to Kalle in a way that he found not entirely unpleasant. It was a long time since someone had cosseted him. He accepted an invitation to lie down on the sofa while Elvy brought him coffee and biscuits.

Flora had told Kalle that Hagar was more or less up to speed with the whole thing, and she went through everything that had happened since she and Kalle went to the Heath together for the first time.

When Flora got to the bit about how Kalle had dealt with the doctor, which won him an admiring glance from Elvy, Kalle's phone rang. ROLAND was showing on the display. Kalle excused himself and went into the kitchen so that Flora could finish the story without him. He sat down and took the call.

'Hi Roland.'

'Hi there. I just wanted to…how did it all go?'

Roland's voice sounded like the morning after the night before, and Kalle looked at the clock. Half past ten. Presumably Roland had just woken up; Kalle hadn't even managed to take in his own tiredness yet.

'Well, it went…it went…'

'Have you got a cold?'

Kalle snorted, and only a small amount of air came out through the hole in the plaster with a whistling noise. He gave Roland a shortened version of the story, missing out the bit about the fly and the bird disappearing into the visitor's mouth. He tried to gloss over the supernatural elements of the whole thing in general;

Roland already thought it was weird enough. But he had seen what he had seen.

'OK,' said Roland. 'This is all completely crazy. But there's a box in my garage. What am I going to do with it?'

That particular problem hadn't crossed Kalle's mind. After their experiences in the Heath, any other worries had seemed unimportant. But that wasn't the case for Roland, of course, who had a box full of body parts in his garage.

'I've got someone from one of the weekly celebrity gossip magazines coming at three, and…well, the whole place stinks even though the garage doors are shut.'

'A gossip magazine?'

'Yes, what can you do? But you can bet your life they'll…the last time they wanted to know why I had a swing in the garden when I haven't got any kids, I mean it's there for my brother's kids, but then the article made it look as if…anyway, that doesn't matter, but they're bound to ask questions.'

Kalle couldn't help smiling. *What's the smell in Roland's garage? Roland says it's so-and-so, but our reporter…*

'I'll call you back,' he said, and hung up.

In the living room Flora had finished telling her story, and the three of them were sitting talking, their heads close together. Flora looked up as Kalle walked in.

'Who was that?'

'Roland. It's the box. He…he wants to get rid of it.'

Hagar, who was slightly hard of hearing, looking enquiringly at Flora. 'Who are you talking about?'

'Roland,' said Flora. 'Kalle's boss. From Tropicos.'

'Did he just call here?'

'Yes, he—'

Hagar clapped her hands. 'But that's fantastic!' She raised one forefinger in the air to emphasise her point: 'Now *he's* one of the few really stylish men left in this country. What did he want?'

Elvy raised her eyebrows meaningfully; Kalle went over to Hagar and said in a louder voice, 'He wants to get rid of that box!'

Hagar looked around as if she couldn't work out what the problem was.

'Oh?' she said. 'Well in that case we'd better go and get it, hadn't we?'

On the way out to Roland's place they stopped at Bauhaus and bought two sacks of peat-based compost. Hagar had an idea that it ought to be quicklime, but none of them knew where to get hold of it, or what it was actually used for. It had something to do with the decomposition process, but that wasn't really the problem here.

Kalle still thought they ought to go to the police, particularly after seeing his father's reaction when the police were mentioned, but both Elvy and Flora were dead against the idea.

'I'm more or less one hundred per cent convinced,' said Elvy, 'that if we turn to the authorities we'll end up being the guilty party. In one way or another.'

Kalle couldn't suppress a huge yawn. The lack of sleep was beginning to make itself felt. Flora was resting her head on her hand, her eyes half-closed.

'I don't get it,' said Kalle. 'This Association. Who are they? What do they want?'

Elvy snorted. 'We'd better ask your father.'

Before Kalle had the chance to say anything, she placed her hand on his shoulder. 'No offence. The sins of the fathers and so on. I don't believe in all that.'

'Good,' said Kalle, who had no idea what she was talking about.

When they reached Solberga, Hagar started pointing and exclaiming at the charming houses. Elvy, who had remained quiet for a while, suddenly said to Kalle, 'Profit. The greatest possible profit. I think that's what they're after. As if everything were a machine, and it has to work as efficiently as possible, spitting out as much profit as possible. That's it. Profit and usefulness.'

'Like the government recommendations on healthy eating,' said Kalle, turning into Roland's drive. This earned him the first laugh he had heard from Elvy. A high, chirruping laugh that blew away a fraction of his tiredness.

They got out of the van and Roland came towards them from the house. It was obvious that he had already started to get ready for the interview. His hair was neatly blow-dried, and in spite of a hard night his face looked fresher and less lined than the previous evening. When he caught sight of Elvy and Hagar he grew a little taller and threw his arms wide.

'You must be Elvy and Hagar. I've heard so much about you.'

Kalle and Flora glanced sideways at one another. Kalle had mentioned Elvy and Hagar for the first time in his conversation with Roland an hour and a half ago. Flora unloaded the bags of compost while Roland shook hands with the ladies. Hagar bobbed a little curtsey and said, 'You look even better in real life!'

Roland inclined his head. 'It must be a good twenty years since anyone said that! But thank you. You've made my day!'

Before Hagar could expand on her theme, Elvy said, 'This box.'

Roland's smile dimmed only slightly as he made a sweeping gesture in the direction of the garage, inviting them to follow him. 'I really do apologise for putting you to all this trouble, but it's impossible for me to keep it here.'

Roland looked around. 'Kalle, could you back the van up?' The rest of the group moved towards the garage door, and Roland pointed at Kalle's face. 'You look like shit.'

'Thanks,' said Kalle. 'I don't suppose you could spare some of that cream you use?'

Roland smiled, and the laughter lines that had survived various treatments became visible. 'It doesn't work miracles,' he said, following the others.

Kalle reversed the van up to the door and got out. Even though the back seats weren't folded down, there would still be room for the box. He took a deep breath before he walked into the garage.

Elvy and Flora were busy pouring the compost into the box, while Hagar and Roland stood to one side, mouths covered with their blouse or shirt collar. The stench inside the garage was like walking straight into a wall, and Kalle swallowed a couple of times to stop himself from throwing up.

He waved to Roland and Hagar to indicate that they might as well go outside, and they gratefully complied. Elvy and Flora had emptied the contents of the sacks into the box, and it was now full to the brim. Kalle found a roll of gaffer tape and they cut up the plastic sacks and taped them over the top of the box. When they had finished they glanced at each other, then ran outside to breathe.

A short distance away Roland and Hagar were walking around the garden. She had tucked her arm through his and Roland was chatting away, pointing out various trees and shrubs. Kalle shook his head. *He never turns it off.*

Elvy nodded back towards the garage. 'That was hell. What a mess.'

'Do you think...' Kalle began, then didn't know how to continue. 'What?' asked Flora.

Kalle made a vague gesture somewhere in between Flora and Elvy. 'Do you think your...your grandfather...your...might be...?'

'I don't know,' said Elvy, compressing her lips into a thin line. 'I didn't look.'

Kalle dropped the subject and opened the back doors of the van. The three of them managed to manoeuvre the box over to the van and heave it inside. Roland and Hagar came back, and Kalle asked, 'Roland, I don't suppose you've got anything to put over our mouths?'

It would be unbearable to travel with the box in the back of the van, and Kalle wished he'd thought of it when they were in Bauhaus. Fortunately Roland slapped his forehead and said, 'Of course. Idiot.'

He went into the garage and rummaged through various drawers until he found what he was looking for: an unopened pack of dust masks. He handed it to Kalle.

'I was going to do up the bathroom, but...' He shrugged his shoulders, and Kalle realised the bathroom renovation had suffered more or less the same fate as the plans for the cutting torch. An idea that came to nothing, as was so often the case with Roland.

Roland looked at his watch and clapped his hands.

'I don't really know what to say.' He looked at Elvy and Hagar and bowed. 'Lovely to meet you. If I can be of any further assistance, then I am at your disposal.' The memory of what had been said during the night lingered on, and Roland knew it. In a more serious tone of voice he added, 'Truly.'

When they got in the van the stench wasn't as bad as Kalle had feared. The compost and the plastic helped. They wouldn't even need the masks; driving with the windows down would probably be enough. Roland waved as they set off, and they all waved back. Kalle caught one last glimpse of Roland outside his house—the image that would no doubt turn up in the gossip magazine sooner or later.

As they pulled out onto the motorway Elvy leaned over to Hagar, who was gazing blankly into space, and asked, 'Did you get his autograph?'

'Better than that,' said Hagar, patting the pocket of her blouse. 'I got his phone number.'

Flora turned around. 'Hagar, please!'

'What's the matter?'

Kalle groped for Flora's hand and squeezed it reassuringly. It was one of Roland's foibles that he gave out his phone number right, left and centre, which meant he had to change the number roughly every six months. Women called, and in the worst-case scenario he ended up in Södertälje in the middle of the night. It was a mixture of egocentricity and thoughtlessness. Instead of a lock of his hair, he gave away his number. Same idea, but with more complicated consequences.

After a quarter of an hour Kalle was reversing up to their destination, Hagar's garden shed. They stowed the box in among garden tools covered in cobwebs, then camouflaged it with an old oilcloth tarpaulin. Hagar's first husband had built and used the shed, and since their divorce thirty-five years ago it had never been touched.

When they had closed the half-rotten door and dusted off their hands, they stood outside the shed in a disparate little group. Kalle's brain wasn't working properly; he suddenly felt completely exhausted. He looked at Hagar's unassuming functionalist house thirty metres away, seeing faces and shapes in the crumbling plaster.

Hagar broke the silence by clapping her hands and saying, 'So! What now?'

There wasn't really a satisfactory answer to that question, so they went inside for tea and sponge cake while they talked things over. Something had to be done, but nobody knew exactly what. What bothered Elvy most was 'reinforcements in the enemy camp', as she put it: the man who had come to visit Kalle that morning.

'Perhaps you two should come and stay with me for a while?' she suggested. 'Just to be on the safe side.'

Flora gathered up a little pile of cake crumbs, tossed them in her mouth and said, 'Until?'

'Until when?'

'Exactly. Until when?'

'Oh, you mean...well, I don't really know. Until...things settle down.'

'And when will that be?'

Before Elvy had time to come up with an answer, Kalle chipped in, 'I've got a feeling it...that thing would find us anyway. Wherever we are.'

Elvy looked at him sharply. 'On what are you basing this feeling?'

'I just...that's how I feel.'

Elvy's eyes were locked onto his, but after a few seconds she sniffed, nodded, and said, 'Fine.'

Kalle yawned. The back of his neck was about to give way, and his head kept drooping down towards his chest. He went over to the sink and sluiced his eyes with cold water, trying not to wet the dressing. The blood was throbbing underneath it, sending out constant pulses of pain that sparked flashes of orange before his eyes. He turned to the others.

'OK, we need to make a decision. I want to go home and get some sleep.'

Nothing was decided. Kalle and Flora went home to sleep. As they drove away from Hagar's house, Kalle glanced back and said, 'Your grandmother...she's pretty tough, isn't she?'

'Yes,' said Flora. 'And she really wants to do something. She... kind of messed up last time.'

'What do you mean, last time?'

'Last time we had a chance. Before they closed the Heath.'

A cold draught was blowing through the apartment when they walked in, and they were both on the alert straightaway. However, it was just that the window the man had opened was still ajar. Kalle closed it and fell into bed without getting undressed. He closed his eyes and heard Flora lie down next to him. Then he heard nothing more.

It was dark outside when he woke up. He was alone in the bed. He could hear the music to the video game Double Dash playing quietly in the living room. He lay there for a while looking at the streetlight outside the window; it seemed to be floating all by itself like the smallest moon in the universe, orbiting around Kalle Liljewall. His nose felt blocked, and he tentatively tried blowing air through it, but without success. He pressed a little harder and a thin stream of air forced its way out of the battered channels and the hole in the dressing.

Daddy. My very own darling daddy.

Pain stabbed through his stomach, and he suddenly felt very sorry for himself. Nothing he did turned out right. Everything just went wrong, however hard he tried. He had finally met someone he liked, and where had that taken him? You only had to summarise the events of the past twenty-four hours to see that it had taken him even further down the toilet than he had been before.

Why can things never be simple?

His childhood, his mother, his youth, his…everything scrolled past, and he just wanted to curl up in a ball beneath the covers and never come out again. If you stick your nose out, it gets smashed. Lie low. Lie low, for fuck's sake.

I want to be alone.

He was more suited to being alone, he wasn't made to be with someone. He could sit here in his apartment, watching his TV programs and feeling bloody sorry for himself, but at least he would have some kind of order in his life. Yes. Sit in an armchair, let the hours go by. Be alone. That would suit him.

When Flora came in half an hour later, these thoughts had been going round and round in Kalle's head in an ever-descending spiral, and as she sat down on the bed he said, 'Flora. I can't do this anymore.'

She didn't answer. She gently pushed back his hair, laid her hand on his forehead. Kalle let it happen. He had nothing more to say. He was curled up inside, and he didn't want to come out. After a short silence she simply said, 'It's you and me against the world.'

Her expression was totally serious. Kalle sighed.

'Isn't that some pop song?'

'Yes. But it's still true. Come and have something to eat.'

Flora had made a lentil stew, which they ate with couscous. Candles on the table.

You and me against the world.

Now that Kalle had woken up properly and got some food inside him, he could see his brooding thoughts on loneliness for what they really were: romanticism. A sentimental picture, the fruits of his tragic isolation. If that was the case, it was perfectly possible to swap it for something different, something equally melodramatic: *You and me against the world.*

And the situation in which they were caught up was so extreme that 'you and me against the world' wasn't even incorrect. It was an accurate description of the state of things.

So yes. You and me against the world.

The events of the day had left them both so exhausted that they spent the evening watching a load of rubbish on TV, laughing at stupid ads and actors styled to within an inch of their lives. Flora said Elvy had called to check that everything was OK. Kalle nodded. Yes, everything was OK. Not good or even comprehensible, but sitting here on the sofa with Flora curled up beside him and Buffy the vampire slayer entangled in yet another unbelievable dilemma, it was OK. Very definitely OK.

Before they went to bed at around two o'clock, Kalle took a couple of Alvedon for the pain in his face. Flora fell asleep in no time, but Kalle lay awake, feeling the blood stabbing at the top of his nose.

I am not alone.

No. In fact, he had never felt more as if he were part of a group than he did now. Funkface was a different matter. They rehearsed, they chatted, they were mates. But it was nothing serious. This was different. He, Flora, Roland, Elvy and Hagar, God help them, were involved in something much bigger than themselves. And...

I want to be a part of it.

To his surprise he realised his attitude had completely changed since the last time he lay here in bed. Perhaps it wasn't until now it had happened, the thing Flora had talked about. He wanted to be a part of it. He wanted to do his bit.

The Alvedon started to work and his thoughts drifted off into the great darkness.

He woke up at six and couldn't get back to sleep, so he went into the hallway and picked up the newspaper. It took him a couple of seconds to grasp what he was seeing on the front page, something he recognised so well: a photograph of the gates at the Heath. The headline read: 'Reliving isolated'.

He switched on the coffee machine to warm up yesterday's coffee, sat down at the kitchen table and began to read.

During the previous day the reliving had suddenly become extremely aggressive, for some unknown reason. A number of people had been injured, and in order to improve supervision, all the reliving had now been gathered together in one location. A box at the side of the article gave a series of facts about the course of events and the number of deaths that had occurred when the reliving escaped three years ago. A doctor whose name Kalle vaguely recognised stated that the violence displayed by the reliving was much greater on this occasion; it was sheer luck that no one had been killed.

Kalle poured the black, oily coffee and took a swig, pulling a face at the burnt taste.

What's going on?

The health minister had also made a statement, explaining that alternative methods of dealing with the problem were currently under discussion. The safety of the public was the number one priority.

When Kalle had put on some fresh coffee he went to wake Flora and show her the article. She read it and shook her head.

'This is fake.'

'You mean nothing's happened?'

'No. It's just a smoke screen. They're up to something, and they're trying to...I don't know.'

'But you don't think it could have happened?'

'If it had, would there have been anything in the paper? I mean, they haven't released any information at all for the past three years. Why now, if it's not a deliberate ploy? They're working up to something.'

Flora's mobile rang. Elvy had also read the article, and come to the same conclusion as Flora. When they had finished talking, Flora got out of bed. 'We have to do something. Now.'

'Yes. But what?'

Flora looked at the clock on the bedside table. 'Do you think Roland will be up yet?'

'Hardly. Why?'

'Gran and I were talking yesterday and...we had an idea. It might not be any good, and it might not work. But we need Roland.'

Kalle waited until eight o'clock before calling him. Flora had outlined the plan and it was just as she said: it might not be any good, but it was the only thing they had at the moment.

Roland wasn't awake yet. It had been a bit of a late night with the reporter from the gossip mag, and he needed some time for reflection. Kalle suspected that Roland just wanted to move to a place where a sleeping magazine reporter couldn't wake up and overhear what he was saying.

Bingo. When Roland rang back ten minutes later, the background noise suggested he was out in the garden.

'OK,' said Roland after they'd talked for a while. 'I'm in.'

'To be perfectly honest,' said Kalle, 'I have absolutely no idea how this is supposed to work; it could easily be a complete disaster.'

'Life's a disaster anyway. For me, at least.'

They spent the day getting ready. Kalle had the feeling that he was packing for a very long journey, that he was saying goodbye. His hands were lighter than usual, touching things with more care. Perhaps it was the stress, but he felt a reverence for life that he hadn't experienced for a long time now that he was standing here on the verge of taking his leave of it, if that was what it came to. Flora was inward-looking and focused, gathering her strength.

At four o'clock they parted company: Flora set off for Täby, and Kalle headed for Haninge to swap the van for the big bus. He was anxious. What they were going to do that evening wasn't something normal people did. Criminal gangs, possibly: security van heists and so on. And their planning was usually a lot tighter, with precise knowledge of times and movements, and local factors.

Kalle didn't even know what things looked like inside the Heath now, after what he had read in the paper. And it bothered him that he hadn't heard a peep from either his father or their visitor. In short, they hadn't a clue what was going on and their plan was extremely shaky, a shot in the dark. But it was all they had. Kalle couldn't come up with anything better.

Although the bus hadn't been used for a month, it started first time. So far so good. It wasn't a large bus, perhaps half the size of a normal city bus, but Kalle didn't have a bus-driver's licence. When they'd used the bus in the past, Tropicos had brought in another driver and Kalle had just gone along as a humper.

He drove at ten kilometres below the speed limit, and was overtaken constantly on the road heading towards the E18 and Täby. The roundabouts were the worst; he kept thinking the bus was a metre wider than it actually was, and that it had a will of its own when it was turning and responded to the steering wheel only when it was good and ready.

When he finally pulled up outside Elvy's house and wanted to switch off the engine, his left hand was locked around the steering wheel in a grip so vice-like that he had to prise his fingers off one by one. His head was aching, but he was quite pleased with himself. He'd managed things so far.

The others were already gathered in the kitchen. Maja had expressed the opinion that the entire project was insane, and Flora had had a long conversation with her. Eventually Maja had let her go, but refused to take part herself.

Roland was wearing a Helly Hansen top and a pair of Fristads trousers that looked well worn. Elvy and Hagar, dressed for the outdoors, looked exactly like two elderly ladies setting off to forage for mushrooms. Neither Flora nor Kalle had seen any reason to wear anything different from their normal clothes.

'Hi,' said Kalle as he walked into the kitchen. 'Have you got any Alvedon or anything like that?'

Elvy pointed to one of the kitchen cupboards. Kalle took out the first-aid box, found two Alvedon and swallowed them. As he was putting the box back, he saw a small glass jar containing a piece of paper, a little bit of kitchen paper with brown stains on it. He didn't know if it was rude to ask, but they were a team now, weren't they? He picked up the jar.

'What's this?'

The paper looked like a piece of old parchment. When Elvy saw the jar, she smiled and reached out to take it. She looked at the paper and sighed.

'Well, you could say that this is why we're sitting here. This is where it came from.' Elvy pointed to the middle of her forehead, and Kalle now saw that what he had thought was a wrinkle was in fact a scar, a paler line just above the skin.

'Elvy was given a task,' said Hagar. 'But we misunderstood the implications somewhat.'

'We behaved like idiots,' Elvy corrected her.

'Yes,' said Hagar. 'That too.'

'You must forgive me, ladies,' said Roland. 'But I find that very hard to believe.'

Elvy went through the story briefly, explaining how the figure they now knew as Death had given Elvy the task of bringing the reliving to her, how she had believed these were ordinary, living people she had been asked to guide, and how she had got it wrong and missed her opportunity to put everything right.

'So if it hadn't been for my stupidity, we wouldn't be sitting here now.' She sighed deeply and suddenly looked very weary. Roland placed his hand on hers.

'And we would never have got to know one another.'

Elvy gave a wry smile. She wasn't as inclined as Hagar to swallow Roland's gallant remarks. Hagar, on the other hand, was nodding eagerly, as if the privilege of getting to know Roland definitely compensated for missing the chance to save hundreds of lives.

'Shall we get going?' suggested Flora.

Roland looked out of the window. 'I thought we were going to wait until dark.'

Flora shrugged. 'I don't think it makes any difference. The element of surprise is the only advantage we have. The quicker the better.'

'Just a minute,' said Roland, disappearing into the hallway. He came back with a bottle of champagne, which he placed on the table. He waved at it with a flourish.

'This, my friends, is a Bollinger '66. I daren't say how much it's worth. I've been saving it, and I thought that since this evening's…

activities might mean I will never have the opportunity to enjoy it in the way I'd intended, I would like to share it with you.'

Elvy had no champagne flutes, so ordinary glasses were set out on the table as Roland opened the bottle with a pop and a sorrowful expression. Everyone took a glass.

'Cheers,' said Roland. 'To life and love.'

Kalle hadn't drunk champagne very often, but this was the best he had ever tasted. It hit the soft palate with a little prickle, then dissolved, evaporated in his mouth. His tongue felt slightly numb, and the alcohol went straight to his head. Flora cuddled up close to him, and it might have been the champagne making him sentimental, but Kalle had tears in his eyes; he thought this was the most beautiful moment of his whole life.

When they had finished the champagne, Roland said, 'Kalle, I've been thinking. It might be best if I drive.'

'Why?'

'Because...' Roland looked at Flora, then at Kalle. 'Going for the pathos angle, which I think is appropriate under the circumstances, you've got more to live for than I have, that's all.'

Kalle caught and held Flora's gaze. Then he nodded. 'OK.'

Twilight was falling by the time Roland pulled up on the edge of Järva field. He unhooked the microphone and announced over the bus's PA, 'Ladies and gentlemen, we have now reached our destination. Kindly take your places. May I also take this opportunity to recommend the excellent souvenir shop situated by the entrance. Thank you. Is everyone ready?'

Elvy and Flora moved to the seats next to the door in the middle of the bus, while Kalle went forward and sat by Roland, whose hands were clamped around the steering wheel, his eyes firmly fixed on the gates a few hundred metres away.

'Roland? Are you OK?'

Roland's jaw was clenched, but he nodded. Kalle patted him on the shoulder. When he turned away to go back to the others, Roland looked up at him with a pleading expression and said, 'They won't start shooting, will they?'

Kalle's guess was as good as Roland's, but he gave the answer Roland wanted to hear: 'No,' and went to sit next to Flora. Both Elvy and Hagar had grabbed hold of the handrail in front of them; Kalle and Flora did the same. Roland revved the engine a couple of times. Then he released the clutch.

He increased his speed as they approached the gates. Through the windscreen Kalle could see there were now four guards by the gates. At first, as the bus drew closer, they just stood there staring. A dance-band bus with palm trees and a sunset on the side was heading for the gates. When it was perhaps twenty metres away, one of the guards started waving his hands: Stop! *Stop!* Roland floored the accelerator and ducked.

The other guards reached for their submachine guns, but presumably their orders were unclear, and not a shot was fired before the bus hit the gates. There was the sound of metal snapping, the bus juddered and one of the gates was ripped off its hinges before being dragged along by the bus for several metres; eventually it flipped over and lay still.

Kalle glanced through the back window. The guards were standing in the same spot as if they were paralysed, staring after the bus. This scenario obviously hadn't come up in their crisis training. The engine was roaring frantically, and Roland yelled, 'Left, wasn't it?'

'Yes,' Kalle yelled back. 'Left and then straight on.'

There was a crack running all the way down the windscreen, top to bottom. The gate had been the critical element. Kalle screamed, 'The windscreen! It's going to—'

'I know, I know!'

Roland was hunched over the wheel, and his thoughts flashed

through Kalle's head: *Drive fuck drive drive...left drive.* Roland's thoughts were the wildest and the strongest. Kalle could hear the others too, and behind them a panic-stricken murmur he was unable to identify. But Roland came through loud and clear, and in spite of the hysteria Kalle was also picking up a sense of joy. The happiness of someone who is racing towards the abyss, and doing it of his own free will: someone who has finally arrived.

After another turn they could see the community centre through the cracked windscreen. There were a number of guards gathered outside the main door. Their thoughts struck the passengers on the bus, and were exactly what they might have expected: a mixture of fear and suspicion.

This time Roland did something he had omitted to do at the gates: he sounded the horn. The noise was deafening, and the guards reacted to the oncoming danger as anyone would: they leapt out of the way.

'Hang on tight!' Roland shouted.

He swerved to the right so that the bus ran alongside the wall up to the entrance. The roof was perhaps three metres above the ground, and fast approaching the windscreen. This was the part they were most unsure of. Just before the roof hit the windscreen, Roland slammed on the brakes and the bus went into a skid. Roland was hurled forward over the steering wheel just as the steel roof girder smashed the glass. There was an ear-splitting crash and a shower of tiny shards of glass cascaded into the bus. The metal roof crumpled and was pushed down into the aisle. Kalle just had time to think:

This wasn't a good idea

...before the bus hit the supporting girder on the other side of the roof and came to an abrupt halt. Kalle flew forwards and hit his chest on the handrail, knocking the breath clean out of him.

The bus was motionless, the engine turning over. A piece of metal shifted and a pile of broken glass scattered across the floor.

Outside the bus they could hear the sound of agitated voices: 'Fucking lunatics…what the fuck…'

Kalle coughed and looked around. Both Elvy and Hagar had had the sense to curl up in the emergency brace position, and they were now straightening up. Flora, bleeding from a split lip, said, 'I'm fine.'

'Roland?' Kalle shouted.

No reply. Kalle climbed over metal and broken glass to get to the driver's seat. Roland was lying across the wheel, his back completely covered in splintered glass.

'Roland?'

Roland twitched and raised one hand.

'I'm OK,' he said, and sat up straight. His face was criss-crossed with tiny, bleeding scratches. He grimaced with pain and collapsed again. 'My ribs. I think I need to…have a little rest.'

They heard the voices of the guards: 'Get this fucking thing moved.'

If it was possible to talk about being lucky, then they'd been lucky. A large part of the metal roof had got stuck between the steering wheel and the last supporting girder outside, and this was now preventing the guards from immediately climbing in through the hole where the windscreen had been. But it wouldn't take them long to remove it.

Roland waved his hand. 'I'll be fine. You go.' He lowered his hand and pressed a button. There was a faint hiss, and the middle doors opened. The metal screeched in protest as the guards tugged at it, and through a gap Kalle could see a furious face. He patted Roland on the back. 'Nice driving.'

Roland said, 'Glad to be of service…' and Kalle made his way down the aisle and followed the others. Through a combination of luck and skill the plan had worked: the bus was so close to the wall that it was blocking the entrance to the building, and the only way in was now via the bus.

As Flora walked down the steps, an icicle plummeted through Kalle's stomach. The one thing he hadn't thought about was which way the main door opened. If it opened outwards, they were fucked.

But luck was still on their side. The door opened inwards, and after a couple of seconds they were all standing inside the entrance hall. Kalle and Flora wound the chain they had brought with them several times around the handle, and fastened it with a padlock. It would take a while for anyone to get that door open.

'How's Roland?' asked Hagar.

'Fine,' Kalle lied. 'He just didn't want to come in with us, that's all.'

Hagar nodded and clutched at her head.

'I can understand that. This is just dreadful.'

There were no words to describe the din that filled their heads now they were so close to the source. It was like the moment when Sweden scores a goal in a crucial World Cup match, that moment when thousands of people leap to their feet and let out a roar—but this was long, drawn out, endless. And it was exactly the opposite of that moment. Not joy and celebration, but mass pain and horror.

At the same time, because the din was so overwhelming it was almost easier to deal with than previous experiences. There were no individual sounds, it was like being part of an agonising disease. Their bodies shook and their heads were full of black, screaming mud, but they kept on moving and stuck to their plan.

Hagar stayed by the door to warn them if it looked as though their blockade might be breached. Kalle, Flora and Elvy carried on into the next room, the big hall.

The benches that had filled the room on Kalle's previous visit had been cleared away. Now there was only empty floor space, and here the reliving had been gathered together. All of them. There must have been several hundred people, or what had been people. They were packed close together, pressed up against the walls.

Grey skin, skeletal arms, expressionless faces and sunken eyes. Dead people. There was the same veil over all the eyes; the only variation was in the state of decay of the bodies. Dried-up skin or swollen skin, a mummified face or a face marked with liver spots. Dead people. Corpses that should be at rest, lying down, released into death, instead of standing tightly pressed together, screaming their silent screams, all with their eyes fixed on the empty space in the middle of the room.

A reliving person had just been led into the circle. Three men were standing there. The reliving was a hunchbacked old man whose fingers were bent around something that wasn't there. He was brought forward. Clumps of grey hair stuck out from his head.

One of the men held a box up to the old man's throat. There was a faint crackling sound and the old man fell to the ground, face down. The man with the box stepped back, and the second man stepped forward. He was holding a pair of bolt cutters in his hands.

Elvy took two strides towards the group.

'Stop!' she yelled. 'Stop that! What are you doing?'

The man with the bolt cutters stopped. The third man turned around, and Kalle recognised him. It was the same man who had been in Kalle's bedroom. The Visitor. The same suit, the same tie. There was only one difference: his stomach was even bigger now. He smiled and said, '*That* explains all the racket.' He turned to the wall beside the door. 'Sture. Your son is here. That's nice, isn't it?'

Kalle looked across. His father was indeed there, along with four other men who were walking towards Elvy. Two of them were holding pistols, pistols that didn't look like anything Kalle had seen either in a film or in reality; they looked more like crazy toys.

One of the men pointed his weapon at Elvy.

'Stop right there. Back off.'

Elvy stopped, looked at him and asked, 'What are you doing?'

The man waved his weapon to indicate that Elvy should move away, and she stepped back a couple of paces. Kalle couldn't work out what kind of weapon it was—was it actually a weapon at all?

The Visitor nodded to the man with the bolt cutters and held up a warning finger to Kalle, Flora and Elvy. 'Now don't do anything stupid.'

The handles of the bolt cutters were opened to their full extent and the man wielding them pressed the twin blades into the back of the motionless old man's neck. Pressed again so that the points penetrated the skin. Then he brought the handles together. There was a moist, crunching sound as the blades cut through the vertebrae in the neck and a small amount of viscous blood trickled out. The Visitor gestured to the man with the pistol, exhorting him to remain on his guard. Then he slid his foot under the old man's stomach and flipped him over onto his back.

He stared at the old man's ribcage, waiting.

'This was a particularly demanding situation,' he said. 'It was necessary to carry out research in order to find the correct method.' He looked up for a moment and said in an exaggeratedly high voice, like a small child, 'Even I didn't know what to do, can you imagine that?'

And then it happened. A white caterpillar emerged from the old man's chest. The Visitor crouched down and gazed with delight at the little grub as it twisted and turned, naked and defenceless. After a few seconds it began to change colour. It turned pink. It swelled up. It turned red. It swelled even more. Then it burst. At the very moment when the thin membrane burst, the man quickly bent down and opened his mouth over the caterpillar. It was sucked in, a little clump of red tissue, and it was gone. The man licked his lips, got to his feet, nodded to the man with the box. 'Next.'

He opened his arms wide to Kalle, Flora and Elvy.

'This is what we're doing.'

The next victim was brought forward. A woman this time. She was wearing only a nightdress, and underneath it you could sense the loose skin, falling in folds and wrinkles. The skin on her face was also loose and grey, sagging towards the floor. A greater sorrow than the whole world lay in her empty eyes.

As the box was held to her throat, Kalle realised what it was: an electric stun gun. It paralysed the victim, making the operation easier. Elvy stood there with her fists clenched, and Kalle could feel a lethal contempt crackling in her mind. Flora wasn't there. Kalle quickly looked around.

Flora was standing in front of the wall of the reliving, sending thoughts to them. Kalle felt it in his own head when he turned his attention to her: she was communicating. She was trying to convince them that they should give themselves up; she was sending the image of death into their heads and Kalle saw the shadowy figure, a hand with hooks on the end of the fingers flickering by, different-coloured butterflies, a light.

But the black shadow smothered everything, and she couldn't get through. They were too frightened. They were like a group of animals, waiting patiently to be slaughtered instead of fleeing en masse. Flora wrapped her arms around her body and tried to make the images more beautiful, but her efforts struck a jarring note and she felt it, Kalle felt it, the reliving felt it.

The crackling noise came again, and Kalle gave a start. The woman had fallen to the floor.

I can't be here any longer.

The cacophony of the terror of the reliving, the repulsiveness of the whole situation...he didn't want to be here anymore. He wanted to sink through the ground, run away, cease to exist. His lips were trembling and his body felt like a windscreen about to shatter into a thousand pieces. He would break soon if nothing happened.

Elvy suddenly ran forward beside him. He opened his mouth to say something, but she had passed him before it came out. She ran over to the reliving, shouting, 'Tore!'

Elvy pushed her way through the front row and reached a man who didn't look any different from the rest in Kalle's eyes. A big, heavy body, broad shoulders and a colourless, expressionless face, which Elvy took in her hands.

'Tore,' she said. 'Tore, you mustn't...you have to...'

She shook his head from side to side, but got no reaction. She pressed her forehead against his as if to gain a better surface contact, and Kalle could feel her sending virtually the same message as Flora. Tore's eyes burned with emptiness.

One of the men with the strange weapons was on his way over to her. He raised the weapon.

'Move away immediately!'

He stopped a few metres away from Elvy, who ignored him completely. Kalle knew the man was about to shoot, and he moved quickly to stand in front of Elvy. He pointed at the pistol.

'What kind of fucking toy—'

That was as far as he got. He heard a faint report and felt a burning sensation in his thigh. He looked down. There was a dart sticking out of his thigh, with a metal cable attaching it to the pistol. He looked up and the second before the man pressed the trigger, Kalle realised what it was. He'd read about it somewhere. The police in the US had—

A quivering stream of lava flooded his body in a fraction of a second; his arms shot out, his fingers spread wide, and it felt as if someone was pulling his hair as the electricity destroyed all muscle control. He was hurled to the ground, incapable of moving; it was as if something warm and solid had been poured over his skin and set fast. Wax, perhaps. His whole body hurt, and a strange calm came over him.

He lay there staring into space and saw the man take a step towards him, pull the dart out of his thigh and press a button to retract the cable. The man bent over him.

'Nice and quiet now, aren't you?'

Kalle would have nodded if it had been possible. He felt utterly calm. He wasn't at all surprised, didn't even jump when something black suddenly came into his field of vision and the man's head disappeared with a thud. He just thought about it calmly, logically, and guessed that it was Flora's boot he had seen, on its way to kick the man in the head.

He looked down and saw that he had guessed correctly. The man was lying on the floor holding his head; Flora picked up his pistol and pointed it at him. Kalle wanted to say something, something appreciative, and his tongue did actually move in his mouth. He scrabbled on the cement floor. His fingers moved. He blinked. He could blink.

The man was so preoccupied with the kick he had received that Flora felt able to leave him; she came over to Kalle.

'How are you feeling, are you OK?'

'I...yes...yes...'

Flora slid a hand under his armpit and helped him up into a sitting position. It felt as if he were a few centimetres outside his body, as if he were slowly moving back into it, discovering it afresh. He nodded at Flora and saw a movement just behind her. He thought: *Look out!* and Flora heard him. She threw herself to the side and the dart missed her by a fraction, hitting the leg of one of the reliving behind them.

Flora turned to the man and raised the pistol. Then they heard Elvy's voice:

'Give that to me.'

Flora looked at her grandmother, standing with her hand outstretched. 'Give it to me. Now.' Flora did as she asked, shaking her head in bewilderment. The man with the second pistol was just retracting the cable, and Kalle managed to summon up enough strength to put his foot on the dart. The man who had been lying on the floor had got to his feet and was swaying. Blood was pouring from one ear.

The Visitor had followed events with amused interest. He said, 'You might as well give up now. This is going nowhere. The one you are seeking will not come.'

The man waved to his other henchmen to take care of the disruption. Three men, including Kalle's father, approached. The dart was jerked from under Kalle's foot and quickly retracted. Suddenly he felt afraid. He might have been calm after the electric shock, but he certainly didn't want another one. He moved slowly backwards, away from the man who was fixing the dart back in its place.

We've had it. We're going to end up in...his belly too...

Kalle heard a muted report behind him, and Flora screamed, 'Nana! No!'

He turned his head and saw Elvy standing there with a faintly surprised expression on her face. She was holding the pistol in her hand, with the cable running straight into her chest. She had fired it into her heart at close quarters and the dart had gone in between a gap in her ribs, penetrating deeper.

'Nana, no, no! No!'

Elvy gave a little smile, then blew Flora a kiss before pressing the trigger. As if she had been a marionette whose puppeteer had suddenly jerked all the strings simultaneously, a spasm passed through her body, all her limbs shot outwards in a convulsion and she collapsed at Tore's feet.

Flora was by her side before her hand fell to the floor. 'Nana, Nana, you can't...'

But Elvy's eyes were already unseeing. The electric shock had stopped her heart, and her body did not react to Flora's kisses and caresses. Kalle felt a hand on his shoulder, and looked up. His father was standing there, his face contorted with conflicting emotions, but the main impression was one of shame. Not shame at his own behaviour, but at the fact that he had a son who was behaving in this way.

'Come on, damn you!'

Kalle thought the buzzing and whining inside his head was coming from his own hatred, but in that case it should have been impossible to locate the noise. But it was possible. It was coming from his left, from the spot where Elvy lay.

He placed his hand on top of his father's, as if he were a penitent son in need of support. He got hold of his father's index finger and snapped it straight back.

His father's screams were drowned out by the shrieking inside his head. It was still coming from the left, and he must not turn his head in that direction. But he did. He was so stunned by the electric shock and by the fear emanating from the reliving that more pain was of no significance.

He saw the white caterpillar on Elvy's breast. He saw Flora, curled up beside it shaking her head. And he saw the shadow. A slender figure, almost attenuated, drawn from the darkness itself, with flowing black hair.

Death...

Yes, it was Death, just as he had imagined death ever since he was a little boy, when he used to think that this same figure used to seep out of his wardrobe at night when he was trying to get to sleep, the figure that had shot out of the train hurtling towards his mother and taken her away. Death.

Death stretched out her hand, and right at the end of her finger-tips were glittering hooks. Thin hooks, not unlike fish hooks, but longer and more...perfect. One of the hooks reached down towards the caterpillar on Elvy's breast, caught it and penetrated the membrane. The caterpillar writhed as if it were in pain, and Kalle didn't understand.

Why this...why is this...better?

Death raised her hand, and even Flora followed the movement with her eyes although they were brimming with tears. Then something happened. Instead of changing colour, swelling and bursting, the caterpillar began to open up, and it was no longer a caterpillar, it was a pupa. A pair of delicate wings emerged through the opening and a butterfly crept out. A tiny, fragile butterfly the same colour as the eyes of the one you love, a colour for which there are no words.

The butterfly flapped its wings a couple of times and then took flight, settling on Tore's hand. Tore lifted his hand and looked at the butterfly from his sunken eye sockets. His mouth was hanging open. Then Kalle felt something inside his head, something that came from Tore, a spark of the same colour as the butterfly's wings.

And he let go. It was impossible to explain how Kalle could feel it, but it was a bit like a hand loosening its vice-like grip on something it doesn't really want, and is only holding onto because it's *mine, mine, mine!* Tore let go and collapsed on the floor.

The Visitor had stepped forward. He was standing with clenched fists, watching what was happening. Death was whirling around him like irritating smoke, and for the first time the man looked unsure of himself.

The caterpillar crawled out of Tore's chest. Death caught it, and the same thing happened again. Another butterfly emerged and joined forces with the one that had come out of Elvy; they fluttered around one another above the heads of the reliving. It was as if a sigh of relief passed through the room, a collective exhalation from deep inside hundreds of bodies.

The dead began to collapse. First one, then two, then a chain reaction, dominoes falling everywhere. The rows thinned out, gaps appeared, more and more fell to the ground and thuds could be heard all around the room, like in an orchard during an autumn storm. They all fell down, and Kalle looked at the Visitor, revelling in the expression on his face.

You're losing.

Hundreds of bodies had now fallen, and hundreds of caterpillars were on their way out. What Kalle didn't understand was how Death was going to be able to catch them all. The Visitor seemed to have the same thought. He moved in among the mass of bodies with his mouth wide open, waiting for what must inevitably happen: some of the caterpillars would swell up and be destroyed before Death could get to them.

They're just our strength, made visible in a way we can understand.

Death tossed her head and her hair flew wide, growing longer and longer, and the strands of hair swept over the bodies. At the very end of each strand of hair there glittered a hook. And the hooks found their mark, pierced the caterpillars and lifted them, leaving the Visitor's mouth without nourishment. He clasped his hands and roared at the ceiling. His prey had escaped him.

As if his rage needed a direction, he turned to Sture. He stared at him and pointed at Kalle, yelling, 'Your son! Your son and his whore!'

Kalle felt the stab of hatred, the command hurled into Sture, and he hauled himself to his feet. Sture seized the bolt cutters and ran towards Kalle, who tried to clear his head, to see the movements, but he was still feeling groggy. Sture swung the bolt cutters at his head and Kalle ducked; he felt them catch on one of his dreadlocks and yank it out, and blood trickled down his scalp.

A red mist descended. When Sture swung his weapon again, Kalle followed the movement and grabbed hold of the bolt cutters as they passed him, ripping them out of Sture's grasp.

Sture's consciousness was still pulsating with the order he had been given, and he hurled himself at Kalle with his bare hands. Kalle didn't think, he simply defended himself with what he had. He swung the bolt cutters, and they hit Sture squarely on the temple. Sture let out a muffled whimper and collapsed. Kalle dropped the bolt cutters.

The butterflies took off. They were perched on the ends of Death's hair, hundreds of them, in every imaginable colour, and some colours that were indescribable. They were striving to get to the ceiling, to the space beyond, and they lifted Death off the floor. The entire ceiling was hidden from view by her hair, by the butterflies' wings, an immense flower coming into bloom.

Kalle looked at his father. Blood was pouring from the wound in his temple, and his hand twitched a couple of times before falling limply to the floor. Death was biding her time, floating in the middle of the room.

When the caterpillar emerged from Sture's chest, Death moved downwards. A hand reached out, the hooks coming closer. Kalle placed his hand over the caterpillar. Death hesitated. She was not allowed to touch him. Kalle could feel the caterpillar swelling beneath his hand. When it was about to burst he picked it up and threw it to the Visitor. The mouth opened and the caterpillar disappeared down his throat.

Kalle looked at his empty palm. It was no longer possible to change his mind. The choice had been made.

Flora came and stood next to Kalle; she put her arm around his waist and leaned her head on his shoulder. Together they watched as the butterflies let go of the hooks and drifted up towards the ceiling, a final glimmer of all the colours, fragments of a rainbow that passed through the ceiling and was gone.

Flora's voice was a muffled whisper as she said, 'Goodbye, Nana. You did well. In the end.'

Silence fell in the room. The dead bodies covered the floor like a carpet of worthless flesh. Life had left them, and taken Death with it.

Only Flora, Kalle and the Visitor remained, along with his five henchmen. They weighed each other up. It wasn't difficult to work out what was going to happen. They had destroyed something he had spent several years building up.

The doors flew open and four guards burst in. One of them was holding Hagar firmly by the elbow. When the guards took in the scene laid out before their eyes they froze, and Hagar seized the opportunity to pull free. She ran to Elvy. Flora followed her, and they fell into each other's arms. Kalle could no longer hear any thoughts, but it wasn't difficult to work out what Flora was telling Hagar. Her grandmother had taken her place among the greatest heroes, but no living person would ever hear her story.

The guards waved their submachine guns half-heartedly as if they had no idea where to start, or who the guilty parties might be.

Kalle was still gazing into the Visitor's eyes. It was like looking through a knothole in a plank of wood. Beyond the hole you suddenly see the desert, or the sea, and it fills your field of vision. Eternity. He was incapable of looking away, and he asked slowly, 'What. Are you. Intending. To do. With us?'

The Visitor appeared to consider the question. He looked away and gazed around the room, contemplating the ruins of his great idea. He shrugged.

'Revenge,' he said, 'is a human invention. It serves no purpose.'

Then he was sucked into himself and was no longer there. Like something you think you see out of the corner of your eye, but when you turn around it's not there. The Visitor disappeared. Kalle was free once more to fix his gaze wherever he wished. He fixed it on Flora.

She and Hagar were crouching beside Elvy's body, wiping away each other's tears.

It's over.

A couple more guards joined the others. One of them was escorting Roland, whose face was still covered in blood from the myriad tiny cuts. He was alive, but it would be quite some time before he was ready for a photo shoot with any of the gossip magazines. Kalle went over to him.

Roland's big blue eyes peered out through the crust of congealed blood. He asked, 'Did it work?'

'Yes,' said Kalle, and just for a moment he glimpsed the rainbow as it disintegrated and drifted away. 'Yes, it worked.'

Afterword to the Swedish edition of 'Let the Old Dreams Die'

When I saw the finished version of *Let the Right One In* at the Gothenburg Film Festival in 2008, I was dumbstruck.

I had visited the sets on three occasions, I had sat with Tomas Alfredsson and looked at various scenes, we had discussed the editing. I had seen a couple of rough cuts on large and small screens. And yet nothing could have prepared me for seeing the final edit, with all the sound effects, on the enormous screen in the Draken cinema.

It was a revelation. All the pieces had fallen into place, and the film was a small masterpiece, both within Swedish film and within the horror genre. This would later be confirmed by an unparalleled shower of awards from across the world, and I am eternally grateful to Tomas Alfredsson for the way in which he treated my story.

There was only one thing that nagged away at me when the film was over, and that was the ending itself. When Oskar is sitting on the train with the box containing Eli at his feet, on his way to a different life.

In spite of the fact that I was the one who had written the manuscript, it wasn't until after the showing at Draken that I actually realised what the ending implies. Which is that Oskar will become another Håkan. Someone who will take on the terrible task of being Eli's human helper, supplying her with blood and a place to live and so on. That was what the ending said. The fact that I hadn't realised it earlier is probably indicative of a certain level of stupidity in my brain.

The American version recently had its premiere, under the title *Let Me In*. I like that version very much as well, but what is only implied in the Swedish film is spelt out in the American one. Håkan has been with Eli since he was a boy the same age as Oskar. Therefore, it isn't difficult to work out what fate awaits Oskar.

Don't misunderstand me. I think it's a perfectly reasonable ending, a fair interpretation of the story and the deliberately open ending I left in the book. But it isn't *my* ending.

I readily admit that I wouldn't have thought of writing the short story that gives this collection its title if it hadn't been for the films. I wanted to give my version.

'Let the old dreams die' has been rewritten several times, but I was able to produce something good only when I accepted that it had to be a story which could stand on its own two legs. A version where Oskar and Eli play only a subsidiary role. A love story, but with different main characters.

And for those of you who are wondering about the title, it's the next line in the song.

Afterword

Rådmansö, October 2005

I CAN'T HELP IT...

I don't know what you think about afterwords like this. Me, I love them. So now I'm writing one.

It might be a bit self-centred, but after a few novels I imagine I have a few readers who are curious about the way I think. Fourteen, maybe. The four of you who came to those two signings at the Science Fiction Bookshop, and another ten.

It's you I'm talking to. The rest of you can go to sleep now. Goodnight, goodnight. Thank you for coming. Nice of you to join us. Sleep well.

There now. It's just us.

Did you enjoy the stories? I hope so. My favourite is probably 'Border', but it's led to divided opinions. When I've finished writing something I have a group of test readers who are kind enough to read the relevant bundle of papers and give me their reactions. They've all had their own favourite. Except 'To hold you while the music plays'. Nobody likes that one, apart from me.

Perhaps it doesn't make sense? If I tell you the original title was 'The Cross', does that help?

A little bit?

Titles are a chapter all of their own.

The first horror story I wrote was about a man who is shipwrecked on an island in the Stockholm archipelago in the autumn. He's freezing to death, and the situation gets even worse when his dead girlfriend floats ashore. And worse still later on, when she isn't where he left her...

I called that one 'Our skin, our blood, our bones' after a line by Morrissey. (Which song? Anyone?)

Later on, when I wrote my first novel, it was called *The Only Friend* for a long time; I wasn't very keen on that title, but I couldn't come up with anything better. Until I remembered the title of my first story. Morrissey. I trawled through my memory and there it was: *Let the Right One In.*

For a long time *Handling the Undead* was called *When We Dead Awaken*, until I realised it was a play by Ibsen. Not good. In order to give the sense of those pages right at the back of the phone book, you know the ones: In the event of war...I renamed it *Instructions for Handling the Undead*, but that was a bit long, so...

The only title I'm really happy with is *Harbour*, which will be my next book. Then again, I haven't written a word of it yet! But I've got ideas! Lots of them!

Enough about that.

Are you interested in these stories? How I came to write them?

(I write this in the knowledge that as I have been compared with Stephen King in various ways in the past, this is only going to make the situation worse. But, as Vladimir and Estragon say: Nothing to be done.)

How many of you are still here? Seven?

OK.

These stories were written between spring 2002 and autumn 2005. The first one, 'Eternal / Love', was written just after I finished *Let the Right One In*, and the last one, 'The final processing', isn't quite finished as I write this. I just need to sort out a couple of things.

'Eternal / Love' was born out of a feeling that for some reason became acute. I started thinking about the fact that we don't live forever, however much we love someone. Obvious, of course, but suddenly I saw it so clearly, and I was horrified. We can keep our love burning, but at some point we still have to part. The first sentence in the story just came to me in all its simplicity, then the pieces of the puzzle came one after another. It's just occurred to me that thematically it's a kind of epilogue to *Let the Right One In*.

'Majken' was special in that it began with a name. I got the name Majken, and it sat there in my head. One day on the way to Arlanda I passed a house with a silver Volkswagen Beetle parked outside, and I knew it was Majken's car. This then linked up with the idea of 'Shoplifters of the World, Unite', and there you go. Perhaps I should also mention that I've adapted the security system at the NK department store slightly to suit my purposes.

I started to write 'The final processing' mainly to make use of the grandiose final scene I had planned for *Handling the Undead*, but for which there was no room. I planned a short novella of perhaps thirty pages, but it ran away with me. Which is actually quite consistent, because I had originally intended *Handling the Undead* to be a novella as well.

I won't go through all the stories. That's enough. There are only five of you still listening to me. I don't really know what to do to hold your interest until I've got the acknowledgements out of the way.

Oh yes, I could tell you about the novella I did the most work on, but it isn't in this collection because I didn't manage to finish it. Would that be of any interest?

Actually I think this is the best format for that particular story, because more than any of the others it was based on an *idea*, on the fact that I had such a bloody good idea. And sometimes that can be a problem. The idea is so good it proves impossible to realise.

I should have smelled a rat, because I actually carried this idea around in my head for perhaps eighteen months without it ever poking its nose out and demanding to be *written*. However, in the end I decided to try to put it together, and after a month of dithering between different variations, narrative techniques, tempos and perspectives I gave up. It just wouldn't work, it was all wrong however I tried.

But what about the idea?

Well, it went like this:

A number of people are locked in a chamber a hundred metres underground. Let's say it was intended for the long-term storage of nuclear waste, but it has been left to its fate. Why are they locked in? For TV, of course. A large number of cameras document their every movement. What they call a reality show.

Not particularly original? Well, a film called *My Little Eye* came along at the same time.

But I haven't finished.

The people in the underground chamber are totally isolated. Everything the cameras pick up is stored on a hard drive which is also in the chamber. During the month the group spend in the underground chamber, they have no contact whatsoever with the outside world, and no one can see them. In addition, there is also a kind of inbuilt reward system. If they can complete certain tasks, they receive alcohol or food or entertainment. A living TV game show. When they return to the surface, the hard drive is brought out and used to edit together a program.

Still not keen? No, me neither. Could easily degenerate into satire. But here's the thing:

Are you familiar with Schrödinger's cat?

Briefly, it's a way of describing quantum mechanics, what is known as wave-particle duality. I won't go into the science behind the whole thing, because not even the scientists are completely clear about it. But the idea is that a poison gas is released or not released into the box containing the cat. And in the world of quantum mechanics it isn't just that we don't know if the cat is alive or dead until we open the box. It's also that the cat *isn't* alive or dead, or rather it's both at the same time, until we open the box.

It's the observation itself that evokes the choice, determining the fate of the cat. Or, to put it another way: 'Curiosity killed the cat'.

Back to the story.

The people in the underground chamber have been in a situation not unlike the cat's. But now they begin to look at the tapes, at the material filmed by the cameras. And at that point reality is changed. They see things on the tapes that don't correspond with what the participants said when they came out. When the tapes are rewound, they have been altered to match the new reality.

Since I write in this particular genre, it was naturally a terrible course of events that began to unfold. Those who are watching the tapes realise they *must* watch them in order to be able to stop this course of events, while at the same time they know that the very act of watching will cause the events to happen. Curiosity killed the participants.

Good idea, isn't it?

I thought so, anyway. Until I tried to write it.

Oh well. At least I've found *some* use for it here. As a little bonus story for the three of you who are still hanging in there.

That's all I wanted to say this time. It'll probably be a while before we hear from each other again. Just one last thing.

I had intended to use a particular quotation as a motto for this collection, but I'm going to use it as the final word instead.

Sometimes I'm asked why I choose to write horror. A journalist pushed the issue so far that in the end I got really tired of it.

'Why did you choose horror in particular?'

I told him.

'Why did you locate a vampire in Blackeberg?'

I told him the truth: my idea was very simple. Something terrible arrives in Blackeberg, I wanted to see what would happen. Then came the follow-up question: 'Why does something terrible arrive in Blackeberg?'

Somewhere around that point I gave up. I had no more variations when it came to answering what was basically the same question.

The following day I listened to Morrissey *Live at Earl's Court* for the first time. And there, in the break between two songs, he suddenly comes out with something that I think can serve as both the answer to the questions, and the motto for my entire production:

'I really can't help it. It's either this or prison.'

I also have some people to thank. Lots of people to thank.

Thomas Oredsson and Eva Harms Oredsson did the proof-reading, and Thomas gave a lovely speech. Eva's laughter echoed across the neighbourhood in the summer's evening.

All my stepsons have read the stories. Their names are Nils,

Jonatan and Kristoffer Sjögren and they're the best in the world, each in his own way. Kristoffer's Emma is called Berntson, and she can walk any distance you care to mention. She read them too.

Aron Haglund stuck with it. Gave me faith in Majken and sent great lyrics by return.

Jan-Olof Wesström and Bob Hansson haven't read the stories, but they're such great guys and good friends that I wanted to say thank you, thank you anyway.

Then there are people who've given me factual information:

Frank Watson corrected some photographic errors in 'Can't see it! It doesn't exist!' in spite of the fact that he happened to share the same name as the main character.

Martin Skånberg and Maria Halla told me a bit about the load-bearing properties of buildings for 'Village on the hill'.

Kurt Ahrén sat with me in the boathouse working out Latin terms for 'The final processing'.

The staff at the customs post in Kapellskär told me about their work for 'Border'.

(If any errors remain it is not their fault, but must be blamed on my lively imagination.)

I wouldn't want to be without my editor, Elisabeth Watson Straarup, nor Malin Morell at Ordfront. Without them it wouldn't be so much fun.

And then there's Mia, of course. Everything is written for her, to be read aloud to her. It burns, flickers, and will never die.

Thanks, all of you.
John Ajvide Lindqvist

PS: Plus you, the very last one, who stuck it out right to the end. Thanks to you too.